Also by Eyre Price

Blue Highway Blues
Rock Island Rock
Star Killer Star
(all part of the Crossroads Thriller series)

SINNER SAINT

A Novel of Francis of Assisi

BETSEY —
BE GOOD

SINNER SAINT

A Novel of Francis of Assisi

Eyre Price

Blank Slate Press | Saint Louis, MO 63116

Blank Slate Press
Saint Louis, MO 63116
Copyright © 2020 Eyre Price
All rights reserved.
Blank Slate Press is an imprint of Amphorae Publishing Group, LLC
a woman- and veteran owned company
www.amphoraepublishing.com

Publisher's Note: This book is a work of the imagination. Names, characters, places and incidents either are products of the author's imagination or are used fictitiously. While some of the characters and incidents portrayed here can be found in historical or contemporary accounts, they have been altered and rearranged by the author to suit the strict purposes of storytelling. The book should be read solely as a work of fiction.

For information, contact:
Blank Slate Press
4168 Hartford Street
Saint Louis, MO 63116

Manufactured in the United States of America
A193049598
Cover photography and graphics: Shutterstock
Set in Adobe Caslon Pro and LTC Italian Old Style

Library of Congress Control Number: 2020941798
ISBN: 9781943075522

For everyone who has ever walked to the very edge of that
terrible precipice, looked down into the dark abyss, and prayed
only for the strength to resist taking that last step;
For everyone who has lost their way and feels there's no hope;
For everyone who has been betrayed in the cruelest of ways;
For everyone who has lived a nightmare and fears they might never wake up;
For everyone who feels marginalized, ignored, reduced, and discarded;
For everyone who has been convinced that they
are worth less than everyone else;
For everyone who feels as if there's nobody who
understands and nobody who cares ...

You're wrong.
I do.
And I wrote this book for you.

1

The knock at the door was so soft and hesitant that he wondered whether he had heard anything at all or if the sound had simply been some trick of his fevered mind.

And then the gentle rapping repeated.

"Come in," trailed off into a deep, barking cough he struggled to contain in a scrap of linen, yellowed with phlegm and stained with blood.

A young man pushed open the door and stuck his head into the room. "Pardon me, sir."

"There's no need of pardons. Or *sirs*. I'm no noble."

"Of course, sir."

The door squeaked opened just wide enough for the young man to slip into the room.

His brown robe identified him as a man of the cloth, but his face and features were still boyish. His left hand fussed nervously with the braid of rope around his waist, while his right held an earthen cup which he offered to the man. "I brought you some wine."

"Wine, but something more," the man scoffed. "You've brought a cup of whatever potion has been slipped into my drink, as if I couldn't taste the bitterness."

"I'm sure the doctor only wants what's best for you." The young friar offered the cup again.

The man gestured to the bedside table. "Put it there. I've no interest in his poison."

"A cure," the friar corrected. "To ease your suffering."

"How foolish, to trade away the sweetness of one last cup of wine in exchange for the bitter lie that some elixir might offer a false escape from the suffering that is a part of this life. No, a man who has lived without seeking those comforts should die that way, too."

A silent moment passed before the friar fully comprehended the implications of those words. When he finally grasped their meaning, his understanding left him bowed and unable to respond.

"Oh, come now, little brother, there's no need to be sad. Isn't our death that single moment for which we live?"

The friar was too young to be certain. "I suppose so."

"And I've lived my life as well as I could." The man took a moment to consider his declaration. "Or at least, well enough that I have no fears of that approaching hour."

"Of course not, sir." The friar set the cup on the table, beside the single candle that lit the room. "But surely there's no need to speak so grimly."

"I have lived a life most men would never dare to dream. But for every step of that adventure, Sister Death was always close at my heels. I have slipped from her cold embrace often enough to know now that she has me wrapped up so tightly in her arms that I will never break free again."

"And there's nothing we can do, sir?"

"Besides stop calling me *sir*?"

"Of course—" The friar hesitated, uncertain what form of address or title would better reflect the depth of his respect.

"Francis," the man said simply. "My name is Francis."

"Of course ... Francis." The young man smiled at the privilege.

"Was there something you wanted, besides delivering me my poison?" Francis asked.

"Oh, I'm sorry. Yes, *sir*—" The friar stopped himself and then deliberately said, "Francis." He basked in the moment. "You have a visitor, if you're strong enough."

"Of course, he's strong enough." A man with a booming voice stepped past the young friar like he wasn't there and moved to Francis' bedside. "Brother!"

Francis said nothing, made no reply at all.

"Aren't you going to greet me?"

"My eyes have been shut to this world for some time and all I can know of you now is your voice, but that is admittedly familiar," Francis said in his own time. "The idea that there is one in this world who would call me brother like we were blood, less so."

The man's broad smile fell, and his tone grew solemn, "It's me, Francis."

"Couldn't resist coming to see me off to my death at last, Giovanni?" A thin smile crept across Francis's cracked lips.

"Stop your talk of parting this world. You'll bury me yet and you know it."

"If you're not here to bid me a final farewell, then to what do I owe the honor of your company? We both know there's some motive behind it. You've never drawn a breath without it furthering one scheme or another."

Giovanni looked around the small room for a place to sit but found none. He settled instead on the side of the bed, its wooden frame creaking beneath his weight.

Francis called out to the young friar, still at the door. "Would you find us a chair?"

"Don't bother," Giovanni said, patting Francis' hand. "This seat will do me fine."

Facing conflicting commands, the young friar was uncertain about which he should follow.

Giovanni wasn't. "Leave us, boy. And close the door after you."

Francis offered a conciliatory, "Thank you, little brother," but the young friar had already done as he'd been told.

Francis turned to Giovanni. "You're still issuing orders."

"And you're still mollycoddling the world."

"I've never understood your contempt for kindness."

"There's so much about this world you never understood."

"Or, perhaps, understood too well." A series of coughs gripped Francis and shook his thin frame. He wiped the spittle from his lips and took a deep breath. "But you didn't come all this way to pose riddles. You've always been a man of purpose, so there must be some goal hidden behind your visit."

"I heard you were ill."

"I have been ill for a long while."

"I heard you were more than ill," Giovanni admitted.

"And you thought … what exactly?"

"Only that you might want someone to talk to. If these are your last hours, then perhaps there's something you might want to share with someone whose confidence you know you can rely upon absolutely. Someone you have always loved as a brother. And who has always loved you in that same way."

"I have not seen or heard from you since Rome."

Giovanni understood the reference—and the accusation it contained. He was quick to brush them both aside. "Brothers fight."

"And now?"

"Now is all the opportunity we have left to us to repair those time-worn wounds. Now is a chance for brothers to share with one another."

"And what would we share? I mean, beyond this brotherly love of which you speak?"

"I'm not a fool, Francis."

"No. You might face a thousand accusations, Giovanni, but foolishness would never be among them."

"You know me to be a man of the world. And I have always known—down deep inside—that despite the role that you played for this world, you've always known how this life works, too."

"It is hard to walk the streets of Assisi or any town and not quickly come to a cold understanding of the workings of this world."

"Exactly." Giovanni beamed proudly, like he'd proven a very important point. But whatever his message might have been, the significance was lost on Francis.

"You'll have to speak more bluntly. Even if I had the patience for your artfulness, I'm certain I no longer have the time. Say what you will, but do so directly."

"All right then." Giovanni adjusted his seat on the bed. "It's a serious situation, I'm afraid. There was a gentleman of wealth and power in Venice who retained my services to guard his wife and property while he was away."

"And did you do so?"

"Oh, I treated the both as if they were my very own." A sly smile crept across Giovanni's lips.

"And this gentleman?"

"Has whispered within his circles of power that he wants my life, blaming me for an unfortunate situation that was entirely of his making."

"How are your misdeeds the fault of this man?"

"Anyone who knows me well enough to trust me with their wife and property must surely understand that I cannot be trusted with either one."

"You're right, the situation is entirely his fault." Francis' sarcasm was lost in a cough.

"Exactly."

"And so why have you come to me to proclaim a stranger's blame?"

"Guilty or not, he remains a man of power, in close relation to others who are similarly situated. I thought, perhaps, this might be an opportune time to take to the road again. My life seems to take its share of turns."

"All of us walk a twisting path."

"And you were the cause of many of mine," Giovanni said with a sharp edge to his voice he'd previously kept sheathed. "Always the detour. Ever the burden."

Francis sensed the change in temperament, but was not affected. "That's simply not the case. And wanting to believe something doesn't make it true, Giovanni."

"That's not even my name. Giovanni is *your* name. It's what they first called you when you were born. But as soon as our father returned from France and saw his newborn son, he had to change that all-too-common name to something suitably special. *Francis.* No, they gave the throw-away name to me. Perfectly suitable for the handmaiden's bastard. Another unwanted hand-me-down from you. *Francis.*" Giovanni stopped himself and tried to quiet his emotional display.

"I did not ask for the name," Francis assured him. "Nor for all that came with it."

"But you got it all just the same, didn't you? The privilege. The favors. The money."

"Your words are too bitter for you to ever live with them. I thought I was the sick one, but your sentiments are like the fever of a disease that threatens to consume you," Francis said.

"What I know is that I have given my entire life to watching over you. Keeping you out of trouble when we were kids. Covering for you with our father. Saving your life at Ponte San Giovanni. At Collestrada. You remember Collestrada?"

"How could you possibly think that a single night has passed since then without me hearing those screams in my head? Even with my eyesight gone, I am not spared those sights repeating over and again in my memory as if I were there to witness them anew."

"And Egypt?" Giovanni prodded. "You make the easy reference, but do you remember how I spirited you out of there before those infidels got their hands on you and took your head or sold you to slavery—or worse."

Even in his weakened state, Francis could not be bullied. "I remember much more about Egypt than I wish to recall right now. Or ever again in this life."

Giovanni sat up, his posture defensive. "And what do you know for sure? The only incontrovertible fact is that I got you out of there. Alive. And here you are."

"Here I am. Is that by your own acts or God's good grace?"

"You owe me." Even Giovanni couldn't hide the faintest tinge of shame in his assertion.

"What debt is that?"

"The debt of a brother. A friend. A comrade."

"And even if your accounting were accurate, with what would I settle that obligation?"

Whatever trace of humility or self-consciousness had softened Giovanni's bluster gave way to frustration. "Stop it, Francis."

"I don't understand."

"You may have the rest of them fooled, but not me. I know the interest Rome has shown in you since your *miracle*." He made no secret of his skepticism. "And I know how they demonstrate such favor. For someone who's always claimed to have no interest in gold, there have always been people putting coins in your hands."

"And they ran right through my fingers like rain, showering down upon others."

"I see what you've built over your lifetime. The followers. The churches. This monastery."

"It was never my ambition," Francis explained, though the exertion was clearly draining. "I never had any aspiration, except to feed as many of the hungry as I could, to make sure the naked were clothed, and to see that the sick knew some comfort in their suffering."

"Spare me. We both know well that there are no treasures greater than the Church's own coffers."

"Alas, as my interests were never theirs, so their fortunes are not mine."

"There must be more," Giovanni said. "Some cache that you set aside for yourself, a wealth amassed that can no longer serve you here on Earth and that you could now share with one to whom you owe so much—and who needs it so badly."

"And now, at last, we arrive at your destination." The realization pained Francis as severely as any of his symptoms. "Am I right? As I fight to keep what little life I have left, you come to my deathbed with a request that conceals the allegation that all my life was a lie? And that I owe you gold, as a result?"

"*Lie* is not my word," Giovanni said artfully. "But no man could be as virtuous as you've pretended to be. There has never been a heart so pure that would allow a man to do all that they say you've done."

"My heart is not as pure as the world would pretend. You're right about that."

Francis's admission shocked Giovanni. "I'm what?"

"You have found me out, my old friend. All that you say is true. I am not who the people say I am—and I never have been. I am just a man. My heart is as tainted as any other, I assure you. Where I should have humbled myself before God, I was consumed by treasures of this world far greater than even you could ever imagine."

"I knew it." Giovanni clenched his fists with excitement.

"Should I share that with you now?"

"You should, brother." The words were eager, like hungry dogs pulling at their chains.

"I think so, too. As I prepare to leave this life, I would like nothing more than to share with you that which I have valued above all else."

"Yes, brother." Like hungry dogs sniffing out dinner scraps.

Francis' trembling hand patted a spot beside him. "Then draw up closer to me now, and I will tell you a tale. Some of which you have lived through yourself, but none of which you could have ever guessed at. Still, I swear that every word is true. And, when I am done, I promise you that I will have revealed my greatest treasure to you—and only to you."

2

The physician stepped out of the room, grateful to be away from the chaos he could not control, away from the madness inside, even if only for a single, stolen moment. Before he had a chance to catch his breath or wipe the sweat from his brow, the lady's handmaiden charged out of the room. "What are you doing out here?"

She was aware the physician was far above her station in every regard and equally conscious that such insolence to a respected gentleman of Assisi might have serious consequences for her, but she had greater concerns than her own welfare. "My lady lies in *there*." She pointed back into the room that the physician had just fled.

"I don't think you understand the seriousness of the situation," he said.

Her name was Maria and her eyes were fierce. "What I understand, sir. Is that the man of the house is away to France on business. Signor Pietro di Bernadone has left the care of his wife, Signora de Bourlemont, in my hands and he is expecting to return home to find that both she and his newborn child are in fine health. He has made it quite clear that my own health is dependent upon this." She caressed her own belly, which was also swollen with child.

"Then I would save your prayers for you and your own child," the physician said. "Because I am certain I cannot save both your lady and her child."

"That may be," Maria said. "But I am equally certain that if you abandon us now, my fate at the hands of Signor di Bernadone with be a thousand-times more merciful than that which he will visit upon you."

The physician was well aware of Signor di Bernadone's reputation. He was equally familiar with Assisi's willingness to indulge its favored citizens' occasional bad acts, including any act of violence that might pass for justice.

"I will try what I can," he assured her and turned back to the room. "But I am afraid I am not entirely sure what else there is left for me to do."

"Then I fear for both of us," Maria replied and followed the physician back into her lady's bedchamber.

The room was more than large enough to comfortably accommodate the enormous bed that dominated the far wall. Intricate carvings of lustful nymphs and wayward maidens cavorted their way up and around the four posters. The silk curtains were all tied back so as to reveal thick layers of fine linens. And in the center of it all, lay Signora de Bourlemont.

Her bed gown was soaked in sweat and her skin was so pale that anyone observing the scene would have concluded she had long since departed this world. The only signs of life were her body's tortured convulsions and the anguished screams that escaped her panting mouth as her only way of managing her unimaginable pain.

The physician approached his patient tentatively, an admission that he had long since exhausted the totality of his education and training. There was more fear in his eyes than in hers.

"Signora," he began. "The child. I am afraid its fight for life is in vain. But with every passing minute that it struggles to resist this inevitable fate, it steals from you what dwindling chance you have to preserve your own life."

The woman's only response to the dire diagnosis was another groan, louder and more urgent.

Maria spoke only because her lady couldn't. "What are you saying?"

"If you let me—" The physician stopped, knowing his very life depended on choosing precisely the right words to convey his proposal. "If I were to hasten an outcome that cannot be changed, if I were to end the poor child's suffering, then that unfortunate event might well prevent a tragedy that would be far, far greater in your lady losing her own life, in addition to the child's."

This time it was the handmaiden who was silent.

The lady spoke. "No!"

"But, Signora," the physician pleaded. "Your child is beyond my help. You, however, are still within the grasp of medicine."

"No!" she screamed.

Maria took her mistress' hand. "My lady, we must save your life. At all costs."

"My life at the cost of my child's? No, that is too dear a price to pay. If my baby has slipped past this world, then I have no use for this life either and we shall be together wherever we go from here. I will not abandon my child, and if that means following it into death's darkness, then I will be grateful to cradle it in my arms."

"You're swayed by your fever, Signora," the physician said.

"I am," she admitted. "But my words are born of faith, not fever. If you would leave my child, then leave me, too. If you would abandon us in this life, then take your things and go."

She turned to her handmaiden. "See that this surgeon is sent on his way. And return instead with a priest. If my child and I are to leave this world on this day, then I would ask that our departure is properly announced."

"Signora—" Maria began.

But Signora de Bourlemont would hear no more. "There is nothing more to say. Go and get the priest. I would gladly put my fate in the hands of God, because I am certain that His mark is already upon my child."

3

Pietro di Bernadone was, indeed, well known throughout Assisi, but echoes of his name had carried far beyond that city's gates. He was a merchant, a seller of silks and other fine fabrics, and so his reputation had spread not only throughout the city-states of the peninsula, but also far, far beyond. From Paris to Constantinople, his name was well-known and well-regarded.

Maintaining such a reputation, however, came at a price.

Building his business, necessitated regular travel to Constantinople and the markets of the East where he bought the silk and linens and other exotic fabrics that were the mainstays of his trade. And then, laden with that valuable inventory, Pietro accompanied his caravan to all of the markets across Europe, servicing existing customers and developing new ones. The endeavor was extremely lucrative, but difficult and dangerous. With the majority of his time spent elsewhere and his attention focused on other matters, returning home often felt to him as if he were just visiting yet another new city and getting to know another group of new strangers he would only half remember in a couple days' time.

This particular occasion, however, was different.

He and his wife had tried for the longest time to begin a family, but it wasn't until the evening before this latest trip that she had finally come to him with the long hoped for announcement that she was with child.

If cancelling the excursion had been a possibility, he might have considered staying until after the child had been born, but such a solution was simply out of the question. All of the arrangements had been made and the members of his company had already been paid a portion of their compensation in advance. There was no going back. Or, at least, it would have been too costly by his calculations.

And so, Pietro had set off on yet another adventure, which by now had become almost routine. This particular trip, however, had been different.

There was no location that he visited that was as foreign or exotic as the prospect of becoming a father, and he explored that new ground with an enthusiasm greater than even that which he had applied to his business. While the rest of his company sampled the local drinks and sought the company of the native women—activities in which Pietro had once happily led the way— this time he spent most (but not all) of those nights lying beside a fire, looking up at the stars, and drifting among those twinkling lights with the imagined adventures he would soon share with his son.

His son—because he knew the child *must* be a son.

So, instead of carousing with his men, Pietro had dreamt away the weeks and months, fantasizing his way over the dusty trails and through crowded bazaars, lost in the wonders of an imagined parenthood. The one thing that hadn't changed, however, was that there was always something about having spent months out on the trail that made the transition from their nomadic existence to domesticity difficult to achieve. Pietro had always figured that this delicate acclamation was more easily accomplished with one last belly-full of wine before setting off for home and this occasion didn't strike him as any different.

There was an inn just off the road to Assisi at which Signor di Bernadone had made something of a tradition for such celebrations. The location was sufficiently within the town's borders to be considered "home," and yet far enough from his own domicile and customary domestic rounds to keep him from familiar (and prying) eyes.

Or so he thought.

He and his companions had only just settled themselves down at a table, with the wine still yet to be poured, when a fellow merchant wandered to the table.

"Signor di Bernadone." It was a heartfelt greeting, but surprisingly solemn.

"Signor Mantegna," Pietro replied, happy enough to renew their acquaintance, but wishing their reunion could have occurred under other circumstances and at another location. If there was a merchant in the area that had realized more success that Pietro himself, it was Signor Mantegna and the encounter made him feel awkward and small.

"I'm relieved to see you here enjoying yourself with friends after—"

"After what?" Pietro's question was tinged not with alarm, but a certain concern.

Mantegna's face seized with regret as he realized his faux pas of having said too much when nothing should have been said at all. "Forgive me, Signor. I had only recently heard that the surgeon had come to your house and I innocently assumed—"

"You assumed what?" Pietro bellowed, but he did not wait for a reply. "A surgeon you say? To my house? How long ago?"

"Last week," Mantegna answered.

Under normal circumstances, Pietro would have stayed at least long enough to extend apologies for his hasty departure to one whose stature and station were slightly, but clearly, higher than his own.

This situation, however, was anything but ordinary.

So, without another word to anyone, Pietro had mounted and taken to the road at a full gallop, too quickly gone to hear the rest of Mantegna's apologies. He rode like the Devil was at his heels, but his thoughts were turned to God. For a man given to moral bartering, the two often kept such mixed company in his head.

Pietro di Bernadone was, of course, a good Christian. A good Christian, but a *practical* one.

He observed the holidays and festivals, held himself out as a model of a man, and always made certain the bishop was aware of his "generous nature." Still, his piousness was always coupled with an understanding that a Christian man was, after all, just a man. Such a practical faith, however, was not enough to weather the prospect of a crisis that seemed far bigger than even he thought he was, so in the time it took Signor di Bernadone to spur his horse all the way home, he found within himself the devout piousness of the truly terrified.

Each thumping beat of his heart was a frightened, fervent prayer and every labored breath was a promise to God that if his wife were spared, then he would

... he would do whatever his Lord and Master might ask of him. And if his wife and his child were spared, then he would gladly do that much more.

Anything.

Anything at all.

"Please, God, *please*."

If God was unwilling to grant his prayer, he was also prepared to deal his soul away. And if God wasn't willing to make the bargain, then he was open to whoever might.

When he finally arrived home, he pulled hard on the reins and dismounted, leaving the frothing steed behind as he burst through the front door and ascended the stairs two by two.

"Pica! Pica!" His voice was desperate like he was calling her back from the darkness that completely consumed the interior of the home. He met the handmaiden on the stairs, but pushed past her like she was just part of the darkness, a shadow to be ignored.

"Pica! Pica!" he cried.

"Signor," Maria called after him. "Please, Signor."

And just then his heart stopped.

He thought he could hear the whole tragic story in just the way the woman had said his name. His shoulders dropped and his fear began to turn to rage. Against her for having failed the orders he'd left her with. Against God, Himself, if He'd had any part in it. And the Devil, too.

"Please, Signor" Maria whispered. "You'll wake my lady."

"Your—"

"She is sleeping, Signor."

"Sleeping?" He was grateful now for the darkness as a cover for the tears welling in his eyes.

"Yes, Signor. I'm afraid the baby had her up all night."

Signor di Bernadone climbed the remaining stairs as if they were obstacles between life and death.

His.

And hers.

The commotion his entrance had caused had already awakened her, and now she stood at her open chamber door waiting for him. The sight of her there was a reward that made him hurry all the more. He threw his arms around her and picked her up as if he'd just plucked her from the depths of death and had resolved he would never lose her again. He peppered her neck with kisses and filled her ears with whispered *I love you*s strained by both emotion and exertion.

He held her at arm's length to get a better look at her beauty and to steal a chance to catch his breath. "You—"

She smiled. "I'm fine."

"They said that the surgeon—" Every attempt he made at expressing the desperateness of his state fell apart even as he tried to give it voice.

She understood. She pressed a single finger to his trembling lips. "I'm fine."

Her reassurances only shook his confidence more and raised a specter that he could not face or speak aloud. "And the ..."

A loud and irritated cry split the silence of the moment. A baby's cry.

"He's fine," she said. "Except that now you have woken him."

"He?"

She nodded. "You have a son."

Pietro released her and went immediately to the child, who was wailing even louder now. He stopped in his tracks. He had travelled from one end of the world to the other in his boundless quest for wealth and riches, and so it was more than a little disquieting to find the greatest treasure of all right before him in his own home.

Pietro picked his son up from his crib and held him to his chest. The child never stopped crying, but the father took that as a sign that his son was strong and full of life.

"My son," he whispered. "My—"

"There were concerns." Pica's voice behind him was soft and low. "They called for the priest."

He turned to face her, terrified that everything that he had gained in that miraculous moment might still be taken away again. He held his breath.

"We're both fine now," she said with a tired smile. "But the priest needed a name in order to perform the Rites. So, I named him Giovanni."

"Giovanni?" He turned from her and looked down on his son. "There are a thousand Giovannis in Assisi alone. That is far too common a name for this child, for my son."

"But I thought—"

"No, no. This boy will travel the world with me, enjoy the finest splendors and have the greatest adventures. He will be sophisticated and confident like the Francs to the north."

When he turned back to his wife, his eyes were wide and bright with inspiration. "Francis."

The name meant nothing to her. "But why?"

"The Francs are a fine people. Wait until you see the treasures that I have brought back from their lands. What better introduction could I give this boy than to name them in their honor?"

"I wouldn't deprive anyone of the honor they deserved," she said, "but I named him Giovanni as it means 'God has shown favor.' And truly, by giving us this child, God has done just that."

"Of course, He has. But God's favor has already been granted, let us name our child that he may receive the favors of this world, too."

Pica said nothing, she knew there was no other argument she could give her husband on the subject. Still, she marked the moment, knowing that all of their lives had been forever changed within her husband's decision to take back from God what she had already given.

4

There are few more foolish than one who has survived a crisis through no work of his own and yet boasts that his good fortune is something solely of his own making. Pietro di Bernadone was not shy in bragging to whomever would listen about the blessings that God—and by this, he meant his own hard work and sharp wit—had bestowed upon him.

He had a flourishing business, a reputation as a man of means throughout Assisi, and significant influence with the Church. His family was the envy of all of Assisi. His wife, Pica, was considered to be a jewel of a woman in a land where all women were beautiful. And his son had been greeted and treated by all not as just an infant addition, but as a prince.

Pietro di Bernadone was a blessed man, indeed. He enjoyed those blessings with an appetite for life that could not be satisfied. He drank the finest of wines, ate the richest of foods, and never once pushed away from life's banquet table that he wasn't soon hungry for more. As his fortune grew, his success only left him yearning for more. And so, he travelled further and further to more exotic locations in search of greater treasures to add to the ones he already had.

On those occasions when he was home, he enjoyed the company of a wife he loved dearly, but not even she was enough to sate his hunger. And he was not a man to be denied. No matter what his appetite demanded.

So, when Pica's handmaiden, Maria, had tearfully confessed to her mistress that she, too, was with child, there was no further discussion of the matter at all within the household. Instead, Pica continued on as lady of the house and Maria went about her duties as if nothing had changed—even if those duties no longer took her outside of the house or beyond the family's grounds.

And when it was time for Maria's child to come into the world, a single midwife attended to her without drawing any more attention to the event. The newborn was laid in his mother's arms, but she did not look down upon her son. Instead, her first reaction was to look up to her mistress with tears in her eyes that each conveyed a thousand unspoken apologies.

"He's beautiful," Pica said, silently offering an apology of her own.

"He is," Maria said, but even those words were tinged with guilt. "I don't know what to name such a child." Maria tears flowed more freely, until she was sobbing under the weight of her new responsibility.

"I do," Pica said with a smile. "We shall call him Giovanni, for surely God has shown you favor with this child."

5

Parenthood is the greatest of blessings. And the worst of curses. It is a bounty of joy and fulfillment. And a state of perpetual loss. Each passing day brings more than its share of magic and wonder, but then slips away under cover of darkness leaving nothing behind but memories. And those days slip past by too quickly. In no time, they become months. And then years.

So it went, until there came a time that whenever Pica and Maria watched their sons at play, each of them silently aware that they had lost forever the babies they'd once held in their arms, the toddlers who had brought smiles to everyone's faces, tripping over one another. They were boys now, young men, and that bittersweet realization left both women desperately hoping that time wouldn't strip that from them, too.

Pietro, however, couldn't wait for the time to put an end to Francis' boyhood completely. Giovanni's, as well.

He was impatient for good, strong men whom he could bring into his ever-growing business. And he took every opportunity that he could find to speed along that process.

On one particular day, a terrible crash that had echoed throughout their villa was traced back to the two boys, who stood wide-eyed and slack-jawed with wooden swords in their hands and the shards of a shattered porcelain vase at their feet.

"It-it-it wasn't me, father," Francis stammered.

At the exact same time, Giovanni claimed, "It wasn't me, Signor di Bernadone."

"And who should I believe?" Pietro asked.

Neither boy had a response, but only cast an accusatory glance at the other.

"As I thought. Then I shall make certain you *both* work off your debt to me."

"Pietro," Pica tried to intercede. "They're just boys."

"And they'll never be anything more if you don't stop coddling them. They are more than old enough to learn that actions have consequences. When they break another's property, they should be prepared to make amends."

He turned to the boys. "Do you understand?"

"Yes, Papa."

"Yes, Signor di Bernadone."

"I will see you both at the very first showing of the sun tomorrow morning, and you shall each work at my stand in the market until I decide that your debt to me has been paid."

6

The sun hadn't even begun to break through the night's black veil, but the di Bernadone house was already bustling with activity. Neither Francis nor Giovanni were a willing part of it, however. In fact, neither had known that such an hour existed before Pietro had pulled them from their beds and marched them down to his stall at the marketplace.

"Did you ever wonder how we are able to live in such a lavish house? To enjoy the life that we enjoy?"

If either of the boys had an inkling, the hour was too early and they were both too sleepy to say so.

Pietro was undeterred by the silence. He gestured to the market stall with enormous pride. "*This* is how we are able to live the life we do. We have so much because I work so hard. This life requires money, lots of it. And if you each work as hard as me, you both might have the same for yourselves."

He showed the boys bolts of fabric from all over the world, linens and silks in a diverse palate of colors and patterns. He lectured them on how to treat their customers and how to draw in those who might stand at the edge of the crowd just looking. But most important of all, he explained to the boys how each item was priced to accommodate a certain amount of haggling; not enough and the price was too soft, too much and the sale would be lost.

"You take their money and put it here," Pietro instructed, pointing out a small wooden box. "At the end of the day, I'll return and the goods missing from my inventory had better be reflected in the money in that box. Do you understand?"

"Yes, Papa."

"Yes, Signor di Bernadone."

And with that, the boys were left alone.

Each of them had been to the market before, of course. But they had never been *a part* of the market before, and that small distinction made all of the difference in the world. The smells were more intense, the sounds louder, and the colors brighter and more vivid. And, of course, the action of buying and selling was quicker than either of the young boys could have possibly imagined.

People snapped at them with questions about their wares and demands for *this* much of the silk and *that* much of the linen. They called to see this spool and then that bolt. But more than anything else, the adults that gathered in front of the stand were quick to try to take advantage of the young boys who had been left on their own, demanding discounts and lower prices.

Giovanni, for his part, was a natural and even quicker to stop them all in their tracks.

"The whole bolt's only worth half that," one would insist, clutching at the fabric they fancied for a larcenous bargain.

"Don't confuse young with stupid," Giovanni would tell them. "I'm young, but you're stupid if you think you're going to steal from me."

Francis, however, was a little slower to pick up on the combat sport of commerce. He had no interest in the haggling and bickering, and more than once he would've let some piece go for a fraction of its worth if Giovanni hadn't interceded.

By the end of the afternoon, Giovanni was handling the stall like he had been working in the trade as long as Pietro, himself. And it was equally clear Francis had absolutely no aptitude for the business. So, while Giovanni stayed at the front of the stall enthusiastically haggling with the crowd and making deals, Francis sat quietly in the back, seated upon a stack of fabric bolts and wishing only that their day in the market would be over soon.

Francis spent this time waiting by watching the people in the crowd. They were funny, he thought. All of them. So excited and agitated to get this bolt of cloth or that frock of garment when they already had clothes on their back. To Francis, that odd behavior seemed like calling for seconds when there was still a full plate already in front of them. The day was almost ended, when he became aware of some rustling movement from behind him.

"Boy." The voice was hushed, not soft, but wary.

Francis turned and was surprised to see that a man had pushed in between the flapping canvas sides of their stall. He was bent with age, brown with sun, and gaunt from many a missed meal. Francis had never seen anyone like him before. At least, not so closely. But Francis wasn't frightened so much as simply curious.

"Yes?" he said.

"I'm ashamed to ask, but I haven't eaten in so long that I'm afraid I might die right here and now."

Francis looked the man up and down and found nothing about his appearance to dispute his claims. "What can I do for you?"

"Could you spare a coin or two so I could get some bread or cheese?"

The request struck Francis as completely reasonable. While his own belly was full with the lunch Maria had packed for the boys, this man was suffering from want. To Francis, it only made sense that those who had so much—like his own family—should give to those who had so little. "Of course."

"Bless you."

Francis got up from his makeshift seat and trotted off to the coin box, which Giovanni had spent the day filling up. Without a moment's hesitation, he opened the box, retrieved a handful of coins, and then shut it tight.

He turned and was started back to the back of the booth, when Giovanni caught him by the arm. "Where are you going with that?"

Francis pointed toward the stranger. "This man hasn't eaten in some time. I was just giving him some money to get food."

"What?" Giovanni's reaction was more anger than alarm.

And before Francis could explain the situation, Giovanni had already pushed past him towards the old man. "Get out of here. Don't you know what happens to thieves like you?"

"I'm no thief," the man insisted.

But "thief" was the only word that the crowd heard.

Immediately, the crowd that had been so intent on taking advantage of the two children turned their collective attention from their larcenous bargaining to the old man cowered in the corner of the tent.

"A thief," they called out in a unified voice of righteous outrage. "Get him."

The mob moved as one toward the rear of the tent. The old man might have been on the cusp of death from hunger, but he had no intention of meeting his end at the hands of the angry townspeople. He dashed out through the hole in the back of the stand and disappeared into the market like a wisp of smoke into a night sky.

Francis could not understand what had caused such a commotion. He looked at the coins in his hand and thought that while such a small amount meant very little to his family, it could mean a great deal to a hungry man.

"The man's no thief, just hungry," Francis called to the crowd.

No one heeded his words, but before he could repeat them, another voice came booming out of the crowd. "What's going on here?"

The crowd parted to let Pietro have access to his own booth, and they all sheepishly slunk off, knowing that any "bargains" they might have been gained from the boys' inexperience disappeared with his presence.

"Francis was giving money away," Giovanni said.

"Money?" Pietro was shocked. "Giving it away?"

"It was only a small bit, Father." Francis opened his hand to show him the coins.

Pietro opened his hand, too.

He slapped Francis to the ground. "I won't tolerate a thief," he growled. "Not even my own son. *Especially*, my own son."

Francis did not cry. He put his hand against his stinging cheek, and then picked up the coins he'd dropped. He stood and looked straight into his father's eyes, not defiantly, but not deferring either. "No man is a thief who helps another man in need."

"And who told you that?" his father asked.

No one had actually told Francis that, not in so many words, but he was certain of it, nevertheless. He knew it had to be true, and so he cited the highest authority he knew. "God."

Pietro laughed. "God? The nonsense your mother pours in your ears is softening you, as I warned her it would. There is a place for God, but that is in the Church. Outside of the Church, this is a world of men, and we live by the rules of Man, not God. God never fed a man and if He doesn't feel the responsibility to do so, why should I?"

Francis looked to his father. "Because you can."

Without another word, Francis turned and ran out of the booth, following the same flapping exit the beggar had used. It took him a while, running as fast as he could, but eventually Francis was able to find the man, curled in the shadows, and looking even weaker than he had when they'd first met just minutes earlier.

"Here." Francis held out his hand and offered the coins. "These are for you."

"No." The man's voice was thin and shaky. "I don't want any of them. I don't want any trouble."

"There's no trouble," Francis assured him.

The man tilted his head. Francis nodded.

"Really? You're sure?"

Francis nodded more emphatically.

But before he could put the coins in the gnarled, outstretched hand, Francis heard Giovanni's voice. "There he is!"

Francis turned and saw his friend running towards him. Pietro came bringing up the rear, red-faced and breathing hard.

"Thief!" Pietro screamed. Without saying another word, Pietro raised his hand. Another slap sent Francis to the ground and the coins scattering across the cobblestones.

"I'm not a thief," the man insisted, thinking the accusation had been hurled at him.

"You come to my stall in the market looking for coins you haven't earned and then claim you're no thief?" Pietro snapped. "No, I suppose you're not. At least, a thief works at his dishonest trade. What do you do?"

"Nothing, sir."

"Then I suggest you go do it somewhere else."

The old man didn't need more of a warning than that. He sprang to his feet with an energy no one would've suspected he could possess and slipped off again into the crowd.

Francis wiped blood from his lip and got to his feet.

His father slapped him back to the dirt at his feet. "Don't get up. You stay down on your knees and pick up every single coin."

When Francis had done as he was told, Pietro took hold of his arm with a grip that could have easily ripped it from its socket. Pietro held out his other hand. Francis put the coins there. Pietro clutched the coins and shook his son with a terrible violence, as if he might rattle even more coins loose from the boy. "Your mother. The priests. They prepare you for a life in the next world. But right now, we live in *this* world and I must prepare you for that."

"But mother says—"

"Mothers say many things, because fathers give them the sort of homes where they can keep those soft concerns. But out here on the streets—where those mothers never need go to find a meal or a place to stay—things are different. The rules are different. And a man must be different, too. Do you understand?"

"I do." Giovanni smiled broadly and shook his head enthusiastically, even though he knew the words hadn't been offered to him.

Francis said nothing.

"Do you understand?"

"But—"

His father's wrath was only just barely contained. "Do. You. Understand?"

"I understand," Francis said finally.

"And so, what did we learn today?" Pietro asked his son.

Francis looked his father in the eye. "That you needed those coins much more than I thought you did."

7

"**O**ne. *Two. Three. Again.*"
Every day Francis was schooled in literature and writing, history and mathematics. There were lessons in Latin and Greek. Rhetoric and religion, too. Sometimes, when Giovanni's chores were done or deferred, he was allowed to observe, too. Francis had a gift for learning, but not a keen interest. Giovanni had neither.

For both boys, the most important lessons of all were reserved for after the day's studies were finished. That was when the *condottiero*, a professional soldier Pietro had met in his travels, would come limping up the cobblestone path to the house to begin another lesson, training Francis in the art of swordsmanship and other martial arts. A partner was necessary for Francis to train and so participating in these lessons was considered a part of Giovanni's daily chores. They were the only obligation he was happy to fulfill.

"*One. Two. Three. Again.*"

It might have been somewhat unexpected, but of the two boys, it was Francis who had the true gift with a sword in his hand. Giovanni was a bullishly aggressive young man and more than game to hack about with his wooden training sword, but it was Francis who was the true artisan with a blade.

He was light on his feet and so quick with his movements that his wooden sword slashed through the air as cleanly as steel. More important still, he had a keen instinct that put him always a step ahead of his opponent. And not just Giovanni. Before two years had passed, he could more than hold his own with his battle-scarred instructor, and by the time he'd reached his teens even that old mercenary acknowledged his gifts.

It was ironic then, that for a boy who seemed completely without purpose or ambitions, Francis' only appreciable talent was for fighting. In fact, everyone who saw the boy practicing his combat skills agreed he had all of the necessary qualities necessary to become a distinguished soldier and make a name for himself among the ranks of the military.

That is, all of the necessary qualities ... except one.

"No!" Pietro exclaimed, although he thought no one could hear him.

Pica came up from behind. "What's wrong?"

"Your son." He pointed down to the cobblestone yard where the Francis and Giovanni were being put through their drills.

"*One. Two. Three. Again.*"

She took a look for herself. "He looks like he's doing fine."

"Fine?" Pietro's question was sharper than the boys' blades. "He's as talented as any man I've ever seen pull steel from scabbard."

"Then I don't understand your concern."

"My concern is that although he has been blessed with a soldier's skill, he lacks the heart to put it to its intended purpose." He winced at something he had seen below. "See there, he has the advantage, as he has had at every turn today, but he lacks the heart to press hard until it leads to victory."

She smiled at the sight. "Our son may lack many things, but heart is not among them."

"The *heart* of which you speak is a softness which will cost him his life should he carry it out into this cruel world."

"Perhaps," she conceded softly. "His mortal life."

"And should he be concerned with another?"

"He should," she said. "And he is."

Pietro shook his head. "He is too much his mother's child and that has always been his problem."

She found a point of pride in the observation, but dismissed it. "Oh, Francis isn't my child."

"Well, who then almost gave her life to give him his?"

She smiled up at her husband. "I gave birth to him, that's true, but he has never been my son. Even on that terrible day when I was certain we both would die, I knew—have always known—he belonged to something far greater than me."

8

A poor man believes money is to be spent, a medium of exchanged used to buy the necessities of life, and then, maybe, to procure a distraction or two. A rich man, however, knows that money's true purpose is to make more money.

Pietro di Bernadone was a rich man.

A very rich man.

He had made a fortune in the mercantile trade, but that princely sum had gone on to generate still more riches. And more riches still. He made loans to other merchants who did not share his business acumen. He was the shadowy owner behind more than a few of the establishments that offered Assisi an opportunity to place a wager, have a drink, or seek the "company" of women. And many of the farmable fields at the outskirts of the city belonged to him, as well. It was one of these tenant-farmers who made his way to Pietro's door, late on a spring afternoon.

The man came with an offering of wine and a request for patience and leniency with that season's payment. His name was Abrezzi, and his bulky body looked like it had been pulled from the very land he tended. He travelled in the company of his son, Albi, who was about the same age as Francis and Giovanni, but bigger still than those two put together. And trailing behind the duo was their dog.

Maremmas are Italian shepherd dogs, as tall at the shoulder as a man at the waist. Their coats are as heavy and white as the snow that covers the mountains in winter. And they are loyal beyond any other consideration, protecting their people and their flock from wolves and bears without any concern for their own safety.

This one was named Orso and behind her trailed four plump pups that were her spitting image. And one straggling runt that certainly was not.

Abrezzi and Pietro talked business for a while. The farmer tried his best to articulate his position, and Pietro was quick to take advantage of the wine— and then the man's lack of business acumen. While the men talked, Francis and Giovanni played with the puppies, all the time under Albi and Orso's equally disapproving glares. The four pups chased the boys around and fell over one another. The little runt fell over itself.

When the sun was sinking low in the sky and the men's negotiations had come to completion, Albrezzi called to the boys and readied the pups to leave.

Pietro smiled at the sight and asked his son, "Do you like the dogs?"

Francis sat on the ground with the puppies jumping over one another, struggling for the chance to lick his face. "I love them all."

"I appreciate the wine," Pietro said to Abrezzi. "As I appreciate you coming to me as you did. Such an approach shows character and an understanding of commerce."

Abrezzi smiled nervously, knowing only too well what inevitably followed a rich man's compliments.

"But do you know what would really solidify our relationship?" The farmer knew better than to answer.

"If you were to give my son one of your puppies here," Pietro said. "That would be a much-appreciated gesture on your part."

Immediately, Abrezzi looked at his own son and a pained, tense conversation passed between them without a word.

"I would," Abrezzi hedged. "But the dog is not mine, she belongs to my own son. And the puppies as well."

Too young to realize that someone of his station could never win such a contest, Albi smiled.

Pietro did not. "You come to my home asking for my patience, asking for my understanding. I do what I can for you, and you can't return my kindness with the gift of a dog? A *dog*?"

The conversation had quickly escalated beyond mere social etiquette. Or even business negotiations. It was now a contest of wills. And money always settles those conflicts.

Abrezzi bowed his head in defeat. "Which one would the boy like?"

"But, Papa," Albi immediately objected. His father silenced him with a glare. "Which of the pups would your son like?" Abrezzi asked again.

Pietro smiled triumphantly.

"Well, tell the man, Francis. Which of the dogs here would you like as your own?"

Francis got to his feet and looked the group over. Four of the puppies leapt over one another in frenzied excitement. Francis chose the one that couldn't. He picked up the runt and held it to the chest. "I want this one."

"No," Pietro said. "That's the runt. She'll never grow up to amount to anything."

Francis knew better. "She'll grow up to be my dog."

Now Abrezzi was the one left smiling. "If that's the one your son wants, please accept it as my gift."

There was no way then that Pietro could refuse the offer without committing a serious social faux pas, so now it was his head that was bowed. "Thank you," he said, although each word burned in his throat.

"It's a pleasure doing business with you," Abrezzi said, still smiling. He turned and led his son and the rest of the dogs away down the road before Pietro had any opportunity to rectify the situation.

Pietro turned angrily to his son. "Do you know what you've just done?"

Francis simply smiled. "Yes."

"And what's that?"

"I've given a chance to a pup that didn't have one."

Pietro shook his head. "You've embarrassed me."

"I didn't mean to," Francis said. "But how could you be embarrassed by an act of kindness."

Pietro threw up his hands. "She's your dog now."

"I know. Thank you."

"You take care of her," Pietro hollered.

"I will."

"Because if you don't, I'll give her the end God intended for her."

Francis was scared by the threat but determined to protect his pup now. He held her tightly. "Clearly, *this* is the end that God intended for her."

Pietro stormed off into the house. Francis put the puppy down and ran about the courtyard. She did her best to follow. In time, the pup became known as Ombra because she followed Francis like a shadow.

9

Most measure a life in years, but Pietro knew that attaining manhood—*true* manhood—was something more than could be accounted for on the calendar. Manhood was a like the foundation of a house, constructed brick by brick with accumulation of certain skills and experiences. And by Pietro's reckoning, Francis was more than a few bricks short.

Francis' failures in this regard troubled Pietro. He knew fatherhood came with a host of responsibilities, but carried with it, he felt, a fair share of corresponding demands a parent might reasonably expect from their child. When he considered this balance between the two parties—he and his son—Pietro was confident he had more than fulfilled his paternal obligations.

The problem, he thought, was that in his estimation, Francis—*not that Pietro didn't love his boy*—had nevertheless failed his father in the bargain. And Pietro did love the boy. He *did*. Still, love did nothing to temper the growing frustrations he felt towards his son or to assuage the mounting fears that maybe Francis' *differences* were too great to overcome and too significant to allow the young man to make his way in the cold, hard world. So, Pietro concluded that if hard work, discipline, and a strong backhand across the face from time to time weren't an effective combination to force Francis into accepting the mantle of manhood, then perhaps there was another way to lure him there instead.

"Francis, get up," Pietro whispered, standing over his son's bed.

Only Ombra, the one-time runt of the litter who had grown to a fearsome size under Francis' loving care, stirred. The dog growled lowly at the intruder in his owner's room.

Pietro took a cautious step back. "Stupid mutt. I should have drowned you when I had the chance."

The growl gained resonance.

Pietro took another step back.

"Father?" Francis rubbed at his eyes. "What hour is it?"

"Late. Or early. However, you look at it. The others in the house have just now retired to bed. Don't worry about the time. Just get up and get dressed."

Francis did as he was told. "Is something wrong?"

"Only that you're going to wake the whole house with your questions. Now, keep quiet and hurry up."

When Francis was dressed, father and son slid out of the house without anyone taking note of their departure—except for Ombra, who let out one last low growl and then circled, circled, and circled some more before settling into the warm spot her master had left in their bed.

The night air was bracing contrast to the warmth of that bed for Francis. "Where are we going?" he asked as soon as they'd closed the door behind them and stepped out into the street.

Although there was no one around to hear his words, Pietro spoke in whispers. "We are going to a secret place, somewhere you must never talk about." There was an unspoken warning of dire consequences in his tone.

"I don't understand."

Pietro offered a smile of resignation. "There's a great deal about life you don't understand, my son. I have tried to tier your education with the more basic aspects of life, thinking we could work our way up to those more complicated elements, but this has not proven as successful as I might have hoped."

Francis sensed every bit of the disappointment contained in his father's words. "I'm sorry."

"But then I think to myself that, perhaps, you are one of those people who stumbles with the lightest loads, but easily carries the heaviest burdens. And so, I've decided that we will start your education with the most complicated of all the lessons you must master to be a man."

"Complicated?"

"The *most* complicated," Pietro corrected.

"And what's that?"

"Women."

"Women?"

"Yes," Pietro said. "The greatest reward and the most grievous punishment for being a man: women."

"I don't understand."

"Who does?" Pietro asked. "But tonight, I am taking you a special place where a very special lady will introduce you to a world that a boy like you could never even imagine."

"A special lady?"

"A very special lady ... who will make you a man."

"Am I not a man already?"

Pietro laughed. "There is one thing you must always remember when it comes to women, and this is true for them all, not just those that you will meet tonight. The perfume you smell is not her true scent. The makeup she wears is not her real face. And her smile, her swooning, and all of the '*I love yous*' in the world are not her authentic self. Every woman has a reason for everything that she does. How she smells, looks, sounds, feels, acts. All of it comes with some endgame in mind, for there is no more cunning predator in all of nature."

Francis' mind was buzzing with a hundred questions, trying to decide which one he should ask next. In that absentminded state, he followed his father around a corner and bumped straight into a figure wrapped in a cloak as black as the shadows from which it had stepped from. The collision took both parties by surprise, but in the instant before Francis could issue an apology for his clumsiness, something shocking happened. Something incredible.

Francis reflexively took a half-step back to get a better look at what had blocked his path, and there he saw ... *her*.

People may very well measure their lives in years, but when all those years have come to an end, every life is really defined by little more than a handful of moments. And this was one of those moments for Francis.

There was a young woman beneath the cloak. She was Francis' age, maybe a year or two older or younger, and so she too was teetering on the knife's edge that separates childhood from everything after. Her eyes were wide with surprise at their collision, and when Francis looked into them, he felt a pull he couldn't resist. Their eyes locked and—for Francis, at least—there was a sudden spark that burned away the blanketing fog that had always shrouded him in disinterest and indecision.

And, in that burst of illumination, he saw *everything*.

And everything that he saw made sense. The meaning he'd always been seeking. The purpose he'd always been lacking. Everything.

It was her.

Just her.

The boy who had always been directionless had suddenly become a man who had discovered his true north.

Then, just as unexpectedly as she had emerged from the shadows, she slipped back into their dark embrace and was gone.

For his part, Pietro hadn't taken any particular notice of his son momentarily bumping into some waif of the night. He'd moved on down the street and continued dispensing his sage advice as he went. "There are women we love and women we want, my boy. As a man, the trick is to know the difference between the two and to always refrain from chasing either one."

There was no response. No annoyingly naïve questions. And that silence was the first indicator to Pietro that he had been left alone. He turned and looked up the street and down, but his son was nowhere to be found.

Francis was gone.

10

The foundations of Assisi stretched back into the very mists of time. Umbrians. And then Etruscans. And then Rome took control of the region in 250 B.C., surrounded the existing settlements with walls built to withstand both invading forces and the ages. Like so many of those cities that were planned out and constructed with such strategic considerations in mind, Assisi's streets and alleys were twisted and turned like a mythological maze so that any wayward wanderer might become helplessly, hopelessly lost in their intertwining trap.

Francis' kept his eyes fixed on the young woman in the black cloak, but she moved quickly from shadow to shadow, turning here and dashing down that alley, then turning there and cutting through this courtyard.

Still, he kept her pace, hurrying after her, pushing his way past what few other pedestrians were out and about at that ungodly hour. Together their footsteps fell in syncopated rhythm, clicking and clacking against the cobblestones, until it seemed as if they were dancing across the city to a song that only they could hear. A *saltarello* performed across the entire city, a dance in which he wanted nothing more than to take his partner in his arms and pull her closer.

And in that spirit of desperate desire, Francis defied the silent sanctity of the late hour and called out to her. "Hey! Wait! Please!"

She did not stop at his plaintive shouts, but quickly turned a corner. Twenty rushed paces later, Francis rounded that same corner but found nothing but more shadows waiting for him there.

But just when Francis thought that he had lost her to the darkness forever, she popped out of her concealment in a doorway and stood there looking at him, not frightened at all, but offering something between earnest anger and quizzical amusement.

"Why are you following me?" she asked.

Everything about the situation took Francis completely off-guard, and he stood flat-footed in the moment trying to find the right words to express all of his racing thoughts.

"I just—" was all that came out.

She grinned, like she'd just won a contest between them. "You just what? Do you have any idea what time it is to be shouting like that, like a madman?"

It was a complicated question, and all that Francis could concentrate on was how beautiful her face was, lit by the moonlight she seemed to belong more among those celestial heights than on earth with him.

"Do you even know my name?" she snapped.

He didn't, of course, but he no idea what to say instead of making that admission. And it wouldn't have mattered anyway. By the time he could open his mouth to let all that silence out, she was already gone back around still another corner and disappeared. Completely vanished this time; disappeared from everywhere but his heart.

Francis, of course, had heard the troubadours sing of the sort of love that comes unexpectedly, all at once, and overwhelms a man, but he had never thought it might happen to him. He'd just assumed that all of their ballads were the sort of nonsense meant only to earn a coin or two from the crowd.

Still, he wandered the streets for hours that night, humming one of their ridiculous tunes, and hoping he might again find the mysterious love of his life.

He didn't.

Instead, he grew cold and hungry and weary for the bed he had left too many hours earlier. When Francis finally made it back to familiar streets and climbed the stairs that led to his home, his father was up and waiting for him.

Pietro shook his head sadly. "What am I to do? I can't even tempt you with the sweetest nectar."

Francis stood silently. The rebuking was much easier to take with his mind so many miles away, where in his imagination he had caught up with the mysterious young woman and they were now strolling, hand-in-hand, through an endless meadow dotted with wildflowers.

"Have you heard even one thing that I've said?" his father asked angrily.

"Yes." Francis smiled. "Women."

11

lthough he had excelled in his studies, Francis never demonstrated any appreciable skills that might lead to their application in real life. Except for the one. And so, Pietro had decided that if Francis would not follow him into the mercantile business, then he would follow Assisi's army into war.

"War. There's always one war or another," Pica said as she tried to straighten the straps that held the cold amour to her only son's chest. "I can't even imagine what all this fighting is about anymore."

"Our conflict with Perugia is complicated. The Ghibellines would recognize The Holy Roman Emperor and deny our Pope." Pietro knew such an explanation was an oversimplification. He shook his head at his wife. "How could I ever be expected to make a woman understand, much less a mother readying to send her boy into battle?"

"It's not a woman who can't understand war," Pica corrected. "It's any human being who has value for another."

Pietro gave her and her sentiment a dismissive wave of his hand. "Value is the very cause of all wars. Don't get me wrong, every conflict has its own causes, but every war is fought for only one reason: those who make war, make fortunes. War is gambling for those who are too rich and too powerful to be excited any longer by dice or fighting cocks."

"Well, I didn't raise my son to raise fortunes for someone else," she said.

"And just what exactly did you raise him for?" Pietro made no attempt to conceal the mocking nature of his question.

She wasn't insulted or deterred. "Something better than this."

"I'll be fine," Francis said. He tried to take his mother's hands, partly to comfort her and partly to stop her fussing over him.

"He'll be fine," Pietro repeated. "Besides, this is the opportunity he needs."

Pietro turned to his son. "You do what your commander tells you to do. You fight well. Fight hard. There is a place to be made in this world for a young man of your position who has established himself as a soldier."

"I'm not doing this for myself," Francis said.

"Then you are a fool," his father retorted.

"I'm doing this for Assisi. For the Pope," Francis said.

"Assisi and the Pope can take care of themselves," Pietro said sternly. "Listen to me for once. This is a chance for you to do something that will allow you to make a life for yourself."

Francis looked at his father blankly.

"You've already proven you're no merchant." Pietro laughed, but neither his wife nor his son found the humor in recalling that story. "So, be a soldier. A man of military rank can earn a good, little life."

"I don't want a little life," Francis said.

"His father scoffed. "Keep up that attitude and all you're likely to have is a short life."

"Pietro!" Pica's voice was filled with horror and reproach.

Pietro went to his wife, because even he knew he'd gone too far. "Oh, don't get so upset. The chances are good they won't even draw their swords."

"Really." Hope lit up her face.

"Really," Pietro assured her. "They'll march off and meet the army from Perugia on a battlefield somewhere. Our commander will meet their commander in the center of the field. They'll make their demands. We'll make our demands. And then, by every expectation, a deal will be struck, and both sides will just march back home again."

"Really?" she asked again.

He smiled like he knew a secret. "Trust me."

"I do." She kissed her husband on the nose and slipped out of the room to ready herself for the trip into the heart of the city.

As she was leaving, Maria appeared at the door. "Signori, you asked to see Giovanni before we left."

"Of course, of course," Pietro said. "Come in, my boy."

Giovanni's armor was not new or shiny like Francis', but the used pieces gave him the look of a man who had seen battle before—and lived. More than once.

"Now *that* is what a soldier looks like," Pietro exclaimed and clapped Giovanni proudly on the back. "Are you ready?"

"I am," Giovanni said. It wasn't just his words that expressed his eagerness for the fight, his eyes were hard and set with deadly purpose.

"Good," Pietro said. He draped his arm over Giovanni's shoulder. "You just remember that when the battle begins, there is only one way off of the field and that is to kill your enemy. Every one of them. For you to live, they all must die."

Giovanni's eyes twinkled just like Pietro's. "I understand."

"I thought you said that there probably wouldn't be any fight at all?" Francis interrupted.

Pietro tossed him a bored glance. "That's something I said for your mother, to make her feel better. Of course, there will be fighting."

Something in that exchange sparked a thought for Pietro, and he turned to his son like he'd forgotten everything else. "I gave you a chance to start in my business and you ran away. I tried to let a real woman make a man of you and you ran away. Now, you march out to battle. If you run away from this, don't come back home." There was no armor that could protect Francis from those words. "I won't run away."

"It would be better for all of us if you fell on the field, than if you returned home a coward," his father continued. "Especially for you."

"I won't run away."

"Good." Pietro slapped Giovanni on the shoulder. "You take care of Francis."

"I always do," Giovanni said.

"You'll do well," Pietro assured them both. "You'll do fine."

Pietro led Giovanni from the room.

Francis followed behind.

12

"It's odd, don't you think?" Francis said as they walked through the crowd.

Pica was quick to indulge. "What's that?"

"Seeking God's blessing so that His children can go off and kill more of His children," Francis said.

"Hold your tongue, boy," Pietro cautioned. "Talk like that will see us all tried as traitors. Or heretics." He took an indignant step or two. "And they are *not* the children of God. They are Perugians. No better than dogs and more deserving of death at the cold, steel blades wielded by the fine men of Assisi."

"That's exactly what we'll do, Signori Pietro," Giovanni said.

"Good, good." Pietro stopped in his tracks and pointed to a group of soldiers that had gathered at the far end of the town center. "That's your company," he said to Francis and Giovanni. "You should go and make yourselves known."

Pica began to sob.

And so did Maria.

"Stop it, both of you," Pietro scolded. "Your little boys have long ago left you and this is not a time for tears."

He turned to Francis and Giovanni. "Go, go. Run along and we will find you after the bishop has given his blessing."

Both young men did exactly as they'd been told. They introduced themselves to the other members of their company. Some of the men assembled there were as eager as Giovanni, but most were as full of trepidation as Francis.

When whispered word circulated through their number that the bishop's procession was making its way, the entire crowd assembled itself so that everyone was facing towards the cathedral in anticipation of his arrival. Banners fluttered in the wind as a large entourage entered the city square.

The bishop, adorned in flowing robes and vestments entered behind, solemnly acknowledging the rousing welcome. He ascended the platform to address the crowd.

"Children of Assisi," he called out to the assembled.

At the northern edge of the crowd, Giovanni quietly nudged Francis. "Don't worry. Everything's going to be fine. Just follow me."

"I'm not worried," Francis insisted, as loudly as he could without drawing reproachful glares from those who were paying closer attention to the bishop than he was.

And that much was true.

He *wasn't* afraid.

Not really.

Not so much frightened as distracted by his own thoughts. He knew that he should be listening to the speech, that there must be something important to be gained in the words a man of his position was offering to the assembled troops and the people of Assisi. Francis tried to focus. Yet the harder he tried, the more his mind wandered like a bird on the wing, with his eyes following after to give chase across the crowd.

And that was when he noticed her.

Her.

He had found *her* for the second time.

13

Francis knew that every good Christian's thoughts should rightfully be fixed on the bishop's words; a drifting mind was a sinful mind. He was equally aware that the men around him were likely preoccupied by thoughts of the battle they would soon be marching off towards—and the prospect that they might not be marching home at all. Francis' thoughts, however, were neither with God nor with Assisi.

His thoughts were with *her*.

And they had been with her ever since the night he'd first seen her. He had chased after her that night, running into the dark with no hope other than to introduce himself and maybe learn her name. She'd eluded him, slipping off into the shadows, but that was the only escape she had managed. In his fertile imagination, he always caught up to her. Over and over again. Visions of her had kept him sleepless at night and caused him to drift off into dreams during the days.

Every day, every night, his thoughts were with her.

So, when he scanned the crowd, expecting nothing but to be disappointed by a sea of lifeless faces, and he found her standing there among them, he naturally assumed that it was just some odd effect of the stress of his situation. An impossibly beautiful mirage in a desert of despair. But there she was, standing at the far edge of the crowd, wrapped in the same black cloak she had been wearing when destiny had first brought them crashing into one another.

Unlike Francis, she must've been a good Christian, because her eyes were fixed on the bishop. Or at least, she didn't seem to notice Francis at all. He understood that Death was a soldier's constant companion, and he knew that he might well meet his end in the coming days. Despite what his father had suggested, and Giovanni had seemed to tacitly confirm, Francis had no fear of losing his life. Or, at least, not much. The only prospect that left him cold from his bones to his soul was the harsh fate of meeting a soldier's end without ever having met *her*, without having her name to gasp with his dying breath.

"Move," Francis whispered to Giovanni, as he pushed past him. "I've got to go."

"Go? You can't go," his friend said, but Francis was already on his way. "You promised your father."

"I'm not running away," Francis insisted. "I'll be right back."

Francis pushed his way through the rest of the line of solders. Some resisted his efforts to move past, others pushed him back and grumbled, but Francis didn't care. He could not be stopped. He worked his way through the crowd until he reached its edge, and then he pushed himself free.

It took a moment to reorient himself, trying to find her again amongst the large crowd. At first, all he saw was just a sea of stern, disapproving faces. His heart dropped and he wondered if his first impression hadn't been correct and that the sight of her had been nothing more than a trick of his imagination. He had just about given up hope and was preparing to return to his spot among the other soldiers when he spied her again at the back of the square.

He moved straight towards her like a lost man returning home.

She spotted his approach, turned, and ran.

They might have been coquettish games she was playing with him or she might simply have been frightened by the soldier dressed out in full armor approaching her purposefully, but whatever the cause, Francis hadn't taken more than a step or two in her direction when she disappeared.

14

Nothing builds determination to achieve one's goals today like the uncertainty of one's tomorrow. By the end of the day, Francis knew he would be marching off with his company, out of Assisi, and towards an enemy waiting for them somewhere beyond the city walls. He had no promise that he would ever return. And although he wasn't as frightened of that possibility as others believed, there was some nagging part of his intuition that was warning him that he was among those who would never make it back to Assisi. So, when she turned and disappeared yet again, Francis was determined to capture, at least, the prize of her name. So, he ran after her.

He stood at an intersection of two streets, looking in all cardinal directions, but there was nothing and no one to be seen. There at the crossroads, exhausted, defeated and desperate, he prayed for guidance. He prayed but remained completely alone.

As Francis had matured into manhood, he'd developed a fondness for the travelling troubadours and their tales of courtly love, and it was through those lyrics that he had come to contemplate his life without the woman he'd never met. If he survived the coming battle, it would be a thoroughly miserable existence without her. Yet there was nothing to do with all of his youthful determination to discover her name. She was simply gone.

He turned to look one last time, heaved a heavy sigh of defeat, and then gave up on everything. And that was when she found him.

"You were following me," she said.

As ethereally as she'd disappeared, he spun around again, and she was suddenly standing there before him.

In the daylight, her eyes were even bluer than Francis had remembered or could have imagined. Long brown hair with sunbaked streaks like late summer honey framed her face. And her smile was more radiant than the sun in the noon sky above. She was more than beautiful; she *was* beauty itself and her presence before him left him speechless and stunned.

"You were following me, weren't you?" There was a touch of impatience sprinkled over her curiosity.

Francis desperately tried to collect his thoughts. "No," he said at first, because his true acts and motivations suddenly seemed to him like a crime he could never admit.

She stared at him.

"Yes," he admitted, realizing his pointless denial of the obvious only made him look guiltier of something even more sinister.

"Yes. No. Which is it?" Her nose twitched slightly as she toyed with him.

"Well, yes. I was following you," he confessed. "But, no, it wasn't like I was *following* you with any dark intention."

"And just what intention did you have?"

"I only wanted—" His desire was simple enough, but words failed its expression.

"You only wanted what?"

"Your name."

"And what would you do with it if I were to give it to you."

He looked straight into her sapphire eyes. "Cherish it forever."

She chuckled.

It was not the reaction he'd expected.

Or hoped for.

"Forever. That seems a very long time," she said. She took light steps around him, like an opponent in a fight looking for the advantage of an opening to strike the first blow.

"Not nearly long enough."

This time she was the one who blushed. "Well, if a name is what you're after, why don't you give me yours first."

It took him a second or two to recall it. "Francis. I am Francis."

"Is there more than that? Or just Francis?" Her full lips turned at the corners.

"Francis di Bernadone."

"di Bernadone?"

"Does that mean something to you?"

"One cannot live in Assisi and not hear of the name di Bernadone."

"So, you live in Assisi then? I thought for the longest time that you were just an angel who only visited us from Heaven."

"Do you talk like this to all of the girls?"

"I don't talk at all to any of the girls."

"I thought as much," she said as she turned from him and began to walk slowly away.

He was quick to follow.

She didn't turn to see if he was beside her, but spoke with the confidence of knowing he would be right there. "You're a soldier?"

Her words were like a reminder of something he'd forgotten. He looked down at his own armor and seemed to be surprised to see it there. "I am, but—"

"But what?"

"That's what I do—or rather what my father would have me do. But it's not what I am."

"Then what are you?"

He longed for an impressive response, but offered the truth instead. "I'm not sure."

"Well, I would like to spend the day talking with you about what you might or might not be, but I have somewhere else I need to be right now." She smiled and quickened her pace.

He stumbled as he followed after her. "Where are you going?"

"Heaven," she said. "I hope. In the end."

"I meant now. Today."

"I told you, I have somewhere else to be."

"Couldn't you be there another day? Tomorrow, perhaps. I am a soldier, after all. I'm marching off to battle."

"And I wish you Godspeed. I do. But the sort of comfort I have to offer is not the kind one would give to a soldier."

He worried that she'd, perhaps, misunderstood his intentions. "No, I'm not a solider. Not like that. I am Francis."

"With your armor and sword, it's hard to tell the difference."

"And that's why I would ask you for this day, just so that I could explain that to you."

"I'm sorry, but as I keep saying, today is not mine to give."

"Then your name, at least."

"I'm sorry?"

"Your name. If you won't give me your day, then won't you at least give me your name?"

She turned without a word and began to walk away.

"Not even your name?" he called after her. "While an army fights for Assisi, won't you give me your name so that I might fight for you?"

"I don't want you to fight at all," she said. "I certainly don't want you to fight for me."

She turned again.

He watched her go, believing in his heart that there was no purpose served to following her any longer.

And when he thought she was gone, that she'd walked right out of his life, she called back to him. "Francis?"

His name on her lips was the sweetest sound he'd ever heard.

"My name is Clare."

Heaven had a name, and its name was Clare.

15

"Clare," Francis called after her, but she was already gone. The armor strapped to his chest made it difficult to run, but the pounding of his heart gave a life to his legs he'd never known before. He raced after her down cobblestone streets, unconcerned with anything but catching up to her again. But despite his determination, she proved an ever-elusive quarry, far faster than he was. In no time at all, he had lost her.

And himself.

At the far edges of Assisi's borders, Francis realized that there were streets he was seeing for the first time. The further he went, the more unfamiliar the terrain became, until finally he wasn't certain he was in Assisi at all. He searched and searched until even someone as headstrong as he was had to throw up their hands and admit that there was no point to continuing the hunt.

With heavy breath and a heavier heart, Francis gave up. And just then, out of the very corner of his eye, he noticed nothing more than movement, a streak of black against the bleak landscape. He turned towards it and saw the tail of a cloak disappear behind the battered door of an old, abandoned church.

He approached the ruins warily. "Clare?"

There was no response, but he could hear movement inside.

With his heart thumping from more than infatuation, he put a hand to the rickety door and slowly pulled it open.

The interior of the church was dark, illuminated only by a few candles placed in sconces on the wall. In their dim illumination, Francis could make out a dozen beds, each of them occupied by a gnarled, groaning exhibit of what disease can do to ravage the human body.

Francis gasped at the grisly sight.

In the far corner, there were a number of standing figures, all of them dressed in black cloaks identical to the one Clare had been wearing. Logic wouldn't let him put all of the mismatched pieces together, but his heart couldn't stifle him from calling out, "Clare?" One of the black-clad figures broke from the group and moved towards him. The flowing fabric of the long garment made it appear as if they were gliding on air, rather that walking.

The figure stopped a distance away.

Francis took a step toward them. "Clare?"

"I'm not Clare." The figure pulled back the hood of its cloak and revealed a woman's face, not beautiful and vibrant like Clare's, but distorted by disease and scarred beyond recognition by leprosy's lethal mark. "You should go. Now!" The shock of the reveal drove Francis back a half step and he tripped over his feet, tumbling to the floor in a loud clattering of metal and man. The woman, now angered, spoke in her full voice. "Go! Now!" Francis pulled himself to his feet, threw open the door, and ran back the way he had come. He did not stop. And he did not look back over his shoulder.

If he had, he might have seen Clare watching him go from behind a corner of the old church.

†

By the time Francis made it back to the city square, the companies of soldiers had all assembled and were readying to begin their campaign. Francis pushed through their numbers, not sure where he belonged or what he should do. Fortunately, before he could find anyone, they found him.

"Francis," Pietro shouted above the din of the crowd.

Francis turned and headed toward the familiar bellowing.

"Where have you been?" his father demanded, with a swift cuff to the back of Francis' head. "Can't you even do this one thing without embarrassing me?"

"Pietro," Pica scolded.

"Woman, I love you. God knows I do. But you have so softened this boy with your constant intercessions that he doesn't even know enough to stay with his company on the very afternoon that they begin a campaign."

Pietro turned to his son. "I told you not to run away."

"I didn't run," Francis stopped. "Away."

"Where did you go?"

"It doesn't matter now. All that is important is where I'm going." And with that Francis kissed his mother. And his father. Pica tried to go to him for one last embrace, but Pietro stopped her. "This is not the time, wife."

She knew he was right and did not resist.

Pietro looked at his son. "Go now." Francis turned and took a step away. "Francis," his father called after him.

Francis turned.

"For God's sake, don't die." Francis could muster only a slight nod in response. "Now, go. Go and fight hard for the glory of Assisi." Pietro waved his son off.

Francis walked away, set in his heart that he would do just exactly what he'd been told.

†

Giovanni stood in the crowd holding the reins to a black stallion, but the mount wasn't his. "There you are," he called out to Francis. "For a moment I thought I was going to be the one riding into battle." He handed over the reins.

Francis had heard it all before. "I told you before, Diavolo was my father's idea, not mine." He looked around at the men gathering for war. "None of this was my idea." He offered the reins back. "You're welcome to ride in my stead."

"I know my place, *Signori*," Giovanni said with a smile.

They might have been as close as brothers, but there were times when Francis was unable to tell when Giovanni's joking verged into some greater, deep-seated resentment. This was one of those times.

Francis mounted the stallion and the beast bucked a bit beneath him, shifting anxiously from hoof to hoof.

"Are you sure you can handle Diavolo?" Giovanni asked. His grin betrayed just how much pleasure he found in Francis' difficulties.

"I'm sure." Francis gripped the reins tighter and prayed that the horse wouldn't make a liar of him.

"Where did you go anyway?" Giovanni asked.

There were other things on Francis' mind. "What?"

"Where did you go when you ran away just now?"

"I didn't run away." The horse began to settle beneath him.

"So, where'd you go?"

"Nowhere."

"It was her, wasn't it?" The grin originally caused by Francis' discomfort grew even wider.

"Who?" Francis bluffed.

"The girl. The one you bumped into on that night with your father."

Francis folded. "Yes."

Giovanni shook his head in disbelief. "I don't understand most of what you do, but your father takes you to visit a courtesan and you go off chasing some waif in the shadows." He chuckled.

"She's not a waif." Even Francis realized that he'd spoken more fiercely than necessary.

"Then what is she?"

"A lady."

Giovanni chuckled some more. "I'll bet she is."

"What do you mean by that?" This time Francis meant ever bit of malice that sharpened the edges of his words.

"The line's beginning to move," Giovanni said. With a nod of his head, he indicated the movement ahead of them.

The columns of soldiers, mounted and on foot, filed out of the city square on their way to battle with their mortal enemies in the neighboring city-state of Perugia. The crowd let out a thundering roar of approving applause and cheers.

"Do you even know her name?" Giovanni asked above the noise.

There was a moment when Francis was tempted to share what she'd given him, just to put an end to the ridicule, but a greater impulse stopped him. She had spoken her name only to him, and that gift was his and his alone.

Francis remained silent. He gave his horse the feel of his heels and endured the beast's protests, pretending he hadn't heard the question at all.

"That's what I thought," Giovanni said, his chuckle building to full laughter, which continued even as he kept pace with Francis. "There will be time enough for phantom girls, my friend. Whatever else you do now, just keep your head."

Francis held tight to the reins, more worried about the potential embarrassment of being tossed from his mount than whatever fate might be waiting for him at the end of the ride. He straightened his back and rode out of Assisi. He did not look to the left or to the right to scan the crowd for friendly faces, and he never looked back.

If he had, he might have seen Clare among the number waving him off and wishing their brave soldiers blessings and God's speed.

16

Life is a tapestry of unimaginable complexity. The threads of one happening are woven with those of a thousand other seemingly unrelated events, all interlaced and knitted together to produce a wondrous design of life and death, love and loss.

The Apennines mountain range runs along the south of Italy's Emilia-Romagna region. High among these snow-covered peaks, on a summit known as Mount Fumaiolo, a pair of springs bubble up from the ground and begin their run to the sea. Just two merging streams of clear, mountain run-off. Nothing could be purer.

And yet, it wouldn't be unreasonable to assert that these crystal founts are responsible for the whole of Western civilization. The triumphs and achievements. And some of its worst atrocities, as well, for those trickling waters that bubble up from these springs run together and grow in volume as they roll toward the sea and become the Tiber River, source of life for Rome.

On the second day of their campaign, the men who commanded the army from Assisi decided to make camp along the banks of the Tiber.

Looking up at the sun sinking in the afternoon sky, they decided the hour was too late to start the crossing and reasoned the riverside would make for a perfect encampment with both an endless source of fresh water and a natural line of protection like a moat.

And the commanders were absolutely right. The night passed without event. Or, at least, the men who had been left on watch failed to take any notice of the invader that slipped in amongst them during the cool of the night.

Camped down by the river, the army from Assisi woke at dawn to find that everything was enshrouded in a thick morning fog coming off of the river, an impenetrable mist that soaked the men to their skin and cut visibility to little more than a hand's length away.

Without breakfast in their bellies and shivering in their soggy clothes, the men grumbled across the Tiber, each barely able to see the soldier directly in front and unseen by the comrade following right behind. When the early morning sun failed to burn away the fog, Assisi's commanders made the decision to trudge on towards Perugia anyway. And so, they stumbled on, drenched and disoriented, and completely unaware of what lay ahead of them.

They were the blind leading the blind—into battle.

Their decision was a foolish one, of course. Pressing on when they couldn't see their hands in front of their faces was the worst kind of strategy. What made it so particularly catastrophic, however, was that this was exact same decision reached by the commanders of Perugia's forces, as well.

The blind leading the blind into battle with the blind.

And so, there was no opportunity for the two advancing armies to take stock of one another from a distance. There was no chance for them to set up their lines in straight rows and then to send their representatives across some field to meet and discuss the terms for a peace that might have allowed each side to just go back home. There was not even the possibility of assessing some sort of strategic plan for whatever carnage might eventually ensue.

There was none of that.

What there was instead were two armies that essentially tripped over one another in the midst of the impenetrable fog, both of them well upon the other before either was aware what had happened. There was no epic moment when the armies, resigned to the inevitability of battle, rushed towards one another and collided in explosions of flesh and steel, bone and blood.

Their encounter was nothing more than a tragic mistake.

And in the moment when each realized that the enemy was already upon them, they were all caught completely off-guard. The men of Assis were as startled as the men from Perugia, as it seemed to both that their foes had come out of nowhere. Confusion consumed them all, as the shouts of comrades trying to warn one another what had happened echoed in the morning air, pierced by the clanging of combatants' reckless swords.

The fog made it almost impossible to distinguish one man from another. Brothers-in-arms looked like foes in the thick haze and more than a few were fallen by swords errantly swung by their own comrades and most trusted friends. Chaos fed chaos, as the two armies, battling blindly, took to one another not in strategic military formations, but as primal beasts deprived of their senses and desperate to defend themselves and kill whatever it was they thought they saw moving as a shadow in the mist.

Men screamed and horses whinnied and neighed. Swords resounded against one another, a sharp tonal contrast to the sickeningly dull sound of weapons striking flesh. And above that terrible din, the screams of men, mortally wounded, echoed out in a growing chorus of anguish, desperation, and resignation.

All of it amplified in the cold, morning mist.

17

Ever since the day he'd been born, Francis' father had doubted his fitness to be a man. He loved him, certainly. Maybe even enjoyed his company from time to time, thinking that perhaps one day they might eventually grow to become friends. But, overall, Pietro had always doubted his Francis' mettle, his capacity to face life's darkest chapters with the ferocity of spirit and strength of character he felt necessary to meet those dire challenges.

Pietro had blamed his wife, of course, and worried that a mother's love had turned their son soft, kept him from developing the calluses on his heart and soul that were an unavoidable consequence of a boy becoming a man. He had always feared that that when *that* moment came, the moment when he was truly put to the test, that his son would fail.

Miserably.

Pietro had been certain of it.

And he'd been completely wrong.

When the battle began, Francis was the who fought most fiercely of them all. On the back of his stallion, Diavolo, Francis rode straight into the thick of the Perugian infantry. His sword slashed back and forth with ferocity, hacking at the men who charged him, cutting down those who turned to flee. Splattered with his enemies' blood, Francis rode like a demon through their ranks, killing every man who challenged him—and every man who conceded that they could not contend. And when he was eventually knocked from his mount, he was quick to climb back to his feet, fighting shoulder to shoulder with the men of Assisi, his sword cleaving through the enemy like their flesh and bone was no more than that morning mist.

Those who have never wielded a sword in combat are often given to the misimpression that a blade is a cold and efficient instrument for dealing death. A parry and a counter, a thrust, and then a quick, gentle death. That is not the case. In actuality, a sword is a savage tool and wielding it requires an unwelcomed intimacy with one's opponent. And with death itself.

In that moment when a blade is thrust into a man, the weapon creates a link between the two foes. The more fortunate of the two, the one holding the grip, can actually feel the last beats of a heart through the steel that binds them together. The swordsman sees the rush of dark blood come bubbling up out of his victim's mouth and smells the sickening stench of death, bile and feces.

He has to struggle to keep his grip on the blood-covered handle when his victim's spasms and the sudden weight of the final collapse threaten to wrench the weapon from his hands.

He hears the last gasps for breath, the gurgling sound of lungs filling with blood, and often that desperate cry for whomever it was that once tethered a soul to this world.

A wife.

A lover.

A mother.

No, killing a man with a blade is a thoroughly gruesome business. For Francis, however, the worst part of that horrible experience was how much he excelled at the task. For a young man who had never shown a particular talent for any endeavor in the whole of his life, it turned out that killing in the chaos of battle was the one thing for which he seemed to have an unnatural gift and for which he showed more aptitude than any other man on the field that day.

Man after man raced to face him in combat and every one fell at his feet. In the midst of the fighting, Francis felt oddly removed from the carnage and the killing came to him an easy practice, a simple science. From that perspective, he quickly learned that every fight was decided long before a single blow was struck. Victory and defeat weren't a matter of skill or strategy or even strength. Instead, there was an energy that flowed between two combatants and the one who was most committed to triumph, who would not accept defeat, but demanded that the whole universe bend to his will, he was the one who took the life of the other—the clashing of blades and butting of heads were all just a formality that followed. And so, as that young man with the long blond hair came charging out of the mist, roaring with his sword held high above his head, Francis knew with absolute certainty that the victory was his and that he was witnessing the young man's final moments on the Earth.

The young man wore armor emblazoned with the crest of Perugia, but he was no seasoned soldier. He swung his sword, not with the requisite murderous intent, but more as if he was terrified *not* to use the weapon. Francis blocked that initial attack easily and, with a single movement, easily disarmed the young man, his blade falling to the ground with a dull thud.

The confrontation was over.

Everything else was just procedure.

The soft spot in the young man's belly.

A sharp thrust.

That was all there was to it.

And yet, for the briefest of moments, Francis hesitated to make the kill.

In the frenzied fury of the battle, it was just a frozen fraction of an instant, but for that slice of time, all other action stopped and the gore-covered field fell deathly quiet.

Not a sound.

Not a movement.

Nothing.

Until it seemed to Francis that he was the only man in the fray who was aware that time had come to a screeching halt. In that uniquely personal moment, when nothing seemed to be alive except Francis, he found himself wondering if the man he was about to kill had anyone to love, if there was anyone who loved him.

A mother?

A Clare of his own?

The dead-man-to-be was slightly younger, but still Francis wondered whether he might already be a husband.

Or a father.

As Francis stood there, awed by the temporal lapse, but still ready with his blade to strike and take the man's life whenever time resumed, he heard a voice cry out. "Don't."

Francis recognized the sweet sound immediately, although he had only heard it once before.

The voice was Clare's.

"Don't. If you love me, you will not kill this man."

Francis knew the situation was impossible, of course.

Clare could not be there with them that morning. She was home in Assisi, more than a day's travel away. He knew that sure enough.

And yet the voice was equally undeniable, as strong and clear as if she were standing right behind him. "If you love me, you will not kill this man."

With time still frozen, Francis looked back to his foe and was startled to notice the striking resemblance that they shared. If not for the simple accident of fate, having been born in different cities, they might have easily been mistaken for brothers, might have been friends.

In fact, as Francis strained his eyes to look more closely at the young man, he thought perhaps that he might be looking into a mirror.

He tried to shake his head clear, but then when he looked again at the young man from Perugia, there was no foreigner staring back.

The young man *was* Francis.

He looked straight back at himself and said, "If you love me, you will not kill this man."

And now the voice took on a resonance of its own as if it was coming from every man on that field.

"If you love me, you will not kill this man," they called out in unison. Francis turned to face them and was shocked to see that they were all versions of himself.

Men of Assisi, men of Perugia.

Every single man on that field *was* Francis.

"If you love me, you will not kill this man."

And then the voice was louder still, as if it was springing from the skies above, and every syllable was a clap of thunder. "If you love me, you will not kill this man."

Dazed and disoriented, overwhelmed and overcome, Francis dropped his sword.

The weapon hit the ground with a dull thud.

And time resumed.

Whenever Francis thought back on it all, the only thing that he could ever remember was standing on that battlefield, unarmed, and watching his young opponent reach for the weapon he'd dropped on the ground. Then he heard Giovanni call out above it all, "Francis, no!"

There was a pounding of hooves. Giovanni rushed towards Francis, and pushed him to the ground. After that, everything went black.

18

Darkness was everywhere. And everything. There was nothing but darkness. And Francis. And then, all at once, he felt a sensation like he was plummeting from the highest point in the sky, falling so far and so fast that he thought he might never stop.

Francis opened his eyes and awoke with a start to find a man leaning over him. Francis could barely speak, but he forced himself to croak out the words, "Is this Hell?"

"No," the man said. "This isn't Hell. This is Collestrada, someplace much, much worse."

Francis tried to sit up, but the man gently held him back. "Don't. You need to rest now."

He had no strength to resist, so Francis lay back down, but was afraid to close his eyes for fear that he might never open them again.

Eyes still closed, he whispered, "Collestrada?" although simply speaking the name was more exertion than he'd expected it would be.

"Don't worry, my son," the man said. "Everything will be all right."

"Stop lying to him, old man."

Francis recognized the voice as Giovanni's. He recognized the anger, too.

"You're in prison, Francis. We're in prison. You did exactly what everyone told you not to do, exactly what I knew you would do. You had one of your fits or spells or whatever it is that happens to you. You dropped your sword on the battleground and when I tried to save your life like the fool I am, we were both knocked unconscious and taken prisoner."

Giovanni let out a shout of rage and frustration.

"We're prisoners, Francis. Because of you."

Giovanni stormed off.

Francis tried to get up to follow, but the old man again interceded.

"Let him go."

"He's my friend," Francis insisted.

"All the more reason to let him go," the old man said. "Besides, how far can he go?"

Francis craned his neck and could make out the shadowy boundaries of all four walls of their cell.

"None of them believed me when I said you were alive," the old man said. "You were on the burn pile."

"The burn pile?" Francis asked.

"The victors bury their dead, but they burn the fallen foes to stop the spread of disease. You were amongst the corpses when I came past. I told them you weren't dead yet, but they only laughed at me." He looked over his shoulder to see if anyone was listening. "Still, I dragged you away anyway."

Francis touched his brow and the gentle contact sent a sharp sting of pain jolting through his system. His fingers were covered with thick black blood when he pulled them away. "I'm not sure whether I should thank you or not."

"I'm not sure either," the old man said with a chuckle. "I've been sitting here beside you for three days while you tossed and turned, fighting and struggling just to stay alive. And the whole time, my only thought was that you were either blessed or cursed, and I couldn't decide which."

Francis took the risk and closed his eyes.

"Maybe both," the old man said. "I think both."

Francis let himself slip back into the darkness.

"Definitely both."

19

Of man's many inhumanities against man, most people would suggest that war is the worst of them all. They would be wrong. And their guess would only reflect the fact that they had never been locked up in a cage. Anyone who has ever been confined knows there is no greater suffering than prison.

War may scorch a soul with the licking flames of Hell, but prison smothers the human spirit forever and sentences any man who has served as much as a day behind bars to the endless torment of the limbo that follows. And so, where war either hardens men's souls like steel or turns them to ash, prison twists all men into some wounded and necessarily malignant version of whoever they once were.

There were twenty-two men held in a stone cell that was no bigger than a single room in the house where Francis and Giovanni were raised. There wasn't a single window for a sunbeam to sneak through or from which to steal a breath of something like fresh air.

Just walls and bars.

And men.

An unhealthy combination.

Giovanni was there, of course.

So was the old man, who said his name was Carito.

The commander of their company, Commander Alevetti, was with them, too; his head always bowed with the shame of defeat.

And a boy, Vincenzo, whom hardly seemed old enough to have left his mother's side, much less go to war.

The rest of the men were strangers to Francis.

They were farmers from the countryside or citizens of the streets whom someone of Francis' station would not have known in the ordinary course of the day. They were all as foreign to him as any of the men from Perugia.

And now they were all locked up together.

"Hey," one of the men shouted to Vincenzo. "Your bowl there," he grunted and nodded at the small wooden bowl of broth and kitchen scraps in the boy's lap. "I want it."

The boy was immediately terrified and started to raise his bowl in compliance.

Francis stopped him and looked up at the bully. "He needs that bowl himself." He thought it was a simple gesture, but Francis hadn't realized that he'd called the brute's authority into question.

The man was an imposing figure by any estimation, with a face that had been badly scarred and a black patch over one eye. He snarled and looked to the other men who had become excited by the palpable tension in the air and the promise of some imminent act of violence to break their boredom and entertain them.

"Then give me yours," the man demanded.

Francis didn't hesitate to offer his portion.

And when Giovanni tried to stop him, Francis restrained his friend and repeated the gesture. "If you need something to eat, then take mine."

"I will." The man snatched Francis' bowl away.

The other men laughed at the exchange and they all talked amongst themselves as their new leader took his prize and the other men's admiration back with him to the darkest corner of the cell.

"Francis," Giovanni said. "You can't do things like that. Not here. You can't afford to be—" He hesitated to find the right words, but when he realized that was impossible, he simply spoke the truth, "You can't afford to be like you are. That has to stop."

"What else can I be?"

"Your entire life you've had the advantage of being ... different. Because people were always willing to protect you, to make excuses for you. Because I was there for you. You can't do this now. I need you to be able to stand on your own here."

"I am able," Francis said.

"You just gave away the only food you're likely to get."

"I fed someone who claimed to be hungry."

"What you fed was his appetite for cruelty. He'll be hungry again in a little while, and he'll come back looking to take more from you and when you don't have another bowl, what do you think he'll want?"

Francis understood, but there was something more important to him. "At least, Vincenzo got to eat."

Giovanni threw up his hands in frustration. "Worry about saving yourself, Francis. You can't save everyone."

Francis looked up to his friend. "But I think we should at least try."

†

There was no sun in the cells at Collestrada, so that meant no time either. Because of this, there was no way of telling for sure just how long the men had been held captive. Still it didn't seem to Francis as if they had been there more than a few days before the cell door clanged open and a half dozen soldiers from Perugia stepped in.

They were led by a man who wore his tattered officer's uniform like it was an emperor's robes. "I am Captain Cruettella. You may think that I am the gatekeeper to Hell." All of the prisoners were silent. "Hell is not the punishment with which I threaten you," Captain Cruettella continued. "Hell will be your sweet release, your just reward only if you obey my words. For I swear to you all on my young son's soul that if you disobey me, I will make sure that Hell is a far kinder fate than the punishment you will receive here from me."

One of the men in the dark corner snickered out loud and spat to the dirt. The captain smiled. And then nodded in the man's direction. An instant later, four of his soldiers had descended on the man with truncheons, striking him again and again until his face was no longer human and his limbs all bent back at odd angles.

"That's enough," the captain shouted. "I don't want him dead. I want him to suffer."

He looked over the other prisoners. "And I want you all to live with his ongoing agony as my promise to each one of you that I will visit upon you something far, far worse."

Francis started to get up to attend to the wounded man, but Giovanni held him back.

The captain looked over the others and then pointed to Francis, "That one."

Two of the soldiers went to Francis and dragged him to his feet. Francis didn't resist, but Giovanni tried to push them off just the same. A soldier struck Giovanni with his truncheon and knocked him to the ground.

The captain pointed at Carito. "That one, too." Two more soldiers grabbed up the old man. The captain's gaze settled on the boy. "And take him." The remaining two soldiers grabbed Vincenzo, who immediately began to thrash about and cry. "No, please. Please."

"You have a sweet voice," the captain said to the boy. "I would keep silent before you bring yourself to the attention of your guards. There is little they enjoy more than the screams of a man from Assisi, but the bleating of a boy from Assisi might tempt them even more."

Then the captain left, and the soldiers took the chosen prisoners with them. The cell door shut and there wasn't a single sound except the low moans of the battered wreck of the man they'd left behind.

20

Francis, Carito, and Vincenzo were all brought to another room, completely empty except for four chairs, with three positioned in a row and the fourth facing them. Each of the three prisoners were forced into one of the chairs in the row and then secured there with ropes around their wrists and ankles.

The captain took the chair across from them. A silent moment passed. When the captain spoke, it was directly to Francis. "What is your name?"

"Don't say a word," Carito said before Francis had a chance to open his mouth.

The captain smiled. And nodded. The guard behind the old man struck him across the back of his head.

"It's rude to interrupt someone when they're speaking," the captain said. "Do it again and I promise you I will teach you the manners that you lack."

Carito fell silent.

"Good." The Captain turned his attention back to Francis. "You were about to tell me your name." Francis said nothing.

The captain nodded his understanding of just what Francis' refusal meant. He forced another smile. "You don't think I can make you talk?"

"I don't care what you do to me," Francis said.

The captain admitted the point with a nonchalant shoulder shrug. "I absolutely believe that you don't."

Francis puffed with pride, thinking he'd put an end to the interrogation before it had even started.

"But you're not here alone, are you?"

Francis looked to either side of him and immediately deflated.

"When I ask you a question, there are only three things that you can do. Just three. You can say nothing. You can lie. Or you can tell the truth." A sinister smile curled the captain's lips. "If you say nothing." He nodded.

The guard behind Carito reached forward with a knife and drew it across the old man's cheek, cutting a bright red wound across greyish flesh. Carito winced but remained silent.

"If you lie to me," the captain continued.

Vincenzo must have concluded what was about to happen, because he immediately began to whimper and plead. "Please, don't. Don't." But his struggles were in vain, and when the captain gave his signal, Vincenzo bore a wound that matched Carito's.

"Now," the captain said. "I've asked you for your name. And I've explained the only three outcomes that can come from this. Which would you choose?"

Carito threw a hard look to Francis, but he did not utter a word. Still, Francis understood and remained silent.

"That was only an opening," the captain said. "I could just as easily take a finger. A whole limb." He paused to consider the infinite possibilities. "Their manhood?" Vincenzo's tears mixed with his blood and dripped off his chin. Even Carito seemed to squirm at the prospect.

"Francis."

The captain smiled. "Oh, come now. Someone with clothes as fine as yours has more than one name."

"I was born Giovanni di Pietro di Bernardone, but I am known as Francis."

"Good." The Captain looked to Francis' left. "And the old man there?"

"Carito."

"And the other one. The crying child."

"Vincenzo."

"See, isn't that better? You answered my question so I didn't need to hurt Carito there. And you didn't lie to me, so I didn't need to hurt young Vincenzo. Do you understand how this works?"

Francis made no response.

"That was a question, Francis. And if you don't answer it, I'm going to take Carito's arm off at the shoulder."

"Yes," Francis answered. "I understand."

"Good. Now we were talking about your clothes. They're fine clothes, expensive clothes."

Francis made no reply, then hurried to offer a "Yes" to save his old friend.

"So, was the armor we took from you." The Captain stopped as if he was considering the implications of his own words. "You are a wealthy man?"

"No," Francis said. "I'm not."

The captain caught on to the distinction. "But your father is?"

Francis didn't reply.

"If you're going to keep silent at the price of your friend's arm, you really should save such costly silence for a question to which the answer is not so obvious. Your father, he is a wealthy man?"

"Yes," Francis said.

"Good. I should hope so, because the only reason that any of you are still alive is that there are some others in our fair city who believe your wretched lives might be worth something to ransom."

"Ransom?" Francis asked.

"Did you ever wonder if your father loved you, Francis?" the Captain asked.

"No," Francis lied.

"Well, soon we will see. We'll see just how much your father loves you."

That was the first time since they'd been imprisoned that Francis felt as if his future was hopeless and his fate damned.

21

Rats are vicious animals. If several are put in a cage, they will quickly turn on one another, fighting to establish dominance and jockeying for whatever illusion of "power" a captive might hold. So, yes, rats are vicious, but men are even worse.

Commander Alevetti had led his men into battle and he'd tried his best to maintain that same level of control behind the iron bars of Collestrada. He did what any man might think to do, but soldiers submit far more readily to discipline than prisoners do.

Soldiers are a part of the world and governed by practical considerations. They are mindful of the pay (or plunder) that follows service and the punishment that results from disobedience.

Prisoners are different. They are banished to a world all their own, beyond rewards or penalties. They will not respect a flag because it flaps in the breeze nor bend a knee for every bit of rhetoric shouted out in patriotic fervor.

In prison there are no rules except those that a man can enforce by his own will or use of violence. And yet that did not stop Commander Alevetti from trying his best.

"Fall in, men," he called with all of the authority he could muster.

The response he got was a noncommittal milling of men around him.

"I said, fall in!" The increase in volume and sharpness of tone did nothing to inspire his troops.

"I will not tolerate this insubordination. No matter what our circumstances," he shouted. "We are soldiers of Assisi."

"We are prisoners of Callestrada," one of those from the dark corner yelled.

Their leader.

He was a burly man named Carlo, and the scar across his left cheek that continued on up over an empty eye socket was a reliable indicator that this was not his first experience in battle. Or prison.

"I am the commander wherever I have men to command," Alevetti replied.

Carlo straightened his back and puffed out his chest. "You have none here."

Francis stepped forward. "You have one."

Carlo gave a contemptuous snort. "You, Little Prince? You've already shown that you can't hang on to your supper."

"And you've shown that you lack the character necessary to demonstrate any loyalty." The voice came from behind the group and everyone turned to find Giovanni, making himself as comfortable as he could, seated on the floor with the stone wall at his back.

"So, someone speaks for the Little Prince." Carlo pushed his way through the crowd. "Get to your feet if you dare. Or would you rather that I took my objections straight to the Little Prince."

Carlo gave Francis a shove.

Giovanni seemed unconcerned. "If you're going to make me get up, realize that only one of us will be sitting back down. The other is going to wind up flat on his back."

"Giovanni," Francis tried to intercede.

Carlo pushed him again and spoke directly to Giovanni. "I think it's the Little Prince, here that you want to see flat on his back."

Those who were friends or acquaintances of Carlo laughed with him as a sign of support.

Giovanni got to his feet.

Francis tried to stop him. "There is no need for this."

Giovanni moved past him. "Francis, I've told you before, your lofty ideals are an extravagance we can't afford in here. In our situation, violence is the only means of communicating effectively."

And then, without turning, Giovanni made his point.

Carlo was a big man. A tough man. A man who was tried and tested in battle.

But he was also a one-eyed man.

While Carlo was still rolling his shoulders and telling his friends what he planned to do to his opponent, Giovanni had already moved on to the fight and his first strike was two good fingers straight into Carlo's one good eye.

In a single instant, Carlo was suddenly completely blind.

And defenseless.

Giovanni knocked him to the ground with a single punch and the set upon him with an unrestrained ferociousness.

Francis rushed to pull his friend off of the man. "Giovanni, stop."

Giovanni only pushed him away. "Francis, I need to do this. And if you understood, you'd know you need me to do it." And, with that, he returned to beating Carlo.

When Giovanni finally got to his feet, there was no one in the cell that would have bet a single coin on Carlo living through the night.

There was also no one willing to cross Giovanni. And because of that, no one was willing to cross Francis either. But none of that mattered to Francis. The only thing that concerned him was the man who lay bleeding on the filth covered floor.

Francis knelt beside him, but Carlo would not suffer the indignation of receiving his help. He pushed Francis away and his friends reluctantly came to drag him back to the dark corner of the cell.

Francis turned back to Giovanni. "You could have killed him."

Giovanni had already settled back to his spot on the floor. "Give it some time."

Francis shook his head. "Sometimes I just don't understand you."

"And sometimes I don't understand how, in a world so hard, your heart can still be so soft." Giovanni folded his arms across his chest, hung his head like he was sleeping, and muttered to himself, "Little Prince."

22

The men were not the only prisoners of Collestrada. Time seemed to be held hostage, too. In its absence, some of the men took to quarrelling. Others, like Giovanni, fell silent, enduring their situation without comment or complaint, but neither offering a word of kindness or support to anyone else. And some like Francis, tried in their own ways to make their unbearable situation, if not better, at least more bearable.

Francis would sit and talk to Carito, long after the others had tired of the old man's ceaseless stories and demanded his silence. He encouraged Commander Alvetti's attempts to maintain military order and, in so doing, to salvage his surrendered pride.

And neither the man whom the captain had ordered beaten nor the one whom Giovanni had blinded would have survived had it not been for Francis tending to their injuries.

Francis had done all that he could, and yet Giovanni had been right all along: not everyone could be saved. Whenever the guards were in the mood for a certain sort of depraved diversion, the iron door would bang open and they would come for young Vincenzo.

The first time it happened, Francis tried to intercede, but the guards beat him to the ground. The second time it happened, Commander Alevetti stood by Francis and together they tried to stop the guards. And together they were both beaten to the ground. The practice went on until it was simply a routine.

Until Alvetti was no longer willing to participate in the ritual and only Francis would summon the resolve within himself to stand up to the nearly nightly beatings.

Eventually, it was Vincenzo himself who came to Francis and asked him to stop, assuring him that he'd appreciated everything he'd tried to do on his behalf, but convincing him that those well-intended efforts just made the situation even worse.

And so, Francis would sit in their cell, his back to the wall, and listen to the boy's cries and the guards' ugly laughter, knowing there was nothing he could do about either.

One night, Carito took a seat beside Francis to pass the awful vigil together. "You're angry," he said. It wasn't immediately clear whether the old man meant it as a question or statement of fact.

Francis scoffed at them both.

"You have every right to be," Carito said. "But you must always remember that only hurt people hurt people."

Francis was more annoyed, than curious. "What is that supposed to mean?"

"It means that hurting someone as those men are doing now to young Vincenzo, that sort of cruelty can only be born from the pain and the rage that come from once having been someone's victim themselves. So, it is easy—maybe inevitable—to hate those men, but if you do so you should always keep in the back of your mind that their viciousness was born first from someone else's viciousness towards them. And on and on. It's an endless chain of abuse and pain and suffering. And you must decide whether you wish to be another link. Or whether you wish to sever the chain once and for all."

"That's easy to say, while we are both seated on this side of that wall," Francis said. The old man snorted. "And you think I was always safely seated, do you? That I have never known the stinging touch of cruelty."

Francis looked in the old man's watery eyes. "I'm sorry."

"You have no need to be sorry, but a man like you should learn how to think."

"A man like me?"

Carito sighed, as if he had something very specific to say, but lacked the words. "When you were on that pile of corpses, ready to be tossed into the flames like so much rubbish, why do you think it is that I came upon you and pulled you free."

"I don't know."

"I'm don't know either," the old man shrugged. "But I am certain that this is what you must figure out for yourself. You were pulled back from the fire. You must find the reason why."

"I don't know," Francis repeated.

The old man smiled ever so slightly. "Well, it certainly wasn't for the brief moment of violent vengeance that you sit here plotting against those guards. You were not given your life back just so you could use it to take another."

Francis resented the old man's intrusion into his personal thoughts. "What other purpose could there be?"

Carito shrugged. "Everything has a purpose. There is no such thing as chance, just reasons ignored or overlooked. When you realize that, you can spend your time more fruitfully by feeling gratitude instead of hatred, by searching for the purpose in your existence rather than a way to end another's."

"Gratitude?" The suggestion offended Francis. "I am a prisoner. What could I possible have to be grateful for?"

"There is always reason to be grateful. Carlo over there is a prisoner too, but now is blind, where you can see. His friend is crippled so that he will never walk straight again, yet you are still fit enough. And I am an old man, with my best days far behind me and Death is my constant shadow, while your life's adventures are still before you."

"You may be right about that, old man, but that's a fanciful way to look at our lives."

"Really? I think it is an infinitely practical way to look at life. Be thankful for what you have. Your body's abilities. Your youth. Your friends. Concentrate on what you are thankful for, and you will soon find that when gratitude fills your heart, it displaces every other darkness of the soul, even the most bitter of hatreds."

"And if you are a prisoner, too, and old, with death waiting for you soon, then what can you possibly have to be grateful for?"

"I'm grateful for the life I have already lived. It was not perfect or free of pain, to be certain, but I tell you it was—" He paused to find just the right word. "Glorious."

"And now? With all of this?"

"With all of this? I am grateful that I've had the opportunity to meet a man like you."

"A man like me? I still don't understand what you mean."

The old man smiled. "You will. One day. Maybe soon."

With that Carito rolled over and pretended to drift off to sleep, leaving Francis alone in the dark.

Francis, however, remained sitting. He sat and thought about what the old man had said, thought about it for a long, long time.

23

It wasn't sleep that consumed Francis. Sleep is a state that brings rest and rejuvenation, but there was no respite to be found in whatever pit of exhaustion into which Francis had fallen. Instead, this was only an unconscious aspect to his suffering. Memories that might have otherwise passed as dreams taunted him with the gory images of the lives he had taken and those others he had simply watched slip away. They came to him, one by one, and showed their faces to him, casting always a pitiful and accusatory gaze in his direction.

And yet, as horrifying as the grisly nightmares might have been, Francis was reluctant to leave them when the guards came and roughly woke him, pulling him from the floor. He struggled to resist, but there was nothing a man in his condition could do. Not even Giovanni could intercede on Francis' behalf. Or, at least, he didn't try.

Francis was brought to the same room where he'd been interrogated by Captain Cruetella. This time there were only two chairs. The captain was in one of them. "Sit."

"I'd rather stand," Francis said defiantly, although his legs were weak, and his head was spinning wildly.

"I didn't ask what you preferred. I told you to sit." The captain nodded casually and one of the guards struck Francis in the back, just at the kidney.

Francis collapsed, but the guard caught him before he hit the floor and threw him in the chair.

"Now that we are all comfortable," the captain said with a sneer. "Do you know why you're here?"

Francis didn't, but he was afraid not to answer. "No."

"I'm here to tell you that word has come back from Assisi, from your father."

Francis straightened in his chair, but didn't make a sound.

"It turns out he *is* a rich man," the captain said. "When we last spoke, you acted as if you weren't sure about his standing, but I'm told that he's very wealthy. Very wealthy, indeed."

"If you say so."

"Oh, I do," the captain said. "I called you here because when we last talked, I had asked you whether you ever wondered whether your father loved you and your only response was a sad, little look of doubt. It struck me strange at the time, but now I understand. I called you here to tell you that a ransom was put to your father, for your life and the lives of your friends, your fellow sons of Assisi. And do you know what he did?"

Francis didn't have a guess, and he wasn't given time to wager one.

"He chose to bargain."

Francis stared back blankly.

"His son rotting in a prison. His son's life in jeopardy every day. And your own father chose to haggle over a better price for your freedom, for your life. Can you believe it?"

Francis could, but didn't say so.

"So, tomorrow you will be a free man—at a bargain price." The captain sneered. "I myself would rather remain forever in prison than know that I meant so little to my father that he sought to bargain away my freedom."

"I suspect that is because you've never been imprisoned," Francis said. "If you had, you might value your freedom at any price. Even a discounted one."

The captain was nonplused. "Perhaps. The fact remains that tomorrow you will be a free man—at a bargain price. But then, I suppose, a father knows his son's worth better than anyone else."

"Is that all you wanted to tell me?"

"Not yet." The captain got to his feet. "You've spent all these many months in prison and still your clothes are fancier than my own."

"Do you want them?"

A bitter laugh. "No. I don't want them. Or your arrogance. How long I have suffered under the smug oppression of the wealthiest men of Perugia, I don't intend to tolerate the same from some spoiled brat from Assisi."

"I have no arrogance for you."

"I am told by the guards that you have taken up a fondness, a protectiveness for one of your fellow prisoners. I believe I met the young man myself once."

Francis gritted his teeth.

"I've been led to believe that, perhaps, my men have been unkind to this young man."

"They have."

The captain shrugged. "I think they've been even more *unkind* to him to you think. Or, perhaps, you already know?"

"I know that only hurt people hurt people."

"What's that?"

"I know that the sort of cruelty your men have brought against that young man arises only as a product of their own experiences as a victim. Yours too, I suspect."

The captain was caught off-guard. "What are you saying?"

"I'm saying that cruelty only comes from cruelty, and I am sorry for whatever was visited upon your men to turn their hearts in this way. I'm sorry, too, for whatever heartlessness stoked these same fires in your own heart."

"How dare you suggest you know anything about me." The captain spat out the words.

"The only thing that I know is that tomorrow we will be free again."

"That's true. And so today, right now, I am giving you the chance to settle all scores."

The captain nodded and the guard standing to Francis' right unsheathed the knife at his belt and handed the weapon to Francis.

"What is this?" Francis asked, taking the handle in his hand.

"Has it been so long that you've forgotten the feel of a weapon when you hold it?"

"There are not enough days for me to ever forget that."

"Then use it. I stand before you completely unarmed." He got to his feet, raised his hands high into the air, and spun around to prove his point. "Here is your opportunity to take your vengeance."

"I don't want vengeance," Francis said. "I already have so many blessings that I couldn't possibly want more of anything, especially vengeance."

"More blessings?" the captain scoffed. "You're a prisoner. You have nothing."

"I have all that I need, and I am grateful. I'm grateful for the opportunity I've had to offer whatever small comfort to that boy whom your men regularly abuse—I suspect, at your direction. I am grateful for having found a strength and a faith that I had always doubted in myself, but which, together, have allowed me to survive this cruel ordeal. And I am grateful for the hope in my heart, because tomorrow I will be free."

"Grateful? Has fear taken your manhood so completely?"

"Quite the opposite," Francis said. "There is no reason to draw a weapon unless one is afraid. We only hate what we fear. We only kill what we fear. I am finally afraid of nothing and, therefore, don't need a weapon. Or vengeance."

"You're a coward," the captain said with a cruel sneer.

"There are many who think so, but their thoughts don't shape who I am—only my thoughts can do that."

The captain let loose a little chuckle, but it was only to vent his rage. "I swear if your safe return hadn't already been negotiated, I would show you fear."

"I'm sure you must be something of an expert on the subject." Francis dropped the knife to the floor, and it landed with a definitive *thud*.

"Get him out of my sight! Now!"

The guards rushed Francis to the door, afraid that they might somehow become the objects of their commander's wrath. But before they could hustle Francis out of the room, Captain Cruettella called out to stop them at the door. "Francis di Bernadone." Everyone stopped in place. Francis turned.

"If you had been a man of honor, you could have stopped me just now," the captain said. "But because your cowardice has spared me, I will be sure to tell your guards that this is their last night with your little friend." He smiled at the devilish thought. "You think of that tonight, when you hear his screams and then you see if you are so smug when the morning comes."

Francis simply turned away. "Only hurt people hurt people."

24

That night was every bit the nightmare Captain Cruettella promised. Even Giovanni, whose heart had calcified over the course of his imprisonment, seemed troubled and unable to sleep as a result of the shrieks and crude laughter that echoed down the stone corridors of Collestrada prison. But even the darkest night has its dawn and that particular sunrise saw the prisoners, including Vincenzo, put in irons and marched single-file out of the prison and assembled in the yard at the front of the stone fortress.

Their imprisonment had begun with twenty-two men in their cell.

Only thirteen were left standing in line that morning.

Having been held captive for so long, none of them could bear even the gentlest light of the rising sun, and they all closed their eyes tightly against the burning brightness. Many had difficulty breathing the fresh air, and they coughed until they were doubled-over, hacking and gagging. And some, including Vincenzo, had so deteriorated during their imprisonment that the short walk out to the yard completely exhausted them and left them wobbling, barely able to stand.

Thirteen men. But free men now.

They stood—or leaned against a friend—in the blistering glare of dawn. Free men who could not do anything but wait.

And wait.

And wait.

The sun was far higher in the sky and the men's eyes had mostly adjusted to the morning sun by the time the captain came striding out into the yard. A dozen of his guards followed behind him in formation.

He turned to face the assembled ex-prisoners. "Men of Assisi, I bring word to you today that your freedom has been bargained for and secured. Today you will be returned to your native Assisi."

If the men had possessed the strength to scream in celebration, they would have done so, but their broken bodies were limited in the expressions of their spirits and so their excitement merely circulated among the small group as a raspy murmur from one man to another.

The captain was quick to cut it off. "I want you all to understand that this is no act of mercy on my part. If I had my way, every one of you would have met a deservedly gruesome death in the days that you were first brought to me. But we don't every time get what we want, do we?"

The men fell silent.

The captain looked straight at Francis.

"No, just as I have demanded your obedience, I must obey my own masters."

The captain began to pace back and forth. "And my masters respect nothing but the rich man's gold. No matter where it comes from."

He came dangerously close to Francis. "More lust for gold than loyalty for Perugia. More hunger for wealth than demand for justice. And so, they have allowed your loved ones to secure your freedom in exchange for nothing more than the equivalent of a handful of silver."

The captain took a ring of keys from his belt and stepped forward to the first prisoner, unfastening the irons around his wrist. He repeated the process, working his way down the line, addressing them as he turned each lock.

"Before you go, I think I owe you an explanation for your treatment while you were under my dominion. You see, overseeing this prison has long been my profession, but your imprisonment was always a personal matter to me."

The captain continued to free the prisoners, one by one.

"For you see, my son was on the battlefield with you that day when you advanced on Perugia. He was there as a soldier of Perugia, and he gave his life to defend her. So, for me to spend every day so close to the one who killed my son was every bit as tortuous for me as your imprisonment was to you."

Finally, only Vincenzo's and Francis' bonds remained. The captain's chose to take the boy's off first. The irons fell to the ground and the captain was left facing Francis.

"Of course, there were so many men on the field that day and it is impossible to determine just which of Assisi's soldiers was responsible for my son's death. When I talked to the men who fought by his side and survived, all that they could tell me with certainty was that when they last saw my son alive, he was engaged in combat with a man who wore armor that was shiny and new and that he had the finest clothes they'd ever seen."

The captain looked into Francis' eyes as he undid the chains that kept him a prisoner.

"Francis di Bernardone," the name came off his tongue like poison he was spitting to the dirt. "I have been warned that your safe return, in particular, is essential to the Judas bargain that my masters have struck. They have made clear to me the consequences of any rash action on my part that would jeopardize their profit. And so, since I may never see you again, but can never forget you, I want to make certain that I, too, am always a part of your life."

Without another word of warning, the captain dropped the ring of keys, withdrew the dagger sheathed at his belt and drove it straight into Vincenzo's heart. Francis gasped and his still-chained hands reached out for his friend. Vincenzo collapsed into Francis' arms and the two fell to the ground together.

The captain stood above them with his blood-covered blade. His wide, wild eyes were evidence that the sight of blood and the taste of vengeance had finally washed away his better senses and robbed him of that last reserve of composure he'd clung to until the very end. All that remained of the man was a grieving father who wanted retribution, without concern for the cost or consequences.

The captain lunged at Francis. In that instant when everyone, including Francis, was certain that he was a heartbeat from death, Carito rushed in front of the mad man, taking the blade instead of Francis. The captain's actions had not been completely unexpected, given his circumstances, and the soldiers had been given their own orders.

Payment of the ransom had been dependent on Francis' safe return and so their assignment was to protect Francis at all costs, even against their own captain. The guards swarmed the scene and restrained their captain before he had any chance of retrieving his knife and renewing his attempts. There was nothing that he could do against so many of his own men and he was quickly slapped into a pair of irons that he had just unlocked.

"I'll kill you!" The captain screamed as he was rushed into the interior of the prison amidst a tirade of demands that he be unhanded and left to seek vengeance for himself and for all of Perugia.

None of his men listened to him, and it was a cold, cruel irony that he had marched out as the captain of the prison of Collestrada and was returned there as a prisoner.

Oblivious to that chaos, Francis held Vincenzo's lifeless body in his arms and struggled to pull Carito to him, as well. He looked up to the others with tear-filled eyes that begged them not for help, but to somehow turn back that which had already happened. There was, of course, nothing that they or anyone else could do and they all bowed their heads in recognition of that sad fact.

Vincenzo's painful life had already come to an end, but Carito's trembling hand took hold of Francis and pulled him close to hear his last, gasping words. "The boy will not die in vain, *I* will not die in vain, if you do not live in vain."

Francis pulled him closer and, in the daylight, recognized features in the old man's face that he had never had the opportunity to notice before. "I know you better than any man, but looking upon you in the light it is like seeing you for the first time, and yet you look familiar to me somehow. Have I known you before?"

"You have," the old man said. "So many years ago, I was starving beggar and a young boy risked all to give me what I needed."

"You?" Francis asked.

Carito smiled weakly. "I have always been there."

A guard rushed to the former prisoners. "There is a cart to take you back to the banks of the Tiber, but you need to leave. Now."

Francis looked up at the man and snapped, "Leave? Two of our own have fallen here. How can we just leave them?"

The guard didn't have options or opinions, just strong advice. "The captain was not alone in his sentiments. Or his losses. I cannot guarantee your safety if you stay here any longer."

"But we have to see to our friends," Francis pleaded.

"The risk is yours," the guard said. "You're free men now. Do what you want. Leave and live or stay and die."

Francis would not be moved by the others' attempts to pull him up and push him forward.

It was only Giovanni who finally got him to move. "We need to go."

"We can't leave them. Not here." With tears and blood smearing his face, he looked back in horror at the edifice that had held them captive for so long. "Not in the dark shadows of this place."

Giovanni was adamant. "Francis, if we stay, we will die. And none of us have the strength to carry them with us."

"No, we can't," Francis sobbed.

"We must," Giovanni insisted. "Neither of them would want you to stay."

"But—"

"You heard what the old man said. Don't cheapen his sacrifice for whatever small statement you might make by staying. If you truly want to honor these men, then honor the old man's words, and do not live your life, the life he has given you, in vain. Leaving now is your first step towards that."

25

For soldiers and prisoners alike, the problem with homecomings is that they often happen too quickly, without any period of adjustment. And when they do, all of the sorely-missed comforts of home—the clean bed and the wholesome food, the family and friends—are little comfort at all. One minute is Hell and the next is just ... normal. And normal is just another shock to an already fractured sensibility. A turn of the lock doesn't always set a prisoner free and peace doesn't always soothe a soul scarred by war.

So, Pica was surprised—and more than a little saddened—to discover they had ransomed their son's return, but not his release.

Pietro had suggested a certain theriac, a concoction of fermented herbs and other exotic ingredients, including *hul gil* or "joy plant," which he had secured in the markets of the Far East during his trade excursions to those foreign lands. The initial benefits of the substance were beyond question, but after a short time the compound seemed to bestow ills of its own.

And then Francis found the wine.

Between his father's special theriac and the household's plentiful wine, Francis' condition seemed to worsen, not improve, and it became a regular occurrence that Pica would be awakened in the night by what sounded to her like the howling wail of some tortured soul boiling in the fiery bowels of Hell. In those dark nights, she would have preferred that some literal demon had been set loose in her house, then to once again be drawn to her son's room only to find him asleep in his bed, contorted in the throes of his imagined agonies.

Pica held bittersweet memories of a time—not so long ago—when she would have gone to her son and gently shaken him from his nightmare, lying beside him and consoling him with whispered promises that everything was all right.

Or that it would be.

Now, she stood at his doorway, sadly aware that he wasn't her boy anymore and dismayed beyond consolation that there was no comfort she could offer to the man he had become. Still, while there might have been nothing she could do to help him, neither could she continue to stand by and watch him suffer so terribly.

That excruciating conflict left her with the same two options afforded to most parents whose children have grown to adulthood only to find the darkest of troubles there: walk away or pray. But then on one particular evening, just as Pica was turning away from the nightly vigil she kept over her son, Francis stopped his somnolent struggles and seemed to find some peace in whatever dreams had swept over him and released him from his terror.

And in that moment, Pica heard him mumble softly, "Clare. Clare. Clare." Then he lay peaceful and silent. Pica was grateful for his peace. And his silence.

And for the name.

†

A week passed.

Francis got no better.

Another week.

And then a month.

Time passed without the slightest improvement in Francis' despondent demeanor or the faintest softening of those shrieks in his sleep. If anything, being at home had only seemed to worsen his condition and suggested that there was only one inevitable conclusion to the tragedy his story had become.

When Pica could no longer resign herself to doing nothing, she resolved to do something.

Making the arrangements took some time, but one morning she entered Francis' room and threw open the curtains to let in the morning sun, something he hadn't seen very much in a very long time.

He reacted much the way he had on his very first morning of freedom, recoiling at the bright invasion.

"What time is it?" he grumbled.

"Past time for you to get out of bed."

"Leave me be, Mother."

"I would be happy to, but I imagine your visitor will be disappointed to find that you are refusing to receive her."

He squinted up at his mother. "What visitor?"

"A lady has done us the great kindness of coming to see you this morning. I expect you to at least look like a gentleman when you greet her."

"Her? Who her?"

Pica went through his clothes and picked out the ones she would have most liked a suitor of hers to be wearing. "She's a fine young lady, the daughter of Flavorino and Ortolana Sciffi, a *noble* family."

Francis was less impressed by the title. "Mother, after everything, I no longer have the constitution to humor some silly girl who thinks her family name will get her through the world."

"I would've thought by now that you would've learned you are capable of so much more than anyone thinks—especially yourself. I have every confidence that you will be the gentleman I raised you to be when you meet this young woman."

She dropped the clothes she'd selected at the foot of his bed.

"Anyway, it's the least you can do. Throughout your ordeal she took quite an interest in you and came to the house on a number of occasions to inquire about your situation. At the very least, you can get out of bed, wash, dress, and come downstairs to give her proper thanks for that significant kindness."

Francis reluctantly started to do just that.

"Sciffi," Francis repeated to himself. "Do we know the family?"

"Not well," his mother answered from the door. "Your father has wealth, but they have wealth and title and those two circles rarely mix."

"And do I know the girl?" Francis asked.

"You said she had come asking about me. Have we met before?"

"I hadn't thought so," Pica answered. "I wouldn't have thought your paths would have crossed, but, as I said, she came to the house on several occasions asking about you, so I suppose you must have met her at some point in time."

"What's her name?" Frances asked.

Pica smiled. "Clare."

She closed the door to his room and left him alone with the name, which sounded in his head again and again.

Clare. Clare. Clare.

There was still some theriac left in a small clay pot by his bed and he took a portion of the remedy just to strengthen his resolve and steady his nerves. He washed the bitter concoction down with some wine from a half-empty bottle and then finished off the contents.

By the time he had readied himself to receive her, he was in no condition to do so.

26

The Francis that had followed Clare across Assisi had been a naïve young man whose heart and head had been turned by his admiration for those traveling troubadours with their songs of courtly love and the perfect woman who might inspire greatness in a man. The Francis who now unsteadily descended the stairs, had been scarred by war and had not yet escaped his personal incarceration. His head could no longer be swayed by a romantic song and his heart was no longer his own.

Between the two, there was a conflict in the man that was apparent even in his appearance. His eyes were dull and sad, reddened and set off by dark circles beneath them. He had never gained back all of the weight he had lost during his imprisonment and so his fine clothes hung loosely from his frame. He was, in all aspects, a shell of the young man he had been when the two had first met.

Still, Francis couldn't help but wonder about the woman waiting for him, whether there could actually be more than one Clare in the world. When he entered the receiving room, everything he had always suspected about the universe was confirmed: There was only one Clare.

She, however, was a completely different Clare from the one whom he had bumped into in the dead of night and followed to lepers' hospice. Her black cloak was gone, replaced by a gown of pink that seemed rare and elegant even to the son of a textile merchant. Her honey-streaked hair was twisted high on her head and there was rouge on her cheeks and lips.

Maybe it was the theriac or the wine, perhaps he was simply awestruck by her beauty, but all he could muster was a single question, "Clare?"

Propriety would have dictated a far more restrained greeting from her, but she left the couch where she'd been left waiting and immediately went to him. She threw her arms around him and hugged him tightly. "Francis."

It wasn't that he didn't enjoy the sensation of her embrace, but he had not been expecting such a warm welcome and his year in a stony prison cell had left him uncomfortable with physical contact that was too close or too intimate. Hers was both.

He pulled away from her as gently as he could. "I don't understand. What are you doing here?"

She tried to hide her disappointment. "I came to see you." She wiped a tear from her cheek, but it wasn't clear whether that was a sign of overpowering joy or a stifled reaction to his deteriorated condition. She sniffled in a most lady-like fashion and then dabbed at her nose with a handkerchief. "I thought I'd lost you forever."

"I thought that was the point of you running away."

"Francis, I never meant to hurt you, but I have to be careful. The work I'm doing—" A horrible thought raced across her mind. "You haven't told anyone, have you?"

"Told anyone what?"

"About where I went and what I'm doing." She didn't wait for his answer. "Francis, if anyone found out, there wouldn't just be a scandal. I'm afraid of what my father might do to those poor people."

Francis was thoroughly confused by her alarm. "What people?"

"The people, Francis. Their suffering is terrible. There are so many sick here in Assisi, but neither the Church nor state will do anything to help them. And so, we are trying our best to take care of those most in need."

At another time, her story might have intrigued him or touched his compassionate heart, but he was a different man now and he stared back blankly.

"But now that you've returned," she continued. "I know if we worked together."

"Work?" Francis scoffed. "When we first met, you were reluctant to even tell me you very name and now you talk of *together*?"

"And what would you have thought of me if I had offered my name to just any soldier who asked?"

"I told you then," his voice was weary, his throat dry. "I was not just any soldier. I was Francis."

"Oh, I know, Francis, in the same way that I know that working together we could do wonderful things to help the people who need it the most."

"Work? Is that what you have planned for us?" He considered her words, but they were drowned out almost immediately by the painful lesson he had learned in Collestrada. "You can't save everybody."

She drew back. "Maybe I can't, but that's no excuse not to try to save *some*body."

"I'm not sure you can save anybody. Not really." He had only been out of bed for a matter of minutes, but he was already exhausted and settled on the couch. "I know I can't save anyone." His thoughts drifted back to the old man and the boy he had failed so completely. "I tried, and I failed."

"What happened to you?" She was young and full of passion about her cause and so her words carried more than a little bit of judgment with them.

He thought maybe it was the theriac that was causing the room to spin, and he blamed the wine for his nausea, but he had no explanation for why he suddenly felt so angry—and sad.

"You couldn't begin to understand, with your clandestine costumes, hiding in shadows. Lady Clare; debutante by day, nursemaid by night. You have no right to ask me what happened to me. Life happened to me. Just as it is happening to those poor unfortunates you think you can save."

He saw the hurt his words brought to her eyes, but it didn't stop him from spilling more. "You can't, you know. You can't help these people, because it's not poverty that has them in their grasp, not disease that is breaking them down. It's life. A life that you and I were sheltered from as children, and a life we can't change as adults."

She came to him and knelt, taking his hands in hers. "You're hurt?"

He shook off the suggestion. "No, the great tragedy of my life is that I am perfectly fine. All of the men I met on the field of battle are dead by my hand. Too many of my friends are gone. Death is all around me, but me? Francis? I am perfectly fine."

She tugged at his hands so that he would look into her eyes. "And none of that is your fault. You're right, that *is* life. I have seen my own share of death.

I have my own terrible collection of sights and sounds that I can never shake from my head, but none of them offer reason to retreat from life. No, they are a call to those with a heart and a conscience to rise to those challenges and meet the cruelest parts of this life directly."

Tears welled in his eyes, and he focused every bit of control he had left in body and soul to hold back the deluge that would certainly follow if he let even a single tear fall.

"Clare, how could I ever help anyone when I can't help myself, when I don't even know who I am anymore?"

"I know," she said, as she squeezed his hands tightly. "I know who you are. You told me once, and I have never doubted it, not once. You are Francis."

27

There were all sorts of stories hidden beneath the di Bernadone's roof, but there was, perhaps, no more complicated relationship in that house than that between Pica and Giovanni.

The young man's mother, Maria, was Pica's great friend, but also her servant. And while Pica tried to the very depths of her Christian heart to understand the circumstances of Giovanni's conception, she was no fool and was not blind to the boy's paternity; and, in that regard, his presence in her house was a repeated slap in the face, a constant reminder of that which she could not forget. But it was more than just the all-too-ordinary array of emotions regarding her husband's forced infidelities.

There was something in Giovanni's very nature that Pica found troubling. The young man, strong and confident, was walking indictment of everything that her own son was not—and all the ways in which she feared she had failed him.

For his part, Giovanni had always regarded Pica as some part of his family, but one that he resented deep in his heart. An aunt who was within her rights to assign him this chore or that, and frequently did. And in that bitter young man's mind—naïve to the workings of the world, but with a deep suspicion of just who had brought him into it—-Giovanni had always regarded Pica as the only obstacle that prevented his mother and himself from being elevated to their proper station, with all of the associated benefits. As a resulted, although Pica and Giovanni had shared that house for more than twenty years, every encounter between the two was always strained and awkward.

Their interaction late that morning was no exception.

"Excuse me, Signora," Giovanni said, his eyes fixed on the floor in front of him.

She feigned a smile. "What is it, Giovanni?"

"You know that I love Francis like a brother, that I only want what is best for him."

She said," Yes, of course," even if she wasn't completely convinced and had from time-to-time harbored suspicions of her own.

"It's only because of that interest, that I feel compelled to share with you something that I think you should know."

But of all the objections she held in her head and heart, nothing troubled her more about the young man than his lapses into obsequiousness. "What is it, Giovanni?"

He smiled weakly. "Only just now, I was passing by the receiving room and learned Francis has a visitor."

Her back stiffened. "A young woman has come to see him, yes."

"Of course," he said. "It's wonderful that he's finally up and receiving guests when he has been so troubled of late."

"Wonderful," she agreed and then remained silent to allow him the opportunity to get to his point.

He understood her unspoken directive. "It's just that as I was passing by, I couldn't help but overhear their conversation."

28

It wasn't so much that Clare had finished her conversation with Francis, as much as it became clear to them both that he'd completely exhausted what shallow reserve he had, and they would need to set some future date to continue the course of their conversation.

He led her to the front door, and she promised that this future date would come soon. He apologized for his deteriorated condition and promised that he would spend the time that passed until they met again, making himself stronger to receive her properly and thinking about everything she had said. She kissed him on the cheek and his spinning head left him unsteady on his feet. He offered her his apologies and left her with her coachman, while he retreated back into the house and the seclusion of his room.

Clare was charmed by his reaction and the deep breath of spring she took brought a smile to her face. It was a brief exchange to be sure, but that moment of connection between them had immediately relieved her of the dread that had plagued her for the year Francis had been gone. His manner and appearance were evidence of the hardships he had endured, but she was encouraged by the spark of life she had managed to kindle in his otherwise lifeless eyes. A spark kindled with just a single kiss.

She was, overall, in much better spirits than she had been when she first arrived at the di Bernardone home. In fact, she felt considerably better than she had in quite some time.

It was only a brief respite.

Pica quietly closed the front door behind her and stormed down the stairs towards Clare. "Just what exactly are you playing at?"

Clare's eyes widened with surprise and alarm. "Signora di Bernardone, I don't understand?"

"A half dozen times you came to my home while my son was away in that hellhole in Perugia. Always, you represented yourself as a good daughter of Assisi, who was only interested in the welfare of one of our city's brave sons. Never once did you represent to me just how well you knew my Francis."

"I can explain my deception."

"Deceivers can always spin webs to conceal their tricks." Pica took a deep breath in an effort to restrain her rising emotions.

Clare was taken aback by the accusation. "I assure you, that wasn't my intention."

"No," Pica snapped. "That was my mistake. I assumed that when you came calling after Francis that your interest was no more than a concern shared by all of the good women of Assisi for a young man who has fought nobly to protect our city. And when I heard him call your name out in his sleep—"

Of all the things that Pica had said, this revelation was the most shocking to Clare. "He called my name?"

Pica ignored the interruption. "I, of course, assumed then that your interest was romantic, that you two had somehow met beyond the sphere of influence of your parents and begun a romance. And fostering that shared passion was my true purpose in asking you here today."

Clare put a hand to her chest. "I promise you—"

"Promise me nothing. Not after what I heard you saying to him today."

"You heard?"

"Not I, but someone else was privy to your conversation," she said. "Don't you have any regard for that fact that this young man is fractured? And you with your nonsense of slipping off to help those who are beyond help and who should be left beyond our reach."

"Madam, with all due respect, no one is beyond our help."

"Then help them if you will, but don't talk nonsense to my son about *duties* and *callings*. A calling? I have nearly lost my son on the battlefield. A year he spent in a prison, treated worse than any you claim to care for now. Do not think that I am going to lose my Francis again to something as wasteful and fanciful as the nonsense you poured into him this morning."

"I'm sorry you think that what I have to say is nonsense."

"I am sorry for the poor and those stricken with illness, but there is nothing I can do to alleviate their suffering. I would be like a grain of sand trying to hold back the tide. And so, would you. And Francis would be still worse."

"I think you underestimate your son."

"I think you underestimate my love for him. As you do my desire that he have a long and happy and healthy life, with a devoted wife and a houseful of children. And if that is possible for him only because of the inequalities of this life, then I can live with that so long as it benefits *my* son. And if you feel that such selfishness fans the fires of Hell, then I am more than prepared any for eternal punishment I might be condemned to. But I am a mother. And I am not fighting every day to draw him back from the brink, only to have you draw him closer to the edge. I will not lose him again, not to war, and not to your foolishness."

"I'm sorry if I have disappointed you."

"You have. Bitterly."

"I only spoke what was in my heart."

Pica scoffed at the sentiment. "If you still believe that speaking your heart will achieve your ends, then I misjudged you. You are nothing but a silly girl, not yet ready for the attention of a man."

"I think you have misjudged me. I do have great affection for you son, just as I have a determined intention to do the work of our Lord, Jesus Christ."

"Then I should advise you to go off in search of the latter and leave my Francis alone. Now and forever."

"I beg your pardon."

"Francis has always been a special child, but after what he's been through, his mind is twisted, and his heart is tortured. His thoughts are not his own. He is vulnerable, and I will not have him fall victim to a naïve girl who fancies salvation can be found in a life wasted in the pursuit of a cause that cannot be achieved."

Clare was sincerely distressed. "I don't understand."

"Do you really need me to be clearer? Fine. I won't have you taking advantage of my son. He clearly has a strong affection for you, but if you don't share an intention to be part of his future, then I will have you relegate yourself to his past."

"I do not believe that there is a conflict between the two. What greater bond could two people share than the desire to—"

"Listen to me. If I see you near my Francis again, I will have no choice but to let your parents know what their daughter is truly up to when they assume that she is within their house and sound asleep. I believe you would find that such a revelation would not only have severe consequences for yourself, but for the shadowy acquaintances whose company you seek out in the dark corners of our city."

Clare's eyes went wide and the color drained from her face. "Please, madam! You mustn't tell a soul. My father would—"

"I will have no reason say anything at all—unless I have the misfortune of seeing you again. Or of learning you are in contact with Francis."

"Please. I beg you."

"Go." Pica took a deep breath to gather herself together. "I thank you for the kindness of responding to my request. And I am sorry I did not state more plainly what I thought was understood by all. If you do not seek to marry my son, but instead seek to draw him into your schemes, then if you should try again to take from me what I love most, I promise I'll shall do the very same to you. Now, go and never return."

29

There are all sorts of prisons. Francis had been released from a cell of stone and iron only to find himself held captive by a promise. He had returned from Collestrada thinking that even if he hadn't died there, he'd certainly lost his life there. But seeing Clare again had reminded him that despite all of the tragedies he had endured, he still might hold the possibility of living a life that was something more than just a day-to-day existence. And so, he waited for her promised return like it was the release from his personal prison.

Days passed, one by one, and he spent them largely by himself, conjuring the memory of figure in her beautiful gown. The luring melody of her voice. The touch of her hand and the scent of her skin.

The days passed, but they did not bring her return.

To those who spent that time with Francis, there were occasions when it appeared his mood had improved, but none realized that this good humor was only nurtured by fantasies of the life he thought he and Clare might share. They were all very much aware, however, that there were still other periods when his thoughts grew even more turbulent, with increasingly darker self-recriminations about why those boyish dreams of a more fulfilling life could never come to fruition in a world so cold and cruel.

He wrote Clare a short note, but got no reply.

He worried that, perhaps, something had happened to her and scribbled off a longer letter asking for an explanation of why she hadn't returned and the promised chance to see her again.

Still, he received no reply.

And so, he waited.

And waited.

And often he washed the empty hours away with a glass of wine.

And then another.

And then a bottle.

And then two.

He sat and he waited and he drank until his dark thoughts twisted his mental portrait of Clare into something far different from the woman he'd thought her to be.

Or, at least, that one he wanted her to be.

His drunken mind plumbed depths he otherwise would have left unexplored. What circumstances, he wondered, had driven her to pursue such a reckless course of action? Why would she risk her family, wealth, and freedom to tend filthy, poor, and diseased strangers? After enough wine, he came to doubt she could truly be such an altruistic person. After still more wine, the answer became obvious: She did it for a man.

Francis convinced himself that, somewhere in the darkness of the shadows in which she traveled, there must be a man waiting for her, waiting to take her into his arms and make her his own.

When the effect of the wine had dulled, he turned again to the theriac of *hul gil* and, under its effect, he convinced himself that Clare's love rightfully belonged to another and that she had only come to him to use him as a pawn, to perform the work that needed to be done while she was occupied with her lover. A lover who was not Francis and never would be.

Never.

And without her love, his life had no meaning. Without her, life was nothing but a cell, even darker and danker than Collestrada. It was a prison from which there was only one escape. And that is how Francis found himself on the roof of his parents' home that evening.

30

There is the blackness of a moonless night. There is the depth of an unplumbed sea. But there is no darker depth in all the world—this or any other—than the personal abyss which beckons beneath the feet of one contemplating bringing their life to its own unnatural conclusion. Those who have never stepped too close to the edge of this abyss, understandably believe that the wayward traveler is catapulted there in a torrent of wild emotions, but this is not the case. The road to one's self-destruction does not end in despair, but in something far more distressing: quiet acceptance and resignation.

With his head drowning in wine and his legs unstable beneath him, Francis stood on the roof of his parents' house, a precipice between his own dark world and whatever might follow.

He looked down at the cobblestone courtyard and wondered only if the distance was sufficient to do the deed.

No more nightmares.

No more memories.

No more longing.

Or hurt.

Or disappointment.

Nothing but nothing.

And at that drunken, tortured moment, the prospect of a short walk off into nothingness seemed to Francis to be nothing more (or less) than the best of all possible solutions to the unmitigated series of failures that had come to comprise his life.

A solution that everyone could live with.

Except him.

Francis thought this unceremonious exit was a fine and fitting plan. And the wine he'd brought with him up to the roof only made the idea seem even better still. But after taking some time on the top of the rook to contemplate his final moments, the elements had turned against him.

He'd been noticed by someone. A neighbor. And then by a well-intentioned passerby. And then another. Eventually, their collective expressions of alarm had alerted Pietro and brought Francis' father out to the courtyard. To make matters even worse, his mother soon followed. Seeing her son up on their roof and realizing at once what he intended to do, she cried and sobbed in Maria's arms as his father shouted commands.

"Francis, you get down here," Pietro shouted. The darkness or the height or perhaps their combination seemed to Francis to amplify his voice. "Climb down. Or jump if you must. But, one way or another, get off my roof."

The cold words only made Francis' mother bawl even more loudly. His father's yelling and mother's sobbing only attracted more neighbors. And more passer-byers. Until, in really no time at all, a crowd had assembled in the street.

"You've got an audience now. It would be a shame to disappoint them."

The voice came from behind Francis, but it was not unexpected.

"Have you come all the way up here to talk me out of jumping, Giovanni?"

"Just the opposite." Giovanni warily negotiated his way across the last few tiles and then took a seat next to Francis. "But that's what they sent me up here for. Your mother. And mine. They're not at all concerned that *I* might slip and lose the life I value so long as I have the opportunity to talk you out of wasting yours."

Francis hated the way that sounded. "It's not like that."

"It's exactly like that, which is why I haven't come here to talk you out of anything. Instead, I've risked my own damned life to offer you some words of encouragement."

"What?"

"That's right. I'm here to share a quick drink of your wine." He took the bottle from Francis. "And then send you off."

"I've never been more serious about anything in my life," Francis insisted.

"Really? Because I've never known you to be serious about anything. I'm glad you finally found something you could commit to." He offered a mock toast and then drank what was left in the bottle. "Here's hoping you don't make the same mess of your death that you've made of your life." Giovanni tossed the bottle off into the night and only afterwards thought to call out, "Look out below."

An instant later, glass shattered on the cobblestones below and sent the assembled crowd scurrying to avoid the flying shards.

"Damn you, Francis," Pietro screamed up to them.

Giovanni turned to Francis. "Now it's your turn."

"What?"

"Go on," Giovanni prompted. "You've gotten us both all the way up here. You have your audience assembled down below. Isn't that what you wanted? What's left but for you to finish what you came up here for? Off into the night air with you and follow that bottle down."

"B-b-but," Francis stammered.

"Don't tell me you can't even get this right." Giovanni leaned forward and looked down. "As far as I can tell it's just a single step."

"Why are you talking like this?"

"Because I want you to do it. I want to be done with Francis. *Francis. Francis. Francis.* My entire life has been Francis. And what of you? Your father gives you opportunities that no bastard-child like me could ever enjoy, and what do you do? You piss on them. You have the well-respected name, while I'm the one they whisper about in the corridors."

"Giovanni, that is not so."

"You know it's the truth, because we've both heard the same whispers. We've heard the rumors and we both know they are fact."

"Giovanni—"

"You ride off to battle on a fine mount and wearing brand new fitted armor. I trudge off behind your horse's ass in dented, rusted hand-me-downs, and still I'm the one who saves your life. Why? Because you can't save your own. Because you freeze up over some apparition or something."

Francis said nothing.

"I'm the one who made it possible for you to survive prison. You would've died that first day. Or worse. But you're the one who everyone worries will collapse under the weight of your memories. *Your* memories? We both have memories, Francis. I was there, too. But I'm not the one up on this damn roof with a bottle of wine in my gut and no sense in my head."

"I don't know what to do, Giovanni."

"Do? What is there to *do*? You live your life."

Francis shook off the advice. "You make it sound so easy."

"There's nothing easy about it. Living is the hardest thing in the world for every single one of us, but stop thinking about doing it and simply do it."

Francis hung his head. "I just don't know."

"This roof isn't going anywhere, Francis. If you go out and live your life only to find that ending it really was your best option, then this roof will still be here waiting for you. But between that dark day and this one, you should face your death with the certainty that you at least *tried* to live."

Francis choked back a sob and then began to cry in earnest.

Giovanni looked around them. "You didn't happen to bring up another bottle up here, did you?"

Francis shook his head.

"Well then, either jump or don't. But I'm off to get more wine." Giovanni got to his feet and began to climb back into the house. "For whatever it's worth, if you do jump, I won't ever forgive you."

It was not what Francis had been expecting to hear. "Forgive me?"

"For backing out on your debt," Giovanni explained.

"What do I owe?" Francis choked out. "And to whom?"

"I saved your life, right? Too many times to count. I figure you owe me. And I won't ever forgive you if you cancel that debt by throwing it all away for nothing."

And with that Giovanni was gone and Francis was alone. He looked up to the star-lit sky, but couldn't admire the majesty or beauty that might have been found there. He was too angry to see anything but the reflection of his own rage.

He was angry at Giovanni for telling the truth. He was angry with his father for a lifetime of trying to change him into this or that, something that he very clearly wasn't. He was angry with his mother for coddling him. He felt betrayed by all of those who had sent him off to Perugia to do the unspeakable. There was no way Francis could contain all of the emotions he felt about what had happened at Collestrada, not just to himself, but to every man imprisoned there.

More than anything, however, Francis was angry with God for having allowed all of that suffering to have taken place in the first place. If he looked into the darkest recesses of his broken heart, the sunless corners where his nightmares bred and his desperation grew, Francis hated God, hated Him for having abandoned him when he needed Him most.

Or, at least, that's what he thought.

The truth of his situation was that Francis, above all the other figures who populated the hate-filled caverns of his decaying heart, was himself the one he resented and loathed more than any other. He hated himself for his pathetic desire to please others, his silent complicity in the sinful schemes of others, and the weakness of his character that made him pliable to others' whims and desires.

But of all of the traits and qualities Francis hated about himself, what he despised most were the personal failings that had led him to so easily lose the faith he had so tenaciously clung to in captivity. He hated the relative ease with which he had abandoned the one thing that had sustained and saved him. He hated that he had failed God.

He hung his head in shame and slunk down off of the roof.

31

When Francis got back down to the ground, his mother wrapped her arms around him in a compassionate embrace while his father offered numerous threats and an assortment of strong admonitions. Francis didn't want anything from either of them. All he wanted was for his legs to stop shaking.

But they wouldn't.

So, on wobbly legs he couldn't be sure wouldn't give out on him with the very next step, Francis pushed his parents away and walked through the crowd gathered to see his spectacle. Without any notion of where he was going, he headed off into the night.

Francis had no interest in a definite destination, knowing that anywhere he might wind up would be better than staying where he was. He now realized his display had brought shame and controversy to his family's front doorstep and exposed him as being entirely unfit for carrying on the family business. He knew, too, that a military career was beyond him now—at least, as an officer of any rank. All that remained for a young man of his station was a life within the Church, and that seemed the least feasible and satisfying of all of his options.

And he also realized that his display and the personal failings they evidenced would eliminate whatever small chance he'd once held for a romance with a member of Sciffi family. If there had ever been the slightest chance of getting a straight answer from Clare or a commitment from her family, he had left them up there on the roof with his professional prospects and his pride.

So, he walked. He wondered the city, one foot after another, until he looked around and realized he didn't know where he was. He stopped, not because he was too tired to carry on, but simply because he couldn't see the point or purpose in taking another step.

This seemed to him to be as good a place as any to end up.

Francis didn't so much take a seat, as he sank to ground as if the legs he'd been unsure of had finally betrayed him. He laid on the ground, drew his knees up to his chest, and, with his face in the dirt, he wept.

They were not tears of sorrow. Or even regret. It was sheer hopelessness that streamed down his cheeks, and he let his tears run freely for there was no reason to restrain them.

"You should get up now."

Francis opened his eyes and found himself staring at a pair of feet.

"There's no reason for you to be lying in the dirt like that."

Francis looked up and found he was staring straight into eyes that he recognized. They were Carito's.

Francis wiped his tears from his eyes and jumped to his feet, throwing his arms around the old man. "How can this be? I saw you die! I held you in my arms."

"Then why are you here?" the old man asked.

"What do you mean?"

"In the yard outside Collestrada," Carito said. "How can you not remember?"

"Not remember? I *can't* forget," Francis insisted. "Not a minute of it."

"And yet you've forgotten the promise you made to me. You promised that you would not live in vain. That was our bargain. And yet here you are—" Carito looked down at the tear-stained cobblestones without finishing his thoughts.

Francis shook his head. "I don't know how."

"What have you tried?"

Francis was silent.

"Very often it is difficult to determine what one should do," the old man admitted. "But when you don't know *what* to do, that's the time when it is most important that you do *something*. Maybe those labors will bear the fruit you seek, maybe they won't. Maybe they'll lead you someplace altogether unexpected. The most important thing is that you do *something*."

"But I don't know what to do," Francis protested.

"Then start by helping one person. Find one person and help him."

The streets were abandoned. "Who should I help?"

The old man smiled. "How about the person right in front of you?"

Francis brightened. "Of course, what can I do to help you?"

Carito considered the offer. "I have never in my life had a proper suit of clothes and I have to admit I have always admired yours."

"Certainly. Come back with me to my home and I will make sure that you get the finest set of clothes in all of Assisi."

"No," the old man said. "You would make sure that your father gave me the clothes. That wouldn't really be *your* doing, would it? It wouldn't require any sacrifice from you."

Francis stood silently confused for a moment and then looked down at himself. "Oh, you meant these clothes I have on." He patted his silk garments.

The old man's smile broadened. "If you insist."

"I would," Francis hedged. "But then that would leave me standing in the streets completely naked and after everything I've been through in the past couple hours—"

"I could give you mine," Carito offered.

Francis looked up and down the street, still deserted. "Well, I suppose. If that's the one thing I can do for you. You're sure you don't want a brand-new set of your own?"

Carito smiled. "Like I've never been sure of anything before."

"Well, all right then." There was apparently no escaping the old man's request, and so Francis found the darkest doorway in which to exchange clothes. Two minutes later, then men were standing in the exact same location, but each dressed as the other.

Francis tried his best to adjust the dirty scraps of cloth that comprised his outfit. When he realized that he couldn't make the ensemble any more comfortable or more modest, Francis turned back to his friend. "Now what?"

"You look tired," the old man said. "Why don't you have a seat."

"I'm fine," Francis protested, but before he could repeat himself, he was seated on the curb and suddenly, almost inexplicably, more tired than he had ever been before in his life and he fell asleep almost immediately.

When Francis woke, Cartio was nowhere to be seen and there was no evidence he had ever been there—except for Francis' new clothes.

The sun was already well on its ascent and the street was filling with people going about their day. Most of them ignored Francis. Some went out of their way to hurl insults as they passed the young man dressed as a beggar. And yet there were a rare few who tossed him a coin or two and advised him to get himself something to eat to start his day.

Francis accepted the alms out of surprise, not need, and before he had even gathered his thoughts, he had a handful of coins in his palm.

He got to his feet and started off in the direction he thought might lead him home and whenever he passed someone who looked as if they had not had a meal in a day or two, he gave them a coin—or two.

32

The sun had already begun its daily descent by the time Francis's meandering path finally returned him to his parent's doorstep, but the darkness was still many hours yet to come and so he was surprised to find that all of the lamps were still lit as if evening had already arrived. At first, he thought his parents were overeager in their preparations for the coming night, but the truth was that they hadn't yet left the previous night's events behind them.

Neither Pietro nor Pica had gone to bed after Francis climbed down from the roof, and the stern looks on their faces made it clear they were not expecting to find rest any time soon. They had spent the whole night and the rest of the day discussing the long collection of Francis' failures and missteps. After hours of tears and talk, the only conclusion the two could agree on was that their situation as parents could not possibly get worse.

And then Francis walked through the door, without his own clothes, and dressed as a beggar.

"Where have you been?" Pietro demanded.

Francis's answer was so soft it barely disturbed the silence. "Searching for something I've lost."

Pietro scoffed at the response. "And what could someone like you, a man who has absolutely nothing in this world, have possibly lost?"

This response was even softer. "Myself."

"Yourself?" Pietro explodedand turned to his wife. "*Himself.* Do you hear the foolish riddles that pour out of his mouth? A man his age should speak words that make sense and have meaning, not this nonsense."

"My words do make sense." This time, Francis's voice was loud and strong. "And they do have meaning."

"Bah!" Pietro swiped at the air dismissively, as if his son's words could be simply batted away with such a gesture. "And do you see how he's dressed?"

"Please, Pietro." Pica pulled on her husband's sleeve to rein in his reaction, knowing that they were quickly approaching the point where actions transcended words, and both become irretrievable and unforgivable.

Pietro, however, could not be stopped.

"Do you see your mother?" he asked Francis. "She's been up all night, worried sick you might be dead." He paused, but only to look the young man over from head to toe. "And when I see you dressed like this, like an ungrateful fool, I half wish that you were dead."

Pica gasped at the suggestion. "Pietro, please, take that back."

Her husband only brushed her off. "I said it. I mean it. I will take back nothing."

"Nor should you," Francis said. "Your wish has come partially true, for I am half dead."

"Francis, no," his mother pleaded.

"Half dead to you both." Francis gestured to the four walls that surrounded them and all of the comforts they contained. "Half dead to this house. To this city. Half dead to this struggle to live a life that is not my own."

"And who do you think has the luxury to live their own life?" Pietro asked. "Not the richest of men. Not the Pope himself. No man lives his own life, because we are all burdened with an understanding of how this world works and weighed down with the responsibilities that come from that."

"Then you are all fools," Francis said.

Pietro turned to his wife. "Do you hear how he talks to me?"

She did. And she tried to stop him, too. "Francis, please."

"And what life would you lead? "Pietro asked. "Would you tarnish the fine reputation I worked so hard to establish for this family, for you? Throw everything away to wander the streets like nothing more than a beggar dressed in rags?"

"I am the same man I was when I left here last evening adorned in silk. Only my clothes have changed."

"And that's the pity," Pietro snapped. "I would have given the world if only you had returned a changed man, instead of the wretch who stands before me now."

Pietro's words brought tears to his wife's eyes. "Pietro, please. I beg you. Hold your tongue."

"If I am a wretch to you now," Francis said, "then that's what I have always been to you. And what I will always be."

"No. You are my son," Pietro insisted. "And by the bones and blood of our Lord, Jesus Christ, I swear that you will start to act like this is so."

"I am not acting, at all," Francis said. "For the first time, I am merely being who I am."

"And tomorrow when the cock crows," Pietro said. "You will rise from your bed as a man, a son of whom I can be proud: a soldier."

The announcement shot Francis with a bolt of surprise. "What are you talking about?"

"By all accounts, you distinguished yourself in the campaign to Perugia. I am proud, at least, of that. You conducted yourself well while you were a prisoner. I had hoped to allow you the opportunity to heal your wounds before you set off on your next campaign, but your behavior makes it clear to me that what you need isn't rest, but more battle."

"You think you know what's best for me?"

"I think that The Count of Brienne, Walter III, has assembled an army, blessed by His Holiness himself. Arrangements have been made. You leave tomorrow for Apulia to join his ranks and serve his cause."

Francis shook his head in dismay. "Another army. Another cause. More battles and more death. For what?"

"For Walter III, Count of Brienne," Pietro said. "For this family's honor. And your future. That's what for."

"That is the future you would wish for me?" Francis asked.

This time it was Pietro whose head shook with disappointment. "I am too old to worry myself with wishes, Francis. This is not the future I want or wish or dream for you. It is all the future I can give you after everything that you've done. It is the future I demand of you."

Pica trembled and bit her lip, fearing that her son's answer might put an end to her family.

But Francis only smiled. "What you *demand*?

"What I demand." Pietro fixed his eyes on his son.

Francis' smile spread. "So, who should I serve, my Earthly father or my Heavenly father?"

"You have only one father," his father snapped, "the one who backs your foolishness with his own hard-earned gold."

Pica pleaded, "Pietro, don't say such things."

But Pietro was too angry to worry about the blasphemy, "You are my son, Francis. Flesh and blood and bone. And tomorrow that same flesh and blood and bone will be contained in armor and astride your mount or you shall have no father at all."

"Is that what you think? That my Heavenly Father would desert me, too?"

"I don't know about any of that," Pietro admitted. "But I'm certain that He won't feed you or shelter you or clothe you."

"Maybe He's simply waiting for my brothers and sisters to do it for Him."

Pietro shrugged at the suggestion. "Then He's been waiting a long, long time."

"He certainly has."

"I tire of your games, Francis. Tomorrow I will wake to wish you good fortune and see you on your way to Apulia or else I will see you escorted you from this house for good and send you on your way to join the company of beggars you seem to prefer."

33

Pica announced herself with a soft series of knocks on Francis' door. There was no response, but she was his mother, so she pushed the door open and went inside anyway.

"Francis?"

The room was dark.

He was dressed again in clothes she recognized, stretched out on his bed, hands clasped behind his head.

"Are you all right?" she asked.

It took a moment before he responded. "I am as you and father want me to be. Isn't that the answer you're looking for?"

If she found his tone to be insolent, she let it pass and took an uninvited seat on his bed. "I know it seems as if sometimes your father is asking a lot of you."

"No. It seems as if he's asking a lot of someone completely different from me."

She sighed softly. "It's just that he wants so much for you."

"He doesn't want anything for me," Francis corrected. "He wants things *from* me. He wants me to add to his own status and reputation. I'm just another possession to him."

"That's not so."

"You know it is, because he treats you the same way."

"Francis—"

"You're the wife he keeps on the shelf to display to everyone so that they can see that a mercantile merchant can at least look the part of a noble man."

"That's enough," she snapped.

He folded his arms across his chest without admitting he'd gone too far.

She took a deep breath. "You have a good heart, and I know that you want to help those less fortunate in this world, but—"

"But how can I help them if father casts me down to their level? I had coins today, Mother."

She wasn't sure exactly what he meant, but she forced an encouraging smile anyway.

"I had coins and I was able to give them away, to help others buy the food they need. I fed people, and it felt good. I suddenly had purpose. But I was only able to do it because I had no need of those coins myself. If I'm starving, then I can't help the hungry."

At some other time, she might have swept the errant hairs from his brow or patted his arm, but she didn't feel comfortable with that contact now.

"I can't help anyone else unless Father helps me," he continued. "And, yes, I'm aware of how hypocritical that sounds."

She didn't add her words to his admission.

"So, what choice do I have? If I stay, I can't help the people I want to help. I won't even be able to help myself. If I go—" He couldn't continue that thought.

"I know what you've been through," she said.

"Know? How could you possibly know?"

"Well, I can imagine," she corrected, although she was annoyed at what she thought was a minor point. "The fact is that your career as a soldier—"

"Career as a soldier? Is that what you think awaits me? A career?"

"If you work hard," she said.

"Work hard at killing people?"

She had finally had enough. "Oh, I don't know, Francis. This is a hard life. And maybe your father is right. Maybe I tried too hard to protect you from its cruel truths and maybe I was far too successful in those attempts. But everyone has to do things they don't want to do. And everyone is afraid—"

"Afraid?" He stopped her dead, and sat up to look at her. "Is that what this is about? You think I'm afraid to go back to war?"

She realized that somewhere in her well-intended words, she'd made a serious mistake, but she wasn't sure when or where and she froze under his piercing stare.

"You don't understand, do you? Neither you nor father understand."

She remained silent.

"I'm not *afraid* to go back to war. I'm afraid of how much I *want* to go back to war. In my whole life, killing people was the only thing I was ever good at. I *excelled* at it. And now I feel a rage in my soul I can barely contain, and all I want to do is find myself again out on a battlefield so I can release that rage and make the world pay for what it's done to me. I want to make men bleed. I want to stand over them and hear them cry out for their mothers. I want to hear them beg for mercy. I want to feel the blade slice through their flesh, feel the mace crush their bones."

His mother stifled a sob.

He lay back on his pillow. "I'm not afraid of losing my life. I would have thought if I proved nothing else last night, I proved my willingness to be separated from this existence. No, the only thing I fear of life is how much I want to take it from others."

Pica looked into the eyes in which she'd lost herself in a thousand times and found no trace of anything familiar.

Or human.

She got up from the bed, not knowing what else to do. "I'll have your things ready to go in the morning."

He rolled over with his back to her. "Fine."

She went to the doorway and stopped without turning back. "Francis?"

"Yes?"

"I'm sorry. About everything."

"I am, too."

She left and closed the door behind her.

34

Assisi's town square was filled with soldiers, their friends and families, and an assortment of curious well-wishers. Everything was just as it had been the year before.

And the year before that. Always, another season and another war. Francis was ready for this new war. New Armor. New weapons. New mount. And new attitude. There was no aura of nervous energy enveloping him the way there had been on his first campaign. This time his eyes were dead and set straight ahead.

He gave his mother a good-bye hug as nothing more than a formality. She cried. He ignored her tears.

His father tried for his own embrace, but Francis resisted the attempt. Instead, Pietro got a terse, "I will do your name proud."

And with that truncated send off, Francis went straight to his horse and made the final adjustments to his gear before climbing into the saddle.

"You're leaving?" The voice that once haunted him now didn't even inspire him to turn and face her.

"There's nothing to stay for." The sword at his side was not his only weapon. He had words that he knew could wound, too.

"I never expected to see you as a soldier again," Clare said.

"And I never expected to see you at all." Francis turned. "Actually, I had expected to see you, but you never came."

Clare's heart sank. "I wanted to, but—"

He scoffed. "Don't bother. I understand."

"No, you don't."

"Then I suppose I never will." His voice was intentionally indifferent.

"It would sadden me to think that you don't already know," she said. "Somewhere down deep in your heart."

He looked straight into her blue eyes. "What heart?"

She looked into his eyes too and was taken aback by what she saw there. Or, rather, by what she couldn't find. "Then I am truly sorry for you."

"Don't be sorry for me. Hold your pity for the one's I'll face in battle."

"I have sorrow enough for you all." She turned from him. "I hope you find your lost heart."

"No need," he said. "You carry it with you."

She turned to him.

"It would sadden me to think that you don't already know *that*," Francis said. "Somewhere down deep in your *heart*."

Her own words twisted against her stung her deeply, but she would not show him the tears that they brought to her eyes. Instead, she turned and ran off into the crowd.

He did not follow. He did not watch her go.

"If you want to go follow her, then go." Giovanni said, watching the path Clare made as she pushed her way through the crowd.

Francis didn't budge. "Here I stand."

"Well, don't. Better that you chase her down, then that you—" Giovanni didn't finish, but only because he thought they both knew what was left unsaid.

Still, Francis dared him to say it. "Better than *what*?"

"Francis." Giovanni had never seen his friend in such a state and the barely-contained aggression made him cede a step backwards.

"No. Don't spare me your words to save me hurt where your silence is more painful. If you have something troubling to say, then share it."

"What do I need to say? That I'm not going to save you. If your mind is with her or wherever else it may roam, I won't be there to save you. Not again."

"You blame me for what happened at San Giovanni?" Francis demanded. "For what happened at Collestrada?"

Giovanni wasn't willing to repeat the accusations he'd made in the past. "Blame is a pursuit for children. I'm only interested in going into battle without distractions, including you if you are distracted."

"I am fixed in my purpose."

"I hope so."

"I never asked for you to save me." Francis' eyes were aflame now. "If that's what you think really happened, then I will curse you for the rest of my life for having *saved* me. Saved me from what? Death? Do you really think that's something I need or want to be saved from?"

"Francis, I only meant—"

"I know all too well what you meant, what you have always meant." There was no calming Francis down now. "You talk about the rumors, the whispers in the shadows about you, like I was too dense to pick up on their meaning on my own. You couldn't be more mistaken. I understood everything that they said about you, about your mother, about my own father. And who ever dared to say them aloud to you in my presence?"

Giovanni was silent.

"All your life you've looked on me with the oddest mixture of brotherly love and cruel envy. Today I have no need or want of any of that combination. You think you saved me? What do you think your life would have been if I had not constantly interceded on your behalf? If I hadn't done everything to let you share my lessons and the benefits of a life I've had to pay for with my very identity? Do you think *our* father would have given them to you otherwise?"

"Francis!" Giovanni was shocked.

"How well do you think you would've borne the pressures of being Pietro di Bernadone's bastard son if everyone else knew the truth? Do you think he would've treated you like the lost son, if I hadn't entreated that you be included in our lives? Or do you think he would've swept you away like the mistake that you were, you *and* your mother?" Giovanni's hand moved the handle of his sword. "You've said too much."

"Is that hand upon your sword intended to stop me from saying more? Think. For once in your life, think. Was there ever a time at practice in which I fought you with all my strength and the intention to win at any cost?"

Giovanni was speechless.

"Every match you took from me, you won because I handed that contest to you. If you think otherwise, then just try to pull that sword free and I will prove to you that I am now and always have been twice the swordsman you are. I have always indulged your bluster for your sake, but if you continue down this course right now, I swear to you that I will take your life before you even free your blade from its scabbard."

There was a moment when Giovanni's pride begged him to rise to the challenge, but his sensibilities quickly convinced him of the truth. And if he had doubts about his own skills, the murder in his brother's eyes was undeniable.

Giovanni took his hand from his weapon.

"You think I owe you a debt for supposedly saving my life; I'd say this act of mercy on my part sets us right." Francis began to mount his horse. "Now, I believe this line is for those of us with mounts. You should probably go find your place with the other foot soldiers."

Giovanni lowered his head and stepped back. "Don't think I don't know my place."

Francis did not respond. He straightened in his saddle and rode off to war without searching the crowd for those watching him leave. His eyes were fixed on the road ahead, and his countenance was like it had been chiseled from stone. And many a person in the crowd commented that he looked like a fine soldier.

35

For as long as man has walked this Earth, he has made war. That is a long and bloody lineage. Yet no assembled army has ever claimed so many lives nor proven so capable of decimating an opposing force as fever and disease. Throughout our bloody, barbarous history, fever and pestilence have claimed far more casualties than any weapon ever could.

Their campaign started inauspiciously, with a number of soldiers vomiting as they marched their way out of Assisi. This was all dismissed as symptoms of pre-battle nervousness. Nothing that a few days spent marching couldn't remedy.

Marching, however, was not the cure.

While there are always stragglers on any campaign, the first hours out of Assisi seemed particularly slow-going, with an unusual number of men complaining of thirst and fatigue. By the time the procession came to a halt to make camp for the coming night, there were half as many men lying in the open field as there were capable of making the necessary preparations.

As darkness descended, the company's condition only worsened. Many lay in the dirt, burning with fever, moaning softly, and many who went about the hard work of building fires and hoisting tents all the while criticizing their lazy brethren for lying about had joined their comrades in the dirt by the time the moon had risen. Those few cook fires that had been lit were mostly left unattended and there was no hot food available that night.

"Here. At least take these."

Francis was reclined and didn't bother to look up at Giovanni. "What is it?"

"Black bread and a skin of wine," Giovanni answered. "I got it especially for you. It will get you through the night."

Francis took the loaf and the skin but did not offer thanks. "I wasn't sure you'd be interested in me making it through the night."

"You said quite a few things today."

Francis looked up at his half-brother. "I don't regret or take back a single one."

"Nor should you. They were all things that should have been given voice years ago. Truths that we both know have always existed between us."

"I'm not sorry for the words, but I regret these divides between us." Francis broke off a piece of the bread and ate it. "And I fear they will always mark the distance between us."

Francis offered some of the bread to Giovanni, but he refused. He shook off the offer to share the wine, as well.

"Whatever may happen from here," Giovanni said, "I am grateful we have set free the truth of that. I would hate to have thought of one of us passing with all of those pretty lies of friendship and brotherhood still binding our hands. It's better now that we understand one another and the reality of how we regard one another."

"I don't know," Francis sighed. "I think I would have kept the lies if I'd had the choice." He washed that regret down with a bit of the wine.

"But you didn't. We have, both of us, been born into certain roles and it is better we live them freely and fully then continue the pantomime. When we meet again, I don't ever want you to hold back. I can't begin to tell you what you have taken from me today by confirming what I must have known all along in the back of my mind and the depths of my heart—that you were the better man."

"Giovanni," Francis started to rise, but his head swam.

"Don't," Giovanni said. "Never again."

Then, just as unexpectedly as Giovanni had emerged from the darkness, he disappeared back into its dark depths.

Francis ate a little more of the bread. He drank a little more of the wine. When he began to feel a growing discomfort in his stomach, he suspected that he might simply be his empty belly rebelling against the introduction of food and drink. He finished off the loaf of black bread Giovanni had given him and drained the wine skin dry, and then laid back on the ground and stared up into the black sky until it seemed to him that the darkness there was pulling him into that celestial void. It was an odd, but not unpleasant sensation.

At some point, he must have fallen asleep. Two or three hours later, when the growing discomfort had turned to a searing pain in his gut, he wondered if maybe there hadn't been something wrong with the bits of bread he'd eaten. Or maybe the wine.

By the time his fevered mind had settled upon the conclusion that they had both been compromised in some way, it was too late to do anything about it. He struggled to his feet, but only made it to his knees. He stayed there for a while, simply trying to gather the energy necessary to stand all the way up.

On all fours in the darkness, Francis heard voices all around him. These were faint at first, but they grew steadily louder and clearer as he was able to recognize each of the voices.

He heard Captain Cruetlla. And the guards from Collestrada. Mixed in the cacophony was his father's bellowing, something about "Francis, this" or "Francis, that." There was another voice, low and raspy; more a bestial growl than human words.

But the loudest voice of all was Giovanni's. "Francis. Francis."

"I'm ready for you," Francis shouted, forcing himself to his feet and feeling around his waist for his sword so that he could defend himself from the attack he knew was coming.

"Francis," Giovanni called out again. "You're fevered."

Francis saw a shadowy figure drawing closer and frantically reached for his sword but couldn't manage to pull the blade free.

"Francis, you need to lay down now. You're burning up and your mind's playing tricks on you."

Francis finally found his sword's grip and clumsily pulled it free.

"No," he insisted. "You're the one playing tricks on me."

Giovanni raised his hands defensively but didn't move his hand to his sword. "You're in no condition for swordplay."

"How is it that you survived Collestrada so well?" Francis asked.

The question took Giovanni off-guard. "What are you asking?"

Francis staggered. "How is it that the captain never came for you?"

"He did," Giovanni insisted.

But Francis knew better. "No, he didn't. He couldn't come for me because they were ransoming me to my father even then. But all the others," Francis thought. "All of the others ... *but* not you."

"You're mad with fever."

"Maybe." Francis tried to hold his sword out in front of him, but the blade was unsteady and the effort soon became too much for his arm. "What was it that you had to give to the captain? You told him who I was, didn't you?"

Giovanni stood calmly. "Are you accusing me of something?"

"Many things," Francis said. He shook his head in a desperate attempt to clear it. "There may be fever here, but I'm under the influence of something else, aren't I?" Francis looked to Giovanni, "The provisions you gave me; bread made with tainted grain? Wine mixed with what?"

"Poison? You think I poisoned you?" Giovanni laughed. "Why would I need to? You are your own poison."

The world swirled, Francis twirled once around, and then everything went black.

36

Darkness. And then, out of the darkness, fire.
Not something made and managed for preparing a meal or keeping one company through the lonely night, but something elemental, raging and wild, contained only by the stone border that encircled it.

The light emitted was painfully bright. Francis had to shield his eyes from the searing brilliance, but as he looked through the narrow spaces between his fingers, he was sure he could make out a number of shadowy figures silhouetted against the blaze, moving around the wicked flames like they were wisps of smoke rising up out of the embers.

There were voices coming from the near distance, from where the shadows and the fire merged and became one. Francis thought he recognized some of these, but most seemed foreign or layered over one another, an unintelligible cacophony of conversations that he could neither understand nor ignore. And so, he inched closer and closer to the raging fire, as close as he could bear, all the while straining to make out the words that he was sure were being spoken about him.

The figures seemed more definite than ethereal as Francis closed the distance between them and called out to them. "Hello. Can you help me?"

There was no response.

Francis edged a little closer and tried again. "Can you help me?"

"No," a voice called back. "You have to help yourself."

"Carito?"

The old man was dressed all in beggars' rags and Francis couldn't reconcile this figure with the one he was sure he had clothed in his own fine silks not more than a few days before.

"Carito?" Francis asked again, looking more for reassurances than identification.

"I have many names and I answer to them all," came the reply. "I am who you need me to be."

"How can you be here?" Francis asked. "This can't be real. I've had some bad bread and poisoned wine. That's all."

"There's a difference between that which makes you see things and that which allows you to witness what is all around us. This is the fire that burns in every heart, which consumes every soul."

"I don't understand."

"And I'm running out of time to explain it all to you."

"I don't understand anything anymore," Francis insisted.

"A coward's lament," the old man snapped. "*Oh, I don't understand anything at all,*" he called out mockingly. "It's a lie. The things you've been struggling with aren't subjects beyond your grasp, they are simply truths you refuse to accept. Like most people, you understand the most important elements of your life, you just won't let yourself accept what you know to be true. There's a difference."

The fire raged hotter, grew higher, so ferocious that Francis was forced to step back. And with the blast of light and heat came a new round of voices, angrier and louder still.

"What should I do?" Francis asked.

"Do?" Carito asked. "What can you do? Run from the fire or walk towards it. Those are the only choices this life offers."

"I'm afraid," Francis said.

"Fear feeds the fire," Carito said.

More voices echoed in the night.

"My father is there, isn't he?" Francis asked, although he was certain of the answer. "I hear his voice loudest of all. He wants me to find success as a soldier. He won't approve of me being here."

"Has he ever approved of anything you've done?" Carito chuckled. "No, I suppose he won't approve. Why does that matter?"

"He's my father," Francis insisted, as if that were the only answer needed.

"That's who *he* is. The question you need to answer is who *you* are. You've spent your entire life trying to be his boy, but is that who you really want to be?"

"You don't understand," Francis insisted. "He's my father, but he's never approved of me."

"No, I do understand. He is your father. And he has never approved of you. But do you approve of him?"

"He's my father."

"Which is just another way of saying, *no*. So ultimately, you're upset because he won't give you something you haven't given him?"

Francis was silent.

"And do you think that he doesn't approve of you or is it more as if he lacks the approval within himself? I don't think it's that he doesn't approve of you, I think he can't approve of you. Or anything else, including himself."

Francis understood the distinction but didn't say a word.

"And what would you do with your father's approval if you ever got it?"

"I don't know," Francis said.

"So, you're standing here by the fire because your father won't give you something that he probably doesn't have to give and you don't know what you'd do with it if you got it?"

Francis shook off what he knew was the absurdity of the situation. "Every son wants his father's approval, don't they?"

"Some do," Carito conceded. "But the point of growing up is that you don't need your father's approval. Or anyone else's."

Francis said nothing.

"And if you've never had your father's approval, then I think it's safe to say that you can do just fine without it—particularly when you don't know what you'd do if you ever got it."

"Then what am I supposed to do?" Francis asked.

"That's what you're here trying to find out," Carito answered. "Why don't you start by telling your father that you're going to do what you need to do."

Francis swallowed hard and took a step forward. "Father."

The flames exploded like someone beneath them had pumped a bellows. "What kind of son are you?" The voice was clearly Pietro's.

"One who's grown to be a man and who is going to do what I need to do."

The flames erupted even higher. "How dare you speak to me like that! You're *my* son. My son. *Mine*. I own you."

A belch of flame and soot.

Francis stood his ground. "No. No, you don't. I am my own man. My own person. Not your son, but *my*self."

The flames subsided.

"Now what?" Francis asked.

"There are still figures around your fire. Why don't you tell me who's there."

Francis turned back to the flames. "The captain. He's there."

"And how does he make you feel?"

"Afraid," Francis answered. "And angry."

"The two are a matched set," Carito said. "So, what are you afraid of?"

"What he did to me."

"And then what are you angry about?"

"What he did to me."

"See? Two of a kind." Carito smiled, thinking he'd proven his point. "And what could you do about all that now?"

Francis was quick to answer, his eyes burning brighter than the fire. "I could kill him."

"You could," Carito admitted. "But that man did what he did because he'd thought you'd killed his son. And so, you'd hurt him and then his loved ones would want to hurt you. And on and on ... " Carito's voice trailed off for a moment. "There's no shortage of violence in the world, and if bloodshed had ever been the answer, mankind's problems would have been solved long ago. Violence isn't the answer. It's just fuel for the fire."

And with those words, the flames rose again like someone had stoked the fire.

"So, what can you do without perpetuating more violence?" Carito asked.

"Nothing," Francis answered.

"That seems to me like a good start," the old man said. "Hatred is a waste, yet people are quick to give themselves over to that particular demon completely. If most people took the energy they invest in hatred and put it into any other endeavor, they might actually accomplish something. Why don't you put your hatred behind you and go out in this world and accomplish something that pays tribute to the loved ones you've lost, that counterbalances all of the pointless violence."

"I don't know if I can just let go of my anger like that," Francis said.

"You've got that twisted," Carito "You're not holding onto your anger, your anger is holding on to you."

"Then what?" Francis asked.

"Tell *him*." Cartio pointed towards the fire.

Francis took a deep breath and saw among the flames the silhouette of the man he hated more than any other who had walked the Earth. "Captain Cruetta," he called out. "I understand your anger. And your loss. I know the pain that was the source of all you did. And I forgive you."

The flames erupted and a booming voice called from the inferno, "You forgive me? I haven't asked for your forgiveness. I'm glad the kid is dead. The old man, too. If I could do it again, I would kill them all over again. My only regret in this life is that I didn't get the chance to kill you ... yet."

Francis nodded sadly, because he saw the truth. "And I would forgive you if you did. Whether you want my forgiveness or not, you have it. And I forgive myself for hurting you, for hating you. I forgive us both. No matter how many times anger might turn your heart—or tempt mine—I will us both forgiveness. Always."

The fire raged still higher and hotter, but then died down considerably.

"Who else is among the flames" Carito asked.

"I'm not sure," Francis said, only because he didn't want to speak the name out loud.

"Who?" the old man demanded.

"Clare," Francis admitted

"Are you sure it's Clare?"

"Of course, I'm sure. Why do you ask such a question?"

"I'm asking if that's really Clare by the fire or if what you see is the vision of what you *want* Clare to be?"

"I don't want her to be anything," Francis protested.

"Now you're just lying to me. And yourself," Carito said. "She hasn't hurt you in any way, hasn't done anything but be herself. Your problem isn't with her, it's with the image of what you want her to be."

Francis stammered a bit, but nothing intelligible came out.

"Don't you think that's hypocritical? Here you are trying to find your true self, and at the same time you resent this woman for nothing more than being herself."

Francis blurted out, "She said she would come back!"

"And why didn't she?"

"I don't know."

"Love doesn't turn to anger over *I don't know*s," Carito said. "But that doesn't matter now, you can't love someone you don't really know. So, perhaps you should spend some time getting to know who she is—who she *really* is—before you come to any conclusions about her. And if you get that opportunity, maybe you should let her be who she is and not try to force her into being who you want her to be."

"So, what should I do now?"

Carito smiled. "This one's easy."

And it was.

Francis approached the fire, but this time it continued to burn evenly as he approached.

He took a deep breath and said softly, "I'm sorry."

The flames died down a little bit more.

There were only two more figures left at the fire. One of them seemed monstrous and less than human, but the other he recognized as Giovanni.

"He betrayed me," Francis said to Carito, pointing at the shdaow.

The old man nodded. "Probably. Or, at least, he will. Do you know why?"

"No," Francis replied. "I've been like a brother to him."

"And isn't *that* the reason why?" Carito asked.

Francis cocked his head in confusion. "What do you mean?"

"You've been *like* a brother to him, but you've never been a brother to him. He's been jealous of you for his entire life and you never did anything about that. Do you know why?"

Francis didn't.

"Because you're jealous of him."

"I'm am not."

Carito shook his head. "You're lying again. You claim to be on a quest to find yourself, but the truth of the matter is what you've really wanted to be—is him."

Francis felt like he'd been gut punched.

"Jealousy is a terrible thing, because like anger and hatred, jealousy is always paired with ingratitude. You're so frustrated and angry about people not appreciating you for who you are, but have you ever stopped to consider the miracle that you are?"

"I just want—"

"And that's precisely the problem," Carito continued. "You want and you want and you want, but you don't ever stop to consider the things that you already have. You have an education and opportunities most people will never know—and yet all you do is complain about the things you don't have. Gratitude is the key. Become grateful for everything in your life and you will never run out of things to be grateful for."

Francis objected, "But Giovanni—"

"Is not you. Don't try to be him. Let him walk his own path. You just be grateful for your path and for the two strong legs you have to walk it on your own, the two eyes you have to see it, and the keen mind you have to appreciate it. Do you understand?"

"Yes."

"Then?"

Francis walked to the fire and the flames roared again. A voice behind the flames called out, "All I have to do is wait for you to be you, Francis. You're your own worst enemy. Sooner or later you'll bring it all down on yourself and I'll step right into your place. Your father. Your fortune."

Francis smiled. "I hope they all fit you better than they fit me."

The flames roared again. "I'll ruin you."

Francis sighed. "No. I'm the only one who stands a chance of doing that."

The flames raged.

Francis thought he understood why. "I love you. Even if you've betrayed me. No matter what. I love you. And you will always be my brother."

The flames died down, and the last shadow figure at the fire was bigger and more menacing than all of the others. A horrible shadow that moved in violent spasms, all the while growling and snarling like a beast.

"What is this?" Francis asked.

"This is the most fearsome demon of them all."

Francis thought about all of those whom he had already confronted. "The worst? Who would that be?"

"Can't you guess?" the old man asked. "This shadow is you."

With those words, the flames grew higher and hotter than they had ever been before, more savage than Francis thought any blaze could possibly be.

"Am I really this demon?"

"That's how you've treated yourself, isn't it?"

"As a demon?"

"Francis, as much as you think of yourself as a man who has grown to hate injustice and inequality, what you hate most—what you've hated most throughout your life—was you."

"That's not true."

"Then why are we here? You've made your life so painful, so difficult, for you. And then when you fall and fail because of your own sabotage, you turn around and blame yourself, pillory yourself. You say you want to succeed, that you don't want to live your life in vain, but there's no proof of that intent. It is, after all, *your* life and you're the one who has placed yourself on this circular path to repeated disappointment. No one else. You."

Francis considered the prospect. "How do I fight myself?"

"I would think that you should know by now," Carito said. "You've been fighting yourself since the day you were born."

Francis inched closer to the raging flames and, as he approached, they furiously leaped to the sky and whipped wildly, as if they sensed his presence and were reaching out to turn him to ash where he stood. Behind the flames, the shadow beast roared and reached out for him with claws formed from the darkness.

And still, there was something subtle in the confrontation that Francis feared more than anything; the knowledge that surviving the beast meant that he would have to slay what he had known as his constant companion. More than facing the monster, he was secretly afraid to be without it for the first time in his life. He wanted to turn and run, but even as he took that first step back, the shadow and the fire sensed his fear and roared with the energy that they drew from it. Francis flinched at the aggression. "I don't know what to do," he called out, hiding behind his outstretch arm.

"We all hate in others what we hate in ourselves."

This time Francis understood and he knew exactly what to say.

The shadow beast he had become was nothing more than the composite of all of the others. To defeat it, he only had to say to himself what he had said to all of the others. "I am my own person. I forgive you for the things you've done wrong. I am sorry for the things that have been unfairly done to you. I regret treating you unfairly and expecting to be something other than what you are. I love you. No matter what. Even when you betray me. I love you always."

There was one last blast of flame and then the fire went out completely.

Carito looked at him and smiled. "You're ready."

"For what?"

"To be what you were always meant to be."

"And what is that?"

"Francis." Carito smiled more broadly. "Simply Francis."

With the fire now extinguished, Francis could begin to get a sense of their surroundings. The first rays of dawn were just beginning to give lighting to a muddied clearing where an army had bedded down for the night.

Francis turned to Carito. "All things considered, I expected something with more grandeur."

Carito smiled. "Cathedrals are built for people who need grandeur. The miracles of the construction of this simple field are far beyond the capabilities of any man and are far more extraordinary than any structure that's ever been raised with brick and mortar. If you can learn to appreciate the incomprehensible wonder that can be found in a single blade of grass, then you will have a true sense of grandeur."

Carito started to walk away.

Francis called after him. "Carito?"

The old man turned. "Yes?"

There were a million things that Francis wanted to say, but he realized they all came down to just a simple, heartfelt word. "Thanks."

Carito nodded. "Don't live your life in vain."

Then the old man was gone.

37

When Francis regained consciousness, the morning sun was high in the sky, but everything else was gone. His clothes. His armor. His sword. His saddle and the horse underneath it. Giovanni. And the rest of the company as well. Everything and everyone was gone. And none of that mattered in the slightest to Francis.

He got to his feet and stood unsteadily in the center of the road with nothing more to his name than his breeches. Still, every road goes two ways and so there was a choice to be made.

The first—and most reasonable—option was that Francis could set out after his company. A single man on foot, even one still weakened from fever (or whatever else he'd been under the influence of) could catch up with a company of that size with little trouble. He could reclaim his gear, maybe exact a bit of revenge, and then proceed on the way to war with all of the opportunities for pillage and position that such a course provided.

The second choice was that he could follow the path his heart had long ago set out for him—a path led back to Assisi.

It was the more difficult choice, but Francis chose the latter and set off alone, confident and content, maybe for the first time in his life. Their slow-moving, fever-ravaged company hadn't covered a lot of ground on that first day of their expedition and so Francis' return trip was fortunately a short one. A short way, but a difficult journey because his bare feet were not used to the rough open road and the day was brisk for a man clad only in linen breeches. By the time the afternoon sun began to set, Francis was completely exhausted and grateful to see the silhouette of Assisi against a sky streaked with violet and orange.

The closer Francis drew to the edge of the city where he'd spent his entire life, the more people he encountered.

Some of them must have been among the throngs that had cheered him marching out of the city as a soldier just a day before, but they marked his return with savage insults aimed at disheveled and nearly naked man. At first, the assault came only as comments thrown his way. But it wasn't long before the harsh words hurled at him came accompanied by clumps of mud and rocks. And then, some of the men he passed along the way began to gather together into groups and talk about what should be *done* with the outsider who had wandered into their midst.

When talking turned to doing and all their grumbling grew to a call for action, Francis wondered if his decision to return to Assisi had been the wrong one after all. And when the growing mob began to move faster toward Francis, far faster than his blistered feet could flee, he became absolutely convinced of his mistake. In the moment Francis was certain he could not escape the crowd, a man called out to Francis from the doorway of a ramshackle building.

"Over here," the man beckoned with an urgent wave.

Francis rushed to the offered sanctuary and slipped inside as the man pulled the door shut behind them.

"Thank you," he gasped, out of breath and weak from his sickness and his hurried flight from the mob. As his eyes grew accustomed to the dim interior, Francis saw that the interior of the building was every bit as decrepit as its edifice, but the benches set up in front of a coarse wooden alter made its purpose clear.

"This is a church?" he asked.

"We fell out of favor." The man went to a cupboard, fished out the well-worn, brown robe of a cleric and handed it to Francis. "Here, this should cover you enough to avoid drawing the attention of those who like to make trouble for men like you."

Francis pulled the garment on, ignoring the roughness against his skin and the strong stench of another man. "Thank you for this."

"I am glad to offer help to any stranger who needs it."

Francis cinched an offered bit of rope around his waist as a belt. "You said you fell out of favor, with whom?"

"It would take less time to tell you who hasn't taken up opposition to me and my work."

"And who would that be?"

The man thought for a minute. "Well, you haven't offered me any opposition. Yet."

"And I won't—" Francis promised, as he waited for the name of his savior.

"Father Leo."

"So, you're a priest?" Francis asked.

"I was. Once." The man reconsidered. "I suppose I am still a man of the cloth, but I'm not the sort of man who does as he's told and that makes it difficult to be a priest." The old man considered his own situation and then nodded at Francis. "Not very different from being a soldier."

"How did you know I was a soldier?" Francis asked.

"Despite your lack of clothes, you seem generally well-tended, unlike most of the other poor souls who turn up at my door. You're not weathered like a farmer or a laborer. And—" Father Leo cut himself off as if he'd already said too much.

"Go on." Francis was eager to hear this man's assessment of him.

"You have a soldier's eyes and they reflect that you've already looked on more death in your young years than any man should see in a lifetime."

"I don't want to be a soldier," Francis said.

Father Leo laughed. "I suppose that would explain your wardrobe. Stripped the uniform off, did you?"

"It's a long story," Francis said.

"Well, we've got time enough." Father Leo got to his feet. "I've got a pot on in the back." He disappeared for a minute and then returned with two earthen bowls.

He handed one to Francis. "It's not much."

Francis took the bowl and held it in both hands. "When you have nothing, *not much* is more than you can imagine."

Father Leo took a sip from his bowl. "So, you're not going to be a soldier anymore. What are you going to do?"

Francis took a look around the fallen down church. "I'm not sure, but I'd like to start by repaying you."

"There's no need for that. I'm happy to offer what I can, but there's no debt."

"I don't feel an obligation," Francis said. "I feel a calling."

"Calling? That's a strong word."

"It's a strong calling."

"I appreciate your offer, my son, I do. But I suspect that you've got enough troubles of your own, I wouldn't want to add any of mine to your load."

"I could help you fix this," Francis said.

"Fix what?"

"Your church. I could help you fix it. I know I could. And then, with a renew structure to work from, I could help you help others. *That's* what I want to do."

"That's a fine thing, my son. But the problem with your proposal is that your friends out there with the rocks and the harsh words don't want that. And that's not what the Church wants either."

"We could change their minds," Francis said.

"Changing a mind is just about the hardest work in the world," Father Leo said. "But changing a lot of minds all at once is almost impossible. Especially when you're trying to convince people to embrace those who have fallen by the wayside. Why, that *is* impossible."

"Nothing is impossible," Francis said enthusiastically. "I can't believe that my finding my way here is any sort of accident. I was directed by a larger hand, to be sure, and I know that together we could do it."

Father Leo shook his head. "You could do it. Or die trying. But I'm too old for that."

"All right," Francis said, undeterred. "Then you could help me, and I'll do it."

"Is that how it is?" Father Leo laughed. "I let you in the door and you're already running the place?"

"I don't want to run anything," Francis said. "I just want to help people."

The old man took their empty bowls. "Well, right now, you should help yourself and get some sleep. You can stretch out on a bench. There's no fire, but maybe a night in the cold will change your mind about accomplishing the impossible and set you straight back on the path to a promising career as a soldier."

Francis stretched out on one of the benches. "I have been through far worse."

Father Leo stopped and looked at the young man making himself at home on the wooden bench. "Looking at you, I believe that's true."

Francis let out a tired sigh and folded his hands behind his head. "Thank you for the food and the roof over my head." He closed his eyes. "Good night."

And for the first time in as long as he could remember, Francis slept soundly.

38

Returning home. The familiar sounds and sights and smells. The experience is either the happiest in the world. Or the saddest.

Francis opened the door of the only home he'd ever known and stepped inside, cautious and slow like a thief in the night. He wasn't sure why each step he took felt like a violation, like a trespass into some place he shouldn't venture, some place he didn't belong. The grand house seemed haunted. He looked around at the luxurious furnishings and felt beside him the ghostly presence of both the boy he had once been and the man he had tried to be. He crept forward, cautious and quiet, and had only taken half dozen steps when he heard his name.

"Francis?"

He froze.

"Francis? Why are you here, son?" Pietro seemed too confused to be vexed. "I had no doubt in the strength of your cause and the certainty of your victory, but surely the battle can't have been fought and won so soon."

Francis turned and found his father staring at him like he could see that same ghost. too. And his mother stood beside him, there in his father's shadow.

"There has been no battle," Francis said. "And there won't be. At least, not for me. I have faced the only enemy I needed to conquer and now would rather sacrifice my life than take another."

Pietro let go a groan of exasperation and disappointment. "Then you should have stayed on the field of battle and done just that. Better to have died with some honor, than to have returned here like *this*." They were just a handful of words, but what started as an expression of mere anger had quickly turned bitter until the last syllable was spat out with deep resentment.

"I don't expect you to understand, Father, but staying with the army, fighting that battle, *that* would've been the easier thing to do."

"Then why wouldn't you do it?" Pietro asked. "When in your cowardly, lazy life have you ever chosen to take the more challenging course?"

"Stop it, Pietro," Pica interceded. "You can't mean such harsh words, not to your son."

"Is this our son? How could I know that? When I ask him to work at my business, he gives my money and my wares away to the lowliest of peasants on the streets. When I secure him a position in the army and outfit him with a fine horse and armor and everything a man could want to make a name for himself in this world, he returns with his head bowed, wrapped in sack cloth. What of him is possibly a reflection of me?"

"I would hope the commitment and character to do what is right," Francis offered.

"Don't talk to me of what is right. Providing for your family is what is right. Honoring your father is what is right. Serving Assisi and the Church. *That* is what is right."

"And I have tried to my best at all those things, Father. But I will not kill another man to do them," Francis said.

"Fine," Pietro snapped. "You won't work in my business. You won't serve as a soldier. Just what is it that you plan to do?"

"I intend to help those in need," Francis said.

"Need?" Pietro did not bother to conceal his contempt. "What help could you possibly give to anyone? You have nothing of you own to offer."

Still, Francis had already faced that fire and was now well beyond it. "There is more to me than you have ever been willing to recognize."

Pietro was left speechless by his son's open defiance.

Pica used the brief silence to her advantage, stepping in front of her husband. "Pietro. Stop it. You're angry."

"I know I'm angry, woman."

She took his hand, stroking it in an attempt to calm him. "And you're going to say something in this moment that you won't be able to take back when your anger has subsided and your love for your son has restored you to your senses."

"What love would that be?" Francis said.

Pica wheeled around and pointed at her son. Her eyes were wild with a sudden anger neither man had ever seen. "No! You do not get to make this situation and then antagonize your father."

"My question stands," Francis said.

"One more word from you," she snapped, "and I swear by the Blessed Virgin Mother that you will taste the sting of my hand on your flesh. I spared you time and again when your father insisted I punish you, but I will not spare you today."

Francis stood silent.

Pica turned back to her husband. "Go!"

"Go where?" Pietro asked. "Out of my own home?"

"Go tend to your business. Or run to wherever it is you slip off to in the late of the evening when you think I'm not aware or awake."

Pietro started to speak in his defense, but she flashed the same eyes she had shown her son and, too, said nothing in retort.

"Go," she said, softer this time. A mother's plea. "Just let me talk to my son. Please."

Pietro stood for a moment, pretending to consider options that everyone in the room knew he no longer had. "Maybe you can talk some sense into him where I failed."

She granted him the moment to let him save face but hastened him on. "Go."

Pietro took a step and then turned back to his son. "Talk to your mother, but you and I—"

Pica gave him another look. "Go!"

And this time he did as he was told.

39

Francis started to speak, but his mother cut him off before he could utter a word.

"Your room." She pointed the way and stormed after him. When they arrived, she slammed the door behind them. "Now what is this all about?" she demanded.

Francis sat on his bed. "I can't be a soldier."

"You told me you were eager to get back to the battlefield."

Her words contained such a mischaracterization from the one person he thought might understand him that they only made him feel sad. And tired.

"I said I wasn't *afraid* of going back to battle," he clarified, hoping he wouldn't need to say more.

"So?" The solution to their shared problem seemed so obvious to her. "If you're not afraid to go off to war, then—"

"I can't do it, Mother. I don't care about the dangers of war to myself, but I cannot take yet another life. I can't bring more suffering into the world when there is already so much. I can't be a part of that."

"Yes," she snapped. "There is suffering in the world. It was here before you were born and will remain long after you have passed. There is nothing you or anyone else can do to ease those pains. You might as well say you want to hold back the ocean's tide or stop the rain that falls from the sky."

Francis nodded sadly, not accepting her point but acknowledging it. "Then I want to help those drowning in that ocean and those who don't have a dry place to go when it storms."

"It was that girl, wasn't it?" Pica exploded.

Francis was confused not only by the sudden shift in subject, but also by the harshness of her words. "What are you talking about?"

"Don't act like you don't know, Francis." Her narrowed her eyes at him. "You're every bit as lousy a liar as your fool of a father."

Francis' confusion only grew. "Mother, I don't know what you're talking about."

"That girl," Pica insisted. "The one I called here to talk to you only to have her try to twist your head with her nonsense."

Francis needed a moment to make sense of the reference. "Clare?"

"Yes, Clare." She spat out the name. "She's the one who's responsible for all of *this*, who put you up to this nonsense." She made a motion with her finger, like she was summarizing everything Francis was in a single gesture and had come away every bit as disappointed with the results as his father. "It's her, isn't it?"

"I haven't seen Clare since that day," Francis said.

"Don't lie to me. I saw you with her just before your company departed the town square."

Francis' encounter with Clare had been so brief and his mind so overburdened, that he had purposefully put that moment out of his mind. "That was nothing."

"I warned her not to—" Pica said, an instant before she caught herself. She turned away, but it was too late.

"You warned her about what?" Francis stood and looked down at his mother.

With her secret revealed, her strategy was to be defiant with her truth. "I know what she said to you. Giovanni told me all about that nonsense with her *calling* and her invitation for you to join her."

"You warned her about what?"

"I told her that if she came back here, if she tried to poison your head with that nonsense, then I would divulge her little secret to her parents, to everyone." Pica glared defiantly at her son. "And don't think I won't still."

"No." Francis took a step toward his mother. "You won't."

Her son's voice was calm, but there was an undercurrent of menace Pica had never heard before, and for the first time in her life, she was afraid of her own son.

For Francis, the crushing implication of his mother's confession was almost more than he could bear, and his troubled thoughts drew a connecting line between his awkward suicide attempt, his decision to return to the army, and his last, cruel words to Clare. He looked at his mother, almost too angry to speak.

"You've ruined everything."

"Francis."

"You've ruined everything."

"I was only thinking of you!" She reached for him, but he stepped away.

"You were thinking of yourself. You want things from me, and you weren't going to let Clare get in the way of getting what you wanted."

"No, that's not it. I love you."

"You may call it love, but that proves you have no idea what love actually is."

"Francis, please. You must understand."

"I do. I understand that all along I thought you were selfless, but I was wrong. You are as selfish as everyone else. Maybe more so. And now you've driven Clare away."

"You shouldn't speak to your mother like that."

"I shouldn't speak to my mother at all."

He crossed the room to his wardrobe and began to gather his clothes into a traveling bag.

"What are you doing?"

"Packing."

"Why? Where are you going?"

"Far from here."

"But your father will want to talk to you."

"Then let this be the last time I disappoint him." Francis shook his head and took a deep breath. "I love and respect you both, but there's really nothing either of you could say to me right now that would mean anything at all."

He closed the bag, hoisted it on his shoulder, and moved towards the door.

At another time, Pica would have stood in front of her son to keep him from leaving, but her fear had not subsided, and she did not recognize the eyes that now looked straight through her. She stepped aside to let him pass.

"Francis," she called after him. "I love you. I only did what I thought was best for you."

Her words echoed in the large, empty house but the only response she got was the slamming of the door.

40

With his bag slung over his shoulder, Francis hurried through the streets of Assisi, heading straight back to Father Leo's ramshackle church. He knocked once on the door as a courtesy of sorts, and then pushed it open, and walked right in like he belonged there.

"Father Leo," he called out. "I've come back."

There was no response.

"Hello? Hello?"

Francis set his bag down on one of the benches, looked around the place, and wondered what to do with himself.

A moment later Father Leo appeared. "What's this?"

"I'm back," Francis announced.

The old priest didn't seem nearly so excited about his return as Francis had expected. "Back for what?"

"Back to start," Francis explained.

It wasn't quite explanation enough. "To start what?"

"Our work."

"We don't have any work," Father Leo said. "That's largely the problem."

"That's all about to change." Francis opened the bag he'd brought and presented it as an offering of sorts. "Do you know anyone who might buy these clothes? They're the finest available."

Father Leo looked into the bag. "I can see that." There was more than a note of suspicion to the old priest's voice.

"These were mine."

"And you're trading them in for a friar's robe?"

Francis looked at the rough, brown garment Father Leo was wearing like he was just noticing it for the first time. "Happily."

Francis thrust the bag into the old priest's hands. "If you'll take these to town and sell them, they should bring us the money we need to get started."

"Get started on what?"

Francis smiled. "Our work, of course."

"Of course," the old priest said, still unsure what to make of the energetic young man with the expensive clothes and the incredible story. "And while I'm out selling your clothes, just what will you be doing?"

"There's someone I have to go see," Francis answered.

Father Leo set the bag of clothes on one of the old church's benches. "My son, I'm not sure what troubles you've gotten yourself into, but I don't want to be a part of them."

Francis refused to take anything back. "There's no trouble. I promise."

Reluctantly, Father Leo accepted the clothes and the promise that came with them. "All right. I'll think about it."

"That's all I ask," Francis said with a satisfied smile. "Now, I'm long overdue to go see someone. I'll be back before nightfall."

The old priest set the pile of clothes down and turned away. "I'll be counting the hours."

41

When Francis had first followed Clare into the makeshift hospital, he had been taken aback by the degree of human suffering, but this time he was prepared for what he knew he would find there. He knocked gently and waited until a woman an older woman, heavy set and thick with age, opened the door.

She eyed Francis from head to toe, and said, "There's nothing for you here."

Francis smiled at what he was sure was a misunderstanding. "I'm—"

"I know who you are," the woman said.

Francis pressed on. "I've come here to—"

"I know exactly why you've come. That's why I'm telling you there's nothing for you here."

"I need to see Clare."

"I don't know anyone by that name."

"No, of course you don't," Francis said. "Well, if you know who I am and why I've come, then the least that you can do is tell me why you're so convinced that there's nothing for me here."

She didn't hesitate. "Because there's nothing here that someone like you deserves."

"Someone like me?"

"A vain and insincere boy."

"You think me a boy?"

"Yes. Vain and insincere, too. Should I add *thick* and *stupid* to the description?"

"And what would it take to convince you of my sincerity?"

"Sincerity isn't something to be proven."

"Nor is charity something that exists in such a judgmental heart as yours. If there are good works being performed here—and I am certain there are—then just as my motivations may be clear to you, it is equally clear to me that your acts are merely the performance of some imagined obligation. Or worse yet, a misguided attempt to barter for salvation."

The old nun was outraged. "You dare come to *my* door to judge *me*?"

"I arrived on your doorstep and you immediately judged me, told me you knew why I'd come, yet—"

Her lip curled in a dismissive frown. "Vain. Insincere. And impudent."

"I plead guilty to the impudence, but I am neither vain nor insincere, and I take the same offense to your words that you have good reason to take to mine."

"How dare you judge me when you could never do for a day that to which I have devoted my life."

"You're wrong," Francis said. "About me. About everything. I would ably and happily assist you today in all that you need done."

She grinned widely and opened the door even wider. "In that case, my vain, insincere boy, please step inside."

If the invitation was a dare, Francis took it as an opportunity and he eagerly stepped across the threshold with a single-minded determination.

The interior of the building was exactly as Francis had remembered it, rows of cots, each of them occupied by someone twisted by disease or consumed by fever. And yet, at the same time, everything about the scene was different. He no longer saw it as a place of human horrors, but rather as a haven for those who had nowhere else to go.

Francis turned to the woman. "Where should I begin?"

She sneered. "Why don't you show me something of the charity you spoke of?"

And so that was exactly what Francis did.

There is a great misconception in healing. It's not the patient, but the disease that requires medicine. What the patient needs is simply someone else to see them through the disease; not a practitioner, but just someone to be there with them with a story or to endure the silence together.

Just *someone*.

And so, not knowing what else he could do, Francis drew up a stool and sat beside the first cot. The occupant was a young woman, whom diseased had robbed of both her beauty and youth. Still, her brown eyes shined liked chestnuts in the autumn sun and the undampened spark he found there made Francis smile.

"I'm Francis," he said.

She tried to speak, but could only cough.

"Don't," he said softly and took her hand. He was surprised how hot it was to the touch. "We'll play a game and I'll guess your name. Would you like that?"

She smiled ever so faintly.

He guessed Giuseppe and they both smiled, for it was a very silly name for a young woman like her.

They ruled out Paulo and Jerome for the very same reason. He guessed Anna and Julia because they both seemed more fitting, but she shook her head no.

Then Francis guessed Angela and told her that was because she looked like an angel. She smiled. So, whether that was her given name or not, that was what he called her as he held her hand and occasionally wiped a damp cloth across her fevered brow.

And just when he thought she'd finally slipped off to sleep, she squeezed his hand tightly and in a hoarse whisper told him, "I'm scared."

"I know," he answered. "It's scary to be alone. And to be sick. And to be both at the same time. I know, because I have been both, too."

She shook her head. He didn't understand. "To die."

"Me, too," he said. "I know I shouldn't be. But I am."

She smiled to think that they shared something more than just that moment.

"I listen to what the priests say, I do. And I believe," he told her. "But in the darkest hours, I'm not really sure what I think about it all."

He could tell from the way that she looked up at him that she understood. And agreed.

"But then I remind myself that there's one thing in this life of which I am absolutely certain. And that's love," he continued. "I am absolutely certain that there is nothing more powerful than love. Not just Our Heavenly Father's love for us, but our love for one another. I believe love binds us together. Forever and always. And so, I promise you that no matter how dark the night gets," he gently squeezed her hand. "I will always love you and I'll never ever forget about you. So, don't you forget about me."

She shook her head, a promise that she wouldn't.

"Then no matter what, we will always have that."

"Love you," she whispered.

Then she closed her eyes and fell off to sleep.

"I love you too," he whispered, grateful that she had found even some temporary peace in sleep.

Francis felt a presence behind him and turned. The old nun stood over him with her arms folded. "You shouldn't give them false hope," she scolded.

"I said nothing of hope. I spoke only of love."

"Your promise of love gives her false hope."

"What is false about Our Heavenly Father's love?"

"You are in no position to speak of such things"

"And you are in no position to take from them what hope for God's love they have," Francis said.

"This isn't a life for hope." Her face was like a stone, making it impossible to determine whether her words were somehow mean-spirited or simply an honest observation.

"But there's no life without love or hope," he said.

"I didn't like you when I first met you," she told Francis. "I think I like you even less now."

"I didn't come here to make you like me." Francis stood and moved past her to the next cot. There Francis found a man named Alessio, who had already lost his wife and three children to the fever. Next to him was Lorenzo, a man who did not seem to be afflicted with anything more than the ravages of old age. And then there was Alicia and Gaberella, twin girls who had been left with nothing to cling to but one another.

Francis sat with them all.

He told some of them exciting stories about adventurous trips he had never taken to wonderful places he had never been, but wished he had. Some he fed and others he cleaned, but with most of them, he simply sat beside them so they would know they were not alone.

The day had all but slipped away and evening was chasing the sun from the sky, but Francis was still busily attending to those who filled the room when he felt a presence behind him again.

Francis had grown tired of the old nun, but he was too tired to stand and confront her again. He remained seated, his back to the interloper. "Yes, I know. You don't like me. You think I'm a vain and insincere boy—"

"All that may be true, except I've never thought you were insincere."

Francis turned to see Clare smiling down at him.

42

The air outside was electric with the energy of life and, after being confined for so many hours in such a dark place of disease and death, Francis and Clare breathed deeply of the intoxicating mix. They headed away from the hospital and walked for a while without exchanging a word. He didn't know what to say, and she was resolved to not say anything until he broke their silence.

They continued on. And on. Until she could stand the silence no longer.

"You've lost your armor," she said, finally.

"I'm relieved to be rid of it."

"So, you're not a soldier anymore?"

"And never will be again."

"I'm glad. I never liked the idea of you being a soldier, and I liked the soldier you were even less."

"I'm sorry," he said. "About the things I said and the way I said them."

She nodded, an acknowledgment of the apology, but not necessarily an acceptance. "When you treated me so harshly," she started.

"I was not myself," he said. "Or, at least, not the self I want to be. I was a mere fraction of the man I can be."

"And yet whatever part of you that may have been, you broke all of my heart."

"And you cannot find it in your broken heart to forgive such a foolish boy?"

"I did not intend to give my heart to a boy, but to a man I thought I knew."

"Then forgive that man as you would the boy. The boy who did not know of his mother's selfish threats, and the man who should have sought the truth before passing judgment."

"I have," she said. "A thousand times over. It is myself I cannot forgive."

Francis stopped and turned toward her. "And of what trespass could you possibly be guilty of?"

"While too many of my brothers and sisters struggle each day with life's great burden of life and death, I have allowed myself to fall into the frivolous diversion of dreaming of love. And worse yet, I fooled myself into give my love to one not ready or willing to receive it."

Her truth was so sad it made him laugh, which took her by surprise.

He stepped forward and took her hand, rubbing his thumb over the softness of her skin. "What is even sadder," he said, "is that I, too, have blamed myself— not for loving you too little, but for having loved you and only you. In my heart, I made no room for anyone or anything else. And when my heart was broken, when you did not return, I—"

She caught her breath and held it.

"Clare, I too have eyes to see the poor and suffering, and in bearing witness, I know that I have been blessed in ways most would envy." His eyes grew distant for a moment as he thought of Carito and the monsters he confronted in the fiery blaze. "I have had the great fortune to witness miracles of both God and man, but never did I look on those treasures of Heaven and Earth with any thought other than the fact that I would gladly trade them all for nothing more than your heart."

The corners of her lips turned ever so slightly to a smile. "It would be a foolish bargain to trade away so much for what you already have—and always will have."

Her smile suggested he should find hope in her words, but he saw something very different in her eyes. He dropped her hand and stepped back.

"I may hold your heart, but I will never hold you in my arms, will I?"

She turned away and started walking before she answered. "You see the work to be done here."

"I do. Of course, I do."

"This is where I am needed, Francis. This is where we are both needed. Whatever I may feel for you, I cannot deny God's calling. Working together, we could accomplish so much, but *being* together ..."

"And is my heart's call to you not as strong as His?"

She shot him a dark glance. "You shouldn't say such things."

"For fear of what?" he retorted. "That I, like Job, should be stripped of all I value, that on top of losing everything, He will rob me of the treasure of my heart?"

"Francis, you must listen to yourself. If overheard, your words would surely lead to your trial as a heretic."

"And what verdict could a court deliver that would punish me more than your words? What sentence could they impose that I would not welcome?"

Clare stopped and clutched his arm. "Don't talk like that, Francis."

Francis closed his eyes and drew in a deep breath. He was quiet for a moment, then he blew out, long and slow. Finally, he looked at her. "You're right. Of course, you are right."

Again, his response took her by surprise and left her without a reply.

"I see now that I went to the hospital today with nothing on my mind but my own desires. I did not go to help those in need, but instead to prove my worthiness to you. I thought I had already learned the lesson of love, but I went in search of the Clare I so desperately want you to be—the Clare that Francis wants, the Clare that Francis needs. The Clare I first met and first loved. If I took you from your work, you would not be the Clare that *you* want to be—the Clare I will always admire and honor and love."

"What are you saying, Francis?"

It wasn't immediately obvious to him either, not until she asked. And then he knew what he had to say. And to do. "Good-bye."

"You're leaving?" The hold she'd had on her brimming tears began to slip.

"I'm leaving you to your work and your calling, because that is the only way I know to show you how much I love you," he said.

She didn't know what to say and so she only asked, "Will I see you again?"

"Our meetings and parting have never seemed to be of our own making."

She sniffed and wiped away a tear. "No. I suppose not."

"We might not have control over the crossing of our paths, but I hope you will always know that wherever my path might lead and whatever my fate may hold, I will always be thinking of you. You are my North Star and that is the only guide that I will ever follow."

She closed her eyes as he bent down to kiss her gently.

"*Addio*," he whispered and hurried down the street. He did not glance back even once, not because he did not want to look upon her face one last time, but because the road ahead was the quickest way back to her.

She stood with her head bowed, and when she finally opened her eyes and looked up, Francis was gone.

43

Francis followed a meandering path back to Father Leo's church and the day was waning when he finally arrived.

"I told you I didn't want any trouble from you," the old man said when Francis appeared in the doorway.

"Trouble? I have brought you nothing but good intentions and a commitment to help you in your efforts to help others."

"You have brought me much more than that." Father Leo held open the door for Francis to step inside.

"Did you really think that you could steal from me?"

Francis recognized the voice even before his eyes could adjust to the dim interior, lit only by a single flickering lamp on the makeshift altar. "Father?" Francis took a step forward and saw the man seated by the altar.

"From me, Francis? You thought you could get away with stealing from me?" Pietro stood and threw a heavy bundle at his son's feet.

Francis looked down to see a bag stuffed with the clothes he'd given Father Leo to sell. "Steal? From you? These are my clothes. I gave them—"

"*Your* clothes? *Your* clothes?" There was violence in Pietro's voice that rattled the windows. "Everything in that house is mine. *Mine.* Including these clothes."

Francis stooped down to pick up the bundle. "Then the mistake was mine. I thought they were gifts from my father and so belonged to me. Forgive me for my presumption of your generosity. I'll gladly return them to you now."

"Oh, it's too late for apologies." Pietro spat out the words. "A thief cannot simply return what he has taken once he's been caught and then be thought an honest man."

From the shadows, four men stepped forward. None said a word, but Francis knew why they were there. "What do you expect from me then?" he asked.

"I expect nothing of you except to pay the penalty for your thievery," Pietro shouted. "And the same for this thief, too." He pointed at Father Leo.

Francis stepped in front of the old man. "He has nothing to do with this."

"One who gives safe harbor to a thief is as guilty of the crime as the man who stole the goods," Pietro said.

"He knew nothing of the clothes I gave him and has done nothing wrong," Francis insisted.

"We will let the Bishop's court decide his fate," Pietro said. "And yours, as well."

"No," Francis said. "If you want to take me back as a criminal, then I am more than willing to go with you now. But I will not let you—" He looked at the other four men. "I will not let any of you put a hand on this man who has shown me nothing but kindness."

"That's not your decision to make," Pietro said.

"If I am to be taken to the Bishop's court, would you have me tell him how you abused this man of God?" Francis asked.

"I haven't laid a hand—"

"Would you have all of Assisi know how you cruelly ripped this humble servant from God's own house?"

Pietro's jaw clenched.

"Would you have all of Assisi know of your own sins?" Francis said. "All of your sins?"

"I have no sins," Pietro scoffed.

"You have plenty of sins just as you have more than one son." Pietro's eyes widened, and Francis knew he'd won. "I will happily explain the situation to the Bishop. To all of Assisi. I will happily explain in public just what kind of a father you are, not just to me but to your other—"

"Enough." Pietro waved a hand at Father Leo. "I will leave the priest, but I am taking you."

"I go with you freely," Francis said.

"You'll go in chains like the thief you are," Pietro snapped. At that, the four men in the shadows stepped forward took hold of Francis, and bound his wrists in chains. One of the men then moved towards Father Leo, but Francis stepped in front of him. One of the men struck Francis across the face and forced him to his knees.

Francis looked up at Pietro. "Is your word so easily broken, Father?"

Pietro took a deep breath and shook his head at his men. "Not the priest." He closed his eyes, hoping to forget the image of his son, bound and kneeling before him. "Get him to his feet," he ordered finally. "And bring the clothes. Evidence of his crime."

A thoroughly rattled Father Leo looked at Francis as he passed. "I hope the Lord will bless you."

Francis' smile was traced in blood. "He already has."

44

Pica's hand shook as she held her lamp high and warily descended the stairs to her cellar. It wasn't the darkness that scared her so. It was what she knew was waiting for her down in the dark.

As soon as she'd opened the cellar door, she'd heard the low, constant whining. There was no relief in discovering that the pitiful sound emanated from Shadow, the old dog Pietro had confined there with a chain around her neck. There was no relief in the discovery because she knew her only child, Francis, was chained there, too.

Her son, her little boy, had pushed aside the cushion and blankets that had been given to him and was stretched out across the stone floor instead. He had crawled as far as his chain would permit to get closer to his dog and, in that position, he seemed more animal than man to her.

She stifled her tears as she approached. Shadow stopped crying and cocked her head at Pica, but Francis did not acknowledge his mother's presence at first. He stayed perfectly still, only opening his eyes to take in her arrival when she was close enough to reach out and touch him. She saw his eyes in the flickering lamplight, but they were unrecognizable. She gasped and choked back a sob. It wasn't her son's discomfort that troubled her so. To the contrary, it was the ease with which he embraced the misery of his situation, as if he and suffering were long-lost friends and he had welcomed its return warmly.

"I would wipe away your tears, Mother, but—" Francis raised his arm and showed her the iron cuff around his wrists which attached him by a chain to a metal ring embedded in the floor.

"Francis," his name escaped from her lips like a breath she could not re-capture or replace.

"You should not call me that," he told her. "Any jailer will tell you that the first thing you do to a prisoner is to take away his name. It is the first step in robbing him of everything that makes him human."

She knelt by his side. "I should not call you that because it is not your name. Francis is a foolish, vain name, given to you by your father to sing his own praises as a worldly man. I had named you differently. Given you a common name. A humble name." She let go a sigh of resignation. "But even as I gave it to you, I knew you were not mine to name."

"Not your son?"

"You were never my son, Francis. Not really." She felt the question he was about to ask and answered it before he could give it voice. "You are the child I gave birth to, of course, but even the surgeon warned me that you would not live. And when you did, I thought I had defied him, defied God, Himself. I thought your life was a miracle—and it was—but it was not my miracle, not mine to keep."

"I will always be your son."

She smiled at what she knew was a lie told with the best of intentions. "You will be as kind to me as you always have been. Maybe, in a while, you might even love me again. But somehow in wanting to hold on to you, I have lost you completely." She pulled a key from her bodice. "And now I've come to set you free."

"Mother—"

"You once told me that I had ruined everything in your life," she said. "I see now that I was right about that, so let me set that right."

"They were words spoken in a moment of anger. Everything is fine, Mother. My life is not in ruins. I am exactly where I am supposed to be."

"You must go, Francis. I cannot live in a home that is also my son's prison."

"But Father, he will—"

"He will bellow and bluster, but in time he will be glad I set you free."

"No," Francis said. "I only meant that Father will only find me again. How far could I run? And where to? No, I appreciate the sacrifice you're prepared to make on my behalf, but my freedom cannot be gained with a key."

"Francis," she pleaded. "I have some money, money your father knows nothing about. You could go to Rome maybe, just until his temper has calmed."

"The only freedom I will ever find is in whatever punishment waits for me after Father has had his way."

"But he means to take you before the Bishop," she said.

"I know."

"If they find you guilty—" She couldn't finish.

"I know the penalty I face."

"And you would have a mother watch her son freely walk to that destination?"

"I would have you trust the God that saved me the day I was born and that has provided for me every day since."

She looked down at the key in her palm. "It's so hard to trust in God when I hold the key to your freedom here in my hand."

"Fear and faith cannot coexist," he said. "Fear will strangle faith like weeds strangle flowers in an abandoned garden, but faith is like the gardener who pulls the weeds and makes way for faith to flourish. In faith there is freedom, for fear forges chains of its own, chains that are much harder to break than these made of mere steel." He held up his hands.

"I want to believe, Francis, but seeing my son held prisoner by his own father, I …" She could not continue.

He nodded toward the key in her hand. "In my head I am screaming for the key, but in my heart I am certain. And if you love me, you must let me follow my heart."

Her shoulders slumped. Without a word, she returned the key to her bodice. "And you would have me just leave you there, chained like a … like a dog." She looked over at Shadow who had resumed whining.

"Yes." He smiled at her.

She stood and looked down at her son. She could not bring herself to tell him that she loved him or to say anything at all. So, she left him there, chained in the cellar with his dog, but she was the real captive. She was trapped in a prison her husband had built around her. One from which she could never escape.

45

The crowd assembled in the city square was far larger than anyone would have expected for an ordinary trial before the Bishop, but everyone knew this was something different.

Originally, word had circulated throughout Assisi that the pending charges had been brought by a father against his own son and the crowd grew through the grimmest of curiosity. Then rumor spread that the father was no other than Pietro di Bernadone, whom many in the town regarded as a fine, upstanding citizen, but far more thought of as a boastful bore of a man; and so, the crowd grew some more, swollen by those who wanted to see the braggart in such a humiliating position.

And then people began to identify the defendant as that weird, young man who had gone crazy as a prisoner of Collestrada, who had once stood on his father's rooftop threatening to jump, who was recognized dressed as a beggar. And as the one who had abandoned the army that had just marched out from Assisi. With that last tidbit, the crowd grew to numbers that had not been seen for such a proceeding in as long as most people could remember.

The size and character of the crowd made it a restless and volatile collection of citizens, but they quieted as soon as the Bishop appeared in the courtyard with his entourage in tow.

"Good people of Assisi," he called out to the assembled. "As you know, I am empowered by Rome and our most Holy Father to hear all controversies and complaints. I might have settled this matter without these elaborate proceedings, but I chose to entertain this call for justice because it raises a question that concerns not just one household in Assisi, but a great many others.

"This case is about an allegation of theft," the Bishop explained. "But the matter before me today is not simply an accusation of one man taking the belongings of another. Rather, this is a father who accuses his son—" A chorus of boos and cheers broke out drowning out his words. Alarmed, he glanced at the head of his guards and then raised his hands to quiet the crowd. His voice booming with authority, he called out, "Please, citizens of Assisi, refrain from judgment until we have heard the evidence presented." The crowd quieted, and he went on. In these times, many houses in Assisi are divided—father against son. And so, it is vital that the Church hear this matter to render a decision that will not only guarantee the delivery of justice, but also stand as a precedent for every household in Assisi."

The Bishop gestured to Pietro. "You have brought these charges today, is that correct?"

Pietro, dressed in his finest silk, shimmered in the afternoon sun like a bejeweled idol in some long-forgotten temple. "Yes, Your Excellency, I have."

"And the charge you bring is thievery, is that right?"

"Yes, Your Excellency."

"And the individual you are prosecuting is your natural born son, is that also correct?"

Everyone's attention turned to Francis, who stood, chained at the wrists. He had been forcibly dressed in fine clothes at his father's instruction but having spent his last few days on the basement floor, he looked like something wild wrapped in a silk cocoon.

"And the items you accuse your son of stealing, they were clothes that you yourself had given to him as your child. Is that right?"

"That is right, Your Excellency. I had given them to *my son*," Pietro's chin was held high as he spoke, as if he had made a critical distinction key to his prosecution.

"I have spoken about the importance of this case to our city," the Bishop said, "but tell me why you believe these charges should not be handled as a family matter, settled behind closed doors, instead of before this court and the citizens of Assisi."

"Because, Your Excellency, what has been stolen here is far more than mere clothes. Rather, what has been stolen is what these clothes represent, the care and effort—and, yes, money—that a parent invests in a child, only to have all those assets cruelly taken away and squandered."

The Bishop's countenance betrayed nothing, and so Pietro, who had bought and sold his way across two continents turned to the crowd to pitch his story as if they were potential buyers of fine fabrics.

"How many of you in this crowd today are parents?"

A rumbling murmur came back that suggested a large number of the assembled had children of their own.

"And how many of you have given to your children? Given them everything you could? Given them far more than ever was given to you when you were children?" The murmur became louder and the Bishop watched the crowd carefully.

"And what was the return for your investment? Was it a child willing to honor you, to take care of you? Or was it bitterness? Was it a child who resisted your efforts to provide for their comfort? A child who wanted to make their own marriage contract? A child who wanted to live a life that excluded you? Was your reward a child who refused to recognize that you were the very one who made everything possible for them in the first place?"

The murmur became a roar. The Bishop was unconvinced of Pietro's argument, but he knew the dangers of crowd aroused by rhetoric, and the last thing he wanted was to release that collective unrest back into the streets without first giving them the show that they had come to see for themselves. He held up a hand to quiet the crowd and nodded to Pietro to proceed.

"Fine people of Assisi," Pietro said, "many of you know me, know that I have worked hard my entire life to provide for my family, especially my son, Francis." He gestured over to where the young man stood bound by chains.

"I put a roof over his head. Kept him safe. I put food in his belly and clothes on his back." Pietro held up the bundle of clothes he claimed Francis had stolen. "I gave him advice and made sure he had an education. I gave him everything he needed to inherit my business or have a business of his own, and what did he do? He tried to give away my money and goods to some beggar on the street." The crowd let out a collective *boo*. "I outfitted him to serve as a soldier in the army of Assisi." A cheer went up, twice as loud as their boos. "And when he was captured at San Giovanni." More boos. "And imprisoned on Collestrada." Louder, more emphatic boos. "I paid the ransom those heretics demanded for his safe return and for the return of other men of Assisi held hostage." Louder, more emphatic cheers.

"But when I outfitted him to return to his military life, he abandoned his post just days later and came slinking back home, dressed like a beggar. So, when he defied me yet again and stole the clothes that I had given him out of a father's love, it seemed to me that he had stolen far more than just those items of silk and linen. It seemed to me that what he had really stolen was my love as a father. And *that* is what I would have you judge him on, Your Excellency. Not just the theft of these clothes—expensive though they are—but for the crime of taking from me over the course of his entire life without ever repaying me with that gratitude or obedience to which I am entitled. What I accuse my son of today is the theft of my love."

This argument was new and unexpected, and a murmur of debate spread through the crowd. The Bishop tried to read the crowd, anticipating its reaction, but found it impossible to do so with the sort of certainty that he felt the situation demanded. He had made plenty of edicts and pronouncements during his tenure—and he knew he would need to make many more in the future—and some of those would necessarily be unpopular with the people of Assisi. And for that reason alone, he was determined to resolve this case in a way that the resolution would please them.

The Bishop looked to Francis. "Do you have anything to say for yourself?"

The crowd grew silent as Francis stepped forward. "Yes. I do."

46

Francis held out his hands, wordlessly requesting that he be set loose from the irons that constrained him, and the Bishop nodded his assent. A soldier stepped forward and put key to lock.

"Thank you, Your Excellency," Francis said, rubbing his wrist.

The Bishop looked the young man up and down, but was moved to neither contempt nor compassion. "If you have a defense to the charges your father has brought against you, declare it now."

"I do have something to say, Your Excellency, but I have no words to offer in my defense. My father is an honorable man and all he has said is true."

The Bishop frowned and Pietro squirmed uncomfortably.

Francis cleared his parched throat and tried to speak loudly enough for everyone in the crowd to hear. "I take issue, however, with his allegation that I stole his love. Love is something that can only be given—and given freely. Whatever he thinks I might have stolen, it must certainly be something other than love."

A murmur spread among the crowd, and the Bishop made a mental note.

"I love my father. I love him still, and I give him this love without any expectation of receiving something of equal or greater value in return. So, I think my father is confused about just what it was he gave *to me* that required something in return *from me*. Whatever it might have been, it was not love, and if it created a debt, with interest accruing, then I am surely guilty of not paying it."

The Bishop thought there might be an easy way to resolve the matter. "Should I take your words as an admission of guilt, then?"

"What my father said was true. I took the clothes he gave me and gave them to another."

The Bishop peered down at Francis. "You realize that more than one thief who has stood before me has gone shortly thereafter to meet his Final Judgment for much the same crime?"

"I have no fear of your verdict or of my Final Judgment."

The Bishop leaned forward. "Pray, Francis di Bernadone, tell me why you do not fear my verdict or your Final Judgment."

"I do not fear man's tribunal, because if I have violated the laws of Man, it was only because I was keeping God's own law. And what sort of man fears punishment for keeping God's law?"

The Bishop sat back and steepled his fingers together. Francis' words—and his attitude—were dangerous and had to be handled delicately. After a moment, he inquired, "And what could someone like you presume to know about God's own law?"

Francis held out his hands like a supplicant. "I don't begin to suggest I understand what other men make of God's word or how they turn those words to say things *they* wish them to say. I only know how Jesus acted and lived within those laws."

The Bishop's brows furrowed. The proceeding was not going as he'd expected, and despite himself, he found the young man before him intriguing. "And tell us your understanding of how Jesus acted and lived within those laws."

"With love, kindness, and concern for nothing but the welfare of his brothers and sisters," Francis answered quickly. "And so, if I have broken the laws of man, then my crime was wanting to give food to those who were hungry and had no hope and clothing to those who were naked and had no dignity. I am guilty of acting as Christ instructed all men to act."

"What about leaving the campaign, deserting your post, and abandoning Assisi in its time of need?" the Bishop asked.

Some in the crowd called out cruelly, but most stood silently waiting for his response.

"I have not abandoned Assisi. Indeed, I love this city and returned from the campaign to serve her and her citizens. But, yes, what my father says is true. I am guilty of leaving the campaign. I left not because I was afraid or because I am a traitor. I left because I was good at killing my fellow man. Too good. As anyone who knows me will attest, I am skilled with a sword and wielded it well on the battlefield. My sword and my soul is forever stained with the blood of others I cut down in Assisi's name." Francis paused and looked straight at the Bishop. "But I will never again take the life of another—even if that means another will take my own."

There were no taunting calls from the crowd, only silence.

"Your Excellency," Francis said. "I am guilty of taking those clothes—clothes I honestly thought were my own—but only because I thought they were the last worldly possessions I would ever have, and I wanted to exchange them for whatever coin they might bring so that I could put those funds to work rebuilding the old church at the edge of town and furthering its mission of charity for those who need it most."

"I know the place," the Bishop said.

"So, if you will convict me, convict me of that. But should you do so, then as you consider a fitting punishment, I would only have you keep in mind that no matter how long I might spend in a prison's bowels, once freed, I will only continue to do what I can to help those in need. And if the sentence to address such crimes will take my life, then I will gladly add my life to the cause that took His life too. I can think of no other way to live and no better way to die."

"You speak boldly," the Bishop said.

"No, Your Excellency," Francis said. "I speak humbly. And so that I should not go to my fate taking more from the gentleman I called my father, I humbly thank him for the use of all the garments he has loaned to me over the years, including the ones I wear now. But as it seems that he needs them all more than I do—and more than the unclothed of Assisi do—then I return them all to him now, for him to do with them as he will."

With that, Francis stripped off his clothes and stood before the crowd as the naked as he'd been on the stormy night he was born. The crowd was abuzz. Francis folded the clothes neatly, crossed the stage, and added them to the pile of garments Pietro had already offered as evidence.

"I love my father, but I am not my father. Nor his father. Nor his father before him. I am my own man and that is how I will live or, if it be your will, how I will die. But whatever my fate may be, I will live and die as I am now and not as anyone else would have me be."

The crowd erupted. Some shouted in outrage at Francis's nudity, but they were nearly drowned out at those shouting loudly and enthusiastically in Francis's favor. Outraged, Pietro began to move towards the front of the crowd to resume presenting his case, but the Bishop raised a hand to stop his advance. The most powerful man in Assisi had not earned his position in the Church through strategic action, not penitent prayer, and the miter on his head reflected his mastery of politics, not scripture. If Pietro was oblivious to what had just happened, the Bishop was not. Francis had deftly transformed the nature of the trial and the Bishop was not eager to be cast in the role of Pontius Pilate before a raucous crowd. Still, he too was looking for some easy resolution that would allow him to wash his hands of the entire matter.

The Bishop looked down at Pietro, who was still holding Francis' freshly folded clothes. "Your son has moved me with the conviction of his words. I hope that he has touched you, as well, and inspired you to drop this matter and welcome him back into your home."

"My home, Your Excellence?" Pietro asked, his voice laced with scorn. "The child who robbed his own father? Who has tarnished my name? Who took everything I gave him and repaid me with nothing but cruel ingratitude?"

Francis stepped forward and addressed the Bishop. "May I speak directly to my accuser?"

Grateful for the opportunity to further distance himself from the outcome, the Bishop nodded. "Please."

Francis turned and looked directly at Pietro. "Father, what you say is true. I did take from you, but what was it that I took? The deficit you accuse me of creating has not harmed you in any way. Are your clothes less grand? Are you not well fed, with a fine supper waiting for you at home beside a warm fire? You have no need of the garments you hold in your arms, and were it not for your anger with me, you would never have missed them. Any of it. And yet every piece of gold they would have earned would have given me the ability to change a poor soul's course on this Earth, to feed them, give them hope." Pietro stared at his son as if he was a stranger.

"Have I tarnished our family name?" Francis continued, his voice loud enough for all to hear. "I hope I have not. I hope the good people of Assisi will continue to hold you in the highest esteem, as they do now, and that their only comments about me will be to note that I have forsaken a life of wealth and privilege to live the life of Christ. And I hope that, in so saying, my deeds will only serve to embellish our family name as honorable men of God. But if I have tarnished that name, then I return it to you with my most sincere apologies. I will not use it again nor will I consider it to be the name of my family any longer. I will go forward as if I have no family anymore. None besides the poor and the sick and those in need. None besides my true brothers and sisters."

Pietro was speechless.

"Of all you have said today," Francis said, spreading his arms as if to draw the crowd in, "the one charge to which I will not own is that I am ungrateful. Nothing could be further from the truth. That I have not fully appreciated the trappings and privileges of your position may be accurate, but I am now and always have been immensely grateful for everything you have given me. Your time and attention. Your wisdom and counsel. And most of all, your love. I am now and will always be, nothing but grateful for having had you as my father, and that is as true today as it will be should my life should end shortly or on some far-off day."

Pietro's brushed at his eye, but if anyone had suggested it was a tear, he would have called them a liar.

"And if you still think me ungrateful, I can only offer you this." Francis approached his father without concern for his nakedness and threw his arms around the man. He kissed him once on each cheek and looked into his eyes. "Thank you, Father. I will love you always and carry you in my heart wherever I may go, in this life and in the next."

Then Francis turned back to the Bishop. "I have said all I have to say, Your Excellence. I am guilty as my father has charged, and I await the justice of your sentence."

The audience was a living thing, buzzing with passionate comments and arguments, debating Francis's fate as if their own lives hung in the balance. The Bishop considered the situation silently for a moment, measuring the likely consequences of the options he had at his disposal. Finally, he reached the decision he was certain would be most favorable for his own position.

"Francis di Pietro di Bernardone," he began, before recalling the young man's pledge to foreswear his name and all that accompanied it. "Francis, I have arrived at the only sentence fitting for a man such as you. And that sentence is life."

Francis did not flinch. The crowd murmured uneasily. Some brave members at the far edges offered calls that were critical, but carefully constructed not to be considered heretical. The Bishop raised his hands to quiet all who cried out.

"Bring this man a proper robe," the Bishop said to one of his attendants, who hurriedly disappeared into the building adjacent to the square. Everyone waited until the attendant reappeared, panting and out of breath, and holding a robe of brown wool. He gave it to Francis, who pulled it on over his head. The attendant held out a rope belt, and Francis cinched it about his waist.

"Not a life spent in prison," the Bishop continued. "No, I sentence you to the life you have chosen for yourself—or, rather, the life God has chosen for you. The real crime here would be any arrangement that would prevent you from performing God's work. The real offense would be in preventing you from exercising your zeal to put our Lord's words to deeds by helping your brothers and sisters in need. *That* is your life sentence. Go and live it well."

Francis bowed his head. "Thank you, Your Excellency."

"But, Your Excellency," Pietro interjected.

"That is *your* sentence life sentence as well," the Bishop said, eyeing him with unspoken condemnation.

"But I have committed no crime," Pietro pleaded.

"The pettiness that has brought you here before this tribunal is the worst of crimes. And I find it a fitting punishment that you will live out the rest of your life without the presence of a true and loving son. While so many fathers of Assisi have lost their sons and would give all that they have to trade places with you, I cannot think of any penalty that could be crueler than to allow you the time to contemplate your own selfishness and the emptiness of your heart."

"But, Your Excellency—"

The Bishop held up a hand and glared down at Pietro. "I would counsel you to accept my words and go before your behavior causes me to rethink my decision. Every word out of your mouth now will be considered evidence of a greater offense and more pernicious betrayal than anything your son did."

Pietro's shoulders slumped and he bowed his head in defeat. "Yes, Your Excellency."

The Bishop got to his feet and called out to all who had assembled. "Go with God."

And that's exactly what Francis did.

47

"**F**rancis. Son." Pietro's words were not the usual bold declarations of a man of wealth and privilege, but the meek plea of a broken soul who finally realized he had lost the one thing he had long held most precious. "I would give you whatever your heart desired, whatever you might long for, if only you would return home with me now."

Alone, with the crowd dispersed, Pietro made no effort to hide the tears he wiped from his cheek.

"I did not speak a single word today that arose from anything but my love for you," Francis said. "And yet you know—as strongly as I do—that I must continue on this journey alone."

Pietro choked out a small laugh. After having spent so much time and effort trying to make a man of Francis, he realized that, perhaps, he had succeeded too well. "This was not the life I wanted for you."

"No son lives the life his father would choose for him," Francis continued. "Nor does any man live the life he would choose for himself. Not really. But this is the life that God has chosen for me. And for you. And I show you more respect by my honest rebellion than I ever could have with feigned submission. I can never return to your house, but I am forever your son."

"You are my son?" Pietro's voice quivered. "Then, please, you must come home with me."

"What I must do is walk the path God gives me."

"And what should I tell your mother? What of her?"

"Tell her what I tell you now," Francis said. "That however imperfect I may have been as a son—and I fear I was terribly so—I have always loved you both with all of my heart. Always. I am the benefactor of your kindness and patience and nurturing. Whatever good I can bring to this world is not my own doing, but merely an outpouring of your efforts on my behalf. And I hope that knowing this will fill your heart—both of your hearts—with a love for me in the same way my heart is filled with love for you."

Francis threw his arms around his father.

On any other occasion, Pietro might have regarded the emotional display as a sign of weakness and rejected the embrace, but this was no other occasion. He wrapped his arms tighter and tighter around Francis, in the vain and desperate hope that if he held on long enough, then maybe not even God could take his boy from him.

"I need to go," Francis whispered.

Pietro knew that was true. He resigned himself to that truth and released his boy.

"I love you," Francis said, then turned and walked off into the gathering darkness.

Pietro stood and watched him go.

It was only when Francis had already disappeared, that Pietro managed to whisper, "I love you, too."

48

When Francis reached the old church, the door was open wide, but he stood on the doorstep, hesitant to enter.

After a few moments, Father Leo called out from the darkness within. "What are you waiting for? I'm not about to carry you across the threshold."

Francis took a deep breath and stepped inside. "I'm sorry about the trouble I brought to this door when I said I would bring none."

"Trouble? No. It was a not-so-subtle sign from our Father to shake a foolish old man out of his fearful complacency."

"And you don't have any reservations about welcoming me now?"

"My door is open wide. And so are my arms, Francis." The old man smiled. "Welcome home."

Francis shook his head sadly. "I'm afraid I don't have anything to offer but my own effort and commitment. I don't even have those old clothes to fund repairs or to provide for those who would seek our help."

"You underestimate yourself, my son."

"How is that?"

"I was in the city square today."

"You were?"

"I am not a favorite of the Bishop's disciples, but I am one nevertheless. I wanted to be on hand in case you needed my intercession before we saw you turned over to some dire fate."

Francis smiled. "Thankfully, it did not come to that."

"No, it did not. What you said today … your words moved me."

"I only spoke what was in my heart."

"That's a sadly uncommon show of strength these days, when most people give their tongue over to whatever deceit they think will further their own cause."

"My only cause is others," Francis said.

"I believe you," the old priest said. "More important, so do many of those that you spoke to today." He got up and showed Francis a handful of coins.

"What are these?"

"Donations left for the young man working to fix the old church, the young man who actually walks in Christ's path."

Francis looked up at Father Leo, a smile brightening his face. "A happy, unintended consequence."

The old man shook his head. "Nothing is unintended. Everything has its purpose. Your trial and humiliation and suffering, none of that was in vain. Your example of true faith will now make it possible for us to help others in Assisi."

"Then it was more than worth the trouble," Francis said.

"Don't lose your humility though," the old priest cautioned. "There is still much work to be done."

Francis put his hand on Father Leo's shoulder. "Then let us stop talking and get to work."

49

Everything takes time. The greatest masterpiece is just a collection of brushstrokes, one laid down after another. And so, days turned to months, then to seasons, and then to years, and eventually, Father Leo's church was rebuilt, brick-by brick, board-by-board, and was accompanied by a rebirth of the congregation, as well.

Some of the new followers had heard Francis present his defense before the Bishop and were moved by the words he'd delivered in those dramatic moments. Others were persuaded by the legends they'd heard of the wonders he performed. But most had simply come across an unassuming man in the ordinary course of their day and had been swayed by his soft-spoken words or his simple acts of kindness.

Whatever their reasons or motivations, the old church became crowded with those who were intent on following in Francis's path. He let them follow, even though he was uncertain about how to lead—or even if he should lead anyone anywhere.

"Sheep need a shepherd," Father Leo told him.

"God is our shepherd," Francis said. "I am following God's path. Let them all do the same."

"There is nothing more powerful than a gathering of men—and nothing more dangerous. The need for a leader is part of human nature, and those who have followed you to this house need one, too. The question is whether you will be that leader or if you will cast them adrift to find another."

"Another would serve them better."

Exasperated, Father Leo shook his head. "Probably. But you are the one they chose—and the possibility of who might take your place and where they might lead these good people worries me more every day."

"But I did not choose to be a leader," Francis protested. "I do not want to lead an ungainly force of men that must be managed with all of the tedious daily routines of any other business."

"But you are in business. Saving lives and souls is a business is like any other. Could you really have thought that you could feed and clothe and house and heal all those in need solely by yourself? Not even you could be that foolish."

Francis shrugged and looked down at his bare feet. "Well, if I have shown nothing else over the course of my life, it is that I have a boundless capacity for foolishness." With a long sigh, he turned and headed for the door.

"Where are you going?" Father Leo called after him.

"Out."

"Out where?"

"Out to talk with someone who might understand my position better than you do."

"I do understand." Father Leo followed Francis to the door. "I understand there is work here that needs to be done and men who need to be organized in order to do it."

"Then my first act of leadership is to put you to it. Organize. Manage. Work."

"That's not my job," Father Leo objected.

"No, that's not the job you chose. It was the job chosen for you. A wise man told me something about that once."

"Well, you've been chosen to welcome the Pope's emissary. He's due to arrive today and we're preparing a dinner to mark the occasion."

Francis shook his head. "The dinners we prepare should feed the hungry, not celebrate those who are already well-fed."

"This world doesn't turn on *should*'s. You know that."

"I do."

"This is important, Francis."

"Well, if it's important," Francis said. "I suppose I should be there."

A relieved smile spread across Father Leo's broad face.

"I *should* be there," Francis said pointedly.

"Wait!" Father Leo said, but the only response he got was a closing door.

†

Lost in thought, Francis eventually found himself in a thicket of trees and sat down in the shade to rest. He closed his eyes and began to repeat the same phrase over and over again. "*Mio Dio, Tuto mio.*

Mio Dio, Tuto mio

Mio Dio, Tuto mio."

Francis repeated the words over and over again until each lost their individual meaning and his consciousness began to rise up and away from his physical self. He did not experience the passage of time, and had no idea how long he'd been there before his serenity was disturbed by the passing of a shadow across his face.

A man cleared his throat, and Francis grudgingly opened his right eye and peered up at the man. Dressed in the finery that marked him as a nobleman or a member of the very upper echelons of social class, the man studied Francis. "You are Francis, the son of Pietro di Bernardone?"

"I am my own man, but there are some who call me Francis."

"Do you know who I am?"

Francis looked the man up and down. "You're a friend of my father's."

"I think more a friend in his estimation than my own, but yes, I know your father. My name is Bernard of Quintavalle."

Francis nodded and then closed his eyes to renew his meditation.

"*Mio Dio, Tuto mio.*

Mio Dio, Tuto mio.

Mio Dio, Tuto mio."

The man cleared his throat again. "May I ask what you are doing?"

Francis answered without bothering to open his eyes. "I'm praying."

"Praying? But you're just repeating the same words over and over again. I know many prayers, but they are all long and complicated."

"The recitation of complicated words often becomes just that, complications. Those who fancy themselves as faithful repeat them again and again until they know them by heart, but they never actually take them to heart. Praying isn't really about rote recitation. Do you think God hasn't heard it all before? Or that He's impressed by your performance?"

Bernard was silent.

"No, the true purpose in praying is to establish a connection—a oneness—with God. That's not a situation created through the eloquence of man, but rather by focusing on the simplest of words which contain the truest of sentiments.

"*Mio Dio, Tuto mio*. My God, my Everything. What more is there for any of us to say?"

"May I join you?" Bernard asked.

"Why?"

Bernard sighed and looked up at the canopy of leaves above them. "I was born to wealth and power and prestige and over the course of my life I have amassed even more. And yet, as I look at the sunset of my life, I realize I have nothing at all. For all of the luxuries I have enjoyed and all of the wonderous things that I have witnessed, it seems to me that the only person I have ever seen in this world who was truly fulfilled was you ... at your trial."

"My only contentment in that moment was found in not wanting anything at all," Francis said.

"Exactly!"

Francis gestured to the forest floor. "This ground is not my own." Bernard looked around and then lowered himself to the ground, watching as Francis began his recitation again.

"*Mio Dio, Tuto mio.*

Mio Dio, Tuto mio.

Mio Dio, Tuto mio."

Quietly, Bernard joined in, and the two men sat together yet apart as each resumed their individual quests to discover something higher than themselves, and ultimately, through the repetition of the simplest of words and the banishment of mundane thoughts, they found themselves united in something greater.

50

Reluctantly, Francis rose to his feet. The sun was low in the western sky, and the responsibilities of the world intruded upon the peace he'd momentarily found.

Bernard looked up. "Are we done?"

"No. We're never done with contemplation. It's part of discovering who we really are."

"And now?" Bernard asked, pulling himself to his feet.

"And now, I'm sorry to say that I have responsibilities to which I must return."

"What responsibilities could a man as free as you have?"

"You'd be surprised what obligations come with trying to walk away from this world," Francis said. "This time it's something about a Papal emissary."

"Your name carries all the way to Rome and then returns with His Holy Father's representatives in tow," Bernard said, his words filled with admiration.

"You speak of it like these events were the fulfillment of some ambition, but I assure you that this was not the path I intended to walk," Francis. "I have gone to great lengths to distance myself from the politics of man and the business of belief." He stared down the path that led back toward the church. "But now it seems as if following my vision has left me destined to assume the role I have always defied."

"Sometimes the things we flee are the ones that follow most closely."

Just then a small bird lighted on a branch not far from the two men.

"You said you envy me," Francis said and pointed at the bird. "I envy that bird, one of the smallest of God's creatures."

The bird tweeted again. Francis smiled. In a pouch at his belt was a small piece of bread. He took it out and tossed several crumbs of crust to the ground. The bird descended from its perch and pecked at the bits of bread.

"All it needs in this world is some crumbs of bread, a song in its heart, and God smiling down on him." Francis tossed some more crumbs to the ground.

Another bird flew to the spot.

And then another.

And another.

"And now he has followers, just like you," Bernard said with a smile.

When the birds were done with the crumbs on the ground, one of them noticed that some crumbs had fallen on Francis' robe as well. Before too long, the birds were perching on him and taking the bits of bread directly from his hand.

Bernard laughed gently at the sight. "And now his followers are your followers, too—whether you want them or not. Just like me, huh?"

"No one is unwelcomed," Francis said. "I only wanted to make clear that I am hardly worthy to be followed."

"If not a man like you, then who else might be worthy?"

"No man is worthy," Francis said. "God comes to us each in our own way, and we should follow Him as we see fit."

"I would keep those sentiments to yourself if you're meeting with representatives of the Pope," Bernard warned. "I've heard that the cruelest of fates have fallen on those who have voiced far less."

"Proof of my point," Francis said. "But no matter, I have seen too much bloodshed in my lifetime to ever fear shedding my own."

Is that right?"

Francis and Bernard were surprised to look up from their conversation and see six boys standing at the edge of the clearing. The biggest and oldest was standing with his hands on his hips like he was waiting for an answer to the question he had posed.

"I'm merely preaching to my congregation," Francis said, stretching out his hand to show off one of the birds perched on his finger.

"He's preaching to birds," the leader said and the other boys laughed. "There's a tax for that."

"A tax?" Francis raised his hand and his feathery converts took flight. "For what?"

"For preaching on our highway."

Bernard tensed and took a step back from the group, but Francis offered him a reassuring smile.

Francis spread his arms to take in the small clearing. "I'm not preaching on the highway,"

"Then travelling it," the young man shrugged. "Just give us the gold," he said, producing a knife like it was proof of both his intention and resolve.

Bernard cringed at the sight of it, but Francis appeared not to take any notice at all.

"The gold? What gold?" Francis asked.

"What kind of fool do you take me for?" the young man snapped. "This one looks like he's rich enough." He gestured at Bernard with the blade. "But everyone knows they send men of the Church with pouches of gold from town to town along this highway."

Francis chuckled. "Only a fool would rob a man who preaches to birds and has no gold."

The young man could feel the eyes of the other boys on his back. "Your robes, then. Hand them over."

Bernard's hands flew to his buttons, but Francis put out a hand to stop him.

"If you had need of it," Francis said to the boy with the blade. "I would gladly give you all that I have. It would not be the first time I've stood before the Lord exactly as He made me. But none of you has any need of my clothes or my friend's and so you shall not have them."

The young man realized he risked losing the respect of his crew, so his threats grew louder and his movements wilder. He waved the knife toward Bernard and shouted, "I said give me your cloaks or I'll—"

And in the blink of an eye, it was a very different Francis who stood before them. He took a step forward. "It's time to stop this. My friend and I have somewhere to be and a short time to get there."

"You may be stupid enough to preach to birds," the young man said, "but you can't be dumb enough to think the two of you are any match for all six of us. If you don't do like I say, then my boys and I will—"

"I do preach to the birds," Francis interrupted. "And I walk with the Lord, so I'm not afraid of you. Any of you. All of you. A boy's threats are wasted on me and I have no time to barter for your mercy—of which I am certain you have none. Now I'll ask you one last time to leave me, my friend, and my feathered congregation in peace."

"And I'm going to tell *you* one last time," the gang's leader insisted, the trembling in his voice now evident to even his followers.

Francis shook his head. "You stand there terrified, wondering what I must have up my sleeve to be so unafraid of you."

"I'm not terrified," the young man said, although everyone—even his own crew—knew he was lying.

"A thief *and* a liar," Francis said. "You stink of fear. I can smell it from here, and that is saying something given the natural stench you arrived with."

"I should kill you just to take the tongue from your head," the young man screamed.

"I understand your need more than you know," Francis said.

"You understand what?"

"Your need to appear to be something you're not."

"You want to know who I am?" The young man took several violent swipes through the air. "I'm the man with the knife."

"You're a boy trying to protect yourself from a world that's already hurt you too deeply and too often. Those who try their hardest to seem frightening are always those who are the most frightened on the inside."

The comment was like a staggering blow to the young man. "I'm not frightened."

"Then why do you need the knife?"

"I don't need a knife to take care of someone like you!"

"Then let's get rid of it, shall we?"

A person may pick up a trick or two and then forget them just a quickly, but martial skills are different. Once learned, they are forever ingrained into bone and muscle. Years had passed since Francis had stepped onto a field of battle, but the warrior's instincts remained with the man in monk's robes and he quickly grabbed the young man's wrist and firmly twisted back until the weapon came free. As the knife fell to the ground, Francis snatched it out of the air and with a flick of his wrist threw it, burying the steel blade in the bark of the tree he'd been leaning against.

All of the boys' eyes went wide at the display.

With a single step forward, Francis easily swept his would-be attacker's feet from beneath him and sent him to the ground, and an instant later, Francis' foot was on the young man's chest, pinning him to the ground.

The young man squirmed like a tipped turtle. "What are you doing?"

"Saving your life." Francis removed his foot from the young man's chest and offered his hand instead. "If you'll let me."

The young man looked at the offered hand, as if he had a decision to make and there was some other way up from the ground. "My life?"

"I understand why your words form a question. It's not much of a life, is it?" Francis asked.

"At least, it's mine."

"That's a lie," Francis said.

"People don't talk to me like this."

"Only because they don't care enough to bother. I do. And I know that you've been hurt. Badly. Often. From your earliest memory."

Silence was the young man's only response.

"And now you take to drinking wine to dull your pain and robbery to buy your wine. But there's only a moment of respite to be found in the bottom of a cup. And then you need more. And that takes coins. So, you rob and you steal and you try to make the world the victim it's already made of you. And that calls for more wine, until at last you live for the numbness of drunkenness. And that's not much of a life, at all."

"It's the only one I've got." There was no more defiance in the young man's voice.

"More lies," Francis said. "This is the life you're willing to settle for. But it's not the life you want. And not the one you deserve."

"You're wrong," the young man said. "This is the life I deserve."

"No. You deserve much more than this." Francis turned to face the others. "You all deserve more than to live a life centered on finding a way to numb yourself and selling yourselves to feed those habits. That life leads to hanging by the end of a rope. Or to skewering by the point of a blade."

"The world thinks swinging from a rope is exactly what we deserve," one of the other boys said.

Francis looked directly at him. "The world is wrong about many things. Every one of you deserves a better life."

Yet another boy spoke up. "A life following you?"

"I am no leader and want no followers."

"Then who should we follow?"

"The one who has never deserted you," Francis said simply. He looked west toward the lengthening shadows. "But now I think it's time you get off of this highway and come with us. I know where you can all get a hot meal this evening. And this road is notorious for its robbers."

Francis set off with a grateful Barnard at his side. The older man glanced behind them at the boys following in their footsteps. "No man is worthy of following?"

"Not one," Francis said. "Only God is worth following."

"Maybe with the best of people," Bernard said. "It's the same thing."

Francis smiled, and walked on in silence. Above them, a single bird sang as it followed, flitting from tree to tree.

51

By any standard, the group Francis led back to the church that evening was a mixed bunch. As a gentleman of rank and wealth, Bernard was dressed in opulence while the young men were dirty, dressed in rags, and obviously hungry. When they approached the church, the men working there grabbed whatever they had nearby that could be wielded as a weapon and marched out to meet them, determined to save Francis and the stranger with him from the ruffians most likely looking for a ransom.

Francis held up his hands to stop them.

"What is this?" He asked the approaching men.

"Have you not been accosted by thieves? These are surely ruffians out for trouble."

"I was accosted," Francis said, simply and calmly. "And they are thieves."

Their suspicions confirmed, the men raised their makeshift weapons and pressed forward.

Francis stepped forward. "Brothers, there's no need for you to react like this."

Brother Paolo, the biggest of the group, was quick to express his devotion. "Wouldn't you have us save you from them?"

"Save me?" Francis asked. "Haven't you been listening to anything that I've told you over the years? How could you possibly save me from my brothers, whether they are thieves or not?"

"We only thought to defend you," Brother Paolo said. "Perhaps we misjudged them."

"No," Francis said. "They are every bit what you thought they were—I think, perhaps, even worse— and they had certainly meant us harm, but you misunderstand what I've tried to teach you. I wasn't telling you there was no need to react violently to these young men because they were harmless, I was telling you that there was no need to react violently ever—not even to thieves. Violence is the last resort of fear. And no one who is truly grounded in the Lord can lose their faith to fear so as to move their hand to violence."

"But Francis—" Brother Paolo tried to object.

"Besides," Francis interjected. "Would you have stopped their violence with yours? Or would you have only added to it? And what then? Their families and friends would seek arms to address your acts. And then we would respond in kind again? And again? And again? That is how wars are begun, not from issues of weight and gravity, but from the smallest of offenses that are allowed to fester and grow. Violence breeds violence."

"But Francis—" Brother Paolo tried again.

"And in the same way that wars are too often begun with a single act of violence, we can all play a part in bringing peace by simply extending our hand in fellowship."

"But, Francis—"

"Now make sure they all have something to eat. And a place to sleep," Francis said, before quickly adding, "And for our new Brother Bernard, as well."

"But Francis—"

"It's been a blessed day to have made these new friends, but it has been a long one, too," Francis said. "Do you need to contradict me at every turn—"

"But Francis—"

"I have said all that I wish to say, Brother Paolo," Francis said when his patience had reached its end. "There is no 'But.'"

"Brother Francis, I do not mean to contradict you. I only wanted to let you know that you have a visitor."

"A visitor?"

"Yes."

Francis knew of the engagement, of course, but he debated whether he wanted to meet yet another Church emissary or nobleman who wished to assuage his conscience with a charitable donation. "No. Not today. I am tired of the constant parade of emissaries from here and there, who come with kind words and good causes, but only want to extend our service when we are already struggling to meet a demand that would otherwise go unfinished."

"She is not an emissary," Brother Paolo said.

"She?"

"I told her she could wait in the vestibule, but she said she'd prefer to be in your room."

"And?"

"She was not a woman that could be denied."

52

More than a few years had passed since Francis had felt that certain mixture of fear and elation, the racing heart and flipping stomach, and so the return of that once-familiar sensation was a shock to his system.

"Clare?"

"It's good to see you, Francis." She turned from the window, the last of the setting sun's rays playing up the golden streaks in her auburn hair.

"You have come all this way alone?" he asked and then immediately regretted the question, which was pointless at best and patronizing at the worse.

"I have," she answered the obvious, without indicating exactly how she'd received his question.

"That's a dangerous endeavor," he said. "Why, I myself came across a group of thieves on the road just now. You should take greater precautions with a trophy so precious."

"I am no one's trophy," she said with a huff. "And my life has never been consumed by precaution."

"But," Francis stammered. "I only thought—"

"You didn't think at all."

"I am guilty of that frequently," he admitted.

He had meant the self-deprecating admission as a lighthearted comment to break the tension between them, but her eyes didn't twinkle with amusement. Instead, she bristled, and Francis could tell she found his words to be an insensitive dismissal of the times he'd broken her heart through that same thoughtlessness.

She straightened her back and cleared her throat. "I am joining an order of nuns and pledging my heart and my hand to God."

Francis felt as though his stomach had dropped to the floor. His throat was dry, and he was suddenly cold. His hand reached out for something to hold onto and found the back of his chair. He pulled it out and sat down heavily. "But surely your family insisted—"

"They did," she said. "But the more they insisted, the more I resisted."

"Oh."

"You seem disappointed."

"No, no."

"Would you rather I—"

"Clare, I'm only surprised, not disappointed." Many years had passed since he'd told a lie, and he felt this one like a punch in the gut.

"I am, too."

"How could you be surprised by your own calling?" Francis asked. "Particularly, if you heard it so strongly that it drowned out the pleas and commands of your family."

"How can a man as blessed as you be so blind?" She shook her head her head in disbelief. "You don't see a thing, do you?"

Francis sat back in the chair. "I don't understand?"

"Obviously. I'm not surprised by my calling, Francis. I'm disappointed by the difficulty I have in answering it fully."

"What difficulty could there be?"

"I hear another voice; every bit as loud as the command of my Lord."

"What voice?"

"It's the call of my heart, Francis," she said, though the tone of her voice conveyed the resentment she felt for having to say the words out loud. "The voice is yours."

"But, Clare. The vows you've taken—"

"Francis, I have not yet taken those vows," she said. "And I can't. Not like this." She crossed the room and went to him, taking his hands in hers. "But if you were to tell me now that your heart does not feel the same as mine, then I could return to my convent, swear my oath, and never regret a moment of my service."

Francis wondered how her eyes could be so blue.

"But I could never spend a single moment under such a commitment," she continued. "I could never serve anyone, not even God, if I wasn't certain about … about your feelings for me."

Francis was as shocked as if she'd confessed doubt about the ground beneath her feet. "I've never made any secret of where my heart lies."

"I've heard what you said." She knelt before him. "I'm asking how you feel?"

"You should have no doubt about how I feel." He cupped her chin in his hand. "But you're the one who said our fates are more complicated than what our hearts crave."

She looked into his eyes, hoping to find what she searched for. "I think these complications were of our own making, mistakes of youth. I'm certain now that all we need is to find the courage to—"

There was a loud knock. Then, before Francis could respond, the door swung open and Brother Paolo stuck his head into the room. "Brother Francis, the emissary from Rome has arrived."

Francis and Clare both stood and backed away from each other.

"Tell them to wait," Francis said.

"I did," the friar answered. "They won't."

The door swung open further, and a man in fine robes strode into the room like he belonged there—or, at least, as if he went wherever he chose.

"Brother Francis. I am Jean du le Rennes Montague. I've been sent here to retrieve you by His Holiness himself."

Francis's jaw clenched. He was unimpressed by the man and his mission and frustrated by his presumption and his timing. "Retrieve me?"

"Pope Innocent III requests an audience with you immediately."

Francis looked to Clare and then back at the intruder. "I'm afraid you'll have to tell His Holiness that I have other more pressing obligations at the moment."

"More pressing than His Holiness?" Montague asked the question as if he were suffering a fundamental failure to comprehend what was happening—and who was making it happen.

"Yes," Francis said. "More pressing than anything in this world."

"I'm afraid you don't understand. The pontiff has assigned you a most important task," Montague's tone suggested he was talking to a child who was both insubordinate and not very bright.

Francis, however, was only insubordinate. "It's you who does not understand. I have no interest in His Holiness—or you, and I am otherwise occupied at the present moment."

"There is great unrest in the Holy Land," Montague said, ignoring Clare's presence and Francis's words.

"And there has been for ages," Francis said. "What is that to me?"

"His Holiness wants you to go there."

The suggestion made Francis take a step back. "Where? Are you joking?"

"No, I'm not joking at all." Montague looked like a man who had never once let a smile twist his lips. "Pope Innocent has come to learn that word of your work has spread across the distance that separates us from that heathen world. More exactly, The pontiff has learned that al-Malik of Egypt has become enamored of stories about you, and it is thought that if the Sultan were to meet you, he might be inclined to discuss the possibility of reaching some terms of peace."

"You must send another," Francis insisted. He looked to Clare. "I have more urgent possibilities to discuss."

"There is no other," Montague said. "The Sultan knows of *your* works, would agree to converse with *you*. Only you. There is no other."

"I simply cannot go. Not now." There was a clear finality in Francis' words.

Montague looked as if he didn't understand the language Francis was speaking. "But you must go."

"And if I don't?"

"If you don't?" Montague had to stop to consider the question. "In all of the years that I have served the Church, I don't think I have ever been asked about the perils of defiance. I suppose the terribleness of those consequences have always gone unspoken. Still, I'm hoping that the strength of your conscience will not make that necessary, and all I need to do is remind you that if you go and establish some peace between Christendom and the Saracens, then there are tens of thousands, maybe even hundreds of thousands of souls who might be saved. Pilgrims and heretics alike. If you refuse, they will all most certainly die. Whatever obligation you have that is more important to you than your obligation to the Pope, I hope it is not more important than the lives and souls of some hundreds of thousands of your brothers and sisters."

"It is not," Clare said.

Francis turned to her. "But—"

"We've concluded our business here," she said, careful that not even Francis would see the tear threatening to betray her. She cleared her throat, breathed deeply, and took a step away. "I'm sure Brother Francis will be prepared to leave with you immediately."

"No," Francis said. "Brother Francis is not prepared to go anywhere."

Clare turned to Montague. "Might we have a moment? Perhaps while you prepare yourself for the trip back to Rome?"

"But, of course." Montague stepped into the hallway and politely closed the door he had opened so rudely.

"Clare," Francis said before she could say a word.

She, however, could not be stopped. "I told you that I could not survive if I hesitated to tell you what was in my heart."

Francis took her hands in his own. "But now that you have—"

"Now that I have, I could not survive if I was the cause for you not going on this mission that God has set before you."

Francis took a step back. "And so, what am I to do? Forget that you've come to me now?"

"Exactly that," she said.

"And you?"

"I will return to my order," she said. "And now I can do so without regret. I came to speak with you—and God answered."

Francis took her hand. "Then you are the only one leaving with a light heart."

"No, I'm the only one not wallowing in the depth of their remorse," she corrected. There was the slightest trace of a smile at the corner of her mouth.

"And if I return from this mission?" he asked.

"*When* you return," she corrected, and choked back a sob.

He nodded and ran a thumb down her face, wiping a tear from her cheek. "When," he confirmed. "You told me that our comings and goings were controlled by something larger than either one of us, and I've come to know that's true. Still, if you had ever doubted me, then you now know my heart. And I know your heart. Neither of us can see whether our paths will cross again or not, but we both know we will never truly be apart."

She threw her arms around his neck, and there was nothing that he wanted more in the world than to hold her, to keep her there with him, forever. But she pushed herself away, and he let her go.

53

As soon as Clare closed the door behind her and disappeared down the hallway, Francis immediately went to find Brother Paolo.

"The woman leaving just now," Francis said.

"What about her?"

"I want you to gather a small group of friars and follow her until she is safely at her destination."

"I will go and catch up to her now."

Francis put a hand on Paolo's arm. "No. She'd never forgive me. Don't let her see you, but don't let any harm come to her."

Francis handed the man a staff. "Whatever you need to do, you make sure that nothing disturbs her."

Brother Paolo took the weapon. "But you said that there was never a call for violence."

"You are right," Francis admitted. "I remember what I said. But what I meant was that there was never a call for violence in defending one's self—or, at least, defending me. But this woman is a completely different matter. Keep her safe at all costs."

"But if I were to strike another in her defense?"

"If there's a sin to be committed in protecting her, then I would be only too happy to take that upon my own soul if it keeps her safe."

Brother Paolo looked into Francis's pleading eyes, and then nodded solemnly. "I understand."

†

"The trip would go much more quickly if you would only ride the horse we provided for you," Montague said from astride his own mount.

"Would it?" Francis looked back at the others walking behind them.

Montague pulled back a little on the reins in order to keep his horse on pace with Francis. "They're big, certainly, but not nearly as frightening from up here as they seem from down there."

"What?" Francis asked without looking up.

"Horses."

"You think it's fear that keeps me on the ground?"

"What other reason could there be?"

"I was taught to ride before I could walk. I promise you, I'm more at home in the saddle than most men are on their own two feet." Francis looked over his shoulder at the dozen guards, porters, and others who made up their group, all of whom were on foot. "The others we travel with, do they all have horses to ride?"

Montague looked back at the servants accompanying them like he was just noticing them for the first time and was surprised to see any of them there. "Of course, not."

"Do you know what causes so much of the world's unrest?"

Montague was game to have a guess, "Heresy?"

"I'd like to think that *heresy* is a term based on one's perspective, for those whom we call heretics think that we are the godless apostates."

"Is that what you think?" Montague's eyes narrowed.

"I think the trouble with the world isn't so much heresy, whatever that may mean, as it is inequality."

"And that bothers you, your perceived inequality?"

"Perception?" Francis asked. "I think that horse sways your perception, and that at the end of our travels today, you will look around the camp, and wonder why these others are so tired even though you were carried the whole way. And our companions will look at you across the fires and think on how sore their feet are because they were not carried the whole way. *That* is the trouble of the world."

"And that is why you're walking?"

The answer was simple enough for Francis. "Everyone rides or everyone walks. That way we all travel together. We share the experience. And we arrive together."

"Does that mean you want me to walk?" Montague asked.

"It means I want you to make your own decision, just as I have made mine."

Montague rode on in silence, but only for a while. "Because I can walk if you want me to."

"Would you rather walk?" Francis asked.

"No, I'd rather ride, but ..."

They fell back to silence. A quarter mile later Montague dismounted and led his horse by the reins. "Is this better?"

"Better for whom? My position hasn't changed," Francis said. "I was walking before and am walking now. The question of whether anything is better would be left to you."

They walked on in silence.

"I don't understand how this has improved anything for anyone," Montague said when the quiet became burdensome for him.

"Perhaps, you would understand if you were to offer the old cook back there the opportunity to ride for a while," Francis said.

Montague looked back at the old man porting his bundle of pots and pans on his back. "Him?"

"He looks tired and pained with every step," Francis said.

Silence.

"I don't think you realize who I am," Montague said finally.

Francis stopped and turned to him. "You've made it abundantly clear that you have quite a few names, but what's the cook's name?"

Montague paused for a moment to consider the question. "He's the cook."

"That's what he *does*," Francis said. "I asked you who he was. Maybe it's not that I don't realize who you are, perhaps the problem is that you don't know who the old man is. Or who any of these people who serve you are."

Montague stopped in his tracks.

Francis continued on alone.

When Francis next saw Montague, he was still leading his horse by the reins, but now the old cook was in the saddle.

Montague turned to Francis. "His name is Olio."

Francis smiled and turned back. "It's a pleasure to meet you Olio."

And that was how they travelled the rest of the way to Rome.

54

On the second night, their procession was about to make camp when they made the happy discovery that they were just outside the small village of Gubbio at the lowest slope of Mount Ingino. The entourage pressed on toward Gubbio, and before the sun had fully set, they were greeted by dozens of villagers who were overwhelmed to learn that "the man from Assisi" was among the travelers. His arrival in their midst had been a complete surprise, but they received Francis as if they had been expecting him and that his visit had come as a direct response to their prayers and pleas, and soon a large group of villagers had gathered around Francis.

The village's mayor was a round, red-faced man named Gabriano, who was quick to embrace Francis heartily. "You are the holy man we have heard of?"

"I don't know about holy," Francis said. "I am just a man."

Montague, fearing that Francis' flat response might temper the villagers' hospitality, cut through the crowd and stepped forward. "Don't listen to him. He's the one that you've heard of. This is Francis of Assisi."

Francis looked suspiciously at Montague.

"They say you preach to everyone," one of the villagers said.

"Yes, that's right," Montague answered.

"They say you preach even the lowest of the low."

Francis chuckled. "I don't believe any of our brothers or sisters are any lower—or higher—than any others. We are, all of us, equal in the eyes of Our Heavenly Father."

"Even the animals?" one of them asked. "We have heard you even preach to animals."

Another villager objected. "Don't insult our guest. No man would preach to animals."

"I preach to whomever will listen," Francis answered. "Whether that's The Pope, himself, or the horse our cook rode in on. Who—or what—makes no difference to me."

The comment troubled some of the villagers—and confused others. "Is he comparing the Pope to a horse?"

"No." Montague was quick to clarify. "Of course, he's not comparing our Holy Father to a horse."

"Of course not," Francis said with a smile. "The horse can carry much more upon his back."

Most of those assembled laughed. Montague was among the few who did not.

Francis continued, "I simply believe God's message of love is one for all of His creatures."

"And what about Satan's creatures?" Gabriano, the mayor, snapped.

"God is the creator of all of the birds of the air and the beasts of the field," Francis said. "They are His dominion alone."

Gabriano disagreed. "You may say that sitting here in the comfort of our village, but in the hills and woods surrounding us here we are under attack by a monster straight from Hell?"

Francis was unaffected by the man's rising level of intensity. "I doubt that."

"You doubt me?" Gabriano exploded.

"No. He doesn't doubt you," Montague corrected, but it was already too late by then.

"Last week, I was hunting in the hills for the beast that has been taking our lambs from the field and terrifying our children," Gabriano said. "As evening began to move across the sky, stretching the shadows, I thought I had wasted my day and decided to return home."

"Tell him about the twigs," one of the villagers said and they all settled in, waiting for the good parts of the story they had obviously heard many times before.

Gabriano nodded. "I had just turned around to start my descent back down to the village when I heard—"

"The twigs," an old woman interrupted.

The outburst only annoyed Gabriano. "No, before that I heard nothing. Absolute silence. Not a bird in a tree. Not even the wind through the leaves. And *then* I heard a twig break."

They all gasped.

Except Francis.

"I stopped and listened," Gabriano continued. "I only heard more silence. I took a careful step and then another. I listened again. Nothing. I felt better for a moment, like I had only tricked myself into hearing something that wasn't really there at all. And then—"

"The monster!" An overeager listener exclaimed.

Gabriano grimaced at the interruption. "Then I heard another twig snap and I realized I wasn't alone. I could feel eyes upon me and suddenly I realized that I was the one being hunted. And I felt my very soul turn cold as ice."

Everyone in the crowd shivered at the image. Everyone except Francis.

Gabriano rose from his seat to heighten the tension. He crouched as if still in the woods. "I turned to face the sound and there, beneath a growth of trees, was a shadow darker than any shadow could be and from the heart of this blackness. I heard a growl."

"Tell them about the growl!"

"A growl like the snarl of a demon. And then I saw—"

"The eyes. Tell them about the eyes!" Someone else in the crowd called out.

"Right in center of this darkness I see eyes. Red eyes glowing in the pitch black like two coals from Stan's own furnace."

A murmur spread over the group.

"And that's when it lunged!" Gabriano said in such a way that many in his audience who had heard the story a thousand times before still jumped with fright.

But not Francis.

"A wolf as big as a bear. Bigger again. It lunged at me with all its evil might and we fought right there amongst the trees. If I hadn't been protected by the Lord, I would've been killed for sure by a demon from Hell!"

"It was no demon," Francis said with certainty.

Gabriano's eyes flashed with anger. "Are you saying I'm a liar?"

"I'm only saying that was no monster, from Hell or any place else. It was a just wolf."

"I won't suffer that insult, not even from a holy man," Gabriano shouted.

Francis smiled. "I told you, I'm no holy man."

"If it was just a wolf, I would've killed it then and there on that very day, just as I have many others," Gabriano boasted. "And I will go back into the woods and kill all of the wolves; every single one of them, until they bother us no more."

"So, you are quite the hunter?" Francis asked.

"I am the greatest hunter in this land. My reputation is well known."

Francis chuckled to himself.

"What is that supposed to mean?"

"It only means that the problem here isn't the wolf in the woods, but men like you," Francis said.

Montague grew nervous. "What he really means—"

"Is exactly what I said," Francis continued. "Nature exists exactly as God has created it, with enough for all, including all of us. But then there are those who would take from it more than they need, who would take advantage of it for their own selfish ends. With concern for nothing and respect for no one, they take more than they deserve from God's own kingdom. And when they take all that they can, they leave the world out of balance. And then they make up stories about *demons* to excuse their own greed."

Gabriano puffed out his chest. "I don't care who you are. No one talks to me like that." He reached for his sword.

Francis didn't flinch. "Sit down."

Montague tensed with anticipation and his soldiers took a step forward.

Gabriano thought better of his decision and let his sword slide back into the scabbard, although he tried to save himself by throwing a hard look at Francis. "If it wasn't for your soldiers—"

"Don't put up your sword because of these soldiers," Francis said. "Put up your sword because I am not threatened by your blade, and I'm not frightened by all of your bellowing—or your stories."

Gabriano smoldered silently while the villagers murmured uneasily amongst themselves, unsure what was happening.

"There's no need for you to take your fear disguised as rage into the mountains to kill the innocent," Francis said. "Tomorrow I will go there myself and find your *demon*—"

Montague stepped forward. "Actually, we have a commitment to keep and we are already running late, so we will be on the road early tomorrow." Francis ignored him. "I will go into the woods tomorrow and talk to the wolf for you."

"Talk? To a wolf?" Gabriano encouraged the others to laugh along with him. "If you go into the hills, then you will die."

Francis nodded like he was bored. "If that is so, then I should get a good sleep tonight." He got to his feet and addressed the others in the village. "I am most grateful for the hospitality you have shown me and the others I am travelling with."

"Are you really going into the hills?" one of them asked.

"Yes," Francis replied. "It seems the least I can do to repay the warm hospitality of your wonderful village. But more important, I want the chance to show this bully what can be accomplished if one is only willing to extend some kindness—even to the beasts who dwell in the mountains."

55

The last ebony vestiges of night still clung to the sky and the villagers were still asleep in their beds when Francis began to make his way the mountainside. Birds chirped as they flitted from branch to branch and a soft breeze rattled the leaves like castanets.

Francis followed the path up and up until he came to a small clearing where, for some reason unknown, the trees had not grown, and the ground was left bare to the sky above. When he reached the center of the circle, Francis stopped to listen.

He heard absolutely nothing. And this, Francis knew, was the place he was looking for. He sat in the middle of the clearing and closed his eyes, basking in the morning sun which was now well into its daily ascent.

He sat and thought about the wolf. His method wasn't intended to give him a predatory advantage over the animal, but rather to put himself in the beast's position. He saw himself stalking through the woods. He felt the earth beneath his paws and the wind in his fur. He pictured the pack and the pups and imagined the spirit of community existing between them all. And he felt the fear. The sounds and smells of men in his woods. The piercing howls and cries of those he loved and the smell of blood thick on the air. He felt the pangs of hunger in his belly and the inconsolable loneliness in wandering the hills alone.

And when Francis felt he finally understood the wolf, his loves and his fears, he knew he was ready.

"I've come to meet with you," he called out across the clearing.

No one answered, of course, but Francis knew he wasn't alone. It wasn't so much what he saw, as what he *didn't* see. Or, to be more exact, what he *almost* didn't see. For just out of the corner of his eye he caught the ghost of a figure, slipping from shadow to shadow at the wooded edge of the clearing.

There was enough of a presence that Francis was certain something watching him from the protection of the woods, but not so much that he was able to determine what exactly it was. Still, Francis was content to sit in the morning sun and wait until the other party felt comfortable enough to approach him.

Hours passed. It wasn't until dusk began to fall and the shadows across the forest floor began to swell with the setting sun that Francis realized he had been right all along.

He was not alone. There were eyes on him. And under the cover of the gathering darkness, his watcher moved stealthily, closer and closer.

A certain sort of man might have notched an arrow in his bow or readied his staff or spear. Even a man without a weapon might have frantically foraged the area for whatever tree limb or rock he could find at his feet that could be converted to a weapon and means of defense.

Francis simply remained seated. "I mean you no harm," he said to what he could not see.

His shadow companion settled amongst the grasses on the far side of a large boulder just ahead.

"But I am alone in that resolve," Francis added.

Silence.

"And so, you can talk with me and we can see what sort of peace might be arranged."

Silence.

"Or you can add my life to the list of those you have taken. And, in turn, the village below will use my death as the final provocation they need to send men with bows and arrows and swords and spears to fill these woods and there will be no place for you to hide. No matter how many you kill, they will send more. Believe me when I say that once they begin, there is never any end to the men with weapons. They cannot be deterred. And once they are invoked, your fate is either to fall at their feet or to drown in a torrent of the blood you spill. Either way, your days will be dark and numbered. And those of your children, too."

There was a slight stirring from behind the rock. A nervous rustling.

"But come to me now. Not with claw and fang, but as a brother. Come and sit with me. Share what little I have to eat. And together we shall reach a peace that will allow us all to share God's bounty. And allow us all to live as He intends us to do."

There was no movement at all.

Francis stayed still and silent. He shut his eyes.

He could hear the slightest sounds, grass bending beneath some weight, a shallow, panting breath. And Francis could sense movement in his direction, but still he did not open his eyes.

It wasn't until he felt a blast of hot, sour breath upon his face that he opened his eyes and found himself staring directly into the eyes of another. Not red and demonic, but yellow eyes filled with sadness.

The wolf was tall, but thin; sinew and muscle stretched over its bones. Its mouth was pulled into a taut snarl to reveal its fangs as it growled low and menacingly.

"Brother Wolf," Francis said calmly. "Thank you for listening to my words. Now let me listen to your story."

56

Francis and the wolf sat together for a long while—until the sound of snapping branches and trudging feet pricked up the wolf's ears.

"It will all be well," Francis said. "But for your sake, it is for the best that you now take your leave. I promise I will tell them everything."

The sounds of intruding footsteps nearing their shared sacred space grew louder, and a second later it was as if the wolf had never been there at all. Francis rose from his position and headed toward the edge of the clearing. He could hear soldiers in the distance, bumbling about in the gathering darkness, but at the edge of the woods, Montague stood alone, waiting.

"What has astounded you so?" Francis asked.

"I just witnessed a miracle," Montague whispered, as if the woods—or the wolf—might hear. "I came upon this clearing and there you were, sitting side by side with a wolf. A wolf! It was almost as if you were speaking to each other."

"Communication is easy when participants don't fear one another and are not looking to take advantage of the other. This is true for man *and* beast," Francis said, as he kept walking past Montague.

His escort turned and quickly followed after.

"What are you doing this far from civilization's comforts?" Francis asked.

"You forget, I'm responsible for bringing you to Rome. The lives of thousands depend on it." Montague said as he struggled to keep up with Francis.

"And so, you came looking for me with your soldiers?"

"I'm responsible for you," Montague repeated.

"How many soldiers?"

"All of them."

"With instructions to do *what* if you found the wolf instead of me?"

"Kill it, of course."

"Why?"

"Because it's a wolf and wolves are dangerous."

"And did I appear to be in danger?"

"Well, no. But—"

"But you would have killed it anyway, even though it wasn't dangerous."

"It was still a wolf."

"Ah, now we are getting to the heart of it," Francis said. "You were ready to kill my new friend not because it was dangerous, but simply for being what the Good Lord made it. Don't you see? Too often we react—to beasts and people alike—not on the basis of anything more than *what* they are."

"But he was still a wolf," Montague insisted.

"You would've killed the poor beast simply because he scares you. Your violence comes from nothing other than your own fear."

Montague was reluctant to admit to anything that sounded so cowardly, but he wasn't sure what to say instead so he stayed silent.

Francis continued. "But don't you understand that you scare the wolf too? Does that give it the right to kill you?"

"No, of course, not." Montague clearly thought the suggestion was ridiculous.

So did Francis. "And so, people—like you, apparently—want to apply one set of standards to their own behavior and another set of standards to someone else's. Peace demands equality among all creatures. Is this not the very essence of the command that we should *Do unto others?*"

"You speak of equality," Montague said, "But I'm just emissary of the Pope's, I'm not his equal."

"Why not?" Francis asked. "He is just a man; the same as you."

"But everyone acknowledges that His Holiness is above us all."

"Maybe that's part of the problem." Francis smiled. "And you are mistaken. Not everyone acknowledges his superiority over anyone else—or your superiority over my friend, the wolf."

The consideration stopped Montague in his tracks. "I don't know what's braver, talking to a wolf or saying things like that."

"There is always danger in walking the path that has been set before us all, but that is no reason to abandon the way or diverge onto some other course you think will be easier. You should walk in His footsteps anyway, regardless of the dangers. Be not afraid. I go before you always."

Francis kept on walking. "Now, let's collect the rest of your soldiers and get back to the village. I have good news to share."

57

As mayor, Gabriano took it upon himself to gather his friends and neighbors around him when he received word that Francis had come down from the hills.

"You were gone so long, I thought for sure you were in a wolf's belly by now," Gabriano said to Francis, following up the comment with a hearty laugh. "I told you that you would never find that demon wolf and that you wouldn't survive if you did."

"You were wrong on both accounts," Francis said.

"What?" The round, red-faced man looked to Montague and the soldiers for confirmation.

Montague nodded his head. "As a servant of His Holiness, The Pope, I swear it's true. When I came upon him, he was sitting in the middle of a glade talking to the wolf."

A gasp went up from everyone gathered. But Gabriano was unfazed. "Talking? To a wolf? That's impossible."

"Nothing is impossible when one acts with faith," Francis said.

The mayor laughed, and with a voice laced with scorn said, "And just what did this wolf tell you?"

"First, I told him what you said, how you'd claimed he'd appeared before you as a demon from Hell."

Gabriano chuckled nervously.

"The wolf said you were a liar."

Gabriano sputtered as his face went from pink to crimson. "No one speaks to me like that!"

"He did," Francis said. "And I do, too. He said you ran like a coward as soon as you laid eyes on him."

"Lies!" he said. "All lies. I swear the wolf stalked me like a hound from hell."

"He is not happy eating your livestock," Francis said to the crowd. "But Gabriano and his friends have hunted all the game on which the wolf once fed his pack. He would rather not take from your flocks, but he has no other choice except to starve."

"So, I hope you told him to go ahead and starve then."

"No, I told him that you would feed him from now on," Francis said.

Gabriano exploded. "You told a wolf we would feed it?" He looked around to his friends and fellow hunters. He knew he needed to save face, but no one stepped forward to stand with him.

"No," Francis said. "You're not listening to me, Gabriano. I told him that you, Gabriano, would feed him from now on."

"Me? You told a wolf I would feed it?"

"That's exactly what I told Brother Wolf." Francis said. Then he turned to Montague, who was quick to vouch for him.

"As I said, when I came to the clearing, the two of them were sitting almost nose to nose as if they were in a conversation."

"I don't care," Gabriano said. "I am not going to feed a wild beast that preys—"

"The wolf only wants to survive and provide for his family," Francis said, looking around the gathering. "Are there any here who don't share this simple ambition?" A low murmur spread among the crowd.

"To survive, we must eat. The only question is whether you will willingly share the bounty you have or if you will greedily hoard all that you take from his home on the mountain. Will you share or force Brother Wolf to seek his meals from your bounty." Francis looked around the gathering again and this time his gaze was not so benign.

There was a low murmuring of discontent with this option.

"To survive, yes, the wolf must eat, but I will go up the hill tomorrow and solve that problem for him," Gabriano boasted.

"Or he will solve it for you," Francis suggested.

"What?"

"I told him that I would do my very best to convince you to feed him, but that if I failed in this endeavor, you were the one he should eat first."

Gabriano's mouth fell open.

"So, if you go up into those hills again with your bow and your arrow or your traps, you should be forewarned that he knows why you are coming, and he is prepared."

Gabriano's eyes widened. He tried to speak, but nothing coherent came out.

"Besides, a wolf on your mountainside will keep other more dangerous wolves away," Francis said. "If you were to kill this wolf, what would that accomplish? Such a grievous action would only open the area for new and different wolves. Maybe wolves that would be even more vicious, even more blood-thirsty."

The murmuring was louder and more discontent.

Gabriano finally rallied his wits. "Then I will take my bow and—

"I know, I know. You would kill all of them, too. And I suppose it is true that you could, over time, kill them all—but not before they continued the terror that has plagued you until tonight. Ask yourselves, what is more dangerous, these surrounding woods populated with a well-fed and contented wolf or with a hungry one?"

Gabriano was flummoxed. "But if we feed the wolf—"

Francis stopped him there. "Would that one act of kindness diminish you as the proud people you are? No, only your cruelty and selfishness could do that. You can choose kindness and generosity and put an end to the struggle. Or you can choose more violence, but I promise you that this will only bring more terror in the night."

Francis looked right at Gabriano. "And rather than the young and the weak that you have been cowardly content to sacrifice, I promise the fattest and fittest of you will be the first casualty in any further fight you want to bring up that hill."

Gabriano said nothing, and Francis went to stand beside him, placing a consolatory hand on the man's shoulder. "The choice is simple. You can care for the wolf and let him return that consideration or you can both destroy one another."

Francis looked to the other villagers. "Which do you suppose God would have you all do?"

And that is how the village became famous throughout the region for having a wolf that protected their pastures and who shared in their prosperity as their brother; an equal to their number.

58

Francis, Montague and the others in their party left Gubblio the next morning, but their trip on to Rome did not go any more quickly after that. No matter how swiftly their group travelled, word of Francis and his deeds always spread faster. So, there was always some village where the people wanted to meet the man who spoke to wolves or the monk who preached to birds. There was always some town where the afflicted sought his comfort and the deprived begged for his assistance.

Francis never turned any of them away or denied their requests, whatever they might be.

When Montague objected to the distractions and tried to hurry him along, Francis made clear, "Your mission does not take precedence over my own, for ultimately mine is an obligation to the higher master."

Because Francis' unshakable interest was focused on charity not haste, they reached Rome not days late, but weeks after their scheduled arrival. And still Montague was ecstatic just to see The Eternal City again.

The silhouette of the city was cut against a sky layered in the orange and pink and purples of sunset and, for the first time in their travels, Montague took a deep breath just to savor a moment. "Rome," he exclaimed. "Have you ever seen anything so beautiful in all of your life?"

Francis looked out over the view. "I have seen the smile of a hungry child who has been given something to eat. So, yes, I've seen a world of beauty far greater than the construction that lies before us." Then he continued walking.

Montague hustled to catch up to him. "For weeks I've listened to you talk like that. I won't dispute the importance of appreciating life's smaller moments or dispute the natural wonder of God's majesty in the mountains and valleys, but how can you ignore the magnificence of man's greatest triumph?" Francis looked to either side of the road. They were lined with people, some at work, others not. Still, everyone he saw looked out onto the world with the wide eyes of those who lived in want and despair.

"You talk of man's triumphs, but all I see are the failures."

"These people?" Montague asked. His question was pointed, like he had just won a long-fought argument. "I didn't expect I would ever hear you call these people failures."

"And you haven't," Francis said. "The failures aren't the people who are suffering, but the opportunities that have been missed to give some assistance or comfort to those poor souls. You look out at the world and see man's triumph in building some structure bigger than it has any need to be, but what achievement is that? I would see man's triumph as finally putting an end to suffering."

Montague was tired from the road and reluctant to concede the point. "You're not a very pleasant person."

"Pleasantries are the curtains that the comfortable draw around themselves so they don't have to see the harsh realities of those not similarly situated."

Montague sighed. "Not very pleasant at all."

59

History keeps a disturbing record of the all-too-temporary nature of power and the inevitability of transitions from one "endless" realm to another for those who are willing to read the chapters of a collected past.

The property on which the Lanteran Palace had been built originally belonged to the Lanterani family, a distinguished and noble house known throughout much of the Roman Empire. The property was ripped from the family's hands, however, when one of the Lanterani was accused of treason by the Emperor Nero. When Nero, in turn, met his fatal fate, the property was passed along from emperor to emperor until eventually Constantine built a palace on the site. Over time the palace was given to the Bishop of Rome and became the home of the Papacy.

And so, as governments and men of power change, so, too, do the buildings they occupy.

Over time the Lanteran Palace was refurbished and embellished by succeeding popes as they endeavored to make the structure a representation of their political power and spiritual authority. Pope Innocent III had been keen to partake in these efforts and set about renovations that would reflect his personal position and status. So, when Francis and Montague and their company finally arrived at their ultimate destination, the Palace was covered in scaffolding that made the entire structure appear to Francis like a giant anthill, swarming with workmen and artisans.

They had been expected, of course, and were led directly to a grand room, the likes of which even a son of privilege like Francis had never seen before. With a smug smile painted across his face, Montague watched as Francis, eyes wide and mouth agape, took in the towering gilded ceilings, brilliant frescoes, and magnificent statuary.

"It is magnificent, is it not?" Montague said. "Can you tell me now that none of this resonates with your soul?"

Francis tilted his head back to take in a large painting of a former pope. "Did Christ commission such grand paintings of himself or live in such opulence when he preached the Sermon on the Mount?"

"What?" Montague couldn't comprehend the question.

"How many hungry bellies might have been filled with the money spent to decorate a room so few will ever see. It seems a tragic waste."

"Heresy." The word—spoken with the force of a slap across the face—came from behind them.

Montague and Francis turned toward the voice and found a corpulent, red-faced, crimson-robed Cardinal standing in the doorway. "Your Eminence." Montague said, rushing forward to kneel and kiss the man's ring.

"You believe it's a waste to glorify God," the Cardinal huffed, looking Francis up and down, eyes narrowing as he took Francis's robes and simple sandals and noting that, unlike Montague, the bedraggled man had not rushed paid proper obeisance. "I believe that such an uncharitable attitude will lead you down a very dangerous path."

Francis laughed. "You call this opulence charity? Charity toward whom? The hungry? The sick? The poor in spirit? I attend to all men, for all men are sinners and in need of the love and forgiveness of Christ—especially the hurt and angry and afraid. Unfortunately, these conditions rarely bring out the best in a person's character, and so they must be addressed—if not out of care and concern, then out of caution. For anger and fear spread from man to man just like a plague, and the destruction they cause over time is no less devastating."

The Cardinal's voice was low and menacing. "Are you threatening an insurrection?"

Montague stepped forward quickly. "Cardinal Le Bougre, please accept my apologies for—"

Le Bougre turned his ire toward Montague. "Who is this man who dares to speak such heresy in the very heart of the Church?"

Francis opened his palms toward the cardinal. "I am a simple man who follows in the path of Jesus Christ."

The cardinal scowled. "Then you should mind your tongue and bend your knee in my presence," the cardinal held out his hand for Francis to kiss his ring.

"I will do neither."

"Francis!" Montague grabbed Francis's arm, but Francis stepped away and swept both arms out as if to take in the whole room.

"Tell me, Cardinal, can you quote the scripture describing Jesus's home as a palace like this? Or tell me of his parable of the bended knee and the kissed ring?"

Le Bougre's face turned purple and spittle flew as he sputtered. "Can you wear the robes of a man of the cloth and not be aware of the penalties for such heretical speech and deeds? Perhaps, some time with the Inquisition would convince you of the error of your ways."

Francis shook his head. "I don't think so. The time would convince me of nothing but the depths of your cruelty and, even after having just met you, I need little convincing of that."

Montague struggled to gain control of the situation. "Your Eminence, what he means—"

"Is exactly what I've said." Francis stared at the cardinal. "And I suspect that if His Holiness sent for me, then he has a role for me to play which will likely interfere with my time before your Inquisitor."

"How dare you speak to me like that," the cardinal cried out.

"He's impertinent, I grant you. But he's entirely correct on that particular matter."

Everyone turned to find Pope Innocent III had made his entrance unannounced.

This time it was the cardinal's turn to genuflect.

"But, Your Holiness," Le Bougre continued. "If you could only have heard how this man said to me just now."

"I did hear," the pope said. "Every word. And he's right. About everything. Especially the fact that I have intentions for him that are far more important than whatever may be troubling you."

"But Your Holiness—"

"Are you challenging my authority to assert your own?"

"No, Your Holiness."

The pope smiled contentedly. "Good. I think we all know what the result of such a conflict would be, don't we?"

Le Bougre's head bobbed up and down as if floating on a roiling river. "Yes, yes, Your Excellency."

The pope turned his attention to Francis. "Too often a man's legend far outweighs his presence, but I am pleased to find that your reputation hardly does you justice."

"I am only a man," Francis said.

"A man." The pope stopped to consider what he'd said. "And yet you understand what a difference a single man—*just a man*—can make in this world."

Francis said nothing.

"Come. Let us talk."

60

Pope Innocent showed Francis into private quarters that were more reserved than the opulent room in which they had met.

"You must be hungry from your time on the road. May I have something brought here for you to eat or drink?"

Francis shook his head. "I thank you for your hospitality, but we passed many today who are in far greater need of food and drink than I am."

"And we will get to that in a moment." The Pope offered a reassuring smile. "But before we do, I'd like to talk to you about something else. How much do you know of the Holy Land?"

Francis shook off the suggestion that he knew anything at all. "Only the stories my father told me when I was a boy. He was a merchant, fine linens and silks, and so he travelled there from time to time."

"Yes, I know."

Francis' situational confusion only grew. "You know about my father?"

The Pope ignored the question. "I'm afraid that Jerusalem and the whole of the Holy Land have again fallen into the hands of the Infidels."

Francis acknowledged the news with a nod but didn't offer any greater acknowledgment.

"A tragedy," the Pope continued. "A greater tragedy still that the situation is entirely our fault. We sent an army to liberate the Holy Land, and from the moment they set out, they behaved no better than the Infidels they were intended to route; worse often. And so, I fear that the tragic events that led to the Holy Land slipping from our grasp is God's way of punishing us for our moral turpitude."

"You may be right," Francis said. "But I don't understand then why you would send for me. I am no soldier. Or, at least, I haven't been one in a very long time and I have sworn an oath that I shall never be one again."

"And *that* is precisely why I sent for you," the Pope replied. "There are soldiers enough. Too many soldiers. The last thing we need is another."

"Then what is it that you think I can offer?"

"It's not what I *think* you can offer, but what I am certain you will contribute."

"And what is that?"

"Compassion. Reason. Peace."

"I have no doubt that the situation would benefit from a demonstration of them all, but why me?"

"There are armies encamped just outside of Jerusalem. And more on the way. And there are fools who assure me that this time their efforts will be different, that their efforts will succeed in liberating the Holy Land and keeping it for the good of all Christendom." He paused a moment. "I shouldn't say fools. Perhaps, they are right and this time their armies will succeed. But you and I both know that even in success, these armies will cause—"

"Death. And suffering," Francis said.

"Yes. Death and suffering with no guarantee they will ever recapture the Holy Land. Not even I can stop these armies. But I can send my own forces." The Pope smiled. "An army of one. You."

"Me?"

"You."

"But I could never—"

"With news of this latest expedition to the Holy Land, I was greatly troubled and had difficulty sleeping. Until one night I had a dream. I was wandering along a road and an old man approached me and told me that in order to end war with peace I needed a warrior of peace. He told me about you."

"Me? But what can I do?"

"Word has reached me that for an infidel, Al-Kamil is a reasonable man, with more than a little interest in our ways and culture. And somehow word of you and your deeds has reached his ear and gained a favorable response. I want you to go to the Holy Land and arrange to meet the Sultan. Then I want you to convince him of our peaceful intentions and arrange a peace that would prevent further bloodshed, but permit access to the Holy Land for all Christian pilgrims."

Francis shook his head in disbelief. "No."

"No?"

"What you're asking is impossible."

"What I'm asking is improbable. But if you don't go, then war is inevitable. As are the deaths and suffering that you know follow in its terrible wake. If there is even the slightest chance that you could prevent all that suffering, if you could save even one soul, then I don't see how you can refuse."

Francis stared down at his dusty feet and old sandals, barely able to comprehend what was being asked of him.

"Isn't that the very nature of faith?" the Pope prodded. "To believe that against all the odds, God and righteousness will persevere?"

"Yes." Francis admitted, reluctantly.

"Then I ask you, do you have faith?"

"It's not faith in God I lack."

"Then what?"

"I doubt men's capacity for peace when war is so readily an option."

"You can change that, Francis. I know that you can," the Pope said. "Just think of what could be accomplished if you succeed in brokering such a peace. Not only in the Holy Land, but here at home. If the treasuries for war were not needed, how much of those resources might be used to help the people you serve? If you accomplish such a feat, imagine how your name would echo."

"I am not interested in my name echoing anywhere. I wouldn't even contemplate this for any advantage for myself."

"Of course not, but think how your reputation would grow and with it your influence. The man who single-handedly restored the Holy Land? How, then, could anyone refuse your calls to help the poor, sick, and downtrodden?"

Francis considered the possibilities. "And if I decide to go?"

"I would send a small group with you. Montague, some of his men, and a mercenary with connections in the area."

"Mercenary? You said that this would be a mission of peace."

"Even a mission of peace needs a man who has mastered the ways of war. Besides, this shouldn't trouble you. I'm told you already know the man."

"I know many different kinds of people, but no mercenaries."

The Pope turned to his attendant. "Send the whole party in."

The attendant returned a moment later, followed by Montague and four of his men. Behind them stood a man whose features were obscured by a thick beard. And yet Francis would have known him anywhere.

The Pope raised a hand and beckoned the man forward. "I believe you know Giovanni di Pietro di Bernardone."

Giovanni smiled. "Hello, Brother."

61

There are people and places, smells and even songs, so tied to a particular time in one's past that a glance or a whiff or a snippet of melody can instantly summon the events of that entire era causing them to flood into the present as if they were unfolding around them still.

Francis had labored for years to separate himself from the aimless person he had once been, to leave all that emotional pain behind him and to better himself in every conceivable way. And if humility had prevented him from ever being proud of his efforts and the results he had achieved; he was nevertheless aware that he'd found a degree of contentment that seemed to elude others.

And then Giovanni walked into the room, and Francis found himself hurtling back into the same pit of emotional disturbance in which he had been so mired as a young man. And Francis knew that Giovanni, rougher, broader, and with a new scar across his cheek, saw every emotional twist and turn play out on his otherwise placid features.

Francis finally dragged his eyes away from Giovanni and turned to the Pope. "What is he doing here?"

"He's the mercenary who will accompany you."

Francis' confusion spiked. "How could you possibly know about—"

"That would be me," Cardinal Le Bougre said, stepping forward. "On my last pilgrimage to the Holy Land, our party encountered some *difficulties* along the way. Signori di Pietro di Bernardone was instrumental in resolving the situation and ensuring our safe return. He was a godsend."

Giovanni offered a sweeping bow. "It was nothing, Your Eminence."

"You're too humble," the Cardinal said with a smile. Then he turned back to Francis and his smile disappeared. "When His Holiness first heard of your name and reputation and began to consider his mission of peace, I was the first to suggest that he might enlist my friend, Giovanni, to oversee your safety—having, as you do, a familial connection."

The Pope studied the changing emotions on Francis's face. "I was led to believe that the two of you were quite close. Brothers. I thought you would rejoice at the opportunity."

Francis' instinct was to respond immediately, but over the interceding years he had learned the benefits of taking a moment to collect one's thoughts before speaking. Meanwhile, everyone waited.

"You're right, of course." Francis forced the words out. "This reunion was more than a little unexpected, and I was only taken aback because it's been so long since I last set eyes on my brother. Of course, if there is a chance this journey might have the impact you desire, then I must have faith that God will provide the means—even if that were to mean journeying into the Holy Land with the Devil himself."

Giovanni's lips curled into a sly smile. "You flatter me, brother."

Francis held his gaze. "Do I?"

The Pope clasped his hands together. "So then, it's decided. You will depart tomorrow with the dawn."

†

Giovanni took his sword belt off and laid it across the back of a chair. He smoothed out his fine leather vest and looked Francis up and down as if appraising a new horse. "It's been a long time, brother."

"Long enough that 'brother' has become a term of affection for me."

Giovanni chuckled at the dig. "I can't say you look well, but you look exactly as I pictured you would."

"I could say the same of you," Francis said.

Giovanni touched the thick red scar that started just below his right eye. "There were a couple of close calls." He laughed. "It seems we have both escaped the gallows."

Francis tried not to wince.

"And, how are your parents?" Giovanni asked with a barely-hidden smirk.

"It has been so long since I last saw them that I cannot answer."

"And my mother?" Giovanni's voice took on an uncharacteristically earnest tone.

"Again, I can offer nothing but memories."

Giovanni nodded. For a moment he almost seemed sad. Almost.

And then the two who had been raised as brothers fell silent.

"I'm not going to say I'm sorry," Giovanni said after a while. "About anything."

Francis shook his head. "I haven't asked for your apology. Or for anything else from you."

"I know. I just want to make clear that there won't be some emotional moment in which I tell you I'm sorry and beg your forgiveness—not for all of the nonsense you've imagined I've done or for whatever I may actually be guilty of."

"It would be meaningless to me if you did."

"Things just are what they are."

"Agreed."

"We have a long road ahead of us."

"We do."

"And as you said, the mission is the most important thing."

"You're right."

The silence returned.

"I had a moment just now," Francis said reluctantly. "As the Pope was sharing his goals, when I saw you standing there, and I realized that my life had come to a sudden and unexpected crossroads, and I needed to make a decision which path I wanted to follow."

Giovanni arched an eyebrow in curiosity.

"I chose to love you," Francis said. "Despite everything, I chose to love you. And I do. I love you. But there is a difference as sharp as dagger's blade between love and trust. I love you as a brother and I always will, but I do not trust you, Giovanni."

Giovanni thought on that for a moment. "I can live with that." He laughed to himself. "I see that the passing years have made you a smarter man."

62

Durazzo. Limassol. Acre.

Although each stop on their journey took them further from their homes, none seemed foreign to Francis. He'd heard about them all so often as a boy that it seemed as if he'd already visited each a thousand times.

Francis remembered enduring his father's endless stories about traveling from one kingdom to the next. For all of the problems his lack of interest in the family business had caused, Francis found it painfully ironic that he was now tracing those same routes and roads with Giovanni by his side in the guise of textile merchants. Francis couldn't help but wonder what his father might think of the expedition if he could see it for himself.

And as always, Francis wondered what Clare would think.

On foot and on horseback, by camel and by boat, they moved from town to town, never staying long in one place and always being careful to keep their distance from anyone who seemed to be too curious about the origins, destination, or intentions of the traveling mercantile merchants.

Weeks passed. Then months. Yet as familiar as Francis was with each of the cities they visited—or, perhaps, because he was so well acquainted with each city—he was ultimately confused and dismayed by their final destination.

At Seleucia, Francis had been told by Giovanni that a small ship had been procured and they would be setting sail for Jerusalem.

With this in mind, Francis was completely surprised—and, at the same time, not surprised in the least—when land appeared on the horizon and a much different destination was announced.

"Damietta?" Francis asked when they entered the port. "I thought we were on a mission to liberate Jerusalem."

"The politics of this world are complicated, Francis," Giovanni said. "The liberation of Jerusalem is part of a process, but one that requires that certain steps be taken first."

"What steps?"

"There's little point in attacking Jerusalem now if the Infidels still hold Egypt," Giovanni said in a tone that implied such a strategic consideration should have been obvious.

"There's no point in attacking anyplace at all," Francis said. "We were sent on a mission of peace, not to facilitate the acquisition of lands beyond Jerusalem."

"*You* are on a mission of peace," Giovanni corrected. "You were sent to meet with Malik Al-Kamil. And I've brought you to Damietta because this is where Malik Al-Kamil is."

"I don't understand." Francis looked around at the camps of Christian crusaders. "I thought this city was under siege, is it not?"

"It is. And it's not. Al-Kamil has declared a ceasefire of sorts. And so, a fragile peace has arrived here before you. Are you disappointed?"

"That the city now enjoys the benefits of peace?"

Giovanni smiled wickedly. "That Christendom's appointed agent, the savior of the known world and beyond, Francis of Assisi, was not the one to bestow that peace."

"Is that what you think of me? That I travelled all this way for nothing more than glory? That's more your ambition than mine."

Giovanni clasped Francis's shoulder. "Don't upset yourself so," he said with a laugh. "My words only tease."

"Your words betray the resentment that's always eaten at your heart and soul. That bitterness makes me wonder all the more why we have found ourselves in this unexpected place."

"Feel free to turn back, if that would suit you better."

Francis sighed and looked out on the city. "If there were anything the two of us might agree upon, I fear it would be that it is far too late for that now."

"And that is all the more reason to stop asking questions about things that don't concern you and concentrate instead on finding a way to meet the Sultan."

63

As Giovanni's footsteps receded, Francis leaned against the bow and stared down at the dark water slapping against the hull. Lost in the calming, hypnotic rhythm, he didn't notice Montague's approach until the man was already seated beside him.

"I don't mean to intrude," Montague said.

"You don't. I'm grateful for your company."

Montague huffed out a short laugh. "That hasn't always been so."

"And vice versa," Francis countered.

Montague didn't contest the point. Instead, he looked out at the gentle waves and smiled at the parade of memories that trailed them both from their initial meeting in the old church to where they sat now, together, on a boat off the coast of Egypt. Traveling with Francis had been a trial, but he was thankful for the the unlikely friendship that had grown between them along the way.

Montague nodded in the direction that Giovanni had disappeared. "So that one is your brother?"

"Half," Francis answered. "But we were raised as if we were closer than mere blood."

Montague nodded. "I had a brother like him once."

"Had?"

"He died."

"I'm sorry," Francis said.

"On the gallows. His death was well-deserved. He was a thief and a scoundrel." Montague looked out across the water to avoid meeting Francis' eyes. "Still, I hated to do it."

Equally alarmed and curious, Francis turned to his friend. "Do what?"

"Part of earning my commission was hunting him down. My loyalty to my oath, to the Church, is greater than anything. Even my love for my brother."

Francis said nothing.

"And I don't regret that. There are men, like my brother—" he looked again to the back of the boat "—and yours who have no loyalty to anyone but themselves."

"True."

"It would be a shame if you were to misplace your own loyalty, to compromise yourself or this mission for the sake of one who has loyalty to none."

"I wouldn't do that," Francis protested.

"No, I don't believe you would. Not intentionally. But I believe your brother has gotten the best of you before. It would be tragic if he were to do so again with so much at stake."

"Yes, it would." Francis was struck by the sharp tone of his own words and wondered whether he was defending Giovanni. Or himself.

"I did not mean to offend," Montague said.

"I know. And you didn't."

"My assignment is to protect you. That is my mission and—"

Francis knew the rest. "And your ultimately loyalty."

Montague nodded. "Stronger than anything. Including your love for your brother." Without another word, Montague got up from his seat and returned to his men at the back of the boat.

Francis looked off across the distance where storm clouds gathered on the horizon.

64

Damietta was an Egyptian city and a predominantly Muslim city, but more importantly, it was a strategically important city. Located on the shore of the Mediterranean Sea, it was a launching point for shipping to Europe and the Holy Land, and sitting at the mouth of a tributary of the Nile, it provided access to all the riches of Egypt and beyond.

Christian Crusaders had laid siege to the city, but lacked the numbers, resources, and resolve to take it over completely. And so they could not press that advantage and capture any significant territory beyond their own landing site. For their part, the army of Sultan Malik Al-Kamil was far greater in sheer numbers than the Christians, but those ranks had been decimated by disease. Whatever strength they held in the size became a corresponding disadvantage and drain on their capabilities as soldiers became patients.

And so, the two armies met, face-to-face, in Damietta, and both remained solidly stuck, neither having the ability to advance nor the willingness to retreat. Instead, both camps sat entrenched, waiting for the other to blink. But in that period of unintended détente, Sultan Malik Al-Kamil proposed a cessation of all active hostilities while his fevered soldiers recovered from the disease that consumed them, and the outnumbered Christians were quick to accept his offer.

And so, an odd, unexpected peace had broken out in the middle of a war. But while peace stalled the military forces at either side of the city, life within Damietta continued on with the daily activities that occupy the citizens of any community.

On the day Francis disembarked, a large crowd had gathered to welcome the sultan back to the palace from visiting his troops. The devoted and the curious turned out to show their support, witness the pageantry of his procession, and catch a glimpse of the greatness and wealth none of them would never know.

Giovanni and Francis made their way through the crowd on their own, hoping not to draw attention to themselves. Montague had objected to Giovanni's plan for the two to have set off into the depths of the city without him and his guard, but Giovanni insisted it was the best way, and Francis relented. Together, they left Montague at the edge of the Christian camp, hands planted on his hips, shaking his head, and conveying his disapproval with a scowl.

"Do you have any idea where we're going?" Francis asked after a while.

Giovanni laughed. "You mean an exact location?"

"Yes."

"No."

Francis conveyed his doubt and exasperation in a single glance.

"Look. Christian or Saracen, every city is alike," Giovanni said. "People follow people. If you follow the flow of the crowd, you'll eventually see everything there is to see." And so, in that way, they wandered the city for what seemed to Francis like hours, taking whatever path seemed the most crowded until they eventually found themselves in a crowded plaza that they both recognized was the city center.

"All right, I got you here." Giovanni said, looking around at the bustling crowd. "The rest is up to you."

Francis nodded. "Yes. Now we need to meet the sultan."

"Good. For a minute I thought we were going to have to do something difficult."

"Difficult is just a state of mind," Francis said.

"Is that right? And here I was thinking that difficult was avoiding the suspicion of the guards watching every street corner."

"God provides opportunity to whomever opens his mind to His infinite power and possibilities and then has the courage of heart to follow them fully."

At that moment, the sultan's procession reached the edge of the grand plaza and those gathered moved back to make room for the horses and soldiers as they made their way towards the palace. Francis saw his opening.

Malik Al-Kamil was a tall man, wrapped in shimmering silk robes, with a cape the color of a robin's egg and a turban to match. He sat proudly in the saddle with a prancing black stallion beneath him. And perched on his shoulder was a saker falcon who surveyed its surroundings like any predator on the lookout for easy prey.

Without a word, Francis put two fingers to his mouth and whistled. The sound was so high that it seemed, even to those right next to him, as if he'd made no noise at all.

To the falcon, however, the call was loud and clear. The bird shot into the air, startling the sultan and spooking his stallion with its unexpected departure. In no time, the falcon was so high above the crowd that all heads tilted up to the sky, although none of them could see anything but the smallest figure making loops against a deep blue sky.

Francis whistled again, and this time the bird folded its wings and dove directly toward him. Everyone near Francis—everyone except Giovanni, that is—cowered and covered their heads as the falcon descended like a missile. Just feet above the crowd, the bird extended its wings and lighted peacefully onto Francis's outstretched arm.

"And just how does stealing the sultan's bird help us out?" Giovanni asked.

"If one wants to harvest from the friendship garden, one must first lay the sow the seeds." Francis stroked the falcon gently and then gave it a gentle kiss on its beak.

While everyone around them took a step back in awe and fear from what Al-Kamil may do next, Giovanni just snorted. "Do you ever hear yourself talk?"

"I hear many things," Francis said.

"I'm sure you do."

For his part, the sultan was not amused. Staring straight at Francis, he raised the whistle that hung around his neck and blew until his cheeks reddened. Again, the bird took off from its perch, made circles through the minarets, and then landed on the al-Kamil's shoulder as if it had never left its perch at all. The sultan flashed Francis a hard look, but before he could kick his steed to restart the procession, the bird had left him again. This time, Francis's whistle brought not only the falcon, but the falconer himself.

The crowd parted before the sultan's horse, and those closest to Francis deserted their positions, wanting no part of the trouble they were sure was coming that way. When the Sultan reached the spot, only Francis and Giovanni remained.

The sultan looked down from his mount. "To steal the sultan's property is a serious offense."

"This bird is a living thing, not a possession." Francis made a gesture and the bird fluttered from his arm to the sultan's shoulder. "And I haven't stolen anything."

"It is no less a crime to try to embarrass the sultan in front of his people." His countenance was grim. "Especially for one such as you."

"I meant no harm or disrespect. And certainly, a man as great as yourself could not be embarrassed by anyone—especially by one such as me."

Giovanni groaned and whispered under his breath, "This is how you sow the seeds of friendship?"

Francis ignored him.

"And it is still no less a crime to displease the sultan, whatever the reason. Give me a reason why I should not take your head right here on the spot."

"I can think of several."

"I asked for only one."

Francis looked up and met the sultan's eyes. "Because you are the great Sultan al-Kalim, and you are a man whose honor would not allow you to take the life of an unarmed man who means you no harm, and because your faith prohibits you from taking the life of one who has devoted his life to monastic service."

Al-Kalim's eyes roamed over Francis's expensive garments. "I see no monk before me."

"I assure you that beneath these garments is a man of faith."

"Faith." The sultan was skeptical. "You speak as if you know something of mine."

"I do," Francis said. "But I would like to know more. I have an interest in your faith because I have an interest in peace and peace is dependent upon understanding."

"Tell me your name."

"I am called Francis. I have come this way from Assisi."

There was no sign of recognition in the steely eyes that studied Francis. Giovanni held his breath, until finally, the sultan nodded. "Come along then," he said, and turned his horse back toward the procession.

As they joined the procession, a man stepped in front of the sultan's horse, bowed elaborately, and waved his hand dismissively at Francis and Giovanni. "A thousand pardons, but this dog must not be allowed inside the palace. If the people were to see, they might think—"

"They would think that their sultan is a generous man who welcomes travelers just as Muhammad, blessed be his name, did."

The mullah bowed his head in deference but was not deterred. "Yes, but—"

The sultan's eyes flashed. "But? Are you questioning my generosity or Muhammad's?"

The man's face turned red. "No, sire. Of course not." This time he bowed so deeply that his nose almost touched his knees.

Al-Kamil urged his mount forward. "Then make way for my new friend, Francis of Assisi."

Francis followed the sultan and Giovanni followed Francis.

The sultan again turned in his saddle, but this time he addressed Giovanni. "Where are you going?"

"I'm with him." Giovanni pointed to Francis.

The sultan looked skeptical and turned to Francis, "Is this man a monk like you?"

Francis hesitated, trying to find a truth that would neither betray the sultan's trust nor leave Giovanni at the mercy of the soldiers surrounding them. "He's my brother."

A continuing sense of doubt lingered on his face, but Sultan Malik Al-Kamil nodded his approval anyway. He looked at Francis. "If you vouch for him, that is good enough for me." He turned back in his saddle, and the procession continued across the plaza and through the palace gates.

And Francis and Giovanni followed him inside.

65

Inside the palace, Francis was struck by how similar it was to the Lanteran Palace. The wall hangings and carpets and carvings were astonishing. There was an attendant who took the Sultan's horse and another who secured his falcon and another who appeared with refreshments.

Ignoring them all, the sultan strode over to greet Francis directly. "You have come a long way, Francis of Assisi. Why did you undertake such an arduous and dangerous trek?"

"I came to speak to you."

"I am the great Sultan al-Kamil. My guards have guards. How could you have possibly thought you would get the chance to speak with me?"

"Because I have faith," Francis said with a smile. "And here we are."

The sultan nodded approvingly. To the mullah, however, Francis's words were heretical.

"A false faith, you mean," he said.

"I speak only of the faith in my heart," Francis said. "Surely, if we are ever to find common ground that would allow us to build a lasting peace, such a construction would start on the foundation of the faith each man holds within his own heart."

"Surely," the sultan said.

"But," the mullah interrupted, "you cannot allow the men to see you in a discussion with this dog."

"You may think to insult me, Francis said, "but I have always found the dog to be a wonderful animal, and far more loyal to his master than most men."

"How dare you speak to me in such a way," the mullah blustered and turned to the sultan. "Do you hear what he has said to your servant?"

"Do you think me deaf now?" al-Kamil said. "What I have not heard is your response to his comments about loyalty."

The mullah's mouth hung open, but no words emerged.

"What I have heard from this man are words of courage and compassion. He has travelled far and risked much to talk with me and I would continue that conversation now."

"But the men will think—"

"My men don't think, they obey. They will respect their sultan's decisions and heed his commands." He looked hard at the man before him. "*All* my men."

"Do you doubt my faith?" Francis asked the mullah directly.

"I do, dog." The man spat out the word. "You should prove your faith to the sultan if you are to have his ear in conversation. Otherwise, we should have your head as a treacherous spy."

"Faith, by its nature, cannot be proven, but can only be lived, day by day, a constant striving to follow a righteous path," Francis said. "I have done my best to do this, giving meaning to my words through my deeds. I have come to your sultan with the purest of hearts, seeking nothing more than the opportunity to speak with him. If your sultan doubts this then he should do whatever he feels he must. I will not oppose whatever action he may take. But the faith I hold in my heart is beyond demonstration or proof."

"You're wrong," the mullah said. "I myself have proved my faith time and again by walking the fire."

"The fire?" Francis asked.

"Tonight, I will prepare a fire with coals from Hell itself. And with nothing more than my faith in Allah to protect me, I will walk through these very fires to prove my faith. If your faith is as strong as you claim, you should be able to do the same. If not, the fires will do to you what the sultan in is infinite mercy has refrained from doing by his own hand."

Malik al-Kamil roared with laughter. "An excellent proposal. We shall welcome our guest this evening. And then the two of you—Mullah Issam and Francis of Assisi—will stop this bickering and demonstrate your faith by walking over the fires of Hell."

"If that is what you want," Francis agreed, his voice low.

"I see your faith is already beginning to leave you," the mullah scoffed.

Francis shook his head. "You are wrong. Faith knows no fear."
Giovanni rolled his eyes and sighed.

66

That evening the sultan ordered that there should be a large banquet held in Francis' honor. There was music and laughter in the air and a wide assortment of foods spread across the banquet table.

"You are not eating, Francis" al-Kamil observed that evening. "Does our food not please you?"

"It's not that," Francis answered, looking out at the overflowing banquet table. "Your food is wonderful. Your hospitality is gracious and generous beyond words. But I have already eaten as much as I need, and I have no desire to consume any more than that. Besides, I passed so many in the city today who could use this sustenance more than I could."

The sultan slapped the table so hard that all of the dishes rattled and the convivial conversation came to an abrupt halt. All eyes turned to him, and the air was suddenly heavy with tension. There were more than a few in the room who believed Francis's head would soon bid farewell to his shoulders. Mullah Issam, certainly, was among them, no doubt praying for such a bloody outcome.

"You would sit at my table and tell me that there are some among my people who need this meal more than I do?" Al-Kamil glared at Francis.

Francis met his stare easily. "Yes, exactly that."

The uneasy, silent tension intensified.

And then the sultan broke out into laughter. "You're absolutely right, my friend." He waved his arm toward a row of waiting attendants. shouted orders indiscriminately to the attendants, "Clear this food! All of it. Now."

The attendants hesitated, unsure how to respond to such an unconventional directive.

"Clear every dish, pack it up, and take it out into the city. Now! Make sure every morsel of this feast finds its way into the bellies of those who need it most."

The attendants rushed to do as they were told, taking food away from those gathered around the tables, even those in the middle of their meals.

Mullah Issam rose to his feet. "Sultan!"

"Do you question my generosity?" the sultan asked.

"Of course, not. I only question that one such as yourself should listen to the words of an infidel."

"You spoke earlier of faith," the sultan replied. "I am beginning to wonder if you haven't lost your faith in me. It is time for your demonstration of faith."

"It would be my greatest pleasure." The man got to his feet and led the others outside to a courtyard where a fire had been burning for hours. He gave instructions to his attendants and the remaining coals were spread out into a path twenty feet long. The embers glowed as if they were stoked by the fires of Hell, just as the mullah had warned.

Issam stood at one end of the burning path and gestured to Francis. "It is time for you to show the sultan just how strong your faith is."

Francis walked towards the path and looked down the length. "Why don't you show me how this is done?"

The mullah took off his embroidered slippers and turned to Francis who, as was often his habit, was barefoot. "My faith in Allah will protect me. Will your faith protect you?" He turned to the gathered crowd and raised his hands. "*Allahu akbar!*"

"God is great," came the response.

Then he turned and quickly walked the length of the embers. When he arrived safely at the other end, he raised his hands and shouted, "*Alhamdulillah!*"

"Allah be praised," everyone echoed.

With a triumphant gleam in his eyes, he bowed to Francis. "Your turn."

Francis looked down at the path of coals. "I told you earlier that faith is not something that can be demonstrated. It is—"

"But cowardice is," Issam interrupted.

"As I was saying, faith is not a trick performed for an audience. It is a life lived for others."

The sultan's smile disappeared. A murmur spread across the crowd, and Issam pressed his advantage. "A life lived as a coward, you mean. A deceitful spy who has wormed his way into our midst, too afraid to—"

"I am none of those things," Francis said, and without another word stepped out onto the coals and walked the full length as easily as if walking across a grassy meadow.

The mullah's mouth dropped open in amazement and the sultan's smile returned. "Well done," he said, clapping his hands in delight.

Francis acknowledged the compliment with a nod. "My father is a merchant who has traveled the world. He often returned home with tales of exhibitions such as this. The trick, he discovered, was to simply move across the coals at a normal pace—not too quickly and not too slowly. One who performed this trick told him that you should first order the coals to be raked as the settling ash protects the soles of the feet. So, as long as one steps lightly, your feet are never exposed to the heat long enough to be burned."

The sultan shook his head in amazement. "Truly, you have demonstrated that you are everything others claim you to be. Not with tricks like this," he said with a dismissive motion to the smoldering embers, "but with your actions and your honorable behavior."

"Thank you," Francis said. He looked around at the group gathered in the courtyard, many who were surely, like the mullah, hoping he would fail. "I believe faith is demonstrated in one's daily actions, in what one does when there is no one around to watch. Faith is not how one performs for a crowd or how one speaks to sultans or popes or kings, but how one conducts himself towards servants, the poor, the sick and hungry."

Sultan al-Kamil signaled his attendants. "The festivities are over for tonight," he said, "and a servant will escort you and your brother back to your quarters. But I look forward to talking more tomorrow." The sultan started toward a portico at the end of the courtyard. Then he stopped and beckoned Francis to him. Speaking softly so no one else could hear, he said, "You may wonder why I did not stop Mullah Issam. It is because I had faith you would not fail." Francis started to speak, but al-Kamil held up a finger. "So, now we see that we are both men of faith. And our faith is unfailing."

67

Francis and Giovanni were led down a palace hallway by an attendant who opened door and gestured to the inside of an opulent room. "This will be yours for the evening."

Francis turned to Giovanni, "This is more to your tastes than mine."

"You're not wrong about that," Giovanni said, moving past him.

"No," the attendant said. "This is only for the sultan's guest." He looked to Giovanni and then turned Francis. "Your servant will have to be housed elsewhere."

"He's not my servant," Francis said.

"My instructions were very specific," the attendant said.

"Who gave you these instructions?"

"It's all right," Giovanni interrupted. "I don't mind."

"No. It's not right," Francis said.

"It's fine," Giovanni said. "I'd rather have my own quarters anyway."

Francis was hesitant to let Giovanni be led away, but before he could offer additional objections, bis brother and the attendant were already moving down the hallway and into the darkness.

Francis closed the door of the room behind him and took stock of his accommodations. He was aware that most people had never seen a room so finely appointed, but it reminded him of his childhood home. For the first time in a very, very long time he felt pangs of loneliness that he thought must be homesickness.

He was not in the room for more than a moment or two before a knock came at the door. Three taps, very softly.

Before Francis could respond, the door swung open and a woman stepped inside, quickly shutting the door behind her.

Francis' expression asked the question that he couldn't find the words for in his moment of surprise.

"I am Yasmeen," she said and then without saying a word more, she let the purple silk that was wrapped around her fall to the ground at her feet, revealing herself completely.

Francis took a step backwards. "My child, please, clothe yourself."

"Do you not find me appealing?"

"You are as beautiful as all of God's creatures," he said. "But please." He motioned to the cloth at her feet.

She snatched it from the ground and self-consciously wrapped it around her again. "If I'm not pleasing to you, there are some who have other appetites. I was chosen because I speak your language."

"It's not a matter of language or appetites," he assured her.

"Then what is wrong? Have I done something to offend you?"

"There is no offense and nothing is wrong."

"Then what can I do for you?" she asked.

"There is nothing, my child."

His refusal clearly frightened her. "But I was told that if I did not pleasure you—"

"Rest your mind," Francis said, gesturing to the bed. "And rest yourself. Please have a seat."

She stretched out across the bed and again stripped off her covering.

"No, no." he said. "Please, cover yourself. You are not here for my pleasure."

"But I was sent—"

"You were sent because someone seems intent on testing my faith," Francis said.

"Your faith? Is that what keeps you from seeking pleasure with me?"

"There are many things that prevent me. The first is that you are not here by your choice."

"It is my honor to serve," she said.

Francis shook his head. "No one should be forced to do something that they don't want to do; especially, not something so personal. As a young woman, you should know that your worth is within you, what lies within your heart and head, not what lies between the sheets."

"Pleasing others is my purpose."

"No. Every soul has a purpose, that is true, but no one's purpose is to be used for the amusement of others."

"And is that all that prevents you from enjoying what I have come to offer?"

"That is enough, but my faith certainly leads me away from such temptations."

"So, it is your faith?"

"It is."

"I don't dispute what you have said, but there is something else, isn't there?"

"What makes you say that?"

"I can see it in your eyes," she said. "Most men, when they see me, their eyes turn hard and cold like a snake's. They want what they want and they do what they do—even men who proclaim their faith loudly in public. But you have kind eyes and even now, when you look at me, I can tell you are thinking of another."

He smiled and sighed deeply.

"She is lucky to have someone who cares about her so much."

"I'm not sure that she would agree with you."

Tears began to well up in her dark eyes. "She is luckier than I will be tomorrow."

"What do you mean?"

"You may not think this is my purpose, but there are many who do. And when they see I have failed, they will punish me."

"I will make certain that no harm comes to you."

"But you do not know—"

"I promise I will speak with the sultan himself. I will not let any harm come to you."

She looked at him. "I believe you."

Francis smiled. "Good."

"But I cannot return to my quarters tonight," she said with renewed alarm.

"Please," he said. "Lay back."

She looked at him suspiciously. "You have changed your mind?"

"You stay here tonight and return to your quarters in the morning."

"And you?"

He looked around the room. "These accommodations really don't suit me."

"No." She smiled. "They don't."

Francis moved to the door. "Good night."

"Good night."

Francis went out and found himself a place in the palace courtyard and slept soundly beneath the open sky.

68

"You intrigue me," al-Kamil said.

The words woke Francis from his sleep and he sat up slowly, rubbing his eyes.

"I give you the finest accommodations in my palace and yet I find you sleeping in my courtyard."

"The ground is the only cushion I need; the sky is the only cover."

"Then you are lucky to have been born to your station and not mine."

"You're mistaken, I was not born to the life I am now leading, but chose it," Francis said.

"Chose it how?"

"As I mentioned last night. My father was a merchant and he travelled the world procuring and selling silks and fine fabrics. He became very wealthy and respected in Assisi, and I grew up with all of the benefits of his affluence."

"Why then did you not follow his lead, become a wealthy trader yourself?"

"I felt a higher calling," Francis answered, leaning back against a tree and staring up at the early morning sky.

"But surely you were expected to carry on your family's legacy. Did your father not make demands of you?"

"He did." Francis's voice betrayed the melancholy that often overtook him when thinking of his parents.

"But you defied your father, your family?"

"Yes."

"And abandoned all of the comforts and privileges with which you had been raised?"

"Yes."

"To follow this calling?"

"Yes."

Al-Kamil shook his head as a sad smile touched his mouth. "The more I get to know you, my friend, the more I like you. And the less I like myself."

"How can you say such a thing?" Francis asked.

"I speak only the truth."

"But you are the great Sultan Al-Kalim. People speak your name with the highest of regards. Even your enemies admire you as a man of unquestionable character."

"And I would be the happiest man on Earth if any of that gave me the slightest bit of satisfaction. Unlike you, I did not choose my life. My people—even my enemies—may regard me as a mighty sultan, but none of them realize I am just another slave."

"You underestimate yourself," Francis said. "The ceasefire you've declared has spared innumerable lives."

"And how many lives have I taken?" The Sultan's thoughts drifted for a moment. "Someone like you can never understand."

Francis ran a hand over his face. "I slept well with the hospitality you offered me, but most nights I can't sleep at all and on many occasions, I drift away for a moment or two only to be torn from my slumber by panicked screams. And I wake in the darkness, unable to get their faces out of my head."

"Whose faces?"

"The men I killed in battle."

"Killed? I thought you were a boy of fortune and a man of the cloth?" Al-Kamil's eyes narrowed.

Francis looked down at his hands as if remembering what it felt like to feel the balance of a fine sword in them. "The path between the two was a march to war and time spent as a prisoner.

Al-Kamil stiffened. "And did you go to war against—"

Francis shook his head. "No, no. I never raised a sword in this conflict. My brother and I marched together against another region. Neighbors. Christians against Christians. No differences between us to justify the violence we committed against one another." Tears welled up in his eye, so he shut them tightly. "As if any differences would justify that sort of violence."

The two men were silent. Birds flitted from tree to tree and sang happy songs on the branches above them.

"I see them, too," the sultan said finally. "The same faces you see. The men who have died by my hand. I see them, too."

They were silent together for a long, long time.

69

Over the course of the next few days, Malik al-Kamil made a point of spending as much time with Francis as his other responsibilities would allow. They traded stories of their childhoods and the long, often painful road they had each travelled to manhood. Al-Kamil discussed his love of astronomy, and Francis shared the lessons he had learned from observing the animals around him. Al-Kamil read from the Quran, and Francis quoted from the Bible. Al-Kamil shared his vision for his people, and Francis expressed his hopes for the world.

One afternoon, the sultan said, "There's a question I've always wanted to ask." He diverted his eyes from Francis as if he was talking to himself, unaware his words could be overheard. They'd been sitting in their usual spot in the courtyard in which Francis had slept since that first night, but the sultan suddenly rose and began to pace. "But I've never had the opportunity before. Until you, I'd never met a man I could trust enough to keep my question a secret and yet whom I respected enough to value his answer."

"I'm humbled if you think me such a man, my friend. I would gladly answer whatever you ask," Francis said.

"Do you ever...." Al-Kamil's words trailed off into a silence he seemed to think was preferable.

"Do I ever *what?*"

The sultan's face stiffened, hardened by unspoken regret that he'd raised the issue at all. He remained tight-lipped, either unable to find the words or unwilling to speak them.

"You may trust me," Francis said softly.

Al-Kamil took a silent moment to consider just exactly what posing his question would mean—and then turned, faced Francis, and asked it anyway. "Doubt. Do you ever doubt? We describe ourselves as men of faith, but do you ever find your heart filled with doubt? I love the Prophet. I am devoted to my God. And my people look to me for guidance in all things. I know I need to be unfaltering in my faith, but I look out over fields of bodies and hear the lamentations of widows and orphans and can't help but feel ... doubt."

Francis reached up to pluck a leaf from the branch above him. "Of course, I doubt," he said, turning the leaf over in his fingers. "Doubt is not the enemy of faith, but its constant companion. They must walk hand I hand. Faith must be a constant, conscious decision made in the face of real and earnest doubt. Blind faith is no faith at all. So, it is only the man who lives with doubt always in his heart and yet *chooses* faith over and over again who can truly claim to be among the faithful."

Al-Kamil let out a great sigh and sat back down. "I agree," he said, as if simply hearing the words he'd long thought to himself was a great comfort. "Yet I am aware that standing between us there are many holy men who would take issue with your definition—-and mine."

"There are too many who adhere to a dogma they believe is holy, but whose acts are evil and cruel," Francis said. "Yet if we don't stop the bloodthirst they claim in God's name, what future do we face? Another hundred years of strife? A thousand? To what end? How many more dead? How much more suffering? How many more lives will be sacrificed to feed the churning maw of destruction, when those same souls might otherwise serve the creation of something greater, something truly worthy of our Creator."

"Again, I agree," the sultan said. "But you speak of peace like it was a goal desired by all. I believe as you do and long to repeat those same thoughts, but in times like these, there are fortunes to be made from war and, because of that, there is no greater heresy than the proclamation of peace."

"Not a single heretical word could fall from the lips of a man who serves God as faithfully as you do. When I speak of the possibilities of peace, I speak only of what you have already established here, where all manner of men live together, side-by-side. From this seed of peace that you've planted, we could harvest the bounty of its fruit in your land. And in mine."

"If only there were enough eager souls to tend to such a crop." Al-Kamil reached up and plucked his own leaf from the branch, running his thumb lightly along its edge as if it were the edge of a knife.

"Their number will swell when they see what I have seen. Mankind has already shown an endless capacity to kill. I say, let us take a chance to show them the promise of peace and let them learn the prosperity that can be shared by all."

"I agree with you," al-Kamil said. "I believe that with all my heart. But there is no profit to be made in peace, no territory added, no wealth or power gained. So, even though I rule supreme as sultan—as a king in your land—I am surrounded by those looking for their own advantage. No matter what the law says, a leader deludes himself to think his power is absolute. We both know, that history is filled with stories of great men vanquished by those beneath them. It is a fatal misstep to lose sight of that."

"There may be enemies all around," said Francis. "But you forget your greatest allies."

"Allies? I am sure I have none."

"You are wrong, my friend." Francis put a reassuring hand on the al-Kamil's shoulder and the sultan did not shake it off. "You are the leader of a proud people. The same people whose lives are nothing more than pawns to be played with and sacrificed by those vipers in your court. No, your real power lies with those men and women who count themselves your loyal subjects."

"I pray you are right."

"I have travelled across the known world to be with you now. And along the way, I've enjoyed the great pleasure of meeting all sorts of people, Christian, Muslim, pagan alike. And through my travels, I have come to know one thing to be true—most people want nothing more than to be surrounded by family and friends with a good meal on the table, a drink in their hands, and a song and laughter on their lips. If you would forsake those who would build fortune in the fields of despair and appeal directly to your people, then there is no power that could stop you."

The sultan silently considered Francis's words. After a while, he asked, "Why are you here? Really?" He looked directly at Francis as if the answer would come in something other than words.

"I have come to talk to you about peace."

"At whose request?"

"The pope. Innocent III."

The sultan shook his head warily. "I have already offered the Christians my terms, but your Crusaders have no interest in peace."

"There must be some misunderstanding." Francis was aware of the importance of his words and chose them carefully. "The pope assured me that all they are trying to do is reestablish a connection with the Holy Land so that our pilgrims have an opportunity to worship our Lord, Jesus Christ in the land where He was born, lived and died."

"This is not true," al-Kamil said flatly.

Francis tensed, alarmed at the implications of the conversation. "I would not lie to you."

Al-Kamil waved Francis's words away. "If I thought you were lying to me, my friend, I would have already dismissed this as the treachery of diplomacy and taken your head. It is because I know that you have been completely honest that I am growing concerned about your presence here."

"I am here to talk to you of peace," Francis insisted, "so that pilgrims of my faith might have peaceful access to Jerusalem."

Al-Kamil shook his head. "The terms of peace I have already offered extended free passage to Jerusalem. I asked them only to leave Damietta, which has no significance to your faith. I offered peace and they refused."

Francis stood and looked down at the man he now considered a true friend. "No, this cannot be."

"As you would not lie to me, my friend, I have spoken nothing but the truth to you."

"No, no." As the sultan had done, Francis waved off the suggestion that his friend was lying. "I could never have issue with your honor or your word. I am simply overwhelmed at the prospect that I could have been manipulated in such a brazen fashion." Francis ran both hands down his face and then looked directly at his friend. "I have been a fool. I fear our desire for peace and understanding has been used against us both."

Al-Kamil leaned forward. "What are you saying? What advantage is there to anyone to have you enter my palace and meet with me? Whose purpose does that serve?"

Francis shook his head, hoping against all hope that his growing suspicions were misguided, but knowing in his heart they were not. "I did not enter your palace alone."

"Your companion." Al-Kamil sat back, confused. "He is your brother."

Francis shook his head, blood now pounding in his veins. "We share the same father and were raised as such." He paused and considered his next words. "But the bond between us has been strained in the past. It would break my heart to know I have been an unwitting pawn in a despicable game, but—"

And that was when everything went wrong.

70

The sultan led Francis back to the room he'd exchanged for the garden. From the balcony both men could hear the sounds of chaos approaching, and for a moment, Francis felt the thrill and dread of battle ring in his ears. The sharp clang of steel against steel. The shouts of anger and the screams of pain.

"You should stay here, my friend," al-Kamil said.

"I should stay at your side, because I *am* your friend."

"No, if the fires of war have indeed been lit, then behind this door is the only place I can hope to keep you safe. Stay here, and I will return." Without any more debate, the sultan left the room.

Outside in the near distance the sounds of war were all around him, but true to his word, Francis remained in the room, pacing the length and breadth, peering out from the balcony, all the while waiting for the Sultan's return.

Three times a group of men ran down the hallway, heavy footsteps and angry voices ringing out. Twice they ran past Francis' door without slowing or stopping. It was on their third passing that Francis heard the soldiers stop right outside his door. He thought, of course, that his friend had sent troops to retrieve him and take him to a place of safety, so Francis ran to the door and pulled it open, only to see Mullah Issam, not al-Kamil, waiting for him.

"Seize the dog!" Two of the mullah's men rushed in and grabbed Francis before he knew what was happening.

"We will see how strong your faith is when it is truly put to the test," the mullah growled. "I will break your body and you will renounce your faith before a new day has risen."

"My faith is stronger than my body," Francis answered, instinctively pulling against the men who held him, even though he knew there was little point in the struggle.

"I'll break them both."

No sooner had the words left the mullah's lips, than the two guards on either side of him collapsed to the floor as if they had been marionettes and their supporting strings had all been snipped at once. A second later, Giovanni stepped from behind the mullah, both hands clenching swords dripping with blood.

In that moment of distraction, Francis was able to throw off the guards holding him. There was an opportunity to attack and inflict greater harm, but Francis could not bring himself to follow through. So, one of the guards quickly recovered and got to his feet, sword in hand, ready to run Francis through at the mullah's command. And Francis stood in front of him, arms at his side.

Giovanni, however, did not hesitate. He threw one of his swords, and Francis watched as the blade turned two, three times through the air before striking its target in the chest. The guard collapsed, and Francis snatched up his sword and hit the surviving man on the head, knocking him unconscious. It wasn't that Francis had abandoned his convictions about violence, it was that he knew it was the only way to save the man from Giovanni.

"You're lucky I need you alive," Giovanni said before knocking the mullah to the ground. He turned to Francis. "Hurry. We need to get out of here."

"Go? I can't go," Francis protested. "The sultan told me to wait here for him. We've reached a union of heart and mind. A peace with which we can all live is finally within our grasp."

Giovanni patted a leather satchel hung around his shoulder. "I have coins enough to wager you're very wrong about that, but we don't have the time to debate it now."

"What are you saying?"

Giovanni checked the hall. "There's not going to be any peace."

"But, the sultan and I—"

"Al-Kamil and you are more idealistic than men of your station have any right to be. You won't accept that there's no profit to be made in peace. It's war that fills the coffers and builds a treasury and adds to lands, no matter what faith you profess. And until that changes, there will never be any lasting peace. Right, my friend?" Giovanni pointed his sword at Mullah Issam who glared up at him.

Francis shook his head. "But—"

"And that means there will never be any peace," Giovanni said. "No buts, Francis. The city is erupting."

"Erupting? In what?"

"War. Profit. Opportunities for God and gold and glory—everything that drives men." Giovanni checked the hall again. "And if you don't leave with me right now, then you are very quickly going to find yourself in a situation that not even God can save you from." He glanced down at the mullah who struggled to get to his feet. "Not anyone's God."

"Wait!" the mullah cried out. "The sorcerer was part of our bargain."

Giovanni sneered and kicked the man in the chest, forcing him back down. "There's no bargain in betrayal and no honor between men like you and me."

Francis' heart sank. "Giovanni, what part did you have in all this?"

"The only part you need to worry about right now," Giovanni said, starting down the hall, "is my role in getting you out of here."

"I told you," Francis said, feet planted where he stood. "I have to wait here for the sultan."

"He's not coming back for you."

"What do you mean?"

"I mean there's no peace, Francis. And no room for friendship. If he returns— if he lives that long—it won't be to save you, it'll be to kill you because, like it or not, that is what a king or a sultan or whatever you call them must do when he's been betrayed. What you have to decide right now is if you want to die at the end of your friend's sword or if you want to take your chances with me."

Francis looked down at the men—alive and dead—laying at his feet, and he looked down the hall at his brother. It took him a long moment to decide, but ultimately, he chose Giovanni.

71

The two brothers ran as fast as they could through the plaza in front of the palace, heading for the narrow streets in which they could more easily hide as they wound their way toward the port and the safety of the Christian camp surrounding it. As they left the plaza behind, Francis thought of how he had called the sultan's falcon to him just a few short days earlier. Certain he had been guided by God, now the memory accused him of some craven act of treason. And the fact that he had played no part in the betrayal—at least, no conscious role in the deception—offered scant consolation for his growing guilt over the unintended consequences.

Sickened at the memory, he nevertheless followed Giovanni as they darted from street to street like thieves, knowing that what they had stolen was their very lives. Sword drawn and at the ready, Giovanni swung his blade at anyone who would stop them—or even slow them down. Francis followed close behind with panicked apologies. "I'm sorry. Please. Out of the way. Sorry."

None of those who jumped clear of Giovanni's blade seemed consoled by the offered contrition and their curses followed close at Francis' heels. Still, Giovanni never slowed, while behind them, the skies thickened with smoke.

Suddenly, found themselves at a crossroads with a high stone wall in front of them.

"Left," Giovanni shouted.

"No, right," Francis countered.

"That way is death, Francis. Because if you go that way, you go alone. And if you go alone, you will die. Now, follow me." Without another word, Giovanni renewed his commitment to the street on the left with an all-out sprint.

Francis had the strongest sense that his brother had chosen the wrong way and so he wasn't quite sure why he found himself racing to catch up when his intuition told him he was heading into danger and disaster. And so, it came as no surprise whatsoever that a few heavy footsteps later, Francis found himself running into a courtyard where his brother had already come to a hard stop.

In front of them were a dozen Saracen soldiers, each one with sword drawn.

"I told you it was left."

"I would freely admit you were right and I was wrong," Giovanni said, panting between words, "but I'd hate to have something so bitter be my final words."

The soldiers were unaware of the nature of the bickering between the brothers, unconcerned with anything except their orders to find the foreigners and kill them.

"Giovanni, we can turn and run," Francis said. "There's too many of them," Francis pointed out unnecessarily. "You can't take them all."

"But fighting together, the odds would swing in our favor. With you and me, they wouldn't stand a chance, brother."

"I can't," Francis said, although he knew in his heart that Giovanni was right.

"I'm going to kill this one quick," Giovanni said, nodding at the soldier closest to him. "When he drops, you pick up his sword and then the fight will be on."

"I can't," Francis said again.

"You must, Francis," Giovanni said. "If you don't, we die. Both of us."

"But—"

"Someone's going to die here and now, Francis. The decision of who lies in your hands, but don't think for a moment that your noble death born of your stubbornness will atone for your sins or that there's any way out of here without you getting blood on your hands."

Even if Francis considered that might be true, he never wavered. "I can't."

Giovanni raised his sword. "Then I hope you're prepared to meet that God of yours."

The lead soldier charged at Giovanni and their swords met.

Another soldier moved past the combatants towards Francis, who stood there pleading for peace. "Stop. I'm a friend of Sultan al-Kamil's!"

"That's why they want to kill you," Giovanni called over his shoulder.

There may have been some truth to that, for no sooner had the words been spoken then the soldier swung his sword wildly at his target. Francis dodged the blade, but in doing so felt the wall at his back, no room to duck again. But in that moment when his death seemed inescapable, a chorus of shouts rose up from the far end of the courtyard, and a moment later, Montague and his men appeared, swords drawn and ready for battle.

With the odds now even, the fight turned. Giovanni took his opponent with an unexpected thrust, then spun and cleaved at the soldier who might otherwise have killed Francis.

The soldier dropped at Francis' feet and the sight of the man, twitching and convulsing before giving up his life, stunned him. The crunch of bone and the squelch of split flesh, the stench of spilled blood and opened bellies brought back a flood of memories Francis thought he'd left far behind, and for a moment, he was transported back to the battlefield, to what he'd done there, and to what trapped him there.

"Francis! Francis!" It wasn't Giovanni's voice, but Montague's that pulled him from his thoughts. "You've got to get out of here."

For Francis it was like being jerked awake from a nightmare only to find that reality was worse. The stone floor of the courtyard was strewn with bodies and more soldiers were running into the fray.

"You've got to go, Francis, now!" Montague shouted again.

Francis surveyed the scene. "We all need to go."

"No," Montague insisted, as he deflected a blow and lunged for his attacker, driving his blade through the man.

"I took an oath to protect you," Montague said, sizing up his next opponent. "If you die here today, then all you have learned will die with you. You must live to share the truth."

"Then leave with me now," Francis said.

Montague engaged a charging soldier and drove him back. "Follow your brother. My men and I will hold the line here."

"Francis," Giovanni grabbed his brother's wrist. "Now!"

"There must be another way," Francis said.

"The only way is that you live, my friend." Montague said.

This time Giovanni would not be denied. He grabbed Francis' wrist and pulled. At the edge of the courtyard, Francis looked over his shoulder and saw the blade pierce Montague's chest.

"No!" Francis screamed. But it was a single cry amidst a chorus of chaos.

72

The gathering darkness of night cloaked their escape in a small felucca, but behind them the horizon was lit with a hundred fires.

"How can we just leave them?" Francis asked.

Giovanni groaned with frustration. "There's nothing back there but death."

"We have to help the others."

Giovanni pulled his attention from the tiller and looked hard at Francis. "Sometimes your self-indulgence amazes me. That and your obsession with death. Have I robbed you of your chance to finally martyr yourself?"

"What are you saying?"

"You've always flirted with death. Defying father when we were kids. Crazed fighting on the field of battle, practically daring the enemy to take you on. Challenging our captors in prison. Your performance on the roof. That night in camp. Your theatrics with father and that farce of a trial. Sometimes I think nothing thrills you so much as the thought of your glorious and noble death."

"I want life," Francis protested, "but I want it for everyone, not just me."

"Then dive in. Dive in and swim for it, because I'm not turning around."

Both men, exhausted and on edge, turned and watched the glow of city's silhouette set aflame.

Francis shook his head. "Which one of us did Rome send?"

"What are you talking about?" Giovanni set about rigging the sail to catch the shifting wind.

"Did Rome send you to accompany me on a mission of peace? Or was it a military mission from the beginning, with me as an unknowing Judas goat to get you into the sultan's palace?"

"What do you hope to find in your question?" Giovanni asked.

For Francis, it was simple. "The truth."

"The truth," Giovanni spat out the words like they were poison. "The truth. Good and evil. Right and wrong. Can this world really be that simple for you?"

Francis hung his head. "All hope of peace is lost."

Giovanni barked out a laugh. "What hope do you think there ever was?"

"The Holy Father sent me to—"

"Sent you to do *what*, Francis? Why do you think His Holiness sent for you? Did that question ever cross your mind or were you too consumed by everyone bowing and scraping, treating you like you were God's own son."

"Is that what you think?"

"At least I *think*, Francis. When the pontiff demands my presence, I think *why*? I don't assume, 'Of course, Rome needs me to bring peace to the world.' I may be whatever I am, but at least I'm humble enough to wonder *why me*? And then I think, what's in it for me?"

"And what was in it for you?"

"Does that matter?" Giovanni asked, shaking his head. "We both serve Rome."

"No," Francis insisted. "Neither of us serves Rome. I serve God. I'm no longer sure who you serve."

"Spare me, Francis. Not all of us can subside on faith alone like you. I'm no different than anyone else in this world, I need to get paid and Rome pays better than God."

"That's what this was about? The chaos that has been caused today, the fighting, the suffering was all about a few coins for you?"

"No," Giovanni said. "This was about coins for me, but for others it was about securing the port city to Egypt. For my friend, the mullah, it was about a misguided attempt to seize power from your probably-dead friend, al-Kamil."

"And the men dying now?"

"They are not my responsibility."

"So, you're not responsible for anyone but yourself?"

"No, Francis. Right now, I'd be happier if that were the case, but I feel responsibilities beyond myself."

"To whom?"

"To whom? To you, you ungrateful, judgmental fool. Do you think your safe return was part of the plan? Do you think that you were supposed to escape today? Do you think you're the only one who sees the advantages to be gained in your martyrdom?"

Francis was silent.

"I could've escaped that city before the alarm went out, but I went back for you. *You.* I saved you. For no other reason than you're my brother."

Francis was silent for a moment and then softly said, "I wish you hadn't."

"Right now, that's about all that we agree on."

"I would rather have died than have been a part of this treachery."

Giovanni looked back into the night at the faintest traces of the city fires. "If you jump in now, I think you can still make it."

73

Acre. Limassol. Durazzo.

The return trip was not any easier or quicker, paved as it was with regrets and self-recrimination. And so, when they saw the silhouette of Rome ahead in the distance, both Francis and Giovanni were more exhausted than elated.

Francis stopped to take in the view. "I did not think I would ever see this sight again,"

Giovanni kept trudging forward. "You're welcome."

"I have nothing to thank you for," Francis said. "I only meant that I never thought I'd see Rome again. I never said I wanted to—any more than I wanted you to save me from the chaos that you, yourself, created."

Giovanni stopped in his tracks. "Yet here you are, alive and well, and looking at Rome. So, let me rescue you one last time by giving you one last piece of advice, which you really shouldn't ignore: Just keep going, Francis. Keep going and don't stop until you're back in Assisi."

"And again, it's not really rescuing me if you're the one who put me into danger in the first place."

"Of course, it is. Danger is danger."

"And right is right," Francis insisted. "Whatever you think of me, you know I'm no coward."

"What I think of you is that you're my stubbornly simple-minded brother and all your foolishness—oh wait, you call it *faith*— won't save you from the rack if you say the wrong thing to the wrong people."

"And what could I possibly say that would be wrong?"

"From you? Just about anything that could come out of your mouth would be enough to secure your fate."

"I'll accept that fate if that's the price of speaking the truth."

"Truth," Giovanni scoffed. "The truth isn't determined by men like you, Francis. It's a tool of men with the power to build cities like Rome. What's done is done and nothing you can say or do now will change any of that. It won't stop it from happening in the future—over and over again. All it will do is get you killed. And while that might seem to me like a well-deserved fate for you, we have an unfortunate history of the people who want to kill you wanting to kill me, too."

"And so, what am I to do? Slink off into the night?"

"Yes, exactly that."

"I can't do that."

Giovanni knew better. "It's not a matter of can't. It's a matter of won't."

"You once asked me if there was a difference between the two—"

Giovanni threw up his hands in frustration. "Then go, Francis. Go and tell them what they already know. Go and tell them what they don't want anyone else to know. Go."

Francis started walking again.

Giovanni came trotting after. "What is it you expect to achieve?"

"I expect to tell the Pope everything that happened. And I expect to find out why."

"I already know what you expect to do, what I don't understand is what you it will *achieve*."

"Good people died, Giovanni. Montague. His men. All those civilians in the city." Francis wasn't sure whether or not the sultan should also be added to the list. "I won't let them die in vain."

"Good people die, Francis. It's almost all they ever do, and when they do it, it's almost always in vain. And if it wasn't for a bad guy like me, you would've been among their ranks a long time ago. That's just how the world is."

"Then, perhaps, we need to change the world."

"Change the world?" Giovanni laughed. "The world is what the world is, Francis. What it's always been and always will be. Your refusal to recognize that may be your greatest weakness."

"No, Giovanni. Not my weakness, my strength. The world is what the world is because indifference and selfishness make too many people unwilling to stand up and change it to what we all know it could be—what it *should* be."

"And is that what you're going to do now, Francis? Stand up and change the world?"

Francis turned and looked his brother square in the eye. "Yes."

74

There were four guards at the main gate of the Lateran Palace. Three of them didn't move at all when Francis demanded, "I want to see the Pope." The fourth's only movement was a dismissive wave of the hand and an equally dismissive, "You should leave here before you end up in front of the Inquisitor."

It wasn't until then that Francis remembered the ring Pope Innocent had given him. He pulled it off his finger and held it out. "I am a papal emissary," he said. "I demand to see His Holiness."

"What's that?" the guard asked.

"A seal. Given to me by Pope Innocent III, himself."

The guard plucked the ring from Francis's hand and studied it. "You've been away for a while, have you?"

Francis hadn't given much thought about how much time had passed in their travels, but it suddenly struck him that they had indeed been away for a very long time.

The silence was the only response the guard needed. "His Holiness. Pope Innocent III has passed away." He handed the ring back. "So, this doesn't mean what it did when you left."

Giovanni anticipated what Francis' response might be and was quick to step forward.

"If that bit of silver won't gain us proper respect and entrance, then perhaps this iron will do instead." He withdrew his sword just far enough from the scabbard to reveal that the blade was well worn, pitted in more battles than all four of the guards had seen in their lifetimes combined.

The guard looked at both men and gave a curt nod. "I'll see what I can do."

†

While natural causes had prevented an audience with Pope Innocent III, political considerations prevented one with his successor. That is, there was no advantage to be gained for the new pontiff in meeting with the man who had failed his predecessor. And so, it wasn't the pope who met Francis, but Cardinal le Bougre who received him in the grand drawing where they had first collided so many months earlier.

The cardinal was much the same man he had been, except his round, red face was now thin and grey. Despite the changed appearance—or, perhaps because of it—he was still in the same ill humor. This time, however, his arrogance was not tempered by papal interference.

"I'm surprised to see you again," le Bougre said.

"Surprised that I survived my errand or that, having done so, I felt compelled to return to this place?" Francis asked.

"Both. I assumed that if you were cunning enough to survive your mission in the Holy Land, you would then be smart enough to avoid returning here."

Le Bougre turned to Giovanni, "I suspect that both of these have more to do with your interference than his instinct or the Good Lord's intercession." Giovanni said nothing.

"I was sent on a mission of peace," Francis said.

"I wouldn't know about that." Le Bougre's voice was dismissive. "As I recall, the Pope—God rest his soul—spoke to you in private."

"I was sent on a mission of peace," Francis repeated.

Le Bougre scoffed. "Then it would seem that while you might have survived your mission, you nevertheless failed in its purpose."

"No," Francis said. "It would appear as if I served my purpose only too well." He looked straight at the cardinal and then at Giovanni.

"I see the experience hasn't tempered your insolence."

"Or my commitment to God."

Le Bougre's eyes widened. "And you would stand there and suggest that your commitment to God is greater than my own?"

"I leave such considerations to you since you seem to be wholly dependent upon them." Francis made a point of looking around the ornate room. "But certainly, the nature of your commitment and mine are very different."

"Your name may spread from peasant to peasant with tales of your works, but that tattered reputation does not give you the right to speak to me like that, I am Cardinal—"

"I am well aware of who you are," Francis interrupted. "And I do not speak to you on the basis of my reputation or yours. I speak to you man to man with the hope that somewhere between the two of us is a common ground on which we are both focused on preserving peace and caring for our fellow man."

Le Bougre snorted out a laugh. "I am solely concerned with caring for the Church."

"Then do not let it veer from the path walked by a humble man whose works were spread from peasant to peasant."

The cardinal's back stiffened.

Giovanni reached out to restrain his brother, "Francis, I caution you." Francis shook off the hand. "If I had truly been given the opportunity I had been offered, I could have established a peace. The very same peace Sultan al-Kalim had long ago offered."

"Do not speak the name of that Saracen in this holy place," le Bougre cautioned.

"Why? He is a child of God, no less precious to the Lord than any other man upon this earth."

"You dare lecture me on who is or is not precious in the eyes of the Lord?"

"I do," Francis said. "Just as I dare swear to you that we could have had a precious peace, had your nefarious efforts not destroyed it."

The cardinal smirked. "Instead, we have something far more precious."

"What is more precious than peace?"

"Demettia. A port that opens the door to all the riches beyond. *That*—not peace—was our purpose. And the only reason you are still breathing is that we were successful in achieving our purpose." The cardinal looked over at Giovanni and then back to Francis. "And that your brother obviously thought you worth saving. I hope you have thanked him for that." Disappointment laced the cardinal's voice.

"He's grateful for nothing," Giovanni said with resignation.

"Perhaps, I should be more appreciative, after all." Francis sighed and sank down into a luxurious couch. "It's all the same, isn't it?"

"What's that?" the cardinal asked.

"The workings of an enormous institution like the Church. Or something as small and intimate as a family. Wherever one looks, there are just patterns that follow themselves over and over again. There are always some few who have more than enough, but who still hunger for more, who crave something to fill up the emptiness within, a voracious maw that can never be satisfied."

"I could have you brought before the Inquisition for such talk," the cardinal warned.

"You could. But you won't."

"Are you so confident of that?"

"I am. Not out of any recognition of my service or mercy for me, but because it would not be in your political interests to be responsible to martyr the one whose name is spread from peasant to peasant. You can tax them and control them, but even you cannot afford to anger them."

Francis stood and moved toward the door.

"I have not given you leave," the cardinal said.

"I did not seek it," Francis said. He reached the door and opened it.

"Be aware that I will not hesitate to act should you ever return here," the cardinal warned.

Francis looked oddly amused. "Return? What is there to return to?" He paused and looked around the opulent room one last time. "The great irony of all of this, Your Eminence, is that all the power for which you've sacrificed so many innocent lives—and, I fear, your soul in the bargain—is wasted with you now, for nothing can save you from the infirmities consuming you from the inside."

"I haven't the faintest idea what you are talking about," the cardinal said, stifling a cough revealing him for him liar he was.

"The truth is that even now every breath you take becomes more and more labored," Francis said with a sad shake of his head. "The aching pain that racks your body intensifies with each passing day. And for the first time in your life, you're beginning to think about God, not as a product you can market and sell for your own profit, but with the quietly quaking fear that everything you've cynically manipulated to your own end might actually be true."

"I will not tolerate such talk. I will have you before the Inquisition—" The threat degenerated into a hacking cough that brought blood to le Bougre's lips which he tried to conceal in a linen handkerchief.

"You're too weak to bluff any further," Francis said confidently. "If nothing else, you know that I am a man of God, and, as you face your own inescapable demise, the thought of my blood on your hands no longer excites you—it terrifies you."

The cardinal might have responded, but his coughing fit would not allow him.

"I don't mean to terrify you," Francis said. "I truly feel sorry for you. Like so many others, you've made a fool's bargain, trading away your soul for the promise of a life that is already too fragile and too brief to be worth the bargain." Francis looked to his brother. "Like so many others."

With that, Francis closed the door behind him. He never returned to Rome again.

Ever.

75

Sometimes the most direct path to follow is the one that meanders most. Francis made his way back to Assisi like a leaf drifting on the autumn wind, alighting here and there, then following another gust to somewhere else altogether. He wandered, but his journey was not without purpose.

No matter how many paths he took, how much distance he put between himself and Rome, Francis could not escape the bitterness that filled his heart since his time there. The hard memories of all that had happened to him strangled his spirit, and the darkness within seeped out of him. His eyes became dull and lifeless, his countenance grim and unwelcoming. There were many he met along his travels who had heard of the miracle preacher from Assisi who talked to animals and gave up everything to serve the poor, but there were few who believed the brooding man in their midst could be one and the same.

One of the few who believed that Francis might actually be the kind, holy man they had all heard so much about was a priest who welcomed Francis from a particularly nasty afternoon. "I'm Father Isso," the man said, offering the shelter of his church from the cold rain that had been falling all day.

Francis was too wet and cold to resist the invitation, but he said little more than, "Thank you."

The priest offered a bowl of soup and Francis was grateful for that, too.

"So, you are the Francis from Assisi of whom I have heard so much?" the priest asked.

"And what have you heard?"

"That you preach to all and offer comfort to anyone who come to you with need." The priest hesitated, then added, "I'm told that you were a messenger of peace even to the Holy Land itself."

"And who told you all this?"

"Word of your deeds travels with the people."

"Is that all?" Francis asked as if he already knew the answer.

"There were emissaries of the Church—"

"Ahh, the Church." Francis smiled, satisfied that his suspicions had been confirmed. "You disapprove of those who spoke so highly of you?" Father Isso asked.

"If they sang my praises in the verse, I'm sure it was only because there was some benefit to them in the chorus," Francis said, never taking his eyes from the bowl in front of him.

"I don't understand." The priest shook his head. "You are a man of the cloth and yet you speak so harshly of the Church?"

"I am a man of the people," Francis retorted. "The Church is what the Church wants to be in order to satisfy its own ambition and meet its own needs, but it can do so without me or my assistance."

"You're angry," the priest said.

"Yes, angry for having been used. And angry for being a fool for allowing myself to be so used."

"It's the world that we live in," Father Isso said, offering more bread.

"That's a popular opinion, but not one that I share."

"I'm afraid it's not really an opinion at all. This *is* a treacherous world." There was a sincere note of sadness in the priest's words. "And yet it's a world of wonder and beauty—and, occasionally, endless compassion and kindness. The Church is simply a reflection of that world."

Francis looked up from his soup. "Is that right?"

Father Isso nodded. He took a bite of bread and chewed it slowly. He could feel Francis dark eyes waiting for an answer. "The Church," he said finally, "is easily maligned for the misdeeds of its members. Justifiably so. Our Church is often misdirected by men who would harness its might for their own ambitions and desires. But that is what *men* do. That is not what the Church *is*."

Francis scowled. "You make easy distinctions."

"Not easy at all, I assure you."

"Not easy for you. Impossible for me."

"Then, perhaps, you should try a little harder," Isso said.

Francis put his bowl down and glared at the brazen man.

"If you said to me that there are corrupt men in the world," Isso continued. "I would look at you with incredulous disbelief at your naiveté and say, 'Of course, there are. But can the dark deeds of one man overshadow the good deeds of the many?"

"And I wouldn't know how to answer," Francis said. "Not anymore."

"Really? You've helped hundreds of souls, perhaps thousands. Does the misdeed of any single man negate the good you have done?"

Francis sighed and hung his head. "I'm not sure I've really done all that much good."

"I'm sure you have. And I'm sure that no one's misdeeds can cancel out that work. It's flawed men who are corrupt, not the Church. Just as it is men who can be cold and cruel, not the world. I think the true sin here would be for a man such as yourself to give up on either one simply because of the acts of a despicable few."

"I think it's more than a few."

"I can't believe the numbers matter," the priest said. "But what would your alternative be? Even without the Church, don't you think that these same men would find another means of securing and wielding devastating power at any price? I assure you they would. And then who would do the good work that even you can't deny the Church does through the hands of men such as yourself?"

Francis had finished his soup and tired of the debate. "I'm just so disheartened."

"I understand. It is disheartening to learn there is darkness where there should only be light, but that is just more reason for the souls like yours to shine all the brighter still."

Francis leaned back and crossed his arms across his chest. "You make it sound so easy."

"Oh no, there's nothing easy about it at all. That's one of the problems. People want to rely on the Church like they were children. And they treat God no better. To most people, prayer isn't a time of devotion, but an opportunity to make requests, to ask for what it is they think they need. What they don't understand is that God is like a father, but a good father who prepares his children for life and expects them to live their lives and work to solve their problems. We, all of us, need to take responsibility for ourselves and for our neighbors. We need to take care of one another as good children take care of their brothers and sisters. We need to ask less and do more. For ourselves. For one another."

Francis felt warm. And full. And maybe slightly a little better. "You're right. I've squandered too many days with bitterness and regret."

"But tomorrow's another day," the priest said. "And the possibilities are infinite."

Francis took the blanket that Father Isso gave him and found a corner of the church to stretch out. And there, on a mattress of stone, he slept more soundly than he had in a long, long time.

80

O   When Francis finally reached Assisi, the city he knew better than all others, he was surprised to discover that it struck him like the most foreign of places, with buildings he'd never seen before and too many faces he did not recognize. Even the one person with whom his was most familiar seemed to be an odd and different copy of the original. The Father Leo who greeted him at the door of the old church was not the same man who had rescued him so many years ago. The figure who stood in the doorway regarding him suspiciously was older and frailer than Francis remembered his friend.

"You're back?" The voice was softer and fainter, too.

Francis looked at the structure he had long known as an old, dilapidated church and had difficulty reconciling the imposing structure. "Is that where I am?"

"You've been gone for a long, long while."

Francis tried not to entertain the memories which the statement conjured. "Too long."

"Are you back to stay?"

Francis laughed to himself. "As long as I can."

"I only ask because there was a woman came here looking for you," the old priest said.

Francis tried to suppress those memories as well. "I know. I watched her go before I departed on my own journey."

"No," Father Leo corrected. "This was a different woman. She gave me this and asked that I pass it on to you if I ever saw you again." The old man handed Francis a folded note.

Francis read what was written there without a single word of it affecting his expression. When he was done, he put the note away and simply said, "I have to go."

Father Leto nodded and watched as Francis turned away from the church and hurried down the street.

†

Francis had been away from Assisi for so long that moving deeper into the city created the odd sensation that he was traveling further away. Still, he knew exactly where his every step fell, and he did not get lost or misdirected on the twisting roads he had not travelled since he was another man altogether.

He announced his arrival with a knock at the door, then took a deep breath and waited.

After a few moments, the door came open and there stood his mother. She had aged considerably in the time that he'd been away, and the sight of her was jarring. Francis had, of course, traced his own progression from boy to man, but he'd never considered his own parents were fellow passengers along that journey.

His mother's hair, once as black and shiny as obsidian, had turned as grey as ash and curled about her shoulders as if she no longer practiced her daily ritual of brushing and combing. She looked at him, and for the briefest of moments, there was a spark of joy in eyes which had long since surrendered their sparkle and were now reddened and underlined with dark lines of care and spent tears. "It's good to see you," she said.

If she wanted to embrace her son, she was unable to take that first step forward. "I wasn't sure you would come. They said you were in Rome. For the Pope."

"Of course, I'd come." Francis reached out to hug his mother, but it was not a mother and child reunion. The absence of whatever had once bound them together, now made their embrace an awkward occasion for both of them.

They released each other and he stepped inside. He looked around the house and was struck by a noticeable absence. "Shadow?" His mother was silent. Francis knew the dog would have been ancient by now, but somehow, he had imagined her bounding up to the door to greet him. It was childish, and he felt a prick of tears for his companion and his boyhood innocence. "When?"

"Not long after ... the trial." She touched Francis's arm lightly. "She was a harsh, snarling reminder of you that your father could not abide," Pica said, as if that explanation might bring Francis some understanding.

His fists clenched, his jaw tightened, his teeth ground against one another. He took a deep breath and forced himself to remember why he had returned to his family home. "Am I too late? Is he ..." Francis was surprised how hard it was to finish the question.

"He's upstairs," she said and then pointed the way as if he didn't already know it well.

If time had altered his mother, the passing years had deformed his father.

Confined to his bed, Pietro was no longer the volcano of a man that Francis had known as a boy. If there was still some spirit left in him, his body was like a corpse, both withered and bloated. His nose, once merely reddened by his fondness for the grape, was now swollen and engorged as if drunkenness had been his own personal plague. His eyes were watery and sunk in their sockets and fixed in a maniacal stare at the ceiling above.

Francis had tended to thousands who had been afflicted with far more serious and devastating illnesses and injuries than the mere passing of time, but he'd never been so horrified by the sight of a human being ravaged by the decay that is the most natural part of life.

"His condition worsens each day," Pica said from the doorway, like there was some invisible barrier keeping her from entering and standing beside Francis. "It's been so long since anyone had word from you, I never thought he would survive to see you again. The only thing that the priest and physician agree on is that his desire to see you is the only thing that has kept him alive when any other soul would have long since passed on. He is too stubborn to die before talking to his son again."

Francis turned to her, "Will I do as a substitute?"

She bit her lip. "Don't be cruel. Not now."

He turned back to his father for just a moment, but when he looked back to the doorway again, he found it empty. He'd been left there all alone.

Francis took a seat beside the bed, unsure what else he could do.

His father stirred. "Francis, is that you?"

"Yes, Father. I am here."

"Really? Is it you?" Pietro's dry, white tongue tried in vain to lick and moisten his cracked lips. "Because sometimes I see things, such horrible things. That damn bear."

"Bear?"

"They say there's no bear here." Pietro's voice was barely more than a hoarse whisper. "But I see the goddamn beast, watching me from the shadows. Don't think I don't."

"No, Father. I know you do."

"You see it too, don't you?"

Francis looked into the corner his father had indicated with a nod of his head and thought for a moment about what to say. "Mother said you wanted to speak with me."

"What?"

"Mother said you wanted to talk to me."

"Who?"

"Mother. Your wife."

"I don't trust that woman," Pietro rolled his head rolled on his pillow as he shook his head. "Never did."

"Did you want to say something to me, Father?"

"It's good to see you, Francis. It's been a long time."

"Yes."

"When was the last time?"

"When you brought me before the Bishop."

"I did?"

"Yes."

"I don't remember that." Pietro chuckled to himself, until the chuckles became a series of coughs that stole his breath away. "Sounds like something I'd do," he said when he could.

Francis took a cloth from the bedside and wiped the spittle from his father's mouth.

The old man licked his lips. "Have you seen Giovanni?"

"Giovanni? No," Francis said, unsure whether or not his answer was a lie.

"Always a great boy. Great man." Pietro's eyes warmed for a moment. "He came here quite a bit after you left."

"Did he?" Francis asked.

"He was quite a comfort to me. Not so much to your mother. She never liked him very much. I don't know why."

Francis shook his head. "I can't imagine, Father."

"He's a soldier now."

"Is that what they call them these days?"

"I'm told he serves the Pope, himself."

Francis passed the comment off, "Well, there are so many popes anymore. You can hardly keep track of them. You think you know one and then suddenly there's another."

"Fine man. A man a father could be proud of."

"You always were proud of him," Francis admitted.

"Promise me," Pietro said with a sudden note of urgency in his faint voice.

"Promise you what?"

"That you'll take care of him."

"Giovanni doesn't need me looking after him."

"You'd be surprised who needs you, Francis. You'd be surprised."

Francis said nothing.

"Besides, I have a feeling that once I'm gone—" Pietro paused, to take a breath or collect his thoughts.

"Yes?"

"That once I'm gone, this damn bear will set out after him next. Goddamn bear. It's gold, you know?"

"What is?"

"The bear. Gold bear. It's coming to get me. And when it's done with me, I'm afraid it's going to go after my Giovanni."

"Your Giovanni?" Francis repeated.

"Yes."

And then the old man fell silent and quiet again. Even the wheezing sound softened.

Francis had tended to thousands of the afflicted as they'd each made their ways from this world to another, but he saw no point in staying at his own father's bedside any longer. There was no comfort he could bring to that old man.

Francis put his hand on his Pietro's. "I have to go now, Father."

His father turned to look at him with his bulging eyes. "Do you have to? I was hoping you could stay for a while."

Francis retook his seat. "Of course. If you'd like. I can stay as long as you want me to."

They sat in silence for a minute.

"I don't want it," Pietro said after a while.

"What's that, Father?"

"Your forgiveness," the old man said. "If you've come here to give me your forgiveness, I don't want it. I don't need forgiveness."

Francis nodded.

They stayed silent for a while longer, until Pietro turned to his head and looked up at Francis. "I guess I don't have anything else to say to you after all."

And that was the last thing Pietro di Bernadone ever said to his son.

81

P ica caught her son at the door. "Were you going to say good-bye?"
Francis stopped. "I was hoping it wouldn't be good-bye."

"Would else could it be?"

Francis turned to face his mother. "I'll come back and we'll talk then. It's just that I have other—"

"I understand," she said, although her demeanor suggested otherwise. "Did you and your father talk?"

Francis didn't respond, but he went to his mother and hugged her.

She didn't return the gesture.

He pulled away. "I should be going now."

"You could stay," she said. "If you wanted to."

He walked to the door and pulled it open. "I couldn't. We both know that."

"He wasn't a bad man," she said.

Francis looked at her but said nothing.

"He was always a generous husband. Never cruel."

"Is that how you remember him now?"

Her eyes shifted to the floor. "He was never cruel to me; not like some husbands can be."

Francis forced a smile. "Everyone looks back at the same past, but we all see different things."

"He never meant to be cruel to you," she said. "He just wanted so much for you. And he tried too hard."

"I love you, Mother." Francis thought that was the end of their moment and he moved to the open door.

"When I was a young girl—" Pica's voice trembled. "I had an uncle, my mother's brother. And he did things—" She bit her lip to stifle tears she'd been crying in secret for her entire life. "When I told my mother what he'd done, she—"

After a lifetime of family stories that had left Francis with the impression that he knew everything there was to know about his mother, Francis was struck by the one story he had never heard before.

"My mother slapped me across the face, so hard that I was knocked to the floor," Pica said. If the memory stirred any emotion, her voice was flat. "I pulled myself up from the floor, bleeding from the mouth. And hating her. Hating her even more than my uncle. She told me that I was never to talk about it to anyone, that I should act like nothing had ever happened. I told my father and he hit me, too. Harder. He warned me to never reveal my secret again."

Francis moved to his mother to offer her comfort that she refused.

"For the longest time, I hated my mother. And my father," Pica continued.

Francis reached for her hand, but she withdrew from him. "And the touch of anyone filled me with terror. And disgust. But *I* did what you always refused to do. I did as I was told. I smiled and I behaved and I was the good daughter. The daughter my parents wanted me to be. The wife Pietro wanted me to be. The mother I thought you wanted me to be."

"Mother—"

"My point is that I know what it's like to resent your parents. To hate them even."

"Mother, I don't—"

"But you hate them as a child would because you only understand them as a child. When I was grown to be a woman, with a child of my own, I was able to look at what my parents had done, and as an adult, I understood."

Francis listened, but said nothing.

"If I had told anyone else back then, it would only have disrupted the family on which we were completely dependent. And the only result would have been that I would've been regarded as unfit for marriage and shipped off to a convent or some such place." She looked straight at Francis. "Just like your friend, Clare."

A chill ran down Francis' back, but he said nothing.

"As I child, I judged them. As an adult, I understood that they were only trying to protect me, to do what was best for me. You may look back on your father—and, maybe, me as well—and you can judge us, but only as a child. An adult would understand that everything we did, we did for you."

"Mother."

"Yes?"

"Your parents were wrong," Francis said.

She laughed at the horrible thing he was suggesting. "No. You're saying that as a child, but—"

"I'm saying it as a man," Francis insisted. "I don't hate Father. Or you. I love you both with all my heart. And I forgive you both for whatever you've done that may have hurt me. I have nothing but forgiveness in my heart. For you. For everyone. But forgiveness is not the same as acceptance. Forgiveness comes after the act is addressed, but acceptance is merely turning a blind eye to it. Your parents should have protected you as a child, not from life, but from your uncle. And they should have protected whoever else might have fallen prey to him. We all have a responsibility to protect one another, our children most of all."

She scoffed at him with a bitterness he'd never thought her capable of. "You don't understand the way the world works. You never have. Or you never were willing to. That was the one luxury which our privilege provided you and which you reveled in."

"You're not the first to accuse me of this," he said.

"Did you ever stop to consider what happened to us after your trial before the Bishop. Did you ever think that the price for your noble stand was paid by *us*?"

"I'm sorry if there were consequence. But I did what I thought was right. And if you—and some others—add to my long list of offenses the charge that I have never seen the world's cruelty clearly enough, I promise that you're all wrong."

Francis stepped out into the day.

From the darkness of the house, she called after him. "We did the best we could, Francis."

He did not turn back. "I know."

"We did the best we could," she said again.

And that was the last thing Pica ever said to her son.

82

Francis left his childhood home feeling neither liberated nor alienated. What he felt was numbed. Yet it wasn't his father's tragic last act that had rendered him senseless. Nor was it the details of his mother's confession that bothered him so. Instead, what rang in his head over and over again let he'd been cuffed on both ears was his mother's casual aside. *"Like your friend, Clare."*

There was no mystery to the meaning of the inuendo, but what troubled Francis so greatly was how he could have been so obtuse as to have overlooked it in the first place. He wondered if it might be possible that somehow he'd known all along, but still been completely unaware at the same time. Could knowledge and ignorance co-exist so seamlessly?

What Francis had known for certain was that there had always been a missing piece to Clare's personal puzzle. No matter how she'd given flight to his heart or sparked his imagination, from their very first meeting, he'd been aware that there was something ever so slightly askew about her life, something that he couldn't quite identify or articulate. And it was that mystery he followed from his own house and out further into the countryside where the nunnery was located and where he hoped he might find Clare.

The building itself had been constructed on the ruins of the dilapidated church where he'd first followed Clare all those years ago. The edifice, however, was not the only thing that had changed.

"Oh, heavens!" Even with the addition of years, Francis recognized the old nun who had once done so much to drive him away. This time, however, she seemed eager to welcome him. "We are blessed to receive you. Please, come in, come in."

"You know who I am?" Francis was taken aback by her cheerful disposition and feared she might have mistaken him for someone else.

"Everyone knows of you and your works, Brother Francis. And of your service to the pope, God rest his soul."

Francis wasn't sure whether it was his mission or the old nun's change of attitude that left him so uncomfortable. "I've come to see—"

"Sister Clare?" she finished for him. "I'm sorry. She's not here at the moment."

Francis had been uncertain what might be waiting for him, but he had never entertained the thought that the only thing he'd find would be her absence. "Not here?"

"She's gone on retreat. Several of the sisters have."

Francis nodded. "Where would that be?"

"Oh, I'm afraid she cannot be disturbed. Not even by you."

Francis nodded again. "Do you know when she'll—"

"Return?" she cut him off. Francis nodded.

"Soon, I would think," she responded to her own question.

"Could you tell her—"

"That you came to see her?"

Francis nodded again.

The old nun promised that she would and sent him off with an excited "Good day," even though the moon was climbing high into a darkening sky.

"It's been a pleasure talking with you," she called after him.

Francis smiled. "It certainly would've been."

She returned the smile.

He took a half dozen steps from the door and felt a sudden, sinking feeling in the pit of his stomach. "You won't forget?" he asked.

But the door was already closed.

"Don't forget," he repeated to no one but himself.

83

When Francis returned to Father Leo and the rest of the order, he was quiet. Not just for a day or two or even a week, but for such a duration that even the brothers who had been with him for years understood it was best to let him be than to disturb his silence.

All except one, that is.

"You've had enough," Father Leo said.

"Enough of what?" Francis asked without rising from his meditative position.

"Solitude. Silence. Sorrow. Whatever else it is that you've been wallowing in. You've had enough."

"I'm not wallowing," Francis insisted.

"It's a hard thing to lose a parent—"

"Is this where you join the chorus of people telling me that I don't understand the world?"

The old priest shook his head. "No. I don't think that's true. I think you see the world just fine."

"Then that makes two of us."

Father Leo looked Francis straight in the eyes. "I think what you don't see clearly is yourself."

"What?"

"You try, but you fall short. Always. You see the world just fine, but you're still searching to find yourself."

"That's not true," Francis protested.

The old priest didn't even bother to respond, but Francis couldn't continue to meet his mentor's eyes and looking away was an act of admission.

"You've fought your father for your entire life. Your brother. The world. And that struggle was a large part of what made you a great man," Father Leo continued.

"I'm not a great man."

Father Leo snorted. "Your denial is proof of my point. Your whole life has been based upon that struggle, on fighting that fight. I'll leave to you to decide whether you've won or lost or if any of that even matters now that it's over. But it's over. It has to be, for your sake. Now it's up to you to decide what you want to do for no other reason than you *want* to do it. Or you believe it's right."

"I've always tried to do what I thought was right."

The old priest shook his head in dismissal. "It's a subtle distinction, but there's a difference between opposing what is wrong and doing what is right."

Francis was silent.

"So, the question now is what are you going to do?" Father Leo continued. "You've got this order of faithful men who would follow you wherever you might lead them."

Francis shook his head. "I'm no leader and the order runs itself."

"It doesn't run itself. Other people run it for you because you've chosen not to become involved." Father Leo's voice was tinged with frustration.

"Rules and regulations. Interactions with the Church. These are not the things I'm good at. Not the activities I have a passion for."

"Then there's someone you should meet."

"Who's that?"

"His name is Anthony. An exceptional young man from Padua. And for the longest time he's acted in your stead over the time that you've been away."

"Acted as me?"

"More than that. He's organized the brothers. He's coordinated their efforts and work. The name of Francis of Assisi spreads across the land, but that is in no small degree through the efforts of Anthony of Padua."

Francis understood what the old priest was saying, and all that he had left unsaid. "I'll meet him in the morning."

"Why wait? He's right outside."

†

Anthony followed Father Leo into the room but said nothing. Francis rose from the position he'd taken on the floor for his meditations but said nothing. The two men stood, staring at one another, silently.

"This is the young man I was telling you about," Father Leo said to Francis. "I would say that he has been you for this order during the time that you were away, except that he has faithfully attended to the necessary administrative duties and, in that way, he's been nothing like you."

"I am Francis, by the way." The clumsy introduction was intended in part to lighten the young man's demeanor.

It didn't. "I know."

"You're Anthony." Francis meant the irrefutable statement as an acknowledgement of the young man and his accomplishments, but it came out like a simple observation or, even worse, a recent discovery.

"Yes. I know that, too."

The awkward exchange devolved once again to even more awkward silence.

"I'm told I have you to thank for the success of the order that bears my name," Francis said. If his voice seemed flat, it wasn't that he didn't feel a degree of gratitude, but simply that his appreciation didn't register in his words.

"I haven't done any of this for gratitude or accolades, but merely because the work needed to be done—for the people," Anthony said.

"Whether I owe you thanks or not, you have mine." Francis fumbled for something else to say, but couldn't think of anything at all.

"And now?" Anthony asked after another period of awkward silence.

"Now?"

"Now that you've returned again." Anthony folded his arms across his chest. "What happens now?"

"I'm not sure what you mean. The sun will still rise and there will still be hunger and disease, people will need of comfort and guidance. I can't see what would change."

Anthony nodded, not like he agreed, but like this was the answer he'd expected. "With the exception of the rising sun, there is a lot of work that goes into attending to the hungry and suffering and to offering comfort and guidance to those in need."

"Again, I'm not sure what you mean."

"I mean providing for the brothers. Organizing our efforts to assist those in need. Working with the Church. All of these things require someone—not to take charge—but to—"

"No," Francis was quick to stop him. "You're right, they *do* require someone to take charge. Whatever anyone thinks, I understand that someone needs to assume these responsibilities and, that in my absence, you have been the one to do so. That was why I began our conversation with an expression of thanks."

Anthony reconsidered his position. "I did not mean—"

"In the same way that you do not do your work for thanks, I did not offer my appreciation with any expectation that it would be well received, only that I wanted to express it. If your concern is that my arrival here signifies that I am preparing to take your duties from you, that is not my intent."

"Again, I did not mean to—"

"If the suggestion is that I have not made a fair contribution," Francis continued. "That also was not my intent. But neither was it my intent to grow this order or to accomplish anything more than to renovate the old church and to help as many people as I could. In doing so, I have learned that God pays little attention to our intent."

"I have found that to be true, as well," Anthony said with a hint of a smile.

"If you would like to continue your role in a mission that is far greater than I am capable of, then I would be most appreciative of that assistance— whether you want my thanks or not."

"I'm sorry if my manner came across—"

"You're not interested in accolades and I have no interest in apologies," Francis said. "There is work to be done."

"Yes."

"And as anyone who knows me will confirm," Francis said, throwing a look to Father Leo. "There are many who think I have been blessed, but the ability to follow rules and procedures is not among my gifts. So, if you can continue what you've done so well in my absence now that I have returned, I will press on with my own mission. And I think that would be a fine division of our labor."

"I agree," Anthony said.

Father Leo smiled as Francis moved past him to the door.

"Brother Francis," Anthony called after him.

Francis turned.

"Welcome home."

84

Sometimes life's challenges come one-at-a-time and offer a fair fight. More often than not, the tragedies that break both heart and soul don't travel alone, but rather stalk and attack in packs like wild dogs. If Francis had become more reserved, he'd also worked harder than ever in the days that followed his final farewell to his parents—and his inability to reach Clare.

Certainly, there was much that needed to be done within the surrounding community, but Francis' devotion wasn't entirely altruistic, and he was well aware of his selfish motivation. If he was working, he was thinking about work. And if he was thinking about work, he wasn't thinking about anything else. And distraction was the greatest of comforts at a time when Francis was aware of the dark thoughts being held (just barely) at bay.

This single-minded devotion to each day's work may have been the reason why Francis failed to notice that while he was more driven than ever, Father Leo's pace had begun to slow considerably, and his old friend's coloring had turned ashen, and his breathing labored. And if Francis had taken notice of any of those telltale signs, he might have been able to do something.

There is, of course, no way to deny the inescapable, to prevent the inevitable. But maybe, he might have seized the opportunity to take just a moment or two to tell his friend how much he'd treasured their time together and how that influence and support had transformed his life, and that he was sorry for whatever heartache and trouble he might have caused, and that he loved him very much. Maybe he might have told the old man that, in every way that mattered, Father Leo had been the father Francis had always wanted.

Father Leo was in his chair when Francis opened the door. The old man's hands were in his lap, still holding his prayer book. Francis assumed his friend had simply fallen asleep. "You may have slept through your prayers, but you won't want to sleep through supper."

Silence.

"My friend?"

Silence.

Francis approached, but not with the steps of a man. He walked to the far corner of the room like a frightened child who has discovered something that he wished would stay hidden. He put on hand on the shoulder that had supported him so many times. Nothing.

Francis sank to his knees beneath the weight of a sadness he could not comprehend. He had seen too much death in his days and yet, for some reason, he'd never comprehended that that Fate's cold hand might one day reach out to touch his friend.

And in the man's absence, Francis suddenly felt more alone than he had ever felt in his life.

Abandoned.

Deserted.

And he sobbed, not for his friend who had slipped peacefully from this life, but for himself who had been left there all alone.

Fatherless.

An orphan now.

"Please," he heard himself beg between gasping sobs. "Please."

But there was no one else there to hear his pleas.

No way that anyone could answer his request for just one more moment.

For just the chance to say good-bye.

Or "I love you."

He stayed like that for a while, curled at his mentor's feet, crying like a child. But when he was done, he rose like a man.

He kissed Father Leo on the forehead and whispered, "Thank you."

And "I love you."

Then Francis went to the others and told them that Father Leo wouldn't be dining with them that evening, that he had gone on to the table of the Lord.

85

Sometimes a team functions best when like-minded souls exist in harmony and work in perfect unison. Sometimes opposites are the perfect pairings and the greatest gains are made through conflict. Sometimes, it's a little bit of both.

Anthony ran the business, an inescapable component of every enterprise, even a charitable one. He handled all of the day-to-day matters for which Francis had long demonstrated a complete lack of interest and competency.

In return, Francis rededicated himself to the simplest tasks that had first captivated his heart and soul. He ministered to the down-hearted, attended to the sick, and fed those who were starving, physically and spiritually. And, in this way, Francis was able to generate within their community a certain energy that the devout Anthony was not yet able to inspire on his own.

Between the examples set by both men, the order of brothers prospered, their outreach expanded, and Francis' message was spread across the region, and then far beyond. The larger the order of brothers grew, the greater the number they were able to help. The more they helped; the more Francis' mission was disseminated among them.

That cyclical pattern repeated itself over and over again until the order of brothers had become a body of some significance and Francis' name was known far and wide. But nothing comes alone and as prosperity blessed the order, it brought with it an ever-increasing demand both for the charitable services they offered and for Francis' time and attention. In that way, the full bloom of success brought with it—as it too often does—the seeds of dissolution.

"When Rome sends an emissary, it's important that you show them respect," Anthony said.

Francis had been in prayer and made no movement or other indication to acknowledge that he was no longer alone.

Anthony understood the unspoken message within the silent reception, but being ignored only increased his resolve. "Whether you like it or not, you are the one person who represents everything that all of us have worked so hard to accomplish."

"We've already had this conversation," Francis said, without giving Anthony any more attention than that.

"And I am as tired of initiating this conversation as you must be of dodging it. So, I'm hoping that we can reach an understanding, once and for all."

"I understand," Francis said.

Anthony knew what that meant, too, but he had no choice but to press the issue. "Then understand that when we have papal dignitaries—"

The word was enough to open Francis' eyes wide and spin him around to face Anthony. "Dignitaries?"

"Yes. Dignitaries. That's what they are."

"No," Francis corrected. "That's what they consider themselves."

"There's no difference between the two," Anthony said.

Francis let out a tired sigh. "No man has *dignity* simply because he is dressed in finery, any more than a man loses his dignity if he lacks those same clothes. All men are sons of God and for us to treat one as if he is better than another is—if not an affront to God, Himself—then an affront to me."

Anthony shook his head from frustration. "Francis—"

"If this is the conversation in which you tell me that I don't see the world for what it is, I am even more tired of that one than the one you originally started. I've had it my whole life. With my father. My mother. My brother. Soldiers and prisoners. Cardinals and popes."

"That doesn't make it any less true."

"What's true is that I don't see *your* world." Francis got to his feet. His words rang with an anger that was uncharacteristic for him. "I see *my* world. If that is my sin, then brand me a sinner. I will never repent that particular wickedness. And I will never surrender that vision."

Anthony put his hands up to calm a situation that had unexpectedly become charged. "No one's asking you to surrender, Francis—"

"Francis. Francis. Francis. How I am sick of that name," he exploded. "It's not even my given name! It's just a pretense I've been stuck with my entire life. So, if the pompous, bloated fools from Rome need to have all others bend their knees before them, do not count on me to be among that number. I will not do it. And if that means I am no longer welcome here with you, among my brothers, then I will gladly go and do what I had long ago intended to do by myself."

"Francis," Anthony began and then immediately regretted it. "No one is asking you to leave."

"This is God's domain," Francis shouted. "Not man's. Every day of my life I have supplicated myself to God. I have given Him my life when I would have preferred to have offered it to another. I have done everything in my power to serve His sons and daughters, my brothers and sisters—all of whom He loves equally. And I will not betray Him now by pretending that His kingdom is ruled by anyone else but Him."

Anthony said nothing.

Francis breathed heavily, realizing that he had overreacted. Maybe badly. "I'm sorry."

Anthony nodded.

"I should not have—"

"No, I was wrong to disturb you when you were at prayer. I should have waited to ask you to compromise, if that's what you think I am asking of you."

"I do," Francis said.

"You know, refusing to see the bear in the woods at night doesn't protect you from it."

"No," Francis agreed. "God protects you from the bear."

Anthony considered the response. "I like to think that God gave you two good eyes to see the bear, the common sense to beware of him, and the strong legs to flee when survival calls for running away."

"Perhaps, I want more than *survival*." There was more than a little contempt in the way Francis spoke the word.

"And perhaps that's always been your problem."

"What are you saying?"

"You said you've had this conversation—refusing to see the world as others do—all of your life. With your mother and father—"

"Yes," Francis cut in.

"They weren't necessarily wrong, Francis. None of us are. Maybe it's just that we're all thinking of survival. *Just* survival. And that's never been enough for you. Maybe you've always wanted something more."

Francis stood flat-footed, unable to respond.

Anthony turned and left without another word.

86

A day or two passed with nothing more than a nod of acknowledgment or a quick pleasantry exchanged between Francis and Anthony. And that meant that nothing improved for anyone else either.

"You look troubled," Anthony said when he realized that the silence between them was beginning to seep out into their community of brothers.

Francis shrugged. "Is that how I appear?"

Anthony nodded. "Is it a world of cares or just one that blackens your thoughts?"

Francis pondered the question. "No matter how hard I work, no matter how much we all do, there is never an end to the need. We feed a dozen and there are a hundred more who go hungry. We feed that hundred and a thousand appear with empty bowls held out before them."

"There is much suffering in the world," Anthony admitted. "God's ways are often beyond the comprehension of Man."

"God's maybe, but not Man's. The thousand in need are passed everyday by ten thousand who possess the means to end their hunger. The cure to so much of this suffering is within our grasp if only we would follow the simplest instruction: *Love one another.*"

"I understand your frustrations, Brother Francis, but the darkness of your mood is starting to spread over the entire order, even drifting off into the community. Perhaps, you could use some time away," Anthony suggested.

"It seems to me that I've only just returned from *some time away*. Do you really think the cure lies in distance?"

"I only thought that some distance might be preferable to the close proximity to your dark mood. Perhaps some time away from people, a private conversation between you and God, might allow you to resolve whatever it is that has your heart so unsettled."

"There's much wisdom in your thoughts," Francis admitted. "But I sense another motivation for you sharing them with me."

Anthony did not deny. "The entourage from Rome continues its way toward us and I would anticipate that we would receive them within the next day or two."

Francis raised an eyebrow and smiled. "And you think it would be better for all concerned if I were not here when they arrived."

"I would prefer that you were here to welcome our distinguished guests and to pray for the Church's continued support."

"But you fear—"

"Not fear," Anthony corrected. "We both know what sort of reception you are likely to offer and, in turn, the consequences we all might suffer as a result."

Francis nodded in acknowledgement. "Well, if not the distance, then perhaps the solitude would do much to settle the discontent within my heart since Father Leo's passing."

"I have heard of an island," Anthony offered. "An uninhabited dot of land not out at sea, but within a lake. *Isola Maggiore*. The island is place of great legend where pilgrims often go to separate themselves from the world and to bring themselves closer to God, who is said to have a special presence there."

"And?" Francis coaxed.

"Perhaps travel to and seclusion in such a mystical place might again ignite the spirit within you."

"And?"

"And, maybe, if word of your pilgrimage to such a mystical destination were to be spread among those who are moved by the mere mention of your name, then that message might serve as an inspiration to everyone else—including our visitors from Rome."

Francis nodded, knowingly. "*Isola Maggiore*, you say?"

"Perhaps, a pilgrimage yourself. In the company of some of the brothers here."

"Company is exactly what I am looking to escape," Francis said.

"Then I could ready a number of brothers to leave with you tomorrow, if you'd like. Not to stay with you, but to accompany you there and take you across. You could arrange with them a time and date for your return and then be left alone on the island."

"Perhaps," Francis said. "But not tomorrow. There are a few matters of earthly concern that I think it would be best to resolve before setting off."

"Do what you will, but consider that Rome advances," Anthony said.

"A day or two. Nothing more," Francis promised.

Anthony turned to leave, but Francis stopped him before he got to the door. "Do you ever think about the choices you've made in life, the ones that led you here?"

"No," Anthony said. "Those choices are already made."

"But do you ever regret them?" Francis wanted to know. "Do you ever wish you had chosen another life?"

"I believe I am living the only life I ever could have. So, no."

"You're a lucky man, Brother Anthony."

"I think the same of you."

Anthony walked to the door.

Francis stopped him again. "Anthony? I was wondering if in the past time I was away, if maybe a visitor had come calling for me?"

Anthony was quick to shake his head. "I have not seen her."

87

"Here," Anthony said, handing Francis a pack.

"What's this?"

"Just some things that I've put together for your stay. Wine and bread. A few previsions to see you through. Some other things you may want."

His curiosity piqued, Francis started to open the bundle.

Anthony put a hand out to stop him. "Trust me, I've given you everything you need."

Brother Paolo and three of the other brothers were sent to accompany Francis on the trip to Isola Maggiore. They chattered amongst themselves as they went, but did not direct any comments to Francis, who seemed already to have retreated into isolation.

When the party arrived at the shores of Lake Trasimeno, the sun was already beginning its descent, and they decided it would be best to make camp instead of heading out onto the water.

By the light of the fire, one of the brothers finally gathered the courage to ask, "Are you afraid?"

Francis' mind had been elsewhere. "Me?"

"Yes, Brother Francis, if you don't mind me asking."

"Afraid of what?" Francis asked.

"Of being alone, for all this time."

Francis dismissed the question. "No. I've found myself in danger many times, but never once while I was alone. It's people—not their absence—that pose the real threat."

The brother nodded. "I would find it difficult to be alone for so long."

"Then, perhaps, you should spend more time that way," Francis offered good-naturedly.

Still, the brother seemed frightened by the suggestion and remained silent. Another brother was quick to pick up the conversation. "What do you suppose you'll do for all of that time?"

"People think of their lives in terms of *doing*," Francis answered. "But life is really more about *being*. So, I'll be being. Alone." It was clear that none of the other brothers understood the distinction he was making. "Think of it this way," Francis said. "When you have passed on from this life, do you want to be remembered as someone who accompanied me to this lake or someone who was kind and supportive?"

"The latter, of course."

"Exactly. And if that is how you would wish to be remembered in death, then that is how you must live your life. Don't worry about the things you do—they will take care of themselves—concentrate on what you *are*."

88

By the light of sunrise, the Isola Maggiore's waters shimmered, blue and black against shades of crimson and violet. Francis stood on the banks, with the water gently lapping at his feet. The scene seemed magical and he understood the draw of the location.

There was a boat that was kept as a communal contribution to pilgrims tied at a make-shift dock at the lake's shore. As Francis waited for the brothers to ready the vessel for their crossing, it seemed to him then that he could dive into the depths ahead and emerge not on the island, but in Heaven.

"Brother Francis," one of them called. "Are you ready?"

Francis didn't say a word, but simply climbed into the boat and took a place at the bow. The others pushed off, all of them respecting his contemplative silence. In fact, no one spoke for a long time.

The oars broke the glassy surface without a sound and then slipped through the crystalline waters making no more than whispers as they passed. Not even the birds that filled the trees along the shoreline or soared high above the lake made any sound. It was as if the entire world were observing a memorial moment of silence for something yet to be lost.

The lake was larger than Francis had imagined. And although the brothers put their backs into rowing, their progress seemed slow. In the center of this vast body of water was their destination: Isola Maggiore. Not so much an island, as the tip of some ancient peak that had managed to thrust its way up out of the depths during some seismic activity.

No matter how hard the brothers rowed, it seemed as if the island was always receding before them. They were on the water for the better part of the morning before the bow of the boat groaned as the shore ran up underneath it. Francis was the first to step out onto the island and he was immediately struck by the nature of the place; neither good nor bad, but one of those rare locations that amplifies and reflects the moods and thoughts that a visitor brings with them.

In his dark humor, Francis was tempted to turn around.

"Is anything wrong?" Brother Paolo asked.

"What could be wrong?" Francis responded, concealing whatever his instincts were telling him about turning and heading back to Assisi.

"You just seemed as if ... you stopped," Brother Paolo observed.

Francis forced himself to take a step or two forward. "I've been a long time in the boat and need a moment to get my legs beneath me. That's all."

"Should we come with you?" another of the brothers asked. "To stay, I mean."

It wasn't that Francis hadn't understood the purpose of his pilgrimage was isolation and solitude, but standing on the shore and looking up at the formidable peak looming ahead of him, the prospect of being left alone on the desolate island left him feeling uneasy. Still, not so uncomfortable that he wanted to share his private concerns with the other brothers. So he shook his head and reassured his brothers. "I'll be fine."

It took a moment until Francis realized that they were all looking at him expectantly. "What?"

"If you could just give us a push off then," Brother Paolo said, already at the oars and ready to go.

"Oh, right." Francis put his hands on the beached bow, gave the boat a shove, and then stood back to watch as the craft came free of the shore and drifted backwards.

The brothers at the oars dug in and the boat spun around.

"We'll be back," Brother Paolo called as they pulled away. "Forty days."

"Forty days," Francis called back, but his voice wasn't nearly so certain as the one he was answering. He watched the boat pull farther and farther away with each stroke until, at last, he couldn't distinguish one brother from another or even the brothers from the boat. He stood there on the beach, watching them fade into the horizon until the small boat was just a black spot that he knew wasn't coming back.

89

There was a path that led from the shore up the island to the summit, where one pilgrim or another had built a makeshift shack and subsequent visitors had added an addition here and there. The collection of stones and boards they had assembled over time offered little more than basic shelter from the midday sun and imperfect relief from the rain, but Francis was grateful when his trudging feet finally led him up the steep incline and to its door.

Even with all of its various builders, it was clear that a long time had passed since anyone had made use of the structure, besides the mice that were firmly encamped in the old straw mattress on the floor. Francis looked at one of the rodents, curiously twitching its nose in his direction and asked, "Do you suppose you have room for one more?"

The mouse disappeared back behind the mattress without offering an opinion, and Francis took its departure as a sign of approval and seated himself on the mattress.

He was intending to fast for the duration of his stay as part of the process of spiritual restoration, but the morning climb had left him with a bit of an appetite and he remembered the wine and black bread that Anthony had slipped into his pack.

Francis opened the pouch and retrieved the loaf and wine skin. He took a hunk of the bread and made a rental payment of crumbs to his rodent landlords.

The bread was stale and the wine was bitter, but what caught Francis' attention was the folded piece of paper that had been slipped beneath them both.

He unfolded the page and was breathless at the sight of the script that flowed like a sketch of wildflowers in a field. He recognized the handwriting immediately. His heart raced and his breath fell shallow.

My dearest Francis

It would appear that once again that fate or circumstance or, perhaps, even God Himself has conspired to keep us from one another.

I had word of your return from the Holy Land, but my joy at this news was turned to disappointment when there was no sign of you at my door, as you had promised when you first left. My efforts to see you now have likewise proven for nought and I can only conclude that your interest in what we had discussed at our last meeting has waned.

If there is some other explanation, I can only hope that you will share it with me soon. I had refrained from making a final commitment to the order given our last discussion, but your seeming lack of interest has made me reassess my own position, and I have made arrangements to enter my order. This is a decision I have not made lightly and a commitment that I will not abandon once I have made it.

I only hope that you will offer me the opportunity to continue our discussion before then.

I hope this letter finds you well and that I will find you that same way too in the very near future.

Yours. Always.

Clare.

Francis' heart fell. And with it, the letter she had written dropped from his hand and gently drifted down to the ground at his feet.

He abandoned his camp and ran down the path as fast as he could; faster and faster, until the force of gravity was greater than the speed he could maintain and he tripped over his feet. He pitched forward, scraping his chest and the underside of his chin. He rolled down the rock path until he came to a stop, bleeding and breathing hard.

The injuries didn't stop him.

Francis got to his feet, unconcerned that he was bleeding, and started off towards the shore just as fast as before—if just a little more unsteadily.

When he finally got to the shoreline, his legs were buckling and lungs were burning.

He called out to the brothers in their boat, but they were long gone.

The distance between the shore and the other side of the lake was the only thing separating him from Clare, but given his situation, it could've been the space between the Earth and Moon.

They were, he knew, separated by a void he could never hope to overcome.

Not ever.

Not ever again.

Someone else in his situation might have cried out at the sky above, but Francis could not find the voice for it. Instead, he spoke her name as softly as he ever had, "Clare." And in that single sound he realized that he had said everything he would ever want to say again.

"Clare."

90

All things have their limits. Even the strongest of souls.

The sun was already beginning its descent when Francis finally picked himself up from the ground and began his ascent back up the island's slope. The blood around his nose had blackened and the wounds on his knees were peppered with dirt and small stones, but there was no other alternative.

And so, Francis started on his way back up the path.

Every step was painful step, but he was beyond his own physical suffering, and he made his way up the slope step-by-step until he had again reached the summit and the little shack located in its center.

Francis threw open the boards that had been bound together to form a door only as a formality and stepped inside.

At his feet, he found Clare's letter. One or more of the mice had nibbled at a corner of it and the damage to what he feared would be his last reminder of her set him to a rage he had suppressed for too long.

He kicked the mattress with all of his furious might, sending puffs of dried hay up onto the air and mice scattering in all directions. He picked up the pouch that Anthony had packed for him and swung it like a mace with murderous intent. "You ruined everything!"

In his anger, Francis kicked at the walls and tore off the roof. The humble structure could not stand against his wrath and before he was aware of what he'd done, Francis had rendered his only shelter to nothing more than a pile of debris scattered across the plain.

Not a mouse was hurt, but Francis was distraught when he saw what he had done.

He dropped to the floor.

"I'm sorry. I'm sorry. I'm sorry," he cried out until it wasn't clear from whom he was pleading for forgiveness.

Clare.

Or his parents.

Or the sultan.

Or Montague and his men.

Maybe all of them.

Maybe from himself, too.

†

Night descended, but it did not bring Francis comfort or sleep. He stretched out, not on the mattress he'd kicked apart, but on the bare ground. With no roof above him, he stared straight up into the sky above him, but saw no stars in that heavenly distance—only blackness. He looked longingly into the dark abyss and found within its bottomless depths a temptation to fall headlong into it and, in so doing, find some final release from the pain he could no longer control or abate.

And still, he laid pinned to the earth.

The hours passed, but sleep did not come to offer Francis some temporary release.

At some point, however, Francis must have drifted off because he found himself suddenly with Clare in his arms.

He tried to speak, but she put a single finger to his lips, not to silence him, but to relieve him of the burden of explaining anything.

Or everything.

He looked deeply into her eyes, afraid there would be judgment there, but found only understanding.

She smiled.

Then she put her head on his chest and pulled herself closer still, like she had found the home she had long been searching for and was settling in.

He pulled her to him, wrapped his arms around her as tightly as he could, certain she was the only thing tethering him to this world and that if he ever let her go, he would simply fall off of the Earth and into the celestial void above him that tempted him no more.

"I love you," he whispered.

She buried her head deeper into shoulder. "I know."

"No, not as a sister and child of Christ. Not as one of an infinite heavenly choir. I love you and you alone. Above all others. I love you as the woman you are and as the reason my heart beats and I draw breath. I love you as—"

"I know," she said.

"You do?"

"I do."

"Then I'm coming home to you."

"There's nothing I want more," she whispered. "But you won't."

"I will," he insisted.

"No, Francis," here words were calm, but firm. "Not you. You won't ever leave this island."

Francis woke with a start. Almost immediately, the dream that had been so real began to fade away. He struggled to retain all of the details, to keep her there with him, but the harder he tried, the more quickly she slipped from the grasp of his recollection until, at last, all he had left was the memory of trying to remember.

Without her, the night was darker than dark. And the chill of the sweat upon the small of his back was like the icy touch of Death itself.

"Clare."

There was no answer.

He looked up to the stars above, but their multitude only amplified his loneliness. He closed his eyes, but she was not there.

Just darkness. And loneliness.

And him.

✝

Time passed without any means to mark it. Day bled into night and then turned to day again. And again. And again. And none of it made the slightest bit of difference to Francis.

He sat on his well-worn mattress, looking out from his elevated peak out towards the far shore he could not reach. The impossible destination—so close, so unreachable—seemed like the perfect representation of his life.

"What do you want of me?" he called out to the distance. "Haven't I tried to do everything you asked of me? Haven't I walked the path You made for me? Haven't I tried to resist all of the temptations put in my path, given up everything that mattered to me. What more could I possibly give You?"

The only answer was the whisper of the wind off of the water below.

And so, Francis sat. And waited.

He tried to occupy the time with recitation of prayers, but the words he'd repeated thousands of times, over and over again, tripped his tongue like some unpronounceable foreign language or would not come to him at all.

He tried to let his mind drift to the memories he'd always kept close, both good and bad, but found that he had lost them all.

There was no past.

No future.

No present.

Nothing.

Nothing except, perhaps, a fleeting glimpse at his small place in the enormity of Heaven and Earth. The man he had tried to be. And the one he wound up being instead.

"I've done everything You've asked," he screamed out to whatever might be listening. "I've done Your work. When it cost me my family. When it cost me my honor. I bore every humiliation. I bore all of the suffering. I did everything You asked of me. And all I wanted was one thing out of this life. Was that too much to ask?"

The only response was the distant rumble of thunder from the mountains, echoing across the lake.

"One thing. You give those monsters all of the riches in the world and leave Your children in poverty and disease and suffering. How can You be a loving God when You won't let me be loved?"

Not even the thunder responded.

"I should have listened to my father. I would have been wealthier than him, wealthier by far. With Clare's family, we could have lived a life of such luxury. Respected. Insulated. A life with one another. Children. Everything. *Everything!* And instead You've left me with nothing. Nothing. I have nothing."

There was no more thunder. No lightning. There was no light from the moon. Nothing. There was only darkness.

And Francis knew that he was alone in the depths.

Alone and drowning.

91

This is a life of infinite possibilities, and so, there is little about which anyone can be completely certain. It may have been that an infection had settled into his untreated wounds or, perhaps, some fever that he'd contracted in his ministry and laid temporarily dormant that came to hold him in its grips. The explanation might have been found in the hunger that had become his constant companion. But this is a life of infinite possibilities and it might have been something else altogether.

"Get up."

So much time had passed since Francis had heard a voice that this one startled him. Francis leaned up and tried to shake his head clear. "What?" he asked tentatively.

"Get up."

For a moment, Francis assumed he must have been dreaming, because he had no other explanation for the old man who stood in front of him. "Carito? How can this be? I can't believe it."

"What can you believe, Francis?" There was disappointment in his old friend's voice. "You can't believe what you can't see. And now you can't believe what you do see. Tell me, just what is it that you *do* believe in anymore?"

"I'm not sure," Francis admitted.

"And so, where does that leave you?"

Francis looked around. "I guess, here. Alone. In the dirt."

"And whose fault is that?"

"What do you mean?" Francis was humbled by the implications of the question and his voice was soft.

The old man snapped, "You shout to the heavens that you don't believe in anything and now you whisper you don't understand anything. What I mean is that you're lying there in the dirt like a discarded thing. Whose fault is that?"

"It's nobody's fault, I suppose."

"Well, aren't you kind to yourself," the old man said, each syllable dripping with sarcasm. "You spend your days with a pointing finger for everyone, screaming accusations at Heaven above, but, with all that you've been given in your life, the sad fact that you're lying alone in the dirt is nobody's fault? I'll tell you whose fault it is … yours."

"But—"

"*But*, what?"

Francis was silent.

"Oh, now you don't have a thing to say; but everything else is *My* fault?"

"No, I didn't say that. Or, I didn't mean it." Francis was suddenly pained with confusion. "Wait, what? I don't even know who you are."

"That's not true," the old man snapped. "You've imagined Me this way before—I suppose, because it comforts you—but you know exactly who I am. You said that everything was My fault and you can't take that back now."

"But I never said that." Francis' voice wavered. "Or, at least, I didn't mean it."

The old man was having none of it. "You said it. You meant it. So, tell me, just what exactly is all *my* fault? the sad prospect that you didn't get everything you wanted out of life?"

"No, no, of course not," Francis stammered.

"That's not a tragedy, Francis. That's just life. And that's not my failure, it's yours. I gave you everything you needed. Everything. What you did with those gifts and those opportunities was entirely up to you. What you did was because you wanted to—whatever your reason—not because you *should* have done it."

"I only meant," Francis began to plead.

"A good father gives his child the skills and resources necessary for the child to get what they want and need all by themselves. And I'm a good father, Francis."

Francis said nothing.

"So, if you're disappointed with the outcome of your life, you have absolutely no one to blame but yourself. And before you come to such a grim conclusion about your life, maybe you should give some thought to just what your life has included—and what it has meant to those whom you have touched."

"But—"

"Every starving soul you fed, every suffering person you comforted. Was their relief *nothing*?"

"But there are still so many more," Francis protested.

"Yes, there are so many more," the old man easily admitted. "But their collective number doesn't diminish your importance in the lives of each and every individual you served."

"No, but—"

"And do you think because there are still wars being fought that your efforts to obtain peace were fruitless?"

Francis shook his head. "There are still so many innocents dying—"

"There are. But that's no reason to throw up your hands and surrender. The bloodshed is reduced every time someone walks away from the battlefield like you did, every time someone follows the example you've set. How could you possibly regret that?"

"I can't."

"Just because you can't fix a problem completely and forever isn't reason to do nothing at all. No matter how bad the situation may appear to you, making sure that there is one less suffering soul is still improving that situation. And who knows, maybe if enough people did what little they could do, perhaps some of those problems could be solved in the way that you want."

Francis hung his head.

"Then what is it?" the old man asked, his voice and temperament mellowing. "Is it Clare?"

"She's—"

"I know what she is. And I know what she is to you. Still. Is that what you regret?"

"No," Francis said quickly. "Not regret. I just wish—"

"You love her?"

"Yes."

"And she loves you?"

"Yes."

"A love for the ages?" the old man suggested.

"Yes."

"Then you have a love that will not wither with time or be trampled by jealousy or indifference. Do you have any idea how exceedingly rare—and beautiful—such a love is?"

Francis hung his head.

"Then what exactly is it that you regret, Francis? It would seem to me that you have so much. That you have always held a great bounty. So, tell me why it is you're convinced that I have left you with *nothing*."

"I just—"

"I understand. But, perhaps, what you need to do is see the situation from another point of view."

The old man reached out and touched Francis gently on the forehead, and in that moment, everything went black.

†

Forget everything you think you know about love.

Love is not the seeds cast upon the earth with an expectation of returns and rewards. Love is the rain, which gives everything it has, everything it is, with no expectation for anything other than it will be absorbed completely and disappear in its nurturing gift.

And I love you.

All of you.

Not equally, but individually.

Every single one of you in your own special way.

And that way is every bit as imperfect as each of you.

A father cannot hold His child's hand at every step of life. He must let go. He must watch from a loving distance while the child tries to walk on his own. And sometimes the child falls down. Sometimes they are pushed down.

What can a father do, but send love across the distance and hope that the child will get again to their feet?

And if the child is not aware of the father's presence, that does not change the fact that the father is always there, always loving.

And when the child falls, who do you think hurts more, the child or the father?

I assure you, the father's pain is greater by far. There is no greater pain than to see one you love suffering.

And yet a good parent endures that suffering.

It may seem cruel. Or cold.

I assure you it's neither.

For it is love, not indifference that restrains the father's hand.

Love and the hope that in his stead, the children will come to understand their need to love all of their brothers and sisters and to take care of one another. To love one another as the father loves them.

Because he loves them enough to bear their suffering.

To forgive them when they turn against him.

To love them when they shout at the heavens that they forsake him.

That is love. To expect nothing and to endure everything. That is love.

That is how the father loves everyone.

How he endures everything.

If you think you have known suffering in your lifetime, then imagine for just one moment what it might be like for the father who has felt every bit of pain for every one of his children, who has felt every cruelty, every bit of the neglect. Imagine for one moment what it must be like to look on this world when everyone is your child and every act of cruelty hurts you not only for the victim, but for the aggressor.

Imagine looking on this world, the disease and the war, and understand that your children are doing this to one another.

Imagine that pain.

That is the pain that your father suffers.

All around Francis was dark, but he did as he was told and allowed himself to fall into those words. He imagined for just one flash of an instant what it must be like to look down at a world in which one's own children could treat one another with such cruelty and indifference. And that moment was excruciating beyond any pain that Francis had ever experienced before or could have ever anticipated.

He cried out in anguish. And his cries were heard.

92

Brother Paolo and the others were all alarmed when they reached the shore on the appointed day and Francis was not waiting for them on the shore. They leapt from the boat and called out his name, but got no answer. They looked at one another and then up the path.

A feeling of dread fell over them all.

"Do you suppose something is wrong?" one asked.

"Of course not," Brother Paolo answered, although everyone understood he was only giving voice to their shared hopes.

"Should we go get him?" another asked.

"Maybe he forgot about the day," the fourth suggested. "Or lost track of the days altogether."

They all agreed that this was probably the case, whether individually they believed it or not.

Rather than extinguish that single ray of hope, Brother Paolo and one other set off on their way up the path. The climb was long and steep, but, given the level of their concern, they made the ascent more quickly than either one of them would have thought possible. With both of them panting, they made the summit and were immediately taken aback to see the ruins of the small shack scattered across the ground. The sight of the destruction seemed a confirmation of their worse, unspoken fears.

They were just about to turn and set off to inform the others, when Brother Paolo caught sight of something moving ever so slightly in the tall grass at the edge of the clearing. "Brother Francis?" he called out, fearing whatever might come as a response.

Francis groaned.

The two brothers ran over to his side and pulled him from the weeds. "Brother Francis, Brother Francis, what's wrong?"

When they turned Francis over, the answer to their question was gruesomely obvious. Francis' eyes were fused shut with caked blood.

Brother Paolo was relieved their leader was alive, but he was completely uncertain about what they could or should do next. "Brother Francis, Brother Francis, it is us," he said.

Francis moaned some more, but there were no words discernable.

Brother Paolo took Francis is his arms and tried to bring him around. It was only then that both men realized that there were deep wounds in his hands and a bleeding gash at his side.

"He needs a surgeon," the other called.

"And are you one?" Paolo snapped.

"No."

"Then come in here and help me get him up."

The other grudgingly did as he was told.

"Can you hear me, Brother Francis?"

"Yes," Francis said finally, but the answer was nothing more than a whisper.

"And can you see me, see anything?" Brother Paolo asked.

"No longer," Francis said. "My whole world has gone dark."

"What happened?" the brother asked. "What could have done this to you?"
"I did it to myself," Francis said.

"But how?"

"By doubting. And having faith. All at once," he answered. "I saw. No, that's not right. It was more than seeing. More than feeling. For one wonderful, terrible moment, I was looking through the eyes of our God above."

The brother was alarmed. "Brother Francis, no matter what afflicts you, you shouldn't speak such blasphemy."

"There's no blasphemy in truth," Francis said; his words were strong, even if his voice was weak.

The brothers fell silent.

"All my life I have heard of His sacrifice," Francis said. "I saw the suffering of people everywhere, but never did I consider that God might suffer, too. Until you *feel* His pain like I have felt it, you can have no idea how excruciating it is to witness the sin and suffering of us all. It is an act of love beyond all others. A wonderful miracle, but a terrible burden."

"And how did this happen?"

"Like the ungrateful child I have been, I foolishly accused God of not understanding my suffering. And in my misguided words, He challenge me to experience His own suffering."

The other brother took Francis' hands and then examined the wounds to his eyes. "You did this to yourself then? To get closer to God?"

"No, I never laid a hand upon myself. God did this to me because He wanted me to know that He had never once abandoned me."

"Don't worry," Paolo assured him. "None of us will ever say a word about it."

Francis struggled, trying to get to his feet. "That is your decision, but I will never stop speaking of it."

"Not everyone will believe your story," the other brother said.

"I lived it, and I'm not sure I believe it. Or understand it."

Even though they were completely alone, Brother Paolo lowered his voice. "I'm not talking about skeptics or philosophers, Brother Francis. If word of this reaches Rome—"

"Word of it *will* reach Rome," Francis said.

"And that doesn't concern you?" the other brother asked.

"We all live our lives with concern—a more polite word to clothe our fear—when there is nothing to be afraid of. Shadows and mist, all of it. Our earthly fears are meaningless and that includes whatever wrath Rome might visit upon me for speaking His truth."

"Brother Francis, you should keep those thoughts to yourself," Brother Paolo warned.

"No. That would be the true sin. Fear is the true sin, for it demonstrates a lack of trust in God. I know, I am the guiltiest of all of our brothers and sisters, that is why I have been marked like this. But I tell you that fear is the root of all sin, all evil. All weakness in the hearts of men. Faith isn't the pageantry and ritual of Rome, faith is the opposite of fear."

"You need to calm yourself," Brother Paulo said, as they began helping Francis down to the waiting boat.

"Look at me? What consequence could my upset possibly have?" Francis asked.

"It is exactly that, your health and condition that we must now care for."

"Do you think I'm concerned for my health?"

Neither brother had an answer, but together they managed to get Francis down the path and into the boat. Although the other brothers' eyes were wide with unspoken questions, everyone held their tongues. Brother Paolo instructed them to make a place for Francis, and they rowed him back across the lake and took him home. That was all they could do for him.

93

Francis refused to remain in the bed, but his body was too weak and broken to do much more than to sit in a chair in the corner of his small room. The brothers would bring him meals. And wine. Some would lead him outside for a brief walk, but, more often than not, he did not have the strength for excursions beyond the four walls of his room.

And there were many others who came to visit Francis—or, at least, to see him. Just as he had forseen, word of his condition had indeed spread to Rome. In fact, stories of the monk who had been miraculously visited with the very wounds Christ received upon the cross spread across much of the continent, and everyone who heard the telling was eager to see for themselves. Some made the pilgrimage with blind faith, certain that such a holy man must possess the powers to cure whatever affliction ailed them. More than a few came with nothing but a cynical skepticism in their hearts, wanting desperately to prove that Francis was a fraud. And, of course, there were representatives from Rome who were quick to seize upon Francis' experience as a narrative to further their own campaigns.

But for all the myriad people who came and went in the weeks and months that followed his return, there was only one Francis had really wanted to receive.

"I had expected you some time ago," Francis said. "Or not at all."

"There has been much to do," Anthony said. "And I have been always aware of your care and condition."

"I have no doubts about that."

"Rome has declared your experience a miracle. And with it, your stature has grown. As has the reputation of our order," Anthony said.

"Is that I good thing?"

"I think it is."

"And you've come to me now, because you want what?"

"It is not I who want anything of you?"

"But?"

"There are still more pilgrims, hundreds of them, maybe thousands, who wish nothing more but to touch the man God has chosen to touch," Anthony explained.

"God has touched us all," Francis said. "That was His point in marking me like this." He gestured at his sightless eyes.

"This may be so, but this doesn't change the peoples' desire to come and see God's work for themselves."

Francis turned to Anthony. "And Rome? Just what is it that Rome desires?"

Anthony ignored the question. "If you feel you are strong enough, perhaps you would be willing to meet with some of those who have made the pilgrimage to see you?"

"To what end? They would be better served to think and pray on how God has touched them personally."

"To do what you have always done, to give comfort to those in search of some small measure of comfort."

"How can I refuse when you put it like that?" Francis asked.

Anthony ignored the obvious sarcasm. "Fine. I'll make all of the necessary arrangements."

"I know you will. That's what you do, right? Make necessary arrangements?"

Anthony ignored the bait and walked to the door.

Francis was unwilling to let him go so easily. "Brother Anthony."

"Yes?"

"The letter."

"Which letter was that?"

"The one that was left for me before I went to the island. The one you slipped into the pouch with your stale bread and bitter wine. The one you chose not to give me when you first received it."

"Yes?"

"Why? Why didn't you give it to me when you first received it on my behalf?"

"No matter what any of us do, *You* are the one people think of when they consider our order."

"I never asked for that," Francis protested.

"And yet—"

"And yet I don't understand what that has to do with you withholding her letter from me."

"You *are* the Order, Francis. What you do is what the Order does. It was important to the Order."

"And so, you made all of the necessary arrangements—including keeping her letter from me."

"Would you have gone to the island if I hadn't?"

"You know the answer."

"I do," Anthony said. "And that's also the answer to your question as to why I kept it from you."

"You made the choice for me," Francis said. "Or took it from me. You took control of my life."

"I have no particular interest in your life," Anthony said. "But God apparently does. And I do God's work."

"And depriving me of that letter—of that chance—that was God's work?"
"Preventing you from quitting what you have started here, from leaving the Order and, in so doing, alienating the hundreds who have come to follow you, the thousands whom they shepherd, and the tens of thousands that they in turn serve, *that* was God's work. Preserving your legacy, not just for today but for times in the future until our Lord and Savior returns to us, *that* was God's work."

"God's work," Francis's voice was low, menacing. "To take from me what I valued most?"

"I took nothing from you. Nothing real. I took a dream you've held all your life of what might have been. I took that ethereal illusion, an imagined life, and traded it away for something real, something that feeds and clothes and comforts people. It was a bargain that need to be struck, and I made it. God's work."

"God's work or Anthony's work?"

"Who are either of us to question that?" Anthony scoffed.

Francis heard Anthony's footsteps as he headed toward the door, then stopped. "There was one other thing, Brother Francis."

"Could I refuse you, even if I wanted to?"

"Among the most enthusiastic pilgrims who are currently with us is an order of nuns. I thought you might enjoy meeting with the Mother Superior."

"Please offer my regrets. I don't have the strength or patience for dignitaries at the moment."

"Of this I have no doubt, but I would send her in to meet with you just the same."

"God's work?"

"God's work," Anthony said as he pulled the door open. Francis heard the light steps of a woman come toward him. He could not see the image, but he recognized the presence immediately.

"Clare?"

94

Most loves are temporal in nature, with progressions like the passing of the seasons. A spring when affection first blossoms and a summer when passions burn hot. An autumn when routine leads to complacency and brings with it colder days. And finally, a winter, when frigid blasts and icy storms bring all things to a frozen end.

Most loves.

But there are other loves, too.

Rare loves.

And what bound Francis and Clare together was not subject to time and could not be measured by the calendar. Even though all about him was an impenetrable darkness, Francis knew his visitor immediately. Maybe it was the delicate cadence of her steps across the floor. Perhaps, it was the scent of honeysuckle and sunshine. It might simply have been the sensation that some missing piece of himself had been returned to fill a gaping hole in his heart.

"Clare?" he repeated. His eyes were scarred shut and blind, but still they widened at the imagined sight of her, exactly as they had when he'd caught his first glimpse of her. And though he could not see her, she blushed at his response, just as she had on the first day they met.

She wiped a tear and stifled a sniffle, then took a deep breath to adjust to the shock of seeing him after all that had happened. Another deep breath and then she spoke as bravely as she could.

"I hope I don't come at an inconvenient time. All day long people come from far and wide to see you and many of the friars were busy with word that an emissary from Rome is expected soon."

"People come to see me in endless lines, but I wait here to see you," Francis said.

"Your words are still as sweet as confections," she said, her voice was soft and low, filled with longing and regret. "So much so, that I sometimes wonder if they have substance."

"Whatever I have done, however I may have hurt you, I have never once spoken an untrue word to you," he said.

She knelt before him and took his hand, hoping it was the best way to acknowledge what she knew was the truth. It was only when she held it in her own that she noticed the wound that appeared there and never faded away.

Francis gently squeezed her hand, like that connection was the only thing that still tethered him to the world and if he let go, he would simply drift away.

"I never received your letter," he told her. "Not until it was too late."

"Would it have changed anything?"

"Anything? It would have changed *everything*. But I thought when you did not respond after I called upon you at the nunnery—"

"You visited me?" Her voice was sharp with surprise.

"Did your Mother Superior not tell you?" Francis braced himself for the answer he knew was coming and the betrayal he had never suspected.

"She told me nothing." Clare clasped Francis's injured hand in both of hers and held them to her check. A tear fell on their twined fingers and she kissed it away. "We have both been greatly misused," she whispered.

He reached out his other hand to trace the contours of her face. "And the prospect that our manipulators thought they acted in the interest of the greater good does little to help me accept such treachery."

"What other choice do we have other than to accept," she asked. "Nothing can be done to address any of it now."

Francis knew she was right. "How I wish that once I'd taken your hand in mine and never let it go."

"And what would you have done with it if I had let you keep it?"

"In my heart and in my dreams, I would have led you far away from here, far from all the dark days we have both endured for the sake of others. I would have led you off, to the mountains, perhaps. No, to the sea. To sit beside the changing tides and do absolutely nothing all day but hold this hand."

"I would have followed you," she said, making no effort to pull away from his. "If only you would have been so bold."

"It wasn't boldness I lacked. Nor desire. Was it obligation that stopped me? Or piety? Perhaps the petty fear that if I had done so, we might have gained one another briefly, but as moments turned to days and days to weeks and months and years, the sweetness of our surrender would have turned bitter and we would have lost that which we love the most in one another."

"Not us."

"No," he agreed. "Still, no matter how hard I tried to find my way to you, this life always seemed to present me with opposing forces I could not overcome, like I was drowning in a torrent and could not swim to shore despite all my struggling and thrashing. I'm *just* a man, failed and flawed. But a man all the same, and one who has longed for you since the first moment my eyes saw into yours. A man who longs for you still. I promise you, my lack of action was not an absence of affection, but too many years of denied desire have left me profoundly changed that I cannot possibly understand the failings of the young fool I once was."

"And if we had run off to live by the sea, would that bold trespass have been such a sin that our loving God would have turned us away in our final hours?"

"Certainly not," Francis said with certainty. "Love is God's greatest gift, but you and I were not called to realize that reward, not within the confines of this life."

"And who created those *confines*? God? Or *just* a man?"

"Not *just* a man, far less than that. A fool. A dreamer. A coward, perhaps. But whatever I might have been in my misspent life, I have always been a man in love with you."

"And God," she prompted.

"Yes. And God." he answered. "I'm not sure why it often seemed to me to be a conflict. If that were truly possible, then I have certainly failed in all that I have ever wanted to do and, in so doing, I have failed you both. I suppose what I thought was virtue was really my vice, as dark and empty as any earthly pursuit. A misspent life, for sure."

"You have spent your days in the service of God and there can be no regret for that," she said. "And God, Himself, has recognized you for your efforts."

"No," Francis told her. "The pilgrims may come from far and wide to gawk at what they think is a man of faith, marked by a miracle, but that is not the truth. That is the lie they want to believe. What happened to me was not the Lord rewarding my faith but punishing me for my utter lack."

"Francis, don't say such things."

"I told you, I have never spoken anything but the truth to you," he said. "What happened to me then, what wrecks my body now, it came as a result of the shallowness of my faith, the lack of trust in our Lord."

"How can you say that?"

"I am blind, but I can see now that God wanted me to have faith that—if nothing else—He had already given me everything I needed to live a life of purpose. In doubting myself, I doubted Him. And no heart that holds fear can claim to be filled with faith, as well."

She squeezed Francis' hand as the only way of expressing everything she could not put into words.

"God gave me everything, but I was too lost in my own fear to see it—until I couldn't see anything at all."

"And now?" she asked.

He winced at the question. "I'm no longer afraid."

She held her breath.

Francis forced a smile. "I've just run out of life."

"Francis." She held back her tears.

He was the one who pulled their hands apart. "Live a happy life, Clare. Don't be too afraid to taste the sweetness of those confections from time and time."

"None could be as sweet as what we've shared," she said.

"I was a fool in every way a man can be," he said. "I would offer my apologies but know my words would do nothing to compensate you for what I have inadvertently taken from you. All I can hope is that you can take some small comfort in the knowledge that I have loved you since the very first moment I saw you. In this life, I have loved you and you alone. And, if I am headed now towards my end, I swear upon my soul that death with not stop me from loving you still."

His fingers felt the tears stream down her face, and he wiped them away. "I have no concern for how people will remember me," he whispered. "I only hope that someday a young woman will ask you about the life you have well-lived, and you will smile and say, 'There once was a man who loved me completely, and I was his whole world.'"

She bent to kiss him, knowing all the while that it would only be for a moment—and that it would be the last they'd ever share. But in that instant when she pressed her lips to his, he saw her there. Not as she was, worn with care and age. Not even as a man might picture the object of his heart's desire. Instead, he saw her as she wanted to be, full of life and illuminated against a background of the most brilliant sun.

He saw her there.

Clare.

And that image pierced the darkness that engulfed him and stayed with him, so that while he never again regained his eyesight, he never had any desire to see anything else.

Just Clare.

His Clare.

95

F rancis was quiet for a long moment. He shifted on the bed and felt Giovanni move to make room for him. Finally, he turned his head toward his brother. "And now you know my secret."

"And an interesting tale it was," Giovanni said. "Although I already knew most of it and would take issue with more than a few of your details. Still, you promised me something more. You gave me word of your treasure."

"And I have kept that promise," Francis said. "I have given you every treasure I have."

Giovanni held out empty hands. "But I am no richer."

Francis sighed and chuckled softly. "I have no hidden gold, Giovanni. You were a fool to believe such nonsense. But still I have given you something so much more valuable. I have given you the answer to what all men must seek, the answer to it all. How best to serve God. To live one's life. The answer to it all."

"Faith, fearlessness, and love?" Giovanni asked cynically. "I don't think my creditors are likely to receive any of those to settle my debts."

"Your only debts are to God and to yourself."

"I know at least one gentleman who would disagree with you," Giovanni scoffed

"It's a matter of perspective," Francis said. "When Clare came to visit me, God blessed me with a vision of her. Not as I wanted her to be. Not as a man views a woman. And not of the darkness I was fixated on, but of how He sees each and every one of us. No loving parent begrudges the sacrifices they make for their children or dwells on the pain that may come their way. Loving their children, they see them always as a blessing—no matter what. And so, while we humans take stock of the sins and the sacrifice, God sees each one of us as His own infinite blessing. We think of Him as suffering through our sins and failings as if we were great disappointments to Him. But, in truth, we are his infinite blessings."

"I fear I'm something less than a blessing. Especially an infinite one," Giovanni said with a short laugh.

"You are wrong. You are a blessing to your heavenly Father, just as you were a blessing and a source of pride and joy to your earthly father. To our father."

"Francis—" If Giovanni hadn't convinced himself that he was incapable of shedding tears, he might have taken notice of those tracing their way down his cheeks.

"While I tended to the less fortunate," Francis interrupted. "I was overwhelmed by the enormous suffering I saw before me. It wasn't until I lost my sight that I realized I had failed to take note of the endless compassion beside me. I was never alone in my endeavors, but was instead always surrounded by others helping me, supporting me. It's a matter of perspective, my brother. To truly understand, we must take God's perspective."

"God's perspective?"

"Our own perspective is flawed. We're human. Selfish by nature. So, we spend our lives wanting. And wanting nothing more than to be loved. It consumes us. I wanted our father's love. You did, too. I wanted Clare's love. You wanted the world's."

"Was that asking too much?" Giovani smiled.

"Just misguided. The mistake we make is wanting to be loved. Understandable, maybe; but selfish through-and-through. And ultimately futile, damning us all to a lifetime of yearning, disappointment and regrets."

"I never thought I'd live to hear you speak ill of love."

"Oh, you mistake me. I merely caution about *wanting* to be loved," Francis clarified. "What we should want instead is *to* love."

"Is there a difference?"

"A subtle distinction, but all of the difference in the world. Love—as a thing, a possession, something to hold onto—is not the answer. When love is just another acquisition—like gold or power—it poses the same trap as any other, maybe the cruelest trap of all.

"Loving—as an act—is an unstoppable force that moves one way without seeking compensation or return. To love fully is the key to happiness. Our own and those around us. Loving is the answer. When we love others there is no expectation or possession and that frees us. And that is what any good Father would want for His children."

"You make it sound so simple." Giovani wiped away the tears he couldn't shed.

"It is. Whether we are willing to believe it or not, God has given each and every one of us everything that we need. All we have to do is love one another."

"But Francis—"

"Stay, Giovanni."

"What?"

"There will be work to be done when I am gone," Francis said. "Stay. Stay and do that work."

"I'm afraid I'm too tainted by sin to work for God," Giovanni said. There was no pride in his words and no smile on his face.

"No one knows me better than you," Francis said. "Whatever you think of yourself and whatever others may think of me, there is no darker soul than my own. I know that now that I go to answer for those sins. But if God can work through me, then there is no soul beyond redemption."

"I don't know."

"Giovanni, my brother. You've spent your whole life searching for something you'll never find and that wouldn't satisfy you even if you could. Stop trying to be loved and turn instead to loving others. Stay here and walk your brother's path now that I can walk it no more. Live the life you were always meant to have and find the contentment you've never known in the simple task of loving others. That is the treasure I offer you." He reached out to take his brother's hand. "Will you take it?"

Giovanni made no attempt to hide his tears now. He clasped his brother's hand in his own as if it were the most precious thing he'd ever held. "Yes, Francis. My brother. I will. I promise."

And with that understanding, Francis smiled. He settled back against his pillow and softly let go of his last breath.

Giovanni fell to his knees and sobbed. "Francis. Francis. Francis."

96

There were many who came to pay their respects in the days that followed. There were dignitaries sent from Rome, of course; emissaries come to claim a legacy that they could finally claim for their own. There were townspeople from across Assisi, some who had known him in life and others who had merely heard the stories. And there those whose presence was the only thanks they could offer for the kindness Francis had shown at some point in their life when their needs outnumbered their resources. Those whom he had rescued from hunger or disease or loneliness; they all stood silently in honor of one who had lived a great life, but who was just a man.

Just a man.

The brothers from the order held services in his honor.

Brother Anthony used the occasion as an opportunity to announce his return to his native Padua and left them all with stories of Francis' triumphs over obstacles that most of them knew nothing about. "The mark of a man is not how he acts when all eyes are focused on him," he said, "but on what he does in the middle of the night, when he is all alone, and his choices are his own. Those who came to regard our Brother Francis as a holy man for the acts that he performed in public will never fully know his greatness, because they were not privileged—as I was—to witness his strength in private."

The newest addition to the order, Brother Giovanni, was there, as well, but he did not offer a word to the others. He was, as far as any of the others could tell, a humble and devout man and they took his silence as indication of those qualities.

Of all who came to pay their respects to Francis—and their numbers were in the hundreds, even thousands—what was noticed keenly by those who knew the man most intimately was not who had made their presence known, but rather the one conspicuous absence from their midst.

Some spoke badly of her for failing to attend those services. Others speculated that their last meeting must have ended on a bitter note. Still, the only thing that any of them got right in their observations was that Clare was not among their numbers. And that, for many, was even more tragic than Francis' passing.

In the aftermath, days passed, and life moved on. The emissaries returned to Rome and the beggars to the streets. The brothers continued their good works and the need for their charity continued, as well. In time, the brothers erected a stone in Francis' honor, a memorial of his life among them.

And as days turned to weeks and then to months, those who came to pay their respects at the monument were struck by the miracle that no matter the season, the stone was always clean and there was always an assortment of flowers to be found nearby.

It was, they all believed, Francis' final miracle.

And, indeed, they were right. It was a miracle, of sorts.

No one ever saw her so early in the morning, fussing over the stone by the dim glow of a not-quite-risen sun to sweep away the fallen leaves or brush away new-fallen snow. She never said a word to anyone but the birds in the surrounding trees or the rabbits in the field of the loss she mourned and the love she would always feel.

A rare love. A true love

And love, of course, is the greatest miracle of all.

† †

Resources

When I began this project, what I wanted most was to create a sense of hope for those who needed one.

It's because of this that I want to let you know that while this novel deals with many serious issues framed in fictional circumstances, I'm keenly aware that some readers may wrestle with those same conditions and situations in their real lives. For this reason, I want everyone to know that there are resources out there which are available and may be able to offer whatever assistance is needed. This is by no means an exhaustive list of the organizations providing much-needed services and I implore you to be proactive in seeking the services that you need within your own community.

Take care of yourselves. And each other.

National Suicide Prevention Lifeline
NSPL can all help prevent suicide. The Lifeline provides 24/7, free and confidential support for people in distress, prevention and crisis resources for you or your loved ones, and best practices for professionals. 1-800-273-8255

National Alliance on Mental Health – Help Line 1-800-950-6264

Substance Abuse and Mental Health Services Administration
SAMHSA's National Helpline, 1-800-662-HELP (4357), (also known as the Treatment Referral Routing Service) or TTY: 1-800-487-4889 is a confidential, free, 24-hour-a-day, 365-day-a-year, information service, in English and Spanish, for individuals and family members facing mental and/or substance use disorders. This service provides referrals to local treatment facilities, support groups, and community-based organizations. Callers can also order free publications and other information.

National Child Abuse Hotline 1-800-422-4453 www.childhelp.org

StopItNow If you're an adult survivor of child abuse, you will find resources at www.stopitnow.org or you can talk to someone by calling 1.888.PREVENT. 1-888-773-8368

Rape, Abuse, and Incest National Network (RAINN) National Sexual Assault Hotline - 1.800.656.HOPE 1-800-656-4673

National Domestic Violence Hotline 1-800-799-7233 www.ndvh.org

National Center for Post Traumatic Stress Disorder www.ptsd.va.gov/ This VA link has specific information about PTSD, including assessments, information sheets for families and where to get assistance. This site is good for information and research but does not offer immediate assistance.

PTSD United www.ptsdunited.org PTSD United, Inc. is a non-profit organization dedicated to providing resources for sufferers of PTSD, their friends and family, and anyone else interested in learning more about Post Traumatic Stress Disorder. Their primary method of helping PTSD sufferers is through their free, completely anonymous online social community, which is available twenty-four hours a day, seven days a week where people can go to connect with others living with PTSD .

National Alliance on Mental Illness (NAMI) www.nami.org/veterans 1-800-950-6264 This newly developed link for veteran's issues describes common mental health issues and resources for veterans and families who may be in need. An extensive list of resources is available.

Author's Note

Dozens of historical accounts have been written about the man born as Giovanni di Pietro di Bernardone. There are still more volumes which examine the religious significance of the figure who has become revered all over the world as Saint Francis of Assisi. This novel was never intended to add to the number of either one.

My reasoning in this regard is best explained by asking you to consider your own life. Recall all of the things you've done and said. The places you've gone. The people you've met. If you could ensure the accuracy of all of those dates and quotes, would those assembled facts really be sufficient to comprise the story of your life? Or would that story, even with all of the details in place, be missing something essential?

I believe that each of us is far more than a collection of dates and places and names. No, each of us is flesh and blood, and what matters most isn't those dry facts, but rather the spirit with which we lived our lives.

And that is what I set out to accomplish in writing this book.

So, while I freely admit to taking some factual liberties with what passes for the established history of Francis' life and times, I have not done so lightly. To the contrary, my embellishments were made solely for the purpose of capturing more truly the nature of Francis' spirit—or, at least, what his spirit represents to me.

In the end, it was this spirit that inspired these words and fueled my efforts, not to create yet another historical account of a man who lived almost a thousand years ago, but to tell the timeless story of an (extra)ordinary man whose life of trials and tribulations remains ever-relevant and whose courageous example continues to offer a whispered, but persuasive answer to so many of the questions that plague us today, as individuals and as a society.

Acknowledgements

There are a number of people I need to thank for significant contributions to the pages that follow and the enlightening experience I've had in writing them.

I need to begin with Andrea Cavallaro of the Sandra Dijsktra Literary Agency who placed the most unexpected and fortuitous phone call I've ever received. She changed my life with that call and I can never thank her enough.

I appreciate Jill Marr of SDLA for putting this manuscript out into the marketplace, and. I also owe a great deal of gratitude to Kristina Blank Makansi and everyone at Amphorae Publishing Group who have embraced this project so completely.

Thanks to late Scott Weiland, whose catalogue of music inexplicably became my perfect soundtrack to this book.

Many thanks to my literary brother-in-arms, Robert Pobi. I am grateful for the friendship I have received from Tom Dries and from Eleanor Dries, who is missed and thought of every day. Gracias, mi amigo, Isaac Cuadros. And for showing me that there are angels at work everywhere, thanks to my friend, Joe Loveless.

No story about Francis would be complete without the inclusion of my four-pawed contributors, so big thanks to my constant canine companion, Timber. My feline friends, Karma and Voodoo, frequently insisted on walking across my keyboard and are solely responsible for any typos in this text. The rest of the pack: Bear, Hollie, Kat, Cody, Nate, and Bandit are always in my heart and wait for me, I know, on the other side of the Rainbow Bridge—along with the little one who watches over them for me until I get there to join them all.

My mother, Mary Price, always kept a candle lit for me when the darkness would have otherwise consumed me. It was her voice that I listened to at a time of desperation and her faith and prayers that ultimately delivered me from those depths. I owe her more than I can repay.

My son, Dylan Price, is the finest man I have ever known. They say that every father should be his son's hero, but he is mine. He is the inspiration behind everything I do and every day I strive to be a man worthy of the honor of being his dad.

Finally, when I was a very young man, I fell in love ... and I have never fallen out. That no life could be built from this is my greatest regret and largely the result of my own foolishness and failings, but it was not for any lack of love for her. And, if nothing else, I hope she knows that. Always.

About the Author

Eyre Price was born in Syracuse and raised outside of Scranton, but thinks of America's highways as his home. He's traveled the Blues Highway all the way from Bob Dylan's boyhood Minnesota home to Professor Longhair's shrine in New Orleans. With his son by his side, he's made pilgrimages to Graceland, Sun Studios, Stax, and Chess Records. He's stood at the crossroads where legend says Robert Johnson sold his soul and walked the alley between the Ryman and Hank Williams' favorite honky tonk. The result of these travels was BLUES HIGHWAY BLUES, Price's debut novel that reflected his passion for all American music, from the Delta's blues to Seattle's grunge.

Since then, Price has penned two mysteries, ROCK ISLAND ROCK and STAR KILLER STAR, both part of his Crossroads Thriller series. SINNER SAINT is his first novel with Blank Slate Press and Amphorae Publishing Group.